W9-BDH-306

THE NEXT VICTIM

As Jim clipped his phone to his belt, he looked directly at Bernie. She didn't like the concerned expression on his face.

"I spoke to a Ms. Everett at the college. She said that Thomasina phoned about half an hour ago to tell them she'd had a flat tire and would be running late for her Thursday evening class. They're expecting her at any time."

"Let's go." Bernie headed for the door. Jim followed her outside and straight to her Jeep.

"I don't like this," Bernie said. After crossing the railroad tracks, she took a right onto County Road 157. "We're pretty sure that Stephanie Preston had car trouble the night she was abducted, and now Thomasina Hardy has a flat tire. If she's alone . . ."

Jim grunted.

"If we have a serial killer on our hands—"

"If?" Jim growled the word. "You keep saying if."

"I'm saying if because we're not sure of anything. Yes, there are similarities between the gifts Stephanie received and the things Thomasina said this guy sent her, but maybe it's just some terrible coincidence."

"You don't believe that any more than I do."

Thoughts of what that psychopath had done to Stephanie Preston raced through Bernie's mind. What if he already had Thomasina Hardy? What if they were too late to save her?

Books by Beverly Barton

AFTER DARK

EVERY MOVE SHE MAKES

WHAT SHE DOESN'T KNOW

THE FIFTH VICTIM

THE LAST TO DIE

AS GOOD AS DEAD

KILLING HER SOFTLY

CLOSE ENOUGH TO KILL

Published by Zebra Books

Close Enough to Kill

BEVERLY BARTON

ZEBRA BOOKS
KENSINGTON PUBLISHING CORP.

ZEBRA BOOKS are published by

Kensington Publishing Corp.
850 Third Avenue
New York, NY 10022

ISBN: 978-0-7394-7127-2

Printed in the United States of America

To my husband, Billy . . .
for the love, patience and TLC
I've always been able to count on
through our many years together

Acknowledgments

My heartfelt appreciation to several wonderful Alabama law enforcement officers whose help with research on this book proved invaluable. By sharing their knowledge, they enabled me to "get my facts straight" and, hopefully, present my fictitious Alabama sheriff's department in an accurate manner.

Philip M. Davis, Pelham Police Department, Pelham, Alabama

Lt. Shane Fulmer, Chilton County Sheriff's Department, Clanton, Alabama

Tom Wright, Retired Captain, Anniston Police Department, Anniston, Alabama

Lt. Frank DeButy, Decatur Police Department, Decatur, Alabama

George W. Leak (Retired Alabama State Trooper)

Chapter 1

Please, dear God, let him kill me.

Stephanie Preston lay on the narrow cot, listening to the rapid beat of her heart. Staring up at the ceiling in the small, dark room, she tried to pretend she was somewhere else. At home, with Kyle. Or at work, surrounded by people she knew and trusted. Perhaps at church, where she sang in the choir. Anywhere but here. With anyone but him.

As hard as she tried to mentally remove herself from the reality of this moment, from where she was and what was happening to her, she could not fully escape into her mind.

Try harder. Think about last Christmas. About how surprised you were when Kyle proposed, on bended knee, right there in front of your parents and your sisters.

Just as the image of her smiling parents flashed through her mind, the man on top of her rammed into her again, harder this time. With more fury. And his fingers dug into her hips as he forced her body upward to meet his savage thrust. As he accelerated the harshness and speed of his deep lunges, he voiced his need, as he did every time he raped her.

"Tell me." He growled the words. "Say it. You know what I want to hear."

No, I won't. Not this time. I can't. I can't.

She lay beneath him, silent and unmoving, longing for death, knowing what was going to happen next.

He slowed, then stopped and lifted himself enough to gaze down into her face. She closed her eyes, not wanting to look at him. Not wanting to see the face of terror.

He grabbed her, clutching her chin between his index finger and thumb, pressing painfully into her cheeks. "Open your eyes, bitch. Open your eyes and look at me."

Her eyelids flickered. *Don't obey him. Not this time. Be strong.*

"Why are you being so stubborn?" he asked, a tone of genuine puzzlement in his voice. "You know that I can force you to do whatever I want. Why make it so hard on yourself? You know that, in the end, you'll obey me."

"Please . . ." She opened her eyes and looked at him through a mist of tears.

"Please, what?"

Tears pooled in her eyes despite her determination not to cry. He liked it when she cried. "Just finish it."

"If you want me to finish with you, then tell me what I want to hear. Otherwise, I'll punish you. I'll make it last a long time." Lowering his head to her breast, he opened his mouth and bared his teeth. Before she could respond, he clamped down on her nipple and bit.

She cried out in pain. He thrust into her several times. Harder each time.

When he moved his mouth to the other breast, she gasped, then cried out hurriedly, "I love you. I want you more than I've ever wanted anyone. Please, darling, make love to me."

He smiled. God, how she hated his smile.

"That's a good girl. Since you asked so nicely, I'll give you what you want."

She lay there beneath him and endured the rape, hating every moment, despising him and loathing herself for having given in to him yet again.

This can't go on forever. Sooner or later, he'll kill me.
I hope it's soon. I hope it's very soon.

He stood across the street, on the corner, and watched her get out of her car and walk up the sidewalk to her front porch. She was lovely. He would enjoy sketching her, but before he could begin, he would need to see her up close. When he created the pictures of her, he wanted to get every detail correct. The slant of her eyes. The curve of her nose. The fullness of her lips. Her neck was long and slender; her body nicely rounded, neither skinny nor fat. Just right.

The first thing he would do was call her. Just to say hello. To make contact. He would be able to tell by the sound of her voice if she would be receptive to his overtures. He wouldn't listen to what she said. Women so often lied—unless you forced them to tell the truth. But he could always tell when a woman was interested just by the way she spoke to him.

"Thomasina, Thomasina. Such a lovely name for a lovely lady."

The thought of their courtship excited him. He reveled in the days leading up to the moment before a woman became his completely. It was the prelude to the mating dance that intensified the pleasure, those incredibly delicious events that prepared them for the inevitable.

However, he couldn't begin pursuing Thomasina in earnest until he ended his current relationship. He'd been keeping tabs on her, learning everything he could about her—but from afar. He wasn't the kind of man who would betray one woman with another. It wasn't his style. It wouldn't be easy ending things with his current lover. She was very much in love with him. He had been wild about her in the beginning, when she had posed a challenge to him, when she had led him on a merry chase. And the first time they'd made love had been good, although not all he had hoped it would be. He was certain that she knew their relationship was coming to an end, that they both needed to be free. And soon.

Perhaps tonight he'd tell her.

She would cry, of course. She cried a great deal. And she would beg him, plead with him, offer to do anything he wanted her to do.

Poor darling. It was simply going to kill her when he told her that their love affair was over.

Sheriff Bernie Granger removed her jacket, hung it on the hall tree in the mud room, then took off her holstered gun and hung the strap over her coat. Every muscle in her body ached. She hadn't slept in nearly thirty-six hours, hadn't eaten in twelve, and needed more than the whore's baths she'd taken in the restroom sink yesterday and today. This had been the third search she'd headed up during the past two weeks, each time following a lead that ended nowhere. Trying to stay optimistic and give hope to a family who had all but given up wasn't easy. But damn it all, she wasn't willing to throw in the towel and admit defeat. During the two and a half years she had been the sheriff of Adams County, Alabama, she'd been lucky. Only one murder had occurred in her county while she was in office, and the killer was now serving a life sentence in Donaldson. She'd had to handle four missing persons' cases. The first had ended within twenty-four hours, when they'd found the elderly Alzheimer's patient who'd walked away from home and gotten lost in the woods. The second case had been rough on everyone involved. A missing three-year-old. When they'd found the little boy two days later in a deep ravine, his tiny body bloody and bruised from the fall, she had walked away, found a solitary spot, and cried. In private. Where none of her deputies could see her. She was one of only a handful of women in local law enforcement, so she had to be tough as nails in order to survive. Thankfully, the third missing person's case had turned out to be nothing more than a woman leaving her husband for another man.

And now Bernie was dealing with the fourth missing person's case. Stephanie Preston, a young bride of five months, had been missing for two weeks after last being seen leaving Adams County Junior College, where she attended night classes two evenings a week. Technically, this was an Adams County case, since the woman was last seen in this county and the college campus was not within the city limits of Adams Landing. But the Jackson County Sheriff's Department was also involved since Stephanie lived in Scottsboro, and Sheriff Mays over there was Stephanie's uncle.

"You look like hell," Robyn said when Bernie entered the kitchen.

She glanced at her younger sister and grinned. "I feel like hell."

She and Robyn were as different as night and day. Robyn was tall, model-thin, and possessed a mane of curly black hair. At twenty-eight, she was still single and liked it that way. She had left college without graduating and had flitted from one job to another, one boyfriend to another, for the past eight years. She had finally come home to Adams Landing a year ago and, with some financial help from their parents, opened up a small fitness center that was, surprisingly, doing quite well.

Bernie, on the other hand, was tall, large boned, and sturdily built. She wore her plain brown hair in an easy-to-care-for ponytail most of the time, or she occasionally pulled it into a neat bun. She'd gotten married straight out of high school to her childhood sweetheart and they'd gone off to college together. After four years of marriage, two miscarriages for Bernie, and at least three affairs for Ryan, they had parted ways. Bernie had come home to Adams Landing, gotten a job as a deputy, and then almost three years ago was elected sheriff when her dad retired from the job, which he'd held for nearly thirty years.

Robyn lived at home with their mom and dad, but occasionally she'd spend a few days at Bernie's. This time, when she'd shown up on the doorstep, suitcase in hand, she'd told Bernie that she had to find a place of her own and soon. Being an old-fashioned, church-going Southern lady, Brenda Granger didn't approve of Robyn sleeping around, and when she'd caught Robyn's latest lover sneaking out of the house at five in the morning, Brenda had exploded in motherly outrage.

"Mom has called me every couple of hours to check on you," Robyn said. "She's worried about you."

"That's old news. Mom's always worried about me and about you. We're both single and childless."

Robyn grinned. "Yeah, you'd think the only reason she had us was so we could give her grandchildren."

Bernie trekked across the kitchen, opened a cupboard, and removed a bag of preground coffee. "Have you and Mom talked about things? Have you settled your differences?" Bernie removed the glass pot from the coffeemaker, walked over to the sink, and filled it with cool water.

"You know how it is with Mom—she doesn't talk with you, just to you. And no, we have not settled our differences and we probably never will. Good God, she was living in the fifties when she was a kid, not in the twenty-first century. Do you know what she said to me about having sex outside marriage?"

Bernie clicked her tongue against the roof of her mouth. "Hmm . . . let me guess. Could it have been the old tried and true adage about a man not buying a cow if the milk is free?"

Robyn chuckled. "You'd think she'd at least come up with some new material, wouldn't you?"

Bernie emptied the water into the coffeemaker, turned it on, and removed a cup from the cupboard. "Want some?"

"Huh?"

"Coffee. It's decaf. Want some?"

"No, thanks. I'm heading out any minute now. Paul Landon is taking me to Huntsville for dinner."

Paul Landon? Lord help us! Robyn could do a lot better than Paul. Good looks was about all the guy had going for him. That and a rich daddy. The man had been married and divorced twice, was rumored to have a drinking problem, and the general consensus was that he wasn't worth shooting.

But she supposed it wouldn't hurt for Robyn to date the guy, as long as she didn't get serious about him, and that wasn't likely to happen. After all, it wasn't as if Adams County was running over with eligible bachelors. Bernie's last date had been four months ago with Steve Banyan, a widower with three kids, a receding hairline, and the beginnings of a beer belly. They'd had a total of four dates over a period of a month. She liked the guy well enough, but they had little in common. He was a pharmacist, fifteen years Bernie's senior, and considering how much he talked about his deceased wife, Carol Anne, was probably still in love with her.

"Look, if you two wind up spending the night here, then either the two of you be very, very quiet or just go rent a motel room," Bernie said. "I'm dead on my feet and I've got to have a decent night's sleep."

"This is our first date," Robyn said. "It's highly unlikely I'll let him get in my pants so soon. Despite what Mom thinks, I do have my standards."

Bernie's lips curved into a weak grin. God, she was tired.
All she wanted was a cup of coffee and a sandwich, followed
by a long, hot bath. Then about ten hours of sleep. She'd be
lucky if she got six. She'd have to be at the office early tomorrow morning, ready to meet her new employee. Bill
Palmer retired several months ago, after a heart attack and
bypass surgery, leaving her without a chief deputy, someone
qualified to head up the criminal investigative division.
Originally, she'd thought about promoting from within the
ranks, but that would have been a difficult call since she had
two equally qualified deputies in that division, each with approximately the same seniority. She'd gone to her dad for advice, as she often did, and he had suggested looking outside
the local force.

"You never know when a highly qualified person might
be looking for a change," R.B. Granger had said. In her
opinion, Robert Bernard Granger was the best darn law enforcement officer who'd ever lived. "I've still got contacts in
Alabama, Tennessee and Georgia. Why don't I make a few
phone calls and see what I come up with? In the meantime,
you do the same. Check around. Could be you can bring
somebody in from Huntsville or even Chattanooga. One of
those big-city guys might want to move to a place where the
pace is a little slower."

"Or a gal."

"Huh?"

"A guy or a gal, Dad. Or have you forgotten that the sheriff of Adams County is female?" she'd asked, only halfway
joking. Since her little brother, Bobby, had drowned in the
river on a Boy Scout picnic when he was twelve, Bernie had
been the closest thing her dad had to a son. She'd been the
one who had played high school basketball, soccer, and softball. And she'd played sports more for her dad's sake than
because she loved the games herself. She was the one who

sat around and watched football games on TV with him, went fishing with him, and even went hunting with him once each year.

Bob Granger had put his arm around Bernie's shoulders and said, "You know how proud I am of you, don't you? You're carrying on a family tradition. You're the third generation of Granger to be Sheriff of Adams County."

A car horn honked, bringing Bernie out of her thoughts and back to the present moment, here in her kitchen.

"That'll be Paul," Robyn said.

"Quite the gentleman, isn't he, honking for you instead of coming to the front door."

Robyn groaned. "Now you sound like Mom." She rushed over, gave Bernie a quick kiss on the cheek and flew out of the kitchen, calling loudly as she left, "I love you, sis. Don't wait up for me."

Bernie heard her sister giggling just before she slammed the front door. The moment Bernie was alone, she sighed, leaned her head back and stretched her aching muscles. Just as she eyed the coffeepot, intending to pour herself a cup before she prepared a sandwich, the telephone rang. Her heart leaped into her throat. She had left several of her deputies, along with Adams Landing police officers and several volunteers from Jackson County, still scouring Craggy Point, the area where an eyewitness swore he saw a woman fitting Stephanie's description arguing with a burly black man at the roadside park.

"Sheriff Granger." Her hand clutched the phone with white-knuckled pressure; then she glanced down at the caller ID and groaned.

"Good, you're home," Brenda Granger said. "Have you eaten supper? Taken a bath? Do you need me to come over and fix you something to eat? Or I could bring some leftovers. Dad and I had pot roast for supper and—"

"I'm fine, Mom. I was just fixing to make a sandwich."

"A sandwich? What kind?"

"Peanut butter and jelly." Bernie said the first thing that popped into her head.

"You don't eat right," Brenda said. "That's the reason you can't ever get rid of those ten extra pounds around your hips."

"Mom, I'm really tired. Could we discuss my eating habits and my weight problems another time?"

"Of course." Brenda paused for half a minute. "I'd like for you and Robyn to come to dinner on Sunday."

"All right. I'll be there, if I can. And I'll mention it to Robyn when—"

"Isn't she there?"

Thinking fast on her feet and telling a white lie to avoid further explanations, Bernie said, "She's in the shower. I'll tell her when she gets out, and I'm sure she'll be able to make it for Sunday dinner."

"Good. I've invited the new preacher. He's not married. And I've also invited Helen and her son Raymond. Raymond's divorce is final, you know. Helen and I agree that it's high time he started dating again."

"Good night, Mom. See you Sunday."

"Yes, dear, good night."

Bernie hung up the phone. When she told Robyn that their mother expected them for Sunday dinner, and that she was providing each of them with a potential husband, Robyn would throw a hissy fit. But in the end, she, like Bernie, would go to dinner and endure yet another matchmaking scheme concocted by a desperate grandmother wannabe.

Jim Norton unlocked the front door of his rental duplex on Washington Street. While driving through town, he'd noticed that a great many of the streets in Adams Landing were named for presidents. Washington, Jefferson, Madison, Monroe. Before entering the house, he reached inside and felt for a light switch, which he quickly found. He had rented this place, sight unseen, fully furnished and move-in ready. He stepped inside, dropped his suitcase to the carpeted floor, then closed and locked the door behind himself.

Scanning the living room, he noted the place looked like most furnished rentals. Clean and neat. Furniture, drapes, and carpets slightly worn. Not a home, just a place for a guy to hang his hat. He hadn't had a real home in a long time. Not since he and Mary Lee divorced. He could have bought a house or even rented a nicer place and furnished it himself, but what was the point? While working as a lieutenant on the Memphis police force, he hadn't spent much time at home. Slept and bathed there. And occasionally ate there. If he'd been given joint custody of Kevin, he probably would have bought a house, but Mary Lee had been given full custody and he'd gotten squat. Just visitation rights—and those visits were under Mary Lee's supervision.

He'd driven straight from Memphis this evening, across northern Mississippi and northern Alabama, taking Highway 72 all the way. Adams County was a small county nestled in the northeastern corner of Alabama, a stone's throw from both the Tennessee and Georgia state lines, and the Tennessee River divided the county seat, Adams Landing, from its nearest neighbor, Pine Bluff.

Jim's neck was stiff and his bad knees hurt like hell. He'd made only one pit stop on his journey from his past to his future. His bleak future. Not that his future on the Memphis force had looked all that bright—not since he'd fallen from grace and an air of suspicion had surrounded him ever since.

Jim left his suitcase there by the front door as he walked through the duplex, turning lights on and off as he went from the living room into the small efficiency kitchen. Then he backtracked and went into first one bedroom and then another. The bath was small, but clean, with a shower/tub combination. He'd rented a two-bedroom place despite the added expense because he wanted Kevin to have his own room when he came to visit.

Leaving the bathroom light on, Jim went over to the bed and sat down. He should at least brush his teeth before turning in, but he thought maybe, just this once, he'd forgo his usual routine. After removing his shoes and socks and stripping down to his briefs, Jim flipped back the covers and crawled into bed.

He lay there for several minutes, thinking he'd go right to sleep. But the longer he lay there, the more he realized that until he took something for the pain in his knees, he'd never go to sleep. He had two choices. Both were in his suitcase: either whiskey or the pain-killers the doctor had given him. He chose the prescription medicine. After bringing his suitcase into the bedroom and digging through his shave kit for the plastic bottle, he took one pill and went back to bed. He gazed up at the shadows flickering across the white popcorn ceiling. He had left the bathroom light on and closed the door almost shut. He hated the darkness, especially when he was in a strange place.

He wished the pill would take effect soon. Not just to relieve the pain, but to knock him out. Otherwise, he'd think too much. Thinking about Mary Lee and Kevin and why he was here in this one-horse town was a useless exercise in torment.

He'd met and fallen madly in love with Mary Lee at the University of Tennessee; then they'd married right after he graduated. There had been some good years. They'd been happy. For a while. Kevin's birth had been the greatest day of Jim's life. He'd never known you could love someone the way he loved his son. Back then, Jim had thought he had the world by the tail. Despite knee injuries destroying his dream of playing pro football, he had found a new and satisfying career as a Memphis police officer. He'd made detective fairly young and life had been good. Until his cockiness and stupid arrogance had cost his partner his life. After that, everything fell apart, including his marriage. When he'd found Mary Lee in bed with another man, he had wanted to kill them both. And he almost had. Almost.

He had walked out of his house that day and filed for a divorce two weeks later. Forgiveness wasn't a word in his vocabulary, because as far as he was concerned, some sins were unforgivable.

For the past seven years, Mary Lee had made his life as miserable as possible, at first trying to turn Kevin against him, then later jerking him around about his visitation rights. So it hadn't actually come as a great surprise to him when, after remarrying six months ago, she'd told him that she was moving with her new husband to Huntsville. Kevin's stepdad had recently been transferred to the Rocket City.

"You can drive to Huntsville a couple of times a year to see Kevin," Mary Lee had said. "And he can come stay with you a week every summer."

"No way in hell!"

He had known that going back to court wouldn't do any good. Despite being a whore, Mary Lee wasn't a bad mother. And Jim had proved by his actions years ago that he wasn't such a good father. So he'd realized he had only one choice if he wanted to see his son on a regular basis. He had to move closer to Huntsville. It had taken him six months to find a job—the right job. One that paid him enough to live on and stay current with his child support payments. Being a chief deputy in Podunk was a demotion from being a lieutenant on the Memphis police force, and his yearly salary dropped by over twenty thousand. But he figured he'd do okay since the cost of living here was slightly less than in the big city.

The only thing that mattered to Jim was that he'd now be living less than an hour away from his son.

Stephanie wondered when he would return. Without a calendar or a clock, she had no way of knowing what day it was or what time. It could be twelve noon or twelve midnight. There were no windows in this room and the only light was a bare bulb hanging from the ceiling, too high for her to reach without a ladder. Those first few days after he had abducted her, she had tried everything to escape, but soon realized that there was no way out except the way she'd come in, the single door at the top of the stairs through which he had dragged her. A week ago? Two weeks ago? To her, it seemed a lifetime ago.

He didn't keep her shackled any longer. She was free to roam about in the twelve-by-twelve room, which she felt certain was a partial basement, either under a house or a building of some kind. In the corner, surrounded by a four-foot cinder block stall, was a shower, commode, and sink, as if someone had once planned to turn this area into a spare bedroom and bath. The block walls had been painted yellow, which over time had faded to a dirty cream.

The smell of mildew and mustiness permeated the entire room and everything in it, which wasn't much. A metal bed, a chair, and a desk. He made her sit at the desk to eat when he brought her food, which he did almost every day. At first she had refused to eat; but then he had punished her, telling her that he would not allow her to starve herself to death.

The first time he raped her, she'd fought him; but she soon learned that the harder she fought, the more severe the punishment. He never tortured her to the point where she passed out. At least not yet. Just enough to derive pleasure from her screams. Sometimes he would rape her with a bottle or a wooden phallus before climbing on top of her. And he liked to bite her. She had his teeth prints all over her body, as well as dozens of small burns from where he'd pressed lighted cigarettes on her skin. Most of the burns were on her buttocks and breasts.

He had raped her so many times, tortured her so often, that there was nothing else in her mind, no room to remember her life before this madman had kidnapped her. It wasn't that she had given up easily or that she hadn't hoped and prayed to escape. She had climbed those stairs leading to the outside world numerous times, beaten on the door and cried for help. But there was no help for her. No hope of being rescued. There was nothing ahead for her except more of the same.

She wanted to die. Longed to die. It was the only way she would ever be free of him. But there was nothing in this room she could use to aid herself in committing suicide, so all she could do was hope that he would tire of her soon and kill her.

The lock on the door clicked. Stephanie's body tensed and her mind screamed silently as she stood there, frozen to the spot, knowing the monster would open the door and come down the steps.

Listening, her eyes focused on the bottom of the wooden staircase, she heard his footsteps. Slow and steady. Not rushing. Taking his time.

"Good evening, Stephanie," he said, a self-satisfied smile on his face.

"Is it evening?"

"Yes, it's nearly eleven o'clock."

He gazed at her, studying her from the top of her disheveled hair to the tips of her bare toes. Without being told, she knew what he expected, what he demanded of her. She was allowed to wear nothing except a black silk robe, and only when he wasn't there. With numb, trembling fingers, she undid the tie belt and peeled the robe from her shoulders. It fell to her feet, puddling on the floor like a soft, black cloud.

"My lovely Stephanie."

He came to her, took her by the hand and led her to the bed. Without being told, she lay down, parted her thighs and held her arms open to him.

"Always so willing to please," he said. "I love that about you."

"I love you." She told him what she knew he wanted to hear. "I want you more than I've ever wanted anyone. Please, darling, make love to me."

He quickly shed his clothing, as always very eager. What would he do to her first? He had to inflict some type of pain before he could become aroused enough to rape her.

But apparently not this time. When he stood over her, his eyes wild and his breathing hard, she saw that his penis was already erect.

"Turn over," he told her.

Knowing what he intended and that it was useless to protest, she turned over onto her stomach. She waited for the first blow, but there was none. Instead, his hand caressed her buttocks. Tenderly. And then she felt him as he crawled on top of her. She held her breath. He rammed into her. She whimpered in pain. He rode her with a fury, coming within minutes. Still embedded inside her, he kissed her shoulder, then grasped her hair and jerked her head up off the pillow.

He'd never done this before so she didn't know what to expect next. Suddenly, she felt something pressing against her neck, just below her chin.

"Do you want me to set you free, my darling?" he asked.

And then she realized that he held a knife to her throat.

No, please don't kill me, a part of her begged silently.

That tiny part of her consciousness that longed to live, longed to believe that there was still hope. But the terrified, tormented part of her who couldn't bear to suffer any longer said aloud, "Yes, please. Please set me free."

And with one quick, deep slice of the sharp blade, he ended their relationship.

Chapter 2

Despite living in a new place, sleeping in a different bed, Jim had rested soundly. Thanks to prescription pain medication. It would have been easy to get addicted to the stuff years ago, and God knew he'd come shamefully close a couple of times. But if he'd fallen prey to drug addiction, he might as well have kissed his life good-bye. He was forty, with a couple of bad knees, unmarried, unattached, could barely make ends meet and had to struggle to sustain his father/son relationship with his only child. And here he was on this sunny, clear-blue-sky Thursday morning dreading starting a new job, one that anybody would see as a demotion for a guy who'd been a detective on the Memphis police force.

He parked his seen-better-days Chevy pickup truck in the area of the courthouse parking lot designated for the Adams County Sheriff's Department. After getting out and locking the doors, he glanced around at the other vehicles and grunted. Then he chuckled to himself. *Figures,* he thought. There wasn't another vehicle as old and dilapidated as his. One particular car caught his eye as did one SUV. The car was a late-model white Mustang convertible with the top down. Whoever owned the sporty little ride must have felt confident that it wasn't going to rain today and that nobody would dare mess with his car. He figured the owner to be young—possibly thirty or less—and single. A guy who liked the way he felt when he was behind the wheel of a car other men envied. His guess was that a guy like that usually had a pretty, bosomy gal with him, a looker he could show off the way he did his car.

When Jim passed by the SUV, he'd noticed it because it was clean as a whistle, as if it had just been washed. He knew for a fact that it had rained in Adams Landing very recently, because of the mud puddles he'd seen driving in yesterday. Pausing for a couple of seconds, he looked inside the neat-as-a-pin black Jeep Cherokee. The carpet was clean; the seats and floorboards were void of any clutter, except for a closed black umbrella. Whoever owned this SUV was probably a neat freak, somebody who needed to control every aspect of his life, saw things in a linear way, needed his ducks in a row.

Admitting to himself that he was stalling, Jim ended his vehicle inspections and headed toward the side entrance that led into the north wing of the two-story building. Like so many other towns across America, especially in the South, the Adams County courthouse stood in the middle of town, like the center of a box, with streets crisscrossing in the four corners. The white columned entrance faced Main Street. Two large, age-worn statues of Alabama Civil War generals presided over the green lawn on either side of the brick walkway leading from the city sidewalk to the front veranda. The back of the courthouse faced Adams Street, directly across from the post office, which was flanked by Long's Hardware and Adams Landing Dry Cleaners. The side-porch entrance to the sheriff's department faced Washington, a tree-lined street boasting the local library on the corner of Main and Washington and the county jail on the corner of Washington and Adams. An antique shop and a radio station, both housed in old Victorian painted ladies, sat side by side between the library and the jail.

Taking a deep breath of fresh morning air, Jim squared his shoulders, opened the door and walked into a long, wood-floored hallway. The minute he entered the building, he saw the sign protruding sideways from atop the door frame of the first door on the right: SHERIFF. As he approached the office, he noted that the door stood open, as if inviting people to come inside and make themselves at home. He had no more than stepped over the threshold than an attractive young woman, in the typical brown and tan Alabama deputy uniform, walked toward him, a smile on her face and a cup of coffee in her hand. Slender and blonde. Not pretty, but cute. With short, bright pink fingernails.

"Hi, I'm Deputy Holly Burcham." She transferred her coffee cup from her right to her left hand and held out her right hand to Jim.

He took her hand, shook it, and replied, "I'm Jim Norton."

She smiled warmly. "Thought you were." She glanced at the wall clock. Seven-forty-two. "You're early."

"I wanted to make a good impression," he said, only halfway joking. "First day on the job and all." He offered her a closed-mouth smile.

"Well, come on in and get a cup of coffee and meet a few people."

Holly issued him not only a verbal invitation, but a physical one as well. She took his arm, smiled at him flirtatiously and hauled him over to the coffeemaker placed in a corner across from a large desk Jim assumed belonged to the sheriff's secretary.

After Jim untangled himself from Holly, he removed a Styrofoam cup from a stack on the table, poured the coffee almost to the rim and took a sip. The brew was amazingly good.

"Lisa makes great coffee," Holly said.

Jim's gaze followed Holly's as she looked directly at the small, attractive black woman who had just sat down behind the desk. She glanced up at Jim and smiled.

"Lisa, meet Jim Norton, our new chief deputy for the criminal investigative division," Holly said. "Jim, this is Lisa Wiley, Bernie's administrative assistant."

When Lisa smiled, Jim noted how pretty she was. Probably close to forty. Ultrashort bronze red hair. Slender, small boned, with large black eyes and flawless tan skin.

"Welcome to Adams County," Lisa said. "I hope you'll like it here. I'm sure you'll enjoy working with Bernie. She's the best."

"Thanks." Jim took another sip of coffee. "Has the sheriff come in yet?" He glanced around at the workstation where the "road deputies" did their paperwork for their shifts. There were four deputies already here, and to a man they were sizing him up. He didn't get any specific type of vibes from the officers, neither negative nor positive. He figured most of them would wait and see if the hotshot from Memphis turned out to be a regular guy or a smart-ass.

"Of course she's here," Lisa replied. "Bernie's usually the first one in and the last one to leave. Let me tell her you're here."

Lisa rose from her desk, walked to the closed half-frosted glass door and knocked, then opened the door and announced, "Sheriff Granger, Captain Norton is here."

Jim waited to be invited in, wanting to make sure he started this job off on the right foot. Working for a woman was a first for him, and since he wasn't the most politically correct guy around, he wasn't sure what would or wouldn't offend a lady sheriff.

"Please send him in," a feminine voice replied. He liked the sound of her voice. It wasn't a little girl coo or a nasal whine or a deep, throaty warble. It was strong and commanding, yet Southern soft.

"Go right on in, Captain Norton." Still smiling, Lisa stepped out of the doorway to allow him entrance.

The rank of captain wasn't necessarily the norm for the position he'd taken here in Adams County, but for a lawman with fifteen years' experience, it wasn't unheard of by any means. Getting the rank and the pay that came with it had been one of Jim's stipulations for taking this job. What no one knew was that he'd have taken the job regardless.

"Call me Jim," he told the secretary as he headed for the open door of the sheriff's office.

"Call me Lisa," she said quietly as he passed by her.

When he entered the room, the woman behind the massive old wooden desk stood tall and straight, her gaze directed toward him.

"Please close the door and come on in," she said.

He followed her instructions, then stood about four feet away from her, catercorner to her desk, and waited for her to proceed. They stared at each other for at least a minute.

So this was Sheriff Bernadette Granger. He wasn't sure what he'd been expecting. Maybe someone older and tougher looking. Of course, he hadn't expected a gorgeous babe, which Sheriff Granger definitely wasn't. The lady was tall—he'd guess around five-nine or -ten—big boned and sturdy. His mama would have called her rawboned. She wore brown lace-up leather flats; brown, department-issue slacks; and a white button-down shirt. An acrylic ID badge was clipped to her shirt pocket. She wore her medium brown hair pulled back into a neat ponytail, the tip even with her shoulders, which meant she had really long hair. A pair of small gold hoops dangled from her ears, and her only makeup consisted of a peachy lipstick and blush. Not exactly pretty, but the features were good, the face appealing. And the lady was above all else as neat as a pin.

The black Jeep Cherokee is hers.

"Have a seat." She motioned to one of the two chairs flanking the front of her desk.

Jim took the one on the right. After he sat, she sat.

"First, let me tell you how pleased I am to have you as part of our team. You come highly recommended, and we feel fortunate that you've chosen to join the Adams County Sheriff's Department." She paused, as if waiting for a response, and when he remained silent, she continued, "Our criminal investigative division is staffed with five investigators. A couple of the men on the team applied for the chief deputy position, but I can assure you that neither man will be a problem for you. Both Ron Hensley and John Downs are true professionals."

Jim knew that most sheriffs were equal parts politician and lawman, some more politician than anything else. Sheriff Granger certainly knew how to be diplomatic, a chief tool in any politician's arsenal of weapons. But he would reserve judgment until he got to know the lady better. As for Deputies Hensley and Downs, Jim's guess was that one or both of them would hate his guts on sight. Nobody liked to be passed over for a promotion.

"I'm sure I'll have no problem with any of the deputies," Jim said. It was a bold-faced lie and they both knew it.

Sheriff Granger smiled. He liked her smile. It was genuine. His gut instincts told him that the lady was the same—a no-nonsense, no-frills, what-you-see-is-what-you-get woman. "After you take care of the necessary paperwork and we issue you all the usual paraphernalia, I'll go with you over to the jail and show you your office and introduce you to the others in your department."

"Sounds like a plan."

"After that, I'll show you around Adams Landing, and then take you to lunch. Our DA, Jerry Dale Simms, will be joining us. He's looking forward to meeting you. You'll like Jerry Dale. Everyone does."

"It's very nice of you, Sheriff Granger, to take the time to escort me around personally. I appreciate it." Okay, why were the sheriff and DA taking him to lunch? Not that he minded, but it puzzled him.

As if reading his mind, she said, "You're wondering why the sheriff and DA would take a new chief deputy to lunch, aren't you?" She laughed. "To be honest, Jerry Dale is eager to meet former UT running back Jimmy Norton."

Jim grunted, then chuckled. "Hmm . . ."

She stood and held out her hand across the desk. "Welcome to Adams Landing."

He reached out and took her hand in his and exchanged a cordial shake. Her handshake was strong and self-confident, and the entire time she looked him right in the eyes. Man-to-man, so to speak. Yet there was nothing masculine about Bernadette Granger.

"Holly will show you around the office, introduce you to others and once you're squared away, we'll head over to your office."

Understanding that he had been dismissed, Jim nodded, got up and headed for the door. Just before grasping the doorknob, he paused, glanced over his shoulder and said, "I'm a pretty straight shooter. I'm not a game player and I've made my share of mistakes. I'm not always the most diplomatic guy or the most politically correct. So if I ever say or do anything you consider out of line, just let me know."

Her expression changed. The smile vanished. "You can be sure that I will. I tend to be straightforward and somewhat outspoken, so you'll never wonder where you stand with me."

He nodded again, then opened the door and left her office. He had no more than closed the door behind himself than Deputy Holly Burcham sashayed over to him, all smiles and fluttering eyelashes.

"Come on, handsome. I've been designated as your tour guide."

Any man would find Holly attractive. And he was, after all, a man. But the last thing he wanted was to get involved with a fellow officer, especially right off the bat. He needed time to feel his way around, to get the lay of the land, before even thinking about a personal relationship of any kind. All he wanted was to make a success of this job and strengthen the ties to his son. Only two goals. And he suspected neither would be easy to accomplish.

Bernie sat quietly behind her desk, mulling over her brief conversation with her new chief deputy. Twenty years ago, when Jimmy Norton and Griff Powell had been the golden boys of UT football, she'd been just a kid, but being a tomboy and doing anything to gain her father's attention, she'd watched all the college and pro games with her dad. She remembered Jimmy Norton more than any other player, probably because she'd had a silly schoolgirl crush on him. Yeah, she and how many hundreds of other pubescent and teenage girls in the South? She'd kept a picture of him on her bulletin board alongside one of Tom Selleck as *Magnum PI,* a TV show she and her dad had never missed. So, truth be told, she was almost as starstruck as Jerry Dale was over Jimmy Norton.

But she had to remind herself that she was no longer a kid with a crush on a guy she'd never met in person, and Jim Norton hadn't been a superstar athlete in nearly two decades. Okay, so the guy was still panty-creaming good looking; actually, maturity sat well on his broad shoulders. He was still tall and lean, and she suspected that his body was muscular and toned beneath his clothes. She had to admit that for a couple of minutes while she'd been looking him over, she had pictured him stark naked.

From what she'd learned about him, she hadn't been surprised that he had that rode-hard-and-put-away-wet appearance, but somehow that roughness only made him all the more appealing.

Good grief, girl, get over it, will you? You're thirty-two, not twelve. You've been married, divorced, had your heart broken, and learned the hard way that few men are what they seem. Besides that, you're Jim Norton's superior.

And if those facts weren't enough to throw cold water on her fantasies, the fact that she hadn't felt any reciprocal I'm-attracted-to-you vibes from him should be. Odd that she could so easily admit to herself that she found Jim Norton attractive—very attractive—when she couldn't remember the last time a guy turned her on. It had been such a long time since she'd had sex that she was practically a born-again virgin.

Lost in her thoughts, she barely heard when Lisa buzzed her. "Sheriff Mays on line one."

Dragging herself out of her teenage-crush memories, Bernie punched line one as she picked up the phone. "Hello, Ed."

"Bernie, I don't suppose you have anything new to report on Stephanie, do you?"

"I'm sorry, but no, I don't."

"God, things are bad at my house. My wife's doing what she can to keep her sister calm. Judy keeps telling Emmy not to give up hope, but we're all half out of our minds worrying about Stephanie. She's been missing for two weeks, and between your people and mine, we've scoured most of Jackson and Adams counties."

"Ed, are you sure there's no possibility that her husband killed her?" Bernie wasn't usually so blunt with a family member, but Ed wasn't just Stephanie Preston's uncle-by-marriage, he was the sheriff of nearby Jackson County. He knew how often in a missing person's case it turned out that the spouse had murdered their unaccounted-for mate.

"God, no. Kyle's a basket case. The doctor has put him on

medication and we're making sure someone is with him twenty-four/seven. If Stephanie is dead, that boy's liable to kill himself." Ed paused for a minute. *Checking his emotions*, Bernie thought. "You know they've only been married for five months. He proposed this past Christmas and they had a Valentine's Day wedding."

"I wish I could do more. Just tell me if there's anything, absolutely anything, you want me to do."

"I don't understand how she could have disappeared the way she did, without a trace. The last anybody saw of her, she was heading toward her car after her class that night. But y'all found her car, stilled locked, parked at Adams County Junior College."

"We've gone over the car with a fine-tooth comb," Bernie said. "There was no evidence of foul play. No blood. No semen. Nothing to indicate a struggle. It's as if she headed toward her car and never made it there. Either she decided to go back inside the building or somebody came along and nabbed her. Or she got in her car and back out again for some reason."

"If she got in the car with somebody, then why didn't a single solitary soul see it happen? There were other students going to their cars that night. Why didn't any of them see something?"

"Stephanie's car was not near one of the security lights and it was going on ten when she was last seen. In the darkness—"

"Has that new hotshot detective from Memphis shown up?" Ed asked abruptly.

"He's here now."

"Are you turning Stephanie's case over to him?"

"He's my new chief investigator, so technically that puts him in charge, but I plan to stay involved, to keep close tabs on the case."

"We aren't going to find her alive," Ed said. "And you and I both know it."

"I'm afraid you're probably right," Bernie agreed. But what if they never found Stephanie—dead or alive? Her family would continue to suffer for weeks, months, even years, always hoping beyond hope that out there somewhere she might still be alive. The odds of that were slim to none.

"I don't suppose there's much point in manning another search, is there?"

"I don't think so. If I thought it would do any good, we'd do it, but . . ."

"If anything turns up, you'll let me know immediately."

"Yeah, if it does, you'll be the first person I contact."

"Thanks, Bernie. And say hello to your dad."

"Sure will."

The dial tone hummed in her ear. Bernie placed the receiver down on the telephone base and stared off into space for several minutes. The most difficult part of her job was dealing with her very feminine emotions. Just because she'd been elected sheriff didn't mean she could simply turn off her nurturing, maternal, caretaker-to-the-world instincts. Yes, she was as smart as any man, as good a shot as any deputy on the force, knew the law better than most, and worked diligently to be half as good a sheriff as her dad had been. And although she'd been accepted by the male deputies from day one and she thought she had earned their respect, she knew that because she was a woman, her every action was scrutinized.

A knock on the door gained her attention. "Yes?"

The door opened a fraction and Jim Norton peered into her office.

She motioned for him to come in, but he simply shoved the door open wider to show her that he had his arms filled with the items he'd been issued. Uniforms, "campaign" hat, a Glock 22, Sam Browne belt, holster and cuff case, an ASP, radio, OC spray, badge, and ID card.

"I'm taking these out to my truck," he told her. "After that, I'm ready whenever you are."

As he stood there, she surveyed him quickly from head to toe. He stood six-three. Weighed two-twenty-five. Was forty years old. All info she'd read about him in his file. But nothing in his file described the man's rugged good looks. He wore his dark brown hair cut short and neat. His attire was casual—old jeans, a plaid shirt, and boots. But the one aspect of his physical appearance that Bernie found the most interesting was his eyes. Blue blue. Sky blue. And quite a contrast to his dark hair and tanned skin. "Where are you parked?"

"My truck's in the designated parking lot."

"Okay, you go on ahead. I'll meet you out there in a few minutes. The jail is across the street, at the end of the block. We'll walk."

Upon arrival at the Adams County jail, an updated building that Sheriff Granger told Jim had housed the jail for the past half century, she introduced him to forty-something Lieutenant Hoyt Moses, a burly six-foot redhead with a boisterous laugh and seemingly good-natured disposition.

"Hoyt's in charge here," Bernie said. "He has three sergeants and eighteen deputies working under him."

When they reached the area that housed the investigators' offices, both the criminal and narcotics divisions, she paused in the hallway. "Look, these guys have worked together for years and some of them even went to high school together. They're good men, all of them. They might have some preconceived ideas about you because of who you are. You know, *the* Jimmy Norton. Plus, you were a Memphis detective. But they won't give you any trouble. You treat them fairly and they'll do the same."

"So who's the one the most pissed about being passed over for the promotion?" Jim didn't see any point in pussy-footing around, trying to be diplomatic. Diplomacy was part of the sheriff's job, not his.

The lady frowned. "Brutal honesty isn't always the best course of action."

He shrugged. "It's how I work. It's who I am. Is that going to be a problem?"

She huffed. "I don't know. Guess we'll have to wait and see."

"So, who is he? The guy who already hates my guts for getting the job he wanted."

"Nobody here hates your guts," she said. "The front-runner for the chief deputy position was Ron Hensley, and yes, he was disappointed when I looked outside the department to fill the position. But Ron's a professional and he understands my reasons for hiring you. He's not going to give you any trouble."

Yeah, sure. "That's good to know."

Jim knew that he would have to prove himself to the other deputies, especially to Lieutenant Hensley. He was willing to do his part to get along with the guy, as long as Hensley didn't give him any shit. From the get-go, he needed to make it clear that he was the chief deputy, the man in charge. And he needed to do this in a way that didn't alienate any of his deputies.

"Ron and John are both here this morning, at my request. I wanted you to meet both of your lieutenants."

Sheriff Granger opened the door and breezed into the central office. A couple of uniformed deputies stood talking, each holding a cup of coffee. Jim sized up the two quickly and decided that the short, stocky, slightly balding guy was probably John Downs. He had that easygoing, old-shoes-comfortable look about him. Jim guessed the guy was married, with a couple of kids, went to church every Sunday and liked his life the way it was. The energy he emitted was calm and low-key. The other guy was a different matter. A tad under six feet, slim and fit, with military, short black hair and pensive brown eyes. He presented a flawless appearance—from his handsome, clean-shaven face to his spit-polished shoes. This was, without a doubt, Ron Hensley.

"Morning," the sheriff said. "Ron. John."

Both men turned and greeted her.

"Jim, I'd like to introduce you to Lieutenants Ron Hensley and John Downs." With their gazes fixed on Jim, they both nodded. Downs smiled. Hensley did not. "Gentlemen, this is Captain James Norton."

Downs came forward, shook Jim's hand, and welcomed him cordially. Then reluctantly, after glancing at the sheriff as if to tell her he would do what he had to do, Hensley held out his hand to Jim, but he didn't say anything.

Hensley had a strong, firm grip, but he didn't use the handshake as a pissing contest to prove he was as strong or stronger than Jim. And Jim respected that type of reserve and control in any man. His estimation of Hensley improved because of that one simple gesture.

"Y'all will get a chance to become better acquainted later," Sheriff Granger told the deputies. "I'm taking the morning to show Jim the layout of the department and to give him a tour of the town. Then we're meeting Jerry Dale for lunch. If either of you would care to join us—"

"I'd love to," John Downs said, "but this is Friday, and Cathy, my wife, and I have a standing lunch date every Friday."

"Oh, that's right," the sheriff said. "I'd forgotten." She looked at Hensley. "What about you, Ron?"

"Sure, I'll tag along. Are you taking him to Methel's?"

"Where else?" She turned to Jim. "Methel's is practically an institution in Adams Landing. The current owner is the great-granddaughter of the lady, Methel, who opened the restaurant in the late thirties. It's the best food in town. Down home country cooking like your grandma used to fix."

"You make me wish it was lunchtime already." Jim grinned.

"If you ever want great barbeque, the only place to go is The Pig Pen over on Second Street," Downs told him.

"And if you're ever in the mood for a stiff drink and some loud music, check out the Firecracker on Carney Road," Hensley said.

Jim and Hensley shared a hard look. Not a hostile look, just an understanding that each would reserve judgment of the other until they were better acquainted. *Fair enough.* Jim's gut told him that he and Hensley might have a few things in common.

"Meet us at Methel's around twelve-thirty." The sheriff headed toward the door, but paused halfway there and said, "Ed Mays called me a little while ago."

Downs shook his head sadly.

Hensley glanced at Jim. "We've been working a missing person's case for the past couple of weeks. The missing woman's uncle is Ed Mays, the Sheriff of Jackson County."

"Do y'all suspect foul play?" Jim asked.

"Possibly," Hensley replied. "The problem is, we really don't have a clue as to what happened to her. It's as if she just disappeared off the face of the earth."

"What about the husband?" Jim looked directly at Hensley.

Hensley shrugged. "Doubtful he had anything to do with it."

"No clues, huh? I'd like to take a look at your files on that case this afternoon."

The edges of Hensley's mouth curved into a tentative smile. "I'll be glad to show them to you. Maybe you can catch something we've missed."

"Maybe."

Sheriff Granger cleared her throat. "Captain Norton, are you ready to go?"

"Ready whenever you are, Sheriff."

Chapter 3

Ron closed himself off in the chief deputy's office, the one he'd thought for sure would be his. Yeah, and that's what he got for thinking. He should have known that Bernie wouldn't choose him over John Downs, even if he was better suited for the job. John had seniority over him by only four years, but everybody liked John. Everybody didn't like Ron, which really didn't bother him in the least. He'd take respect and even a little intimidation over being liked any day of the week. But Bernie wasn't about to upset the apple cart in any way, shape, form or fashion. She had her own issues, things she needed to prove. Hell, he didn't envy her the position she was in, although he'd love to be sheriff. Only thing was, here in Adams County, if you ran for the office against anyone with the last name of Granger, you were bound to lose. Bernie's old man, R.B., had held the position for almost thirty years, retiring only after a bout with cancer a few years ago. And from the early forties until his death nearly thirty years later, Bernard Granger Sr., Bernie's grandfather, had been sheriff.

For the time being, Ron had no choice but to grin and bear it, to accept the Memphis detective who'd gotten the job that should have been his. But if Norton screwed up, just once, he'd be the first to shout it to the world. It wasn't that he had anything personal against Norton. He might be a hell of a guy. And if it turned out that he was a great chief deputy, Ron might have to look elsewhere if he ever wanted to be more than a deputy.

Ron removed his cell phone from the belt clip, then eased down into the big, comfy swivel chair and propped his number tens up on Captain Norton's desk. He went to his address book and hit the often-dialed number of his current girlfriend. Although he had dated several different women lately, he was sleeping with only one now. Abby Miller. However, since Abby was married, they had to keep their relationship a secret from the general public.

He didn't make a habit of dating married women, but Abby was different. She had come after him, not the other way around. Usually, he did the pursuing and liked it that way, but with a gal like Abby, he'd made an exception for several reasons. First, the woman was a looker. Built like a brick shit-house, bosomy, vivacious, and flirty. And second, she was horny as hell since her husband's National Guard unit had been sent to the Middle East. The lady was mighty talented in the sack and knew how to keep a man coming back for more.

"Kut and Kurl," Abby said as she answered the phone at her beauty shop, located on West Jackson, two blocks from the courthouse.

"Hi, sugar."

"Hi, yourself."

"I've got to cancel our midday date," he told her.

She whined.

"The new chief deputy's in town, and Bernie invited me to join them and Jerry Dale for lunch today. I could hardly tell her that I couldn't because I was meeting Abby Miller for a quickie in the backroom of her beauty shop."

Abby giggled. "Yeah, that would have gone over like a fart in church. Bernie's all right, but she's a little uptight about her deputies' moral values, if you ask me."

"What Bernie doesn't know about my personal life won't hurt either me or her—or you, for that matter. You don't want your mother-in-law finding out about us, do you? You know that old battle-ax would write Ricky Wayne and tell him you were cheating on him."

Abby sighed loudly. "I don't want that happening." She lowered her voice to a whisper. "If Ricky Wayne found out, he might kill us both when he comes home. You know what a temper he has."

"No point in causing such a fuss over us just having a little fun. It's not like we're actually hurting anybody, right? After all, it's not as if we love each other. And you're sure not making any plans to divorce Ricky Wayne."

"You've got that right. I'm crazy about my husband. I love him to pieces."

"Of course you do. But why should you stay celibate just to prove it, right?"

Abby laughed.

"How about our getting away to Huntsville this weekend?" Ron asked.

"Sounds wonderful, but I can't leave until after twelve tomorrow. I'm booked solid with appointments until eleven-thirty."

"I'll make reservations later today, then get back in touch to tell you where to meet me in Huntsville. I'll try the Marriott near the Space and Rocket Center. You liked that hotel last time, didn't you?"

"Sure did. Sounds great. Look, I've got to go now."

"Too many curious customers wondering who you're talking to?"

"That's right, Martha Dean. Call me later. 'Bye now."

The dial tone droned in Ron's ear. Martha Dean was

Abby's out-of-town cousin, so she felt safe in using her name to cover Ron's identity whenever their phone conversations might be overheard on her end. Since he'd never been involved with a married woman before Abby, this business of keeping their affair a secret was new stuff for him. But if he was totally honest with himself, he had to admit he kind of got a kick out of having a backstreet romance. Besides, Abby was worth a little sneaking around. She was the best damn lay he'd ever had.

Tap, tap, tap. Ron glanced up, searching for the sound, and realized someone was pecking on the door. "Yeah?"

John cracked the door a couple of feet and peered into the office. "I've made some fresh coffee and opened up a pack of bear claws. You interested?"

"Coffee sounds good." Ron slid his feet off the desk, shoved back the chair, and stood. "I'd better stay away from the bear claws." He patted his flat belly. "A single guy like me has to stay in shape."

John chuckled. "I guess it's lucky I'm married to a plump, understanding wife who loves me just the way I am. Otherwise, I wouldn't get to indulge in my favorite pastries so often."

When Ron joined John in the outer office, John poured a cup of coffee and handed it to him, then helped himself to an almond and sugar glazed confection.

"What do you think of Captain Norton?" John asked.

Ron shrugged.

"I know you were expecting Bernie to—"

"I wasn't expecting anything," Ron said. "I'd hoped she would think I deserved the job. Or if not me, then you."

"Nah, not me. I didn't expect it."

"But you wouldn't have turned it down."

"No, I wouldn't have, but . . . well, I guess, in a way, it's my fault you didn't get the promotion."

"How do you figure that?"

"Ah, Ron, come on. You know the answer to that as well as I do. Hell, everybody knows Bernie didn't want to choose between the two of us, and that's why she brought in a 'hired gun' from Memphis. Norton made a name for himself with those murders back last year when some nut job killed that Vanderley woman and that high-priced lawyer Quinn Cortez was involved."

"Okay, sure, I figure Bernie made it easy on herself by looking outside, and I can see why she picked a guy like Norton. But for the life of me, I can't figure out why he'd take this job. Who'd trade being a Memphis police detective for being a chief deputy in Adams County?"

"I guess we could just ask him."

Ron guffawed. "Yeah, you do that, John."

"Nah, not me. I thought you could ask." John grinned at Ron, then took a huge bite out of the bear claw.

He parked on the side of the paved county road, a road he knew well. At this time of day, the odds of any traffic coming along to interrupt him were low. But just in case, he removed the jack and the tire iron and placed them by the back wheel. Then he scanned the road and the area on both sides, soybean fields that had once been cotton fields as far as the eye could see. He pulled the plastic tarp from the back of his vehicle, lifted it gently in his arms, and headed down the old dirt road that led out into the fields. When he reached midway, far enough off the main road not to be seen, yet close enough for his delivery to be easily discovered tomorrow or the next day or next week, he rolled the contents out of the tarp and into the middle of the rut-scarred lane. She spread out on the ground in a most unladylike manner, her lifeless body pale, her dark eyes wide open and staring up at him. After tossing the tarp aside, he knelt down and arranged

Stephanie's body so that one hand covered her pussy and the other arm rested across her breasts.

There, she was decently covered and yet the beauty of her luscious body was not hidden. He lifted her long dark hair and spread it out across both shoulders, the feel of it like silk against his fingers.

"You wanted to be free, didn't you, my beauty? You told me so yourself."

He rose to his feet, then took one final look at his old lover. The only thing that marred her sultry, dark beauty was the slash across her throat, highlighted by dried blood against her flesh.

You're free now. And so am I. Free to love again.

He wished his relationship with Stephanie had worked out, for his sake and hers. He had thought surely she was the one, that he could love her as much as she loved him. But in the end, he had realized that he had no choice but to end things and continue his search. Out there somewhere was the one and only woman for him, someone who would erase all the painful memories, someone who wouldn't disappoint him, someone worthy of his love.

Picking up the tarp and folding it into a twenty-by-twenty-inch square, he headed back to his parked vehicle. Off in the distance, he heard the rumble of thunder. Glancing at the horizon to the west, he noted the dark sky and figured it was raining over in Scottsboro. Back on the paved road, he scanned the four directions hurriedly; seeing and hearing no sign of anyone approaching, he opened the back of his vehicle, tossed the tarp inside, then retrieved the jack and tire iron. After putting everything back in order, he opened the passenger door, slid behind the wheel and started the engine.

He reached out and fingered the note lying on the passenger seat. A love note for his new love. Sighing, he closed his eyes and pictured her. Young and beautiful. Dark hair. Dark eyes. Maybe she was the one. Maybe this time he wouldn't be disappointed. Maybe this time she wouldn't hurt him.

"Ah, my beautiful, sweet Thomasina."

He loved the pursuit, those heady days of getting to know each other, those romantic moments when anything and everything was possible. He would leave the note for her today. And then he would wait. But not for long. He was eager to begin their love affair.

Sheriff Granger stayed in step with Jim as they headed up Main Street, away from the courthouse and toward the restaurant in the heart of downtown Adams Landing. Her long-legged stride easily matched his pace, an advantage of her being a tall woman.

"I did warn you that Jerry Dale was a huge Jimmy Norton fan," she said. "So be prepared. He'll probably gush all over you."

Jim groaned inwardly, but managed not to cringe. It wasn't that he had any hang-ups about his glorious past as a star running back for UT, but God almighty, that had ended nearly twenty years ago.

"I suppose you run into fans all the time, huh?" she asked.

"Occasionally," he replied. "But when it comes to people I have to work with, I don't want them to think of me as Jimmy Norton. To be honest with you, Sheriff Granger, I prefer people get to know the man I am now, just plain old Jim Norton."

She looked at him, a peculiar expression in her brown eyes. "I was a fan, too. My dad and I. Of course, my dad is a big Alabama fan, and the truth is, he really doesn't like UT, but he used to watch every game back when you and Griffin Powell played. Heck, I guess just about every college football fan in the South did."

"You watched college football with your dad? How old were you—ten?"

"Actually, I was twelve your freshman year and turned fifteen your senior year." *And I fell madly in love with you when I was fourteen and spent the rest of my teen years comparing every guy I met to the great Jimmy Norton, a man I'd seen only on TV, in newspapers and in magazines.* Looking back, she supposed one of the reasons she'd started dating Ryan Fowler in high school was because he'd been the team's number one running back, and in her fantasies, Bernie had put him on a level with her idol. Her big mistake hadn't been dating Ryan; it had been falling in love with him and marrying him.

"You're what now—?" He mentally counted the years. "Thirty-two?"

She nodded.

"Was it unmannerly for me to ask your age?" he asked.

"Not as far as I'm concerned."

He liked her attitude. "You're young to be sheriff."

"The youngest Adams County sheriff ever," she told him. "And the first female. Of course, it didn't hurt that my father and grandfather both held the office before me."

"A family tradition, huh?"

"Yeah, something like that."

"Tell me, Sheriff Granger—"

"Bernie."

"Huh?"

"Call me Bernie," she said. "Everyone does."

"Okay. Bernie." Somehow the name suited her. She didn't look like a Bernadette. That name belonged to some petite bit of fluff, not a substantial woman who looked like she could take care of herself in just about any situation. She was no helpless, clinging female. No I-need-a-big-strong-man female. He'd bet when she was a kid, she could beat the living daylights out of all the little boys and had probably put the fear of God into more than one. And he'd lay odds that in a fair fight, she'd hold her own even now.

"I prefer to be called Jim," he said. "Not Jimmy. And James was my dad."

"Jim it is." She paused. "We're here. This is Methel's."

He stopped at her side and inspected the building. His guess was the two-story structure dated back to the late eighteen hundreds and the outside facade hadn't been updated in a good thirty or forty years.

"Local lawyers and courthouse personnel, along with city policemen and our department, keep Methel's in business," Bernie told him. "There's always a huge lunch crowd during the week. If you like down-home cooking, you'll love the food here."

He reached around her, grasped the door handle and opened the door. She jerked back, glanced over her shoulder and smiled at him, then walked into the restaurant. Apparently she wasn't accustomed to men opening doors for her. She had seemed taken slightly off guard by his gentlemanly action.

"We just find the first available table," Bernie said. "There is no hostess." She surveyed the room, which had the look of an old diner, with one row of booths against the left side wall, a counter with six bar stools along the right wall and a dozen small tables situated in between. The waitresses wore jeans, white shirts and tennis shoes, and from the best he could tell, they ranged in age from eighteen to sixty.

Just making conversation, Jim said, "Something sure smells good."

"It's the Friday special. Beef roast." Bernie lifted her hand and waved. "There they are, in the very back booth. Come on. If we don't put in our order before one, we won't get any peach cobbler. It goes fast."

Jim followed her. In his peripheral vision he caught the

inquisitive stares of the other patrons. He figured everybody knew who he was and they were wondering how he would measure up. When they approached the back booth, two men slid off the red vinyl seats and stood. He recognized Ron Hensley, and by process of elimination assumed the other man was the DA, Jerry Dale Simms. Auburn-haired and freckled, Simms grinned and held out his hand. He was taller than Hensley, about six-one, broad shouldered, hefty, with a wrestler's bulky build.

After Bernie made introductions, Jerry Dale grabbed Jim's hand and pumped it as he grinned and talked and slapped Jim on the back. Jim usually hated it when people fawned over him—over who he used to be—but he got nothing but good vibes from Jerry Dale and decided then and there that he liked the friendly good old boy.

"Sit down. Sit down," Jerry Dale said as he slid back into the booth. "We've done ordered peach cobbler for four. Didn't want to wait and risk not getting any."

Ron slid in beside Jerry Dale as Bernie sat and scooted in across from the two men. By the time Jim sat down beside Bernie, their blond, mid-twenties waitress appeared, a cheerful smile on her face, and handed each the one-page, vinyl-laminated menu. Jim had barely glanced at the items listed before the waitress asked, "What'll it be, folks?"

"Today's special," Jerry Dale replied.

"Same for me," Ron said.

"Make that three," Bernie told her.

Jim glanced up at the waitress, caught a glimpse of her name tag—Renee—and said, "I'll go along with everyone else."

"Four specials. And four peach cobblers. Everybody want sweet tea?" Renee looked right at Jim. He nodded. "You the new chief deputy?"

"Yeah," Jim said. "I'm Jim Norton."

"Nice to meet you. I'm Renee Michaels." She glanced over at Ron and grinned, then turned and sashayed off toward the kitchen, swaying her cute little tush.

Jim wondered what the momentary exchange between Renee and Ron was about, but he pretended not to have noticed. He could tell by the expression on the lieutenant's face that the waitress had struck a nerve. His guess would be that at some time in the not-too-distant past the two had been lovers.

"Have you gotten moved in and settled into your new place?" Jerry Dale asked.

"Pretty much," Jim said. "Not a lot to do in a furnished rental."

"I guess not. Later on you might want to buy a house. If you do, just let me know. My Amy is a realtor and she'll be up to date on all the best bargains."

"Thanks, but I figure I'll be renting for a good while. I don't really need much more than a roof over my head."

"No wife? No kids?" Ron Hensley asked, and Jim wondered if the guy really didn't know any of the personal details of his life.

"An ex-wife who lives in Huntsville with my son. Kevin's twelve, and to be perfectly honest, he's the reason I'm here in Adams Landing. He's why I took this job."

"And a good reason it is, too," Jerry Dale said. "I'd move to the moon if Amy ever left me and took our kids up there. How long you been divorced? Did she up and remarry and take your kid away?"

Jim shifted uncomfortably, not wanting to be rude, but at the same time preferring not to go too deeply into personal matters with people he'd just met.

"So how are J.D. and Anna Leigh?" Bernie Granger asked Jerry Dale. "I hear Anna Leigh made the junior high cheerleader squad. I'll bet she's one happy little girl."

"Lord, yes." Jerry Dale went off on a proud papa tangent,

giving blow-by-blow details of how his thirteen-year-old daughter beat out six rivals to win a spot on the squad.

Jim figured Bernie had sensed his discomfort at discussing his ex-wife and son and had diplomatically steered the conversation away from the topic. He'd been in town less than twenty-four hours and he already owed his new boss. Gut instinct told him he was going to get along just fine with the sheriff, that in time they would probably become friends. And that would certainly be a first for him. He'd never been good friends with a woman unless he was screwing her. But there was always a first time for everything.

After lunch with fellow teacher and friend Shannon Tolliver, Thomasina Hardy returned to her classroom at the Adams County Junior College. She'd been teaching here since her graduation from Auburn University five years ago, having taken the job so she could move back home to Verona, a rural community about twenty-five minutes from downtown Adams Landing. She'd never had dreams of living in a big city, away from her family and childhood friends. Some people couldn't understand why, at twenty-seven, she enjoyed living at home with her widowed mother and younger brother, with her two older siblings' homes within earshot of the home place. The Hardy clan was close-knit—mother, four siblings, two in-laws, and three grandchildren. Thomasina hoped that someday she would marry a fine man and bring her own children into the clan. But for now, she liked her life just as it was.

But she didn't love her life and hadn't ever since she and Ron Hensley had broken up about six months ago. She'd gotten a little more involved in their relationship than he had and when she'd made the mistake of becoming possessive, he'd backed off so quickly it had made her head spin. Her heart had been broken and she'd gone into a mild depression for about two months; then she had looked around and realized there were a lot of other men out there—better men than Ron. One man in particular had caught her eye—Brandon Kelley, the art director here at the junior college. He wasn't an Adams County native, wasn't even an Alabama native, and had come to work at the junior college only last year. She didn't know a great deal about him, only the basic facts. He was thirty-eight, divorced, no children, and had come to Alabama from North Carolina.

Once he started teaching at the junior college, enrollment in art classes doubled, and seventy-five percent of his students were female. But who could blame the students for drooling over the guy. He was simply to die for. Chocolate brown eyes, curly brown hair with a touch of gray at the temples and worn just a tad too long. He was handsome in a Greek god sort of way. Thomasina had to admit that she was as infatuated with Dr. Kelley as any of his young students.

After sitting down at her desk, Thomasina pulled out the right-side bottom drawer and placed her handbag inside, then leaned back in her chair and closed her eyes. She had less than fifteen minutes to relax before the start of her first afternoon class and she had found that a quick, ten-minute power nap usually refreshed her and gave her the energy boost she needed to keep her going until the end of the day. But today, for some reason, she couldn't seem to drift off into that semi-asleep state. Her mind kept whirling with thoughts—thoughts about Dr. Brandon Kelley. Her older sister, Amanda, had told her to ask the guy for a date, and she'd been trying to build up her courage to do just that. After all, what was the worst that could happen? He'd say no. And if he did? No big deal. She'd at least know where she stood with him and could move on to someone who was actually interested in her.

Thomasina opened her eyes, grumbled to herself and gave up on getting her daily afternoon power nap. As her gaze traveled over her desktop, she noticed a square white envelope lying in the middle of a textbook she'd put there before leaving for lunch. She stared at the envelope for half a minute, then picked it up and turned it over to the front. Her name—Thomasina—had been printed in bold letters in black ink. Her heart did a nervous rat-a-tat-tat.

The envelope had not been sealed, but the flap had been tucked neatly beneath the V-shaped back opening. She slid the flap up, and with forefinger and thumb eased the one-page note out of the envelope.

Thomasina took a deep breath, then unfolded the paper, which had been pressed in half, and read the brief message.

I worship you from afar, my beautiful Thomasina.

With her heart fluttering and her pulse racing, she gasped. It was a love letter, of sorts. A succinct message from an admirer. But who? One of her students? Possibly. After all, she was rather attractive and had dealt with male students making passes at her on several occasions.

She read the note again; the words were written in bold print and with black ink. But what student could have written something so utterly romantic? None she knew of. It was something a man would have written, not a boy. A worldly man, with the heart of a poet. Or an artist?

What if Brandon Kelley had written it? What if this was his way of wooing her?

Thomasina held the note to her breast and smiled.

After just one bite of the peach cobbler, Jim understood why Bernie and the others had raved about it. Without a doubt, it was the best he'd ever eaten—even better than his mother's, and she'd been a great cook. If he ate many lunches like the one he'd eaten today, he'd either have to work out more or he'd wind up putting on ten pounds his first month in Adams County.

"Amy's going to want to have you over for dinner one night," Jerry Dale said. "She'll be calling you. She's a wonderful little cook."

How did he get out of such a gracious invitation? "That's awfully nice of—"

Jerry Dale laughed. "Nothing nice about it. That wife of mine is a matchmaker. She'll probably invite one of her unmarried friends to dinner the same night. Just warning you ahead of time. And she won't take no for an answer."

Jim swallowed. "I don't suppose there's some courteous way to say no thanks, is there?"

"Not with my Amy. She's a little velvet steamroller."

"When Amy calls you, why don't you suggest that you come for dinner one evening when your son is visiting," Bernie said. "Tell Amy you'd like Kevin to meet some of the kids here in Adams Landing and he could start with Anna Leigh and J.D."

Jim released a silent sigh. Once again, his boss had come to his rescue. Was that just her nature? he wondered. Was she the caretaker type who was always looking out for others?

Suddenly Ron Hensley's cell phone rang—a distinct, loud ring, no catchy tune. He eased the phone from the belt clip, hit the ON button and said, "Lieutenant Hensley."

Jim studied the deputy's facial expressions and figured something was wrong, bad wrong, before Hensley said, "Goddamn it. Who found her? I see. Yeah, we'll be out there as soon as we can. Just don't let anybody touch anything and keep them as far away from the crime scene as possible."

The minute Hensley finished his conversation, Bernie asked, "What was that about?"

"Earl Wheeler found a woman's body lying in the middle

of a dirt road leading into one of his soybean fields," Hensley said. "That was John. He's on his way to the scene now."

"Any idea who—" Bernie didn't get her sentence finished.

"Earl told John that he's pretty sure the woman is Stephanie Preston. Said she looked like the woman in the newspaper and on TV who's been missing for a couple of weeks."

Chapter 4

When they arrived at the crime scene, a small crowd had already formed along the roadside and the rutted lane leading into farmer Earl Wheeler's soybean fields. Jim had seen this happen all too often, thanks to citizens in possession of police scanners. Although several deputies had beaten them there and were doing their best to keep the spectators at bay, Lieutenant Downs was sweating profusely, apparently concerned about keeping the scene secured.

"Look at them," Hensley said. "Swarming like maggots. Why is it that people are so damn fascinated by murder and mayhem?"

Neither Jim nor Bernie replied since the deputy's question was obviously rhetorical.

Bernie parked her Jeep just short of the yellow tape marking the scene, opened the driver's door and hopped out, with Hensley on her heels. She gave the bystanders a hard glare and ordered everyone to keep their distance, then met Downs as he came toward her. Jim, who'd been sitting in the backseat, didn't rush, allowing the sheriff to take the lead. After all, when it came time to speak to the press, she'd be the one to take the heat. And when the case was solved, it was her right to take most, if not all, the glory. As the new chief investigator, this should be his case, but he wasn't about to inform either the sheriff or Hensley of that fact.

After he got out of the Jeep, he stood back, surveying the scene. Bernie paused after speaking to Downs and looked at Jim. She motioned to him with a wave of her hand. He nodded, and then joined the others at the edge of the yellow tape.

"It's Stephanie Preston," Bernie said. "John called Morris Claunch, our county coroner, and he should be here any minute now. He'll be able to give us some basic info, but it seems fairly obvious that Stephanie's throat has been slashed."

Jim stepped over the tape and moved closer to the body, stopping a good five feet away. Stephanie was young, pretty, dark haired, full breasted and slender. With no apparent signs of a struggle and no blood anywhere on the ground near the victim, Jim surmised that she had been killed elsewhere and brought to this spot. And it was apparent, even to an untrained eye, that she had been posed in a somewhat seductive manner. One arm was draped across her breasts and one hand covered her mound, as if although the killer had wanted to expose her lush body, he'd also wanted to present her corpse with a small degree of modesty. The way he had arranged her limbs and long dark hair said that, in his own sick, perverted way, the killer had cared about his victim. Jim had seen this before, usually in cases where a member of the family turned out to be the murderer and in one case where the perpetrator had been a serial killer and posing his victims had been part of his MO.

Just as Jim noticed several marks on Stephanie's otherwise flawless skin, Bernie walked up beside him.

"I have to call Sheriff Mays over in Jackson County," she said. When Jim looked at her questioningly, she added, "Ed Mays is Stephanie's uncle."

Jim nodded. "Take a look at those marks on her." He pointed them out, one by one. "What do they look like to you?"

"I'm not sure. Some look like small burns, as if—" Bernie swallowed hard. "They look like cigarette burns. And the others look almost like bite marks."

"I'd say the body was placed here recently, within the past few hours, so it's hardly likely that any wild animals would have caused those bite marks. If they had, there would be deeper wounds, some tearing, some flesh torn away."

"They're human bite marks, aren't they?"

"That would be my educated guess," Jim told her.

"Someone tortured Stephanie." Bernie closed her eyes for a couple of seconds, then reopened them and cleared her throat.

"It's okay to be upset," Jim said. "You don't have to pretend that it doesn't bother you to know that not only was this young woman killed, but she was probably tortured for a couple of weeks before he slit her throat." He glanced at Bernie and noted how pale her face was. "It bothers me a hell of a lot, too. I'm just better at hiding my feelings."

"I don't have the luxury of crying or screaming. I'm the sheriff. How would it look to my deputies—to anyone for that matter—if every time I'm exposed to something terrible, I break down and boohoo like a . . . a . . ."

"Like a woman?"

Bernie blew out a disgruntled moan. "Since she's naked, do you think that means he raped her?"

"Probably, but it's possible he didn't. An autopsy should tell us everything we need to know about what she endured in the what, two weeks since she came up missing."

"Our coroner, Morris Claunch, is the local undertaker," Bernie said. "He's not trained to do the kind of autopsy we need."

"I figured that. So you'll recommend that Claunch contact DFS, right? Or am I being presumptuous in assuming the sheriff's department usually calls in the state boys when there's a murder?"

"You're my chief deputy, the lead investigator for my department," she told him. "Is it your recommendation that the DFS and the ABI be brought in on this case?"

He looked her square in the eyes. Was she testing him by asking what he thought should be done? "Yeah, it's my recommendation, but you're the sheriff. It's your call."

"Look, I'm more aware than most that law enforcement in many Alabama counties still suffers from a prevailing 'turf' mentality, and some sheriffs and police chiefs are reluctant to call in the ABI. I'm not one of those sheriffs."

"I had a feeling you weren't." The corners of his mouth lifted, hinting at an approving smile.

"Adams County simply doesn't have the resources we'd need to do justice to this type of crime investigation," Bernie told him. "My only other murder case was simple. Cut and dried. The killer confessed. So I haven't worked with the ABI, but my dad knows the ABI area commander in Huntsville, and I've heard him say that he's never had a problem working with the Bureau."

Jim glanced at the cell phone clipped to Bernie's belt, then said, "The sooner the better."

"Right." She removed her phone and scanned through the programmed numbers, then walked away from Jim and farther away from the crowd before placing her call.

Hensley came over to Jim and nodded toward Bernie. "Is she calling in the ABI?"

"Yeah."

"Morris Claunch just drove up," Hensley said. "What should I tell him?"

Day one as Hensley's supervisor and Jim noticed that the guy was already playing by the rules. That was a good sign. "Tell him the sheriff is calling in the ABI and she'll want

DFS involved." Jim looked directly at his deputy. "How long's it going to take to get an autopsy report from DFS?"

"Average time? A week to a month. And for DNA evidence, that could be up to six months or longer. Worst case scenario— up to a year."

"I was afraid of that."

"The DFS guys are overworked and underpaid, and there aren't enough of them to go around," Hensley said. "In the past, we've worked with a preliminary draft right up to the trial."

"Unless the coroner can tell us otherwise, I'm going to work under the assumption that Stephanie Preston was repeatedly raped and tortured before being killed."

A tall, gangly man with thinning brown hair and a decided slump to his shoulders plodded casually over to them; he spoke to Hensley and glanced at Jim. "You the new chief deputy?"

"Yeah, I'm Jim Norton."

The man held out his hand. "I'm Morris Claunch, the coroner."

Bernie replaced her cell phone on the belt clip as she approached them. "A response unit is on its way from Huntsville, along with an agent, a guy named Charlie Patterson." She looked right at Claunch. "I called Dad and he said you and he had worked with Patterson several years back."

"Hmm . . . yeah, we did. Patterson's okay. As I recall, he's a team player. He'll work with you"—Claunch glanced at Jim—"with your chief investigator and his team."

"Once you take a look at the body, I'd like to know what you think," Jim said.

Claunch raised one eyebrow, then nodded before making his way toward the beautiful young woman lying naked on a dirt lane in the middle of a soybean field.

*   *   *

Thomasina Hardy loaded the dishwasher and cleaned up her mother's kitchen, then washed her hands and applied scented lotion. Her brother had a Friday night date and her mother had just left to go to her older sister Amanda's to babysit the children so Amanda and her husband could go bowling over in Adams Landing. So here she was all alone on a Friday night. She and Ron broke up six months ago, so she should be back in circulation by now, shouldn't she? She'd had a total of five dates in the past few months and not once had she accepted a second date with any one of the guys. Yes, she was picky. She might give just about any guy a chance with one date, but if he didn't measure up, she didn't waste her time or his.

Paul Landon, the richest bachelor in Adams County, had thought buying her dinner meant he got to screw her on a first date. The guy was a jerk. Neither his good looks nor his sizable bank account impressed her enough to give him a second chance.

Her mom had fixed her up with widower Steve Banyan, an Adams Landing pharmacist, but an hour into their date, she'd been bored to tears. All the man talked about was his kids and his deceased wife.

Her sister had fixed her up with two different duds—one worked at the phone company with Amanda's husband and the other was a guy on their bowling team.

The only contender in the bunch had been Raymond Long, a recently divorced nice guy. But he'd never called her for a second date. Maybe she simply wasn't his type.

Thomasina picked up the *TV Guide* and the remote control as she sat down on the sofa in the den and contemplated another Friday night alone. As she curled up on the sofa, she turned on the television and laid the remote at her side, then flipped through the guide. She had her choice of cop shows, reality shows and sitcoms, but she decided on a cable channel that showed an attractive young woman undergoing breast enlargement surgery. Although she filled out a C cup, Thomasina had often wondered how she'd look with a set of D or double-D boobs.

Ten minutes into the show, the telephone rang. Thomasina groaned. It was probably one of those annoying telephone solicitors. She hit the MUTE button on the remote, then got up and walked across the room to where her mom had left the cordless phone earlier this evening when she'd made a call to Amanda. Thomasina checked the caller ID. PAY PHONE. A pay telephone? How odd. She knew there were several of those old pay phone booths still around in various areas in Adams County, but she wasn't personally acquainted with anyone who used them. Debating whether to answer or allow the answering machine to pick up, she let the phone ring four times, then quickly hit the ON button and said, "Hello."

"Thomasina?" the unfamiliar voice said.

"Yes."

"Did you get my note?"

It was then that Thomasina realized his voice sounded odd. A deep, throaty baritone.

"Who is this?" she asked.

"I'm your secret admirer."

A cold chill raced up Thomasina's spine. *Don't overreact. Don't assume this guy is some nut job. It could be Brandon Kelley simply being romantic, choosing to woo you as a secret admirer first, before revealing his true identity.*

"Why keep your identity a secret?"

"I will reveal my identity when the time is right," he told her. "But for now . . . sleep well tonight, my beautiful Thomasina, and dream of your secret lover who longs to touch you, to whisper love sonnets in your ear, to fulfill your every fantasy."

Thomasina gasped softly, undeniably aroused by the man's words, by the image his comments painted in her mind. Images of Brandon and her together.

"Please, tell me—"

The dial tone alerted her to the fact that he had ended their conversation.

Thomasina closed her eyes and sighed. Her Friday night wasn't turning out to be so dull and uneventful after all. Will he call back tonight? No, probably not. But maybe tomorrow or tomorrow night. In a way, she wished Brandon would just come right out and ask her for a date, but in another way, she thought it was romantic and rather sweet that he had thought of a unique way to begin an old-fashioned courtship.

But what if it's not Brandon? Of course, it was Brandon. Who else could it be?

She carried the phone with her when she returned to the sofa. After sitting down, she laid the phone beside the remote. For several minutes she stared at the silent television screen and considered the possibilities. If her secret admirer wasn't Brandon Kelley, then who could it be? She couldn't think of another man she knew who would do something so unconventional and romantic.

It has to be Brandon.

She hit the MUTE button again to resume the sound on the TV and tried to renew her interest in the show she'd been watching. But her mind kept wandering, alternating between fantasizing about Brandon and wondering whether she should be flattered or concerned about this little game he was playing with her.

Jim wolfed down a bologna sandwich and swigged on a Dr. Pepper as he tried to decide whether he should shave before heading over to the Adams Landing Hotel to pick up Agent Patterson for a late-evening session with the sheriff. The ABI agent had shown up less than an hour after Bernie had placed her phone call. He came with the crime scene guys, although he'd driven his own vehicle since he'd be staying in town for several days. If they didn't break the case within a few days, Patterson would probably drive back and forth from Huntsville after that, since it was only a forty-five-minute drive. Jim's guess was that this case wouldn't be solved easily, maybe not for weeks or months. Maybe never. He had his own theories, but before mouthing off his opinion, he'd decided to wait until this evening and hear what Patterson had to say and get Bernie's input after she spoke to her father. He wondered how many on-the-job years it would take before she felt confident enough not to run things by her dad. It couldn't be easy for her trying to live up to the old man, living and working in his shadow.

Stephanie Preston's body was on its way to Huntsville. Her family had been notified. Jim suspected that Bernie's call to Sheriff Ed Mays probably had been the most difficult call she'd ever made. Both the ABI and the DFS were now involved due to the type of crime that had been committed, with the two agencies working with the county sheriff's department. Bernie had called a press conference and had faced not only local reporters, but Huntsville newspaper reporters and television crews. She had kept her comments brief and refused to take questions, which was standard procedure this early in the game. Although the statement to the press had been succinct—Stephanie Preston's body had been discovered, the cause of death to be determined by an autopsy, and yes, the death was being handled as a murder—rumors no doubt already abounded. Any of the locals who'd been at the scene could spread the word that Stephanie's throat had been slashed and that she was naked.

After finishing off the Dr. Pepper, Jim wiped his mouth, walked over to the garbage can in the kitchen and dumped the empty cola bottle and the paper towel he'd used as a napkin. He glanced at his watch and saw that he had just enough time to shave, if he hurried. He was supposed to pick up Patterson at six-thirty; then the two of them would go to his office at the county jail, where Bernie, Ron Hensley and John Downs would meet them.

Jim made it halfway to the bathroom before his cell phone rang. Answering the call as he opened the bathroom door, he said, "Yeah?"

"Jim Norton?" He didn't recognize the man's voice.

"Yeah, this is Norton."

"Mr. Norton . . . Jim . . . this is Allen Clark." He paused, apparently waiting for a reaction from Jim. "You know, Mary Lee's husband."

"Yeah, I know who you are. What do you want? Is it something about Kevin? I'm supposed to get him next weekend. Mary Lee hasn't changed her mind, has she?"

"No, no, nothing like that."

"Then what?" Jim flipped on the light and looked at himself in the medicine cabinet mirror.

"I was wondering . . . that is, *we* were wondering if you could take Kevin earlier than we'd planned, say next Thursday?"

"Yeah, sure, but I don't understand what's going on. Why would Mary Lee give me a couple of extra days with Kevin?" Since their divorce nearly seven years ago, his ex-wife had done everything she could to undermine his relationship with his son and never, ever allowed them extra time together.

"Actually, we need you to keep Kevin for several weeks, possibly until school starts in August."

"What's the catch?"

"Look, Mr. Norton . . . Jim . . . I don't know any other way to explain than to just come right out and tell you. Mary Lee has been diagnosed with breast cancer. She's having a mastectomy next Friday, here in Huntsville. Her treatment will probably include radiation and chemo. She needs complete rest."

Mary Lee had breast cancer? The news hit him hard. But

not because he still had any deep feelings for his ex. Nope, that wasn't it. As much as he sometimes hated Mary Lee and had on more than one occasion damned her to hell, she was his son's mother. Kevin loved her. Needed her.

"What's the prognosis?" Jim asked, a tight knot in his throat. Okay, so maybe he did still care about Mary Lee. Maybe he always would. But he wasn't in love with her. She'd killed that years ago.

"The doctor is optimistic. Of course, we won't know for sure until they run tests on the lymph nodes after surgery. But we're hoping and praying for the best."

"Yeah, of course you are. How's Mary Lee?" His ex-wife had always considered herself a sexy woman and had used her body as both a weapon and a reward for the men in her life.

"She's okay. Scared. Upset. Worrying about Kevin."

"Was my taking Kevin for the next few weeks her idea or yours?" Jim asked.

Allen Clark cleared his throat. "Mine, actually. She's concerned that with you starting a new job, Kevin might be alone too much."

"I'll see to it that he's not."

"Then you're okay with my bringing him to Adams Landing next Thursday?"

"Yeah. Sure. But what about Kevin? Have y'all told him—"

"Not yet, but we will. This weekend. And . . . uh . . . I'll call you Monday and set up a time and . . . Thanks, Mr.—"

"Jim."

"Thanks, Jim."

For several seconds after their conversation ended, Jim stood in the small bathroom, his gaze fixed on the mirror in front of him. He no longer saw his reflection, no longer thought about shaving. His emotions were torn between genuine concern about his ex-wife's health and absolute joy over the fact that he was being given the gift of spending so much time with his son.

Jim snorted. Wasn't life always this way? He had a chance for his son to live with him for several weeks, maybe more than a month, and this opportunity came at the worst possible time for him. Just as he was starting a new job that had become exceedingly complicated on his very first day. How was he going to balance giving Kevin the quality time he needed and deserved and giving his all to the investigation into Stephanie Preston's brutal murder?

Chapter 5

Jim had listened, commented when asked a point-blank question and otherwise let the others carry the conversation. He was the new man on the job and despite the fact that he was in charge of this case for the sheriff's department, it was officially now an ABI case. He had sized up Agent Patterson within twenty minutes of meeting him—laid-back and easy to get along with, intelligent without being the least bit cocky. Bernie had informed Jim that Patterson held a B.S. degree in Criminal Justice, as did she, which didn't surprise him in the least. He figured Bernie probably also had, as he had, gone through the ten-week program at the FBI National Academy in Quantico. Besides taking forensic classes, he'd learned something about management techniques during the course.

The four of them—Patterson, Hensley, Bernie and Jim— sat around in Jim's office, everybody on their third cup of coffee and rehashed the situation.

"I think we can eliminate Kyle Preston," Patterson said. "The guy's a basket case. He's been under a doctor's care for over a week now, sedated a great deal of that time, and if I ever saw a grieving widower—"

"I agree," Ron Hensley said. "But without the husband as a suspect, who does that leave us with?"

"It leaves us with nobody," Patterson replied. "At least for tonight. But somebody knows something, even if they think they don't. It's our job to dig deep until we come up with a workable scenario. Some nut job kidnapped Stephanie Preston, raped and tortured her for two weeks, and then killed her. Was he some guy just passing through Adams County or has he lived here all his life? Did he have something personal against Stephanie? Or maybe against her husband or another family member? Or did she just happen to be in the wrong place at the wrong time?"

"And how was he able to kidnap her from the college campus without anyone noticing?" Bernie grimaced. "Where had he kept her for the past thirteen days? If he's done this once, will he do it again?"

"Yes," Jim said.

All eyes turned to him.

"Are you saying that, yes, he'll do it again?" Bernie asked.

Jim nodded. "Is this the first case of its kind in the area that you know of?"

"What are you implying?" Hensley asked.

"You're not thinking we've got the makings of a serial killer on our hands, are you, Captain?" Patterson asked.

"Oh, God." Bernie cringed. "Whatever y'all do, don't repeat that outside these four walls. If the phrase serial killer gets bandied about, we'll have all-out panic on our hands."

Even though Jim's gut instincts told him that there was a possibility that the man who killed Stephanie would do it again and she might not have been his first victim, he wasn't about to go out on a limb on his first day on the job. Not when he'd been wrong in the past and been slapped down for it. Not if the opinion of a seasoned ABI agent differed from his. He could always do some snooping around on his own, if he felt strongly enough about it once they had a few more facts.

"Aren't you jumping to conclusions?" Hensley glowered at Jim. "Shouldn't we wait on the official autopsy report and other forensic findings before we automatically assume anything about this case?"

"Nobody's jumping to conclusions," Patterson said. "And we're not assuming anything. But every opinion counts. We can't rule out anything at this point." He turned to Jim. "It won't hurt to check with neighboring counties to see if there's been any similar murders. But if our killer is nomadic, it'll make solving this case more difficult."

Jim nodded. "I hate to bother her husband and her parents, but I think we should talk to them again and also take a look at her home." Jim glanced at Bernie. "Maybe Sheriff Mays can help us with that."

"You still think the husband might have done it?" Hensley asked.

"No, not really," Jim said. "But it's possible there's something he or her parents haven't told us."

"Why would they have kept anything from us?" Hensley's harsh gaze narrowed until his eyes were mere slits. "They were desperate to find Stephanie. They'd have done anything to—"

"I didn't say they deliberately kept anything from us," Jim said. "But the husband and the parents were under unbearable emotional stress and could have easily forgotten something or dismissed something they thought insignificant. Didn't y'all mention that the husband's been sedated for a good part of the past seven or eight days?"

"I see what you're getting at," Bernie said. "And you're right. I'll contact Ed first thing in the morning and arrange for us to talk to Stephanie's husband and her parents and get Kyle Preston's permission to search the house."

"He'll think he's under suspicion," Hensley said. "Even if he's innocent, he's liable to clam up and hire a lawyer."

"Not if we handle things right." Agent Patterson glanced at Jim. "We have no reason to suspect the husband and he needs to know that up front. But if he refuses to allow us to search his house, well . . ."

Bernie glanced at her watch. Twenty till eleven. "It's getting late. Why don't we call it a night, get some sleep and start fresh first thing in the morning?"

"Sounds good to me." Patterson rose from his chair.

Hensley got up and stretched. "Agent Patterson, do you need a ride to the hotel or do you have your car with you?"

"I think I'll walk back to the hotel. It's not that far and it's a nice night. Besides, I do my best thinking when I take leisurely walks."

Hensley nodded, shook Patterson's hand and said good night to Bernie and then to Jim before heading for the door.

Patterson shook hands with Jim and Bernie. "Is seven in the morning too early for you two?"

"Seven's fine," Jim and Bernie replied in unison, then looked at each other and grinned.

A silly little phrase popped into Jim's mind. *Two fools here and two more coming.* How many times had he heard his father use that expression whenever two people said the same thing at exactly the same time?

As soon as Patterson left, Bernie picked up the empty Styrofoam coffee cups scattered about the room and threw them into the garbage. Jim turned off the coffeemaker, picked up the glass pot and took it into the adjoining bathroom. He emptied the remainder of the coffee into the sink, rinsed out the pot and brought it back into his office.

"You didn't have much to say about this case," Bernie said.

"There's not much to say at this point. We don't have the official autopsy or—"

"What's the official autopsy from DFS going to tell us that we don't already know? Morris examined the body at the scene and told us she'd apparently been raped and tortured, and the cause of death was obvious—somebody slit her throat."

"There's more to it than the autopsy. Patterson hasn't heard back from his crime scene unit yet."

"He should have a preliminary report from them by morning, but you're an experienced investigator. You looked over the scene before Patterson's team arrived. You must have a gut feeling about this case."

"My gut feelings aren't a hundred percent accurate. I've been known to be wrong."

"Haven't we all?"

They stood there and stared at each other for at least a minute. Jim wondered what this in-control, got-it-all-together woman had been wrong about in the past?

"Look, there's something you should know," he said, the comment coming from out of nowhere. He hadn't meant to unburden himself on his boss, at least not yet. But before Kevin arrived on Thursday, he'd have to tell her about the changes in his personal life that might conflict with his duties as her chief deputy.

"Something about this case?"

He shook his head. "No, about me. About something going on in my personal life right now. I hadn't meant to bring it up tonight, but you need to know."

"Is it something that will interfere with your doing your job?"

"I don't think so." He huffed out a disgruntled breath. "No, it shouldn't. Not if I can figure out how to handle being a full-time single father and do justice to my job at the same time."

Bernie lifted an inquisitive eyebrow. "Your son is coming to live with you?"

"Temporarily. My ex-wife . . . Kevin's mother has been diagnosed with breast cancer. Her surgery is scheduled for next week. I know the timing is lousy, what with me just starting this job and our facing this major murder case, but—"

"How old is Kevin?"

"Twelve."

"He won't need a babysitter, just someone to keep an eye on him when you're not at home."

"Yeah, and with this case coming up the way it did, I can't predict what my hours are going to be during the next month or so while Kevin's living with me."

"I see why you're concerned, but I think I have a solution for you."

"You have a solution? What kind of solution?"

"My parents are retired. They both want grandchildren and unfortunately neither I nor my sister, Robyn, has given them any . . . yet. Why not let Kevin spend time with my folks when you're at work? My mother will spoil him rotten. And Dad will take him fishing and play ball with him and—"

"Whoa, hon—slow down." He'd stopped himself just short of calling his boss *honey*. "You haven't even checked with your parents. You can't make that kind of offer without asking them about it first. I can't imagine they'd want the responsibility of looking after my kid. They don't even know me."

"I'll tell you what, come to Sunday dinner. Meet my folks. I'll tell Mom about your dilemma and I'll bet you twenty bucks she'll volunteer for the job of playing surrogate grandmother to Kevin."

Jim felt overwhelmed by this generous offer. *Stunned* might be a better word. He was unaccustomed to people going out of their way for somebody who was little more than a stranger to them. "I don't know what to say."

"Say you'll come for Sunday dinner. My dad's dying to meet you anyway."

"He's dying to meet Jimmy Norton and I haven't been that guy in a long time."

Bernie stared at him, her gaze pensive and penetrating, as if she were trying to delve deep inside him, to figure out what made him tick. "I believe that the child we were, even the teenager and young adult we were, always remains a part of us. Something of who Jimmy Norton was is still a part of you, whether you like it or not."

"You're awfully philosophical for so late at night, or do you always play amateur psychiatrist?"

"Guilty as charged," she told him. "I minored in psychology at Alabama."

"If I agree to come to Sunday dinner and join your dad in regaling my glorious past, will you promise not to try to figure out what makes me tick?" Jim turned off the lights in his office, opened the door and held it for her.

Taking her cue from him, she walked out into the hallway. "Why does it bother you that I want to get to know you better? I've known most of my deputies for years. I went to high school with some of them; some have married friends of mine. You're an unknown, Jim Norton, a bit of a puzzle. And puzzles intrigue me. Besides, I like to really get to know my friends."

"Are we going to be friends?" He kept pace with her as they walked down the hall.

"I'd like to think so."

They exited the jail together, and then paused outside on the sidewalk.

"Don't you want to be friends?" she asked. "Or do you have trouble being just friends with a woman?"

Jim chuckled. "The truth is I've never been just friends with a woman."

"There's always a first time for everything."

"So there is."

She headed toward her Jeep, leaving him standing in the middle of the sidewalk. After unlocking the driver's door, she glanced back at him and smiled. "See you at seven in the morning. You make the coffee. I'll bring sausage biscuits."

"Make mine ham and cheese."

"How many, one or two?"

"Two."

She slid behind the wheel, closed the door and started the engine. Jim stood and watched her until all he could see was the Jeep's red taillights off in the distance. He decided right then and there that he'd definitely like to be friends with Bernie Granger.

He stroked the pearls, loving the feel of their cool, slick surface. These were not real pearls, of course. He couldn't afford real ones like the necklace she had worn. But his lovers didn't seem to mind that the necklace he sent was faux pearls. After all, it's the thought that counts, right? Smiling, his mind filled with memories of her, he closed his eyes and the images grew brighter and sharper. He could see her clearly, almost as clearly as the night he had made love to her. She had been so surprised to see him.

He had foolishly thought she would welcome him with open arms, but she hadn't. And in the long run, it really hadn't mattered. He had gotten what he wanted—actually, more than he'd ever dreamed possible. Satisfaction. Revenge. Empowerment.

Afterward, he had believed her death had evened the score, that killing her had appeased the rage and anger inside him. But he'd been wrong. It had only fueled his need for revenge. That's why he had sought out the other three, prolonging his time a little more with each of them, making them suffer as he had suffered. And when all four of them had been punished, he had thought that would be the end of it. Once again, he'd been wrong.

Just because someone hurts you, disappoints you, breaks your heart, doesn't mean you should stop looking for love, stop searching for the one woman to fulfill your fantasies.

He hummed quietly to himself as he opened his eyes, laid the pearls down inside the white gift box and closed the lid. He would deliver these tomorrow, along with the note.

After pulling out the desk chair, he sat, picked up the black ink pen and stared down at the white note paper. Hmm . . . what to say . . . what words would seduce Thomasina? She was a romantic at heart, so she wouldn't respond well to anything crude and earthy. Not yet.

Please accept this small token of my affection. Pearls for a lovely lady.

There, that should do it. All he wanted to do was whet her appetite for more.

He put the note inside the envelope and wrote her name across the front, then laid the message aside. The note and the pearls were always the next step in his courtship, then the sketch came later. But he was so eager to move things along, not to take weeks to court her, that he felt he should go ahead and send the sketch along with the note and pearls.

He opened the middle desk drawer and brought out his sketch pad and pencil, then closed his eyes for just a moment—long enough to picture her in his mind. His eagerness transferred to his drawing as he quickly sketched Thomasina's face, her flowing dark hair, her sweet smile, her long, slender neck, the curve of her naked shoulder.

There, that's enough. Stop.

He laid the charcoal pencil aside and took a deep breath. Thinking of her naked, of her lush breasts, the nipples peaked, her flat belly, her nicely rounded hips, and that thatch of dark hair between her thighs aroused him unbearably. But he couldn't draw her that way. Not yet. It wasn't time.

Accept the pain. Make it your friend. Remember that waiting for her makes the moment you first come together all the sweeter.

Tomorrow, he'd find a way to deliver his note and little gifts. It shouldn't be a problem. She drove into Adams Landing every Saturday morning and went to Robyn Granger's gym.

Ron went around to the back door and pecked on the glass. When he'd called Abby to cancel their weekend plans, she'd been disappointed, but she'd understood. After all, he was a deputy, and the Stephanie Preston murder case was the biggest thing to happen in Adams County in a good ten years or longer.

He waited for Abby to come to the door; then when she didn't, he pecked again and called her name softly. He had parked down the street and come down the alley, taking every precaution not to be seen. But hell, it was eleven-thirty—who'd be up at this hour staring out their windows?

"Abby, honey . . ."

He heard footsteps inside the dark kitchen, then the distinctive click of the deadbolt being unlocked. The minute she opened the door, he rushed inside, kicked the door shut behind himself, and grabbed her.

"Slow down," she told him, then giggled when he grabbed her ass with both hands and yanked her up against his hard-as-a-rock penis.

"I can't slow down, baby. I want you too much."

He kissed her neck as he rubbed her mound against his arousal.

"You can at least wait till we get to the bedroom," she

said. "I've had a long, rough day and I don't want to wind up with my butt on the floor or slammed up against the wall."

"Ah, baby, you like it any way you can get it."

When he lifted her up off the floor, she wrapped her legs around his hips and tossed back her head when he opened his mouth and covered one breast through the thin material of her shorty pajama top.

Clinging to him, whimpering and talking dirty, Abby encouraged him to hurry as he carried her out of the kitchen, up the hall and into her bedroom. After tossing her onto the bed, he stripped off his clothes, and by the time he came down over her, she was naked and ready. Without saying a word, she reached out, encircled his dick and slid a condom over it. No matter how turned on Abby got, she never forgot to make sure she was protected. He liked that about her, that she took care of herself instead of expecting him to do it.

He thrust into her with one powerful lunge and nearly came right off the bat. She was hot and wet and tight. When she bucked up, he clutched her buttocks and held her for half a second before retreating and plunging again.

"I'm not going to be able to hold it much longer, baby," he told her.

She slid her hand between her legs and stroked herself. "I'll just help things along."

He paused, allowing her to go at it, all the while whispering in her ear, talking the talk, exciting her. In only a matter of minutes, she came in a frenzy, crying, shivering. He jackhammered into her for a couple of seconds, then came, the top of his head exploding as he jetted into the condom.

Once he was spent, he rolled off her and onto the bed beside her. She cuddled up against him and said, "Get some rest. Next time I'm not going to let you off the hook so easily."

Ron reached over and stroked her belly, then delved his

hand between her thighs. She was damp and sticky. When he fingered her clitoris, she whimpered.

"Set the alarm, will you, babe? I need to leave here before sunrise. We don't want to run the risk of somebody seeing me sneak out your back door."

"I'll set it for four," she told him. "That'll give us time for a good morning fuck."

Chuckling, Ron closed his eyes and hugged up to Abby, spoon-fashion.

Chapter 6

Ever since her younger daughter had returned to Adams Landing and opened her own business—Robyn's Fitness Center—Brenda Granger had made a point of taking an active part in several classes Robyn offered. Brenda's favorite was the Saturday morning session where a group of women went from doing stretches together to alternating on all the various equipment—everything from the treadmills to the stationary bicycles. After the first hour, they took a water break, then after the second hour, many of them stayed on and had lunch together. Robyn provided fresh salads with low-fat dressing and yogurt for dessert.

Since Brenda had kept herself in shape all her life and had been blessed with a great metabolism, she hadn't needed to worry about her weight until she went through menopause; then ten extra pounds had crept up around her hips and abdomen before she knew it. It had taken her two months of diet and exercise to get back down to what her husband laughingly referred to as her fighting weight.

As she stood back and watched Robyn, in her much-too-skimpy exercise costume, Brenda sighed, then took a hefty

sip of bottled spring water. Her younger daughter resembled
her a great deal, with a slender figure, full breasts and curly,
jet-black hair. Thankfully, Robyn had also inherited her
great metabolism, as well as her love for physical exercise to
keep her fabulous body toned. She had gotten her height
from her six-four father, just as her sister, Bernie, had.
Robyn was five-eight, and Bernie was just a tad over five-
nine.

Poor Bernie had not inherited her mother's slender build
or her great metabolism. Ever since childhood, Brenda's
elder daughter had been large boned and tended to gain
weight easily, as R.B. did. Bernie was as much her father's
daughter as Robyn was her mother's, in looks and tempera-
ment.

But both girls were equally disappointing to a mother
who longed to see her daughters happily married and pro-
ducing some grandchildren for her. After all, neither she nor
R.B. was getting any younger. A woman of fifty-eight should
already have several grandchildren.

At least Robyn was dating regularly, although Brenda
didn't always approve of the choices she made. Bernie, on
the other hand, dated infrequently and seemed to let every
good prospect slip through her fingers.

Brenda felt it her motherly duty to do what she could to
help both girls find the proper mate. That's why she had invited two very suitable young men to Sunday dinner tomorrow. Raymond Long was a fine man and not bad looking,
despite being a bit of a nerd. He owned the local hardware
store and could provide handsomely for a wife. Luckily, he
had divorced that hussy wife of his before they'd had children. And it didn't hurt that Raymond's mother, Helen, had
been one of Brenda's best friends for ages. The other Sunday
guests would include the new minister, Matthew Donaldson.
Matthew was young, handsome, charismatic, and best of all,
he was single.

"Are you staying for lunch, Brenda?" Abby Miller asked.

"I wouldn't miss it." Brenda smiled warmly at Abby, although she didn't especially like the woman. Abby wore too much makeup, dyed her hair that phony blue-black and wore clothes that screamed trailer trash. And there was a rumor going around town that Abby was secretly seeing another man while her poor husband was off in the Middle East serving his country.

The others staying for lunch began making a circle in the middle of the exercise room floor. Brenda glanced around to ascertain just who was still here so she could decide who she wanted to sit by. One by one, she ruled out the women she did not want to talk to for the half-hour lunch session. Definitely not Abby Miller. She crossed Renee Michaels off her list immediately. That woman didn't have a brain in her silly head. Besides, it was a known fact Renee was a slut. Deputy Holly Burcham was another no-no, but only because she was sitting beside Renee, as was Amber Claunch, whom Brenda liked.

"Hmm . . ." Brenda spotted Bernie's secretary, Lisa Wiley, and started in her direction, but stopped the minute she saw Cathy Downs sit beside Lisa. Cathy was a sweet person, but she would bore you to tears with her incessant chatter. The woman never stopped talking—about her children, her husband Lieutenant John Downs and her latest diet. The plump chatterbox tried every new diet craze that came along and did her best to convince everyone else that this one was the miracle cure for overweight women.

As her gaze traveled the completely formed circle, she suddenly saw her perfect spot, right between Amy Simms and Thomasina Hardy. Brenda hurried across the room, then paused and looked from Amy to Thomasina.

"Would y'all mind making room for me?" Before either could reply, Brenda squeezed in between them, forcing them to separate enough to make room for her.

Amy smiled pleasantly at Brenda. "Yes, please, join us."

"We were just talking about what happened to that poor girl, Stephanie Preston, from over in Scottsboro," Thomasina said.

"It's the world we live in." Brenda shook her head sadly. "When I was a girl, you never heard of anything like that happening around here. Northeast Alabama was one of the safest places on earth to live. Why, my folks never locked the doors and we slept with the windows open and never worried about somebody breaking into the house."

"All the article in this morning's *Daily Reporter* said was that she'd been murdered." Amy looked right at Brenda. "You don't know anything else, do you? Something you could share with us?"

Brenda smiled, hoping her expression conveyed to these ladies that she did, indeed, know something very important about the murder case. Although she knew no more than they did, being the sheriff's mother, as she had once been the sheriff's wife, afforded her the privilege of pretending to be in possession of top-secret information.

"I'm afraid there's nothing I'm at liberty to share with y'all," Brenda said. "There are many things that can't be shared with the public or it might jeopardize the case. I learned years ago, as R.B.'s wife, to keep my mouth shut."

"Oh, Brenda, come on," Amy cajoled. "Isn't there some little something? You know we'd never tell a soul."

Brenda shook her head, then leaned over and whispered to Amy, "Well . . . No, no, I can't. Sorry."

"We understand," Thomasina said. "Besides, I'm not sure I want to know the details. Rumors are that she was naked when they found her, and you know what that usually means— it means she was probably raped. Poor girl."

"Wonder if they think her husband killed her?" Amy said. "I tried to pry something out of Jerry Dale last night, but he wasn't talking. I told him, what good is it for me to be the DA's wife if the DA never tells me anything."

All three women laughed.

"Did somebody tell a good joke?" Robyn asked as she pulled the serving cart behind herself.

"Not really," Brenda replied. "It was just nervous laughter."

"We were talking about that poor Stephanie Preston," Thomasina said.

Robyn retrieved two salads in plastic containers from the serving cart, then handed one to Thomasina and the other to her mother. "You know, when she came up missing and all those searches didn't turn up anything, I had a feeling she was dead. It gives me cold chills to think about what happened to her." Robyn handed Amy a salad.

"We were trying to dig information out of your mother, but she won't tell us anything," Amy said.

Robyn eyed her mother speculatively, the corners of her wide, full mouth turning up ever so slightly. Brenda knew that expression only too well. It was Robyn's shame-on-you-Mama look.

"Being members of the sheriff's family doesn't necessarily mean we're in possession of any more information than the average citizen," Robyn said, then winked at her mother.

Brenda let out a mental sigh of relief that her daughter hadn't given her away. But then Robyn had been Brenda's coconspirator all her life, backing her up, keeping her secrets, sharing in her love for gossip. Bernie had been the tattletale, always telling R.B. everything. Her elder daughter had never learned the art of telling socially acceptable little white lies. Like R.B., she could be too in-your-face blunt and brutally honest. That detrimental trait wasn't very appealing to most men and was probably one of the reasons Bernie couldn't find a husband. That and the fact that Bernie needed to lose twenty pounds.

* * *

Since the Preston home was in Jackson County, Sheriff Mays accompanied Bernie, Jim and Charlie Patterson when they met Kyle Preston and Stephanie's parents at the white vinyl-sided house the newlywed couple had rented near Hollywood. Bernie asked the parents and husband to come outside with her and sit on the porch to talk to her and Ed Mays while Charlie Patterson and Jim Norton searched the house.

The parents sat side by side in the porch swing. The husband sat in one of the two white rocking chairs, while Ed Mays took the other. Bernie remained standing.

"I can only imagine how difficult this is for y'all." Bernie looked at each of them individually. "And I'm truly sorry that we have to question y'all again."

"Ed explained," Jay Floyd, Stephanie's father, said. "We want to do whatever we can to help y'all catch whoever killed our little girl." Tears welled up in the middle-aged man's faded brown eyes.

"We appreciate your cooperation." Bernie glanced at Emmy Floyd, Stephanie's mother, who sat quietly, tears streaming down her cheeks and a glazed expression on her face. She held her hands in her lap and kept twisting her gold wedding band around and around. Dear God, how horrible this must be for her. To lose a child would be bad enough, but to know that child had suffered repeated brutality for nearly two weeks would be something no mother could ever come to terms with.

Bernie turned to Kyle Preston, and she could tell by the glassy look in his eyes that he was still medicated. "Mr. Preston . . . Kyle . . . thank you for allowing us to search your house. I promise that Agent Patterson and Captain Norton will not tear things apart in the search."

"I don't know what they think they'll find," Kyle said. "If I'm not a suspect . . ." His voice cracked. He swallowed hard.

"You're not a suspect, Kyle. Your in-laws verify the fact that you were at their house the evening Stephanie came up missing, that you two had eaten supper there before her night class and that you'd stayed on to help Mr. Floyd work on his tractor."

"That's right," Jay Floyd said. "We expected Stephie to come back by and pick up Kyle, and when she didn't show up by eleven, we called Ed."

Bernie nodded. "I realize y'all have answered a lot of questions since that night, that y'all did everything you could to help us in our investigation then and again yesterday after we verified that Stephanie was dead."

Emmy Floyd keened softly. Her lips puckered; her chin quivered. Jay scooted closer to his wife where they sat in the porch swing and put his arm around her shoulders.

"I hate to go over this again, but it's possible something one of you thinks is totally insignificant might help us in the investigation." Bernie eased backward and braced her hips against the porch banisters. "Can you think of anyone who might have wanted to hurt Stephanie? Someone who was upset with her or had a grudge against one of you?"

"Our girl didn't have an enemy in this world," Jay said. "She was as good as gold."

"Jay and Emmy don't have any enemies," Ed Mays told Bernie. "I don't know a soul who doesn't think the world of them and of all three of their kids, too."

Bernie nodded again. "What about you, Kyle?"

"I don't know of anybody, except maybe all of Stephie's old boyfriends," Kyle replied. "They gotta be jealous because I got Stephie."

"She was a prize," Jay said. "Pretty. Smart as a whip. A good girl."

Old boyfriends. Hmm . . . Was it possible that an old boyfriend hated Stephanie for dumping him in favor of Kyle?

Hated her enough to kidnap her, rape and torture her, then kill her?

"Was Stephanie dating someone she broke up with before the two of you got serious?" Bernie asked.

"I—I wasn't serious about the old boyfriends," Kyle said nervously. "The only boyfriend she ever had before me was Richie Lowery."

"Richie was a good boy," Jay said. "Besides, he's the one who broke up with Stephie."

"He might have been the one who ended things, but I think he wished he hadn't," Kyle said.

"What makes you say that?" Bernie asked.

Kyle glanced at his wife's parents, then at Ed Mays. "Stephie got some notes and some little presents from him last month. She showed them to me and I told her that if he called her or bothered her, she was to tell me and I'd go have a talk with Richie. You know, beat the shit out of him if he messed with her."

"Are you saying Richie was harassing Stephanie?" Bernie looked point-blank at Kyle.

"Nah, nothing like that. After a couple of notes and presents, nothing else happened. I guess when Stephie didn't respond, he got the message that she was happily married."

"Why didn't you tell us about this before now?" Ed asked.

"I didn't think about it," Kyle admitted. "It wasn't anything important. Like I said, nothing more ever came of it."

"Where does Richie Lowery live?" Bernie posed this question to Stephanie's parents.

"As far as I know, he still lives in Hollywood," Jay said. "You don't think Richie . . ." He cleared his throat. "The boy was all right. There's no way he would have hurt Stephie. He wasn't the type."

"I understand," Bernie said. "But it won't hurt to question him."

As she continued speaking with the family, periodically checking her watch and wondering just how long it would take Jim and Charlie to do a thorough inspection of the house, she became more and more certain that Stephanie's parents and husband didn't know anything that could shed new light on the case. That is, other than the information about Richie Lowery, which Bernie's instincts told her probably wouldn't amount to anything. Not unless Kyle wasn't telling her everything. But the guy seemed to be an open book.

After running out of questions, Bernie let Ed take over and she sat back and listened. He talked to the family, reminisced about Stephanie and gave them the opportunity to relive happier days.

The front door opened and Jim peered out onto the porch. His gaze connected with Bernie's. He nodded for her to come to him. She eased up from her perch on the banisters and headed toward the door.

"I believe Captain Norton and Agent Patterson are just about finished," she said. "If y'all will excuse me, I'll check with them and be right back."

When she walked into the living room, Jim closed the door behind her and said, "We found something interesting."

Bernie's heart sank. Oh, please, God, don't let there be any evidence against Kyle Preston. He seemed like such a good guy, a guy in love with his wife.

"Charlie found the items in a box in a cedar chest in the second bedroom," Jim said. "The box was tied with string and had been placed under several quilts."

"What was in the box?"

"Come see for yourself. Charlie's been really careful handling it." Jim held out a pair of gloves to Bernie. She took them, slipped them on and then followed Jim down the hall and into the bedroom.

"Did you tell her?" Charlie asked.

Jim shook his head. "I thought she'd want to see them for herself."

Thomasina got another bottle of water out of the machine at Robyn's Fitness Center before she left. She was warm and sweaty and thirsty, and all she wanted to do was cool off before driving over to the Pig, which was what everyone called their local Piggly Wiggly supermarket, to pick up the items on the grocery list her mother gave her before she left Verona this morning. On the off chance that Brandon Kelley might be doing his shopping this afternoon, Thomasina had reapplied her makeup before leaving Robyn's. She knew she was acting like a silly teenager with a crush, but she couldn't help it. She had even dreamed about Brandon last night. *Sigh, sigh. Be still my heart.*

Hitting the automatic UNLOCK on her keyless entry pad, Thomasina headed straight for her car parked in the back lot behind the fitness center. As she approached, she noticed something hanging on the handle of the driver's door. An advertisement of some sort? Probably. But it was rather large for a flyer.

Stopping and staring when she reached her car, she realized that someone had tied a white plastic bag to the door handle. Her heartbeat accelerated. Thomasina set her unopened bottle of water on the hood of her car, then hesitantly yet expectantly reached out, untied the knot holding the bag in place and grasped it. Standing there in the parking lot, in the noonday July sun, she peeked inside, but all she could make out was a white box and a manila envelope.

She opened the car door, got in and after closing the door and starting the engine to get the air-conditioning running, reached inside the bag and pulled out the note. With trembling fingers, she removed the message from the envelope and unfolded the note.

Please accept this small token of my affection. Pearls for a lovely lady.

Thomasina gasped silently. *Pearls?*

She reached into the bag again and withdrew the small, white rectangular box. She felt like a kid on Christmas morning. After removing the lid, she stared at the eighteen-inch string of pearls nestled on a bed of white cotton. Round and creamy white, with a small gold catch, the pearls weren't real. They couldn't be. But they were beautiful all the same. And such a sweet gift. A gift from a very romantic man.

A gift from Brandon?

She laid the box and the note on the passenger seat, then retrieved the manila envelope and tossed the bag alongside the box.

What could this be?

After opening the sealed envelope, she removed the contents. A single page from an artist's sketch pad. Her heart skipped a beat. Brandon was the art director at the junior college. She turned the paper over and gasped aloud. It was a charcoal sketch of her face. This was the work of a true artist.

Brandon Kelley was that true artist. He was her secret admirer. But why was he courting her in such an old-fashioned, secretive manner? Why didn't he just come right out and ask her for a date?

Because Brandon isn't like other men, she told herself. *He's older, more experienced, worldly wise and undoubtedly one of the last of a dying breed—a romantic gentleman.*

She reached over, lifted the pearls from the box and fingered them lovingly. She would wear them to school on Monday to show him that she liked his gift.

Bubbling with excitement and giddy with expectations, Thomasina attached her seatbelt, shifted into reverse and began humming to herself as she backed up and headed out to the street.

* * *

Bernie handled the items very carefully, taking her time to study the details as Charlie Patterson gave the pieces to her, one at a time. First were notes written in heavy black ink on white note cards, the kind you could buy just about any place that sold stationery. Each note was succinct, flattering to the receiver and eerily romantic.

"Kyle Preston told me that one of Stephanie's old boyfriends sent her some notes and gifts. These must be the notes." But something wasn't quite right about these things. The notes were unsigned, and the wording didn't seem to be something a former lover would write. No, her guess would be the messages were sent from a would-be lover.

"Why didn't he mention these notes before?" Jim asked.

"He'd forgotten about them, didn't think they were important."

"I can't believe a husband could have forgotten about these things," Charlie said. "Especially not the sketches."

"What sketches?" Bernie asked. "Kyle didn't say anything about sketches."

"Then either he's lying or Stephanie didn't share all her little gifts with her husband." Jim pointed to the thin stack of papers Charlie held in his glove-covered hand.

"Let me see those." Bernie held out her hand and accepted the items Charlie gave her.

The first item was a sketch of Stephanie, done in charcoal. Just her face, with a hint of naked shoulder. It was a remarkably accurate sketch; the artist clearly was talented. Bernie shuffled through several photographs of Stephanie, obviously taken at a distance, and it was apparent that she had not been aware she was being caught on film. One photo was of her on her front porch. Another was of her coming out of the grocery store wheeling a cart filled with sacks. There were six photos in all, each taken at a different location and apparently on different days.

"He was stalking her," Bernie said.

"Yeah," Jim replied. "Keep going. It gets worse."

She handed the first sketch and the photos back to Charlie and took a look at the remaining sketches, probably a dozen or so. Bernie did a double take after looking at the first rendering. This was an ink sketch of Stephanie, partially undressed, with one naked breast showing, the nipple tightly puckered. She had one hand slipped suggestively between her upper thighs and her right index finger was stuck in her mouth, pressing her lips apart.

Dear God, had Stephanie posed for this or had the artist drawn it from memory? "We definitely need to question the old boyfriend."

Bernie flipped that sketch and went on to the next. In this one, Stephanie was completely nude, except for a strand of pearls around her neck, and the expression on her face was downright unnerving. She looked like a woman in the throes of an orgasm.

"Lord."

"Amen," Charlie said.

Until Charlie spoke, she hadn't realized she'd uttered the word aloud.

Each successive sketch was more graphic than the one before, and the final four depicted Stephanie in S&M poses. Bound. Gagged. Chained. Her body marred with small, round marks and teeth prints.

Sour bile rose from Bernie's stomach and burned her esophagus on its ascent to her throat. She gagged, then swallowed. *Don't you dare vomit. Neither one of these big strong men is sick to his stomach.*

"Pretty rough stuff," Jim said.

"Disgusting." Bernie managed to get the one word out before she had to clear her throat several times.

"The question is, did the artist use his imagination to

draw these, or at some time either in the past or recently, did Stephanie Preston pose for them?" Charlie looked from Bernie to Jim.

"If you're asking for my opinion, I'd say he used his sick imagination," Jim said.

Bernie nodded. "Unless there was a side to Stephanie that no one knew about, I agree with Jim."

"There are a few other things." Charlie pointed to the open box atop the closed cedar chest. "Little gifts. A string of pearls. A bottle of perfume. A gold ankle bracelet. A tube of pink lipstick and matching nail polish."

"Gifts a guy would give his girlfriend?" Bernie thought about the presents, two pieces of jewelry and three toiletry items. "Why these things?"

"Good question." Jim's gaze met hers. "Were they things he knew she liked? Or were they items he wanted to see her use?"

"Look, you two, I'll get these items to our CSU today," Charlie told them. "While I'm taking care of that, why don't y'all follow up on the old boyfriend? And while you're at it, get a list from her family of every man in Stephanie's life, other than her father and husband."

"That could be a long list," Bernie said. "She worked at McDonald's during the day and went to school at night. Plus, she attended church regularly. The list of men in her life could add up to a hundred or more."

"We'll start with the old boyfriend and then go on to any guy who's shown a particular interest in Stephanie recently," Jim said.

Charlie nodded. "I'll try to get a preliminary report for us and we can go over it tonight. Unless tonight's out for some reason."

"Tonight's fine," Jim said.

Bernie nodded. "Good thing I don't have an active social life."

"Hey, you'll get to spend the evening with two good-looking guys." Charlie chuckled.

"What more could a girl ask for on a Saturday night—two handsome lawmen, takeout from the King Kone and a stack of crime scene photographs?" Bernie rolled her eyes heavenward and sighed dramatically.

Chapter 7

Thomasina had skipped Sunday school this morning, so she'd driven her own car to eleven o'clock church services. When she'd dragged in five minutes late, her mother had given her one of those disapproving glares that only parents can give. She had sat through the sermon, doing her best to relate to what Reverend Donaldson had to say, but the honest truth of the matter was that she'd spent those forty minutes looking at the new minister, actually drooling over him the way every other woman in the congregation was. The man was gorgeous. Black hair, blue-gray eyes that were such a contrast to his darkly tanned face, and a body that would put sinful thoughts into a woman's mind.

Her sister Amanda, who'd been sitting on her right, had nudged her in the ribs and whispered, "He's single, you know."

Thomasina hadn't reacted in any way except to smile. Matthew Donaldson was drop-dead gorgeous and single, facts that under different circumstances would have interested her greatly. But not now. Not when Brandon Kelley was on a mission to woo and win her with a very old-fashioned and utterly romantic courtship. She had hoped to catch a glimpse of her secret admirer this morning, but Brandon wasn't overly religious and came to church on average once a month. Not seeing him had been disappointing, but she consoled herself with the thought that she could make a point of running into him at school tomorrow. She would be friendly, maybe even a little flirtatious, but in a very ladylike way. If she came on too strong, too female-in-charge, she might turn him off and put an end to their romance before it actually began. Taking her cues from him was the wisest course of action. Apparently he wanted their relationship to begin by being sweetly romantic, with an air of mystery.

Thomasina made a point of speaking to Reverend Donaldson and welcoming him to Adams Landing. She figured if Amanda had picked the man out as a potential brother-in-law, her mother had zeroed in on him as son-in-law material. And as every girl knows, it's always best if you can keep your mama happy. Of course, every mother in town with a single daughter over the age of twenty was probably making mental wedding plans for her daughter and the reverend. Young, handsome, successful single men in Adams County were few and far between.

Amanda grasped Thomasina's arm just as she started walking toward the parking lot. "Hold up."

Thomasina paused. "I spoke to him, smiled at him and made friendly. That should satisfy Mama."

"Hmm . . . What are you not telling me?"

"Nothing."

"Come on, I know you. You've got a new boyfriend, haven't you? And it's about time. You should have stopped pining over Ron Hensley two seconds after the bum dropped you like a hot potato."

"He didn't drop me like a hot potato. We just wanted different things from a relationship."

Amanda lowered her voice. "Yeah, all he wanted was sex." She looked directly into Thomasina's eyes, as if daring her to lie to her. "Come on. Who is this new guy?"

"Swear you won't tell a soul."

Amanda giggled. "I swear."

"It's Brandon Kelley, the art director at the college."

"And when did this start? When was your first date? Details, girl. I want details."

"Look, I'll fill you in on everything after dinner today, when Mama takes her nap and the guys and kids are outside playing ball. But I can tell you this—he is so romantic."

Amanda let Thomasina leave without further questioning, probably realizing that they could easily be overheard by any number of people. The church grounds were covered with three fourths of the congregation who lingered to chit chat and gossip before going home.

Despite the clouds blocking the sun, the July heat seeped through and the high humidity created a damp heaviness in the air. On her way to her car, she spoke to half a dozen people and threw up her hand and waved at Robyn and Bernie Granger, who were with their parents. She'd bet Brenda Granger had her eye on the reverend as a potential mate for one of her daughters.

When Thomasina reached her car, she realized that in her haste to make it inside the church on time, she had forgotten to lock the doors. No big deal. She didn't have anything worth stealing inside the vehicle, and who'd want to take her older model Grand Am? She opened the door and started to slide inside, wanting to get the air-conditioning going as quickly as possible. But she stopped dead still when she saw the large manila envelope lying on the driver's seat. Her heart lurched. Was this another gift from Brandon? After picking up the envelope, she got in, closed the door, started the engine and turned up the air-conditioning. Glancing around to see if anyone was watching her, she tried to decide whether to open the envelope now or wait until she got home.

No one was paying any attention to her, so why wait? She opened the envelope eagerly, barely able to contain the fluttering excitement in her belly. Peering inside, she saw a note and what looked like four-by-six-inch snapshots. She removed the note from its envelope.

I love looking at you. You're so beautiful.

Thomasina sighed. Her whole body quivered with pleasure.

Her hands trembled as she reached inside the manila envelope and removed the photographs. Three pictures of her. One taken at the college, one coming out of Robyn's Fitness Center, and one going into the Piggly Wiggly yesterday.

An odd feeling rippled up Thomasina's spine as she realized that he'd been following her yesterday, that he'd been close and yet hadn't made his presence known. It was almost as if he was stalking her. A hint of uneasiness crept into her romantic fantasy of Brandon Kelley courting her with notes and gifts.

You're being silly. There's a difference in a man like Brandon being secretively seductive and some guy she wasn't interested in stalking her. After all, she wanted Brandon to notice her, to take an interest in her, to pursue her.

Taking a deep, calming breath, Thomasina banished every negative thought from her mind. Perhaps tomorrow, at school, Brandon would make his next move and ask her for a date. After all, how long could he continue admiring her from afar when it was obvious what he wanted was to admire her up close and personal.

Jim felt downright awkward coming for Sunday dinner at the Granger house when it was apparent that everyone else here had come straight from church services. Everyone was still dressed in their Sunday best. Reverend Matthew Donaldson still wore his suit and tie. Raymond Long had removed his jacket, but wore a white button-down and blue-and-gray striped tie. Only R.B. Granger looked halfway comfortable, having taken off his jacket and his tie, leaving him in a white shirt, with the sleeves rolled up to his elbows. *My kind of man,* Jim thought. Jim wore khaki dress slacks and a navy blue, short-sleeve, cotton pullover. In comparison with everyone else, he was definitely underdressed. But he usually didn't put on a suit and tie, except for funerals.

"Come on in, Captain Norton." R.B. invited Jim in with a wave of his hand. "Bernie's introduced you to everybody except her mother and sister. They're out in the kitchen getting dinner ready to put on the table."

Jim entered the large den where the others had congregated. This room, like the living room and dining room he had glimpsed when he'd entered the foyer, possessed a sense of hominess. The furniture was a mixture of styles, mostly dark woods and earthy colors, antiques blending with sturdily built, more modern pieces. In many ways, it reminded him of the home he'd grown up in, the place where he'd been happy and at the time hadn't realized what a lucky kid he was. As a boy, he'd had everything he now wanted for Kevin. A happily married mother and father, a kid sister, and a house filled with love.

"Smile, Jim," Bernie whispered to him. "This is Sunday dinner, not a walk to the electric chair."

He forced a closed-mouth smile and entered the den. Bernie had introduced him to everyone, including Raymond Long's mother, Helen, who was at this very minute studying him intently. He couldn't figure out why she was so interested. It was as if she'd taken an instant dislike to him and was searching for a reason to justify her decision.

"Dad, you'll have to keep the conversation going," Bernie

told her father. "I need to help Mama and Robyn. Dinner should be on the table in just a few minutes."

Jim glanced at Bernie as she walked away hurriedly. She wore a two-piece tan suit, with a skirt that hit her mid-calf, but she didn't look all that different today than she had the past two days. Everything about her—from her simple style in clothes to her minimum of makeup and long hair pulled away from her face and secured in a ponytail—was neat, orderly and . . . well, to be honest, plain. Not that Bernie wasn't pretty. She was, but in a plain sort of way. Brown hair, brown eyes, medium complexion, simple clothes, simple hairstyle. Bernie's only outstanding feature was her five-nine height, making her as tall as a lot of men.

R.B. pulled Jim aside and said, "Bernie tells us that you're going to be keeping your son for a few weeks while your ex-wife undergoes surgery and then chemo."

"That's right."

"I sort of know what your ex-wife is facing. I was diagnosed with prostate cancer a few years ago." R.B. grunted. "Cancer. That's a word no one wants to hear in reference to their own health."

"No, sir."

"Look, son . . ." R.B. clamped his big hand down on Jim's shoulder, the two men standing eye to eye, R.B. not quite an inch taller. "Brenda and I talked things over after Bernie explained your predicament, and we're both ready, willing and able to act as surrogate grandparents for your boy."

Jim released an emotional breath he hadn't realized he'd been holding. "That's mighty kind of you and your wife, but—"

R.B. squeezed Jim's shoulder, then lowered his voice and said quietly, for Jim's ears only, "The way I see it, one good turn deserves another." R.B. scanned the room so quickly that Jim doubted anyone else even noticed. "You look out for my kid and I'll look out for yours."

"Do you mean Bernie?"

R.B. nodded. "It's not that I don't think she's doing a bang-up job as sheriff. She's smart and good as any man on the force. But she's young, and well, son, she is a woman. And we both know that a woman thinks with her heart and not her head. Of course, my girl is better than most about using her common sense and seeing things the way we men do."

"Are you concerned about something in particular?" Jim asked.

"Yeah, I'm concerned about this murder case," R.B. told him. "This is a bad one, and we both know it. Unless y'all just get lucky, it may become an unsolved murder. Bernie's not going to accept that easily. She's got a lot to learn, and that's where you come in. You have the experience she lacks. I want you to help her . . . guide her along through this case."

Jim blew out a deeply inhaled breath. No beating around the bush for R.B. Granger. Bernie's father said exactly what he thought. The only problem was that Jim wasn't sure he could make that kind of a deal. "Bernie's my boss. She's the sheriff, I'm just the chief—"

"Dinner is served," a feminine voice called from the doorway.

Taking this as an opportunity not to finish his conversation with R.B., Jim turned his attention to the owner of that syrupy sweet voice. The woman standing in the doorway, smiling, her long, curly black hair framing her beautiful face, all but took Jim's breath away. Tall and willowy, with slender curves in all the right places, the lady was a real knockout.

"Y'all heard my little girl," R.B. announced. "If I know my Brenda, we've got a feast waiting for us in the dining room."

Jim allowed the others to go first, taking his time, bringing up the rear, so he was surprised that when he entered the hallway, R.B.'s "little girl" was still there. When he passed by, he glanced her way. She smiled at him, then reached out and slipped her arm through his.

"I'm Robyn," she told him. "Bernie's sister."

"I'm—"

"Jimmy Norton. I know. I've heard all about you from Daddy and Bernie. I've been dying to meet you."

"Have you?"

When she flashed that thousand-watt smile at him, his stomach muscles tightened. "I hear Mom and Dad are going to be looking after your son. I love kids and I'm a great babysitter. I'll be happy to help out the folks with—What's your son's name?"

"Kevin."

"And how old is Kevin?"

"Twelve."

As they entered the dining room, Robyn whispered to him. "I'm supposed to sit next to Raymond and across from the new minister, but that's Mama's plan, not mine. She's always matchmaking."

Jim noted that the table sat eight, with R.B. and his wife— who was an older, shorter version of her beautiful younger daughter—residing at each end, Raymond and Helen on the left, and Matthew on the right.

Bernie placed a bread basket on the end of the table by her mother, then headed toward the other end with another basket. Just as she started to sit down beside the handsome, young minister, Robyn rushed forward, all but dragging Jim.

"Come on, Jimmy, you sit between me and Reverend Donaldson." She looked at her sister and said, "You sit over there next to Raymond."

Jim glanced at Bernie, whose facial expression didn't alter in the slightest, but he noted something in her eyes. Just a hint of displeasure, so subtle that he felt certain no one else caught it. For a split second she looked right at him, then averted her gaze quickly and took her place at the table beside Raymond Long. Then Jim sat exactly where Robyn had told him to sit, between her and Matthew Donaldson.

During the course of the meal, Robyn didn't pay much attention to the minister or anyone else; instead, she concentrated on Jim. The more she talked, the more he realized she wasn't really saying anything. Her main topic of conversation was herself. Jim offered her an agreeable smile now and then and answered when she asked a question, nodding fairly often and replying yes or no. By the time Mrs. Granger served Mississippi mud pie for dessert, Jim realized that Robyn reminded him of someone. She reminded him of Mary Lee. It wasn't that they resembled each other, except they were both very pretty and had great figures. No, it was more a personality thing. Robyn seemed to be as self-centered and egotistical as his ex-wife. She wanted, probably needed, to be the center of attention. She knew she was pretty, that men found her attractive, and that fact fed her sizable ego.

It wasn't that Jim didn't like Robyn. He did. But he'd been badly burned by one extremely high-maintenance woman and tended to steer clear of others like her. Then again, he might make an exception where Robyn Granger was concerned.

Just as Jim took his first bite of scrumptious pie, Bernie's cell phone rang.

"Oh dear, I wish you could turn that thing off at the dinner table." Brenda sighed. "But I know you can't, your being the sheriff and all. You'd think I'd be used to having my dinners interrupted by business calls."

Bernie scooted back her chair, stood and walked out into the foyer. Jim glanced over his shoulder and watched her as she paced back and forth, doing more listening than talking.

Robyn said something to him, but he didn't understand her because he was too busy keeping an eye on Bernie. "Huh?"

"I said why don't we—"

"Jim, we've got to go," Bernie called to him from the doorway.

When he turned to Robyn, she put on her best little-girl pout. "Business calls," he told her, then laid his napkin on the table, shoved back his chair and stood. "Mrs. Granger, thank you for a wonderful dinner. I appreciate y'all being so hospitable."

"You must come back again," Brenda said. "We'd love to have you any old time."

R.B. stood. "I'll walk you and Bernie out."

R.B. caught up with Jim just as he joined Bernie in the foyer. "So, what's up?" he asked.

She looked from Jim to her father, then replied to her father's question. "That was Charlie Patterson. They've found Richie Lowery."

"This is the Preston girl's old boyfriend, right?" R.B. asked.

Bernie nodded.

"Where was he?"

"I don't know. It seems he heard we were looking for him, so he just showed up at my office about ten minutes ago."

"So he hadn't skipped out on us like we thought when we couldn't find him at home yesterday and nobody seemed to know where he was," Jim said.

"No, apparently not," Bernie replied, then turned to her father. "Dad, we have to go. I'll talk to you later."

"Sure, sure. You two go on."

Once outside, Bernie quickened her steps, as if she couldn't wait to get away.

"Hey, hold up," Jim called to her.

She slowed her pace and waited for him.

"Your car or mine?" he asked.

"Yours. There are several others blocking me in." She glanced at all the vehicles parked in the drive and along the street. Her gaze paused on the old rattletrap truck parked on the street. "Is that yours?"

"Yep."

"Didn't they pay you a decent salary in Memphis?" she asked teasingly.

"Better than what you're paying me," he tossed back at her. "But until my wife remarried, I was paying her alimony, as well as child support. Add to that the fact that I'm socking away as much as I can for Kevin's college fund and . . . you do the math."

She headed toward his truck. When she reached the curb and started to open the door, he reached around her and opened it for her. She jumped.

"Sorry. I didn't mean to startle you," he told her.

Hoisting herself up and into the cab, she replied, "Don't apologize for being a gentleman. It's just that most of my deputies bend over backward trying to treat me like just one of the guys."

"Hmm . . ."

After closing her door, he rounded the hood and got in on the driver's side. As he started the engine, he caught a glimpse of Bernie in his peripheral vision. She sat there beside him, belted in, her back ramrod straight and her gaze fixed straight ahead, as if she saw something interesting on the other side of the windshield.

"Is your sister involved with anybody?" Jim asked.

Bernie didn't respond immediately. Why was she giving her answer so much thought? Why not a simple yes or no response? Finally, after taking a deep breath, she told him, "Robyn's not dating one person in particular."

"Hmm . . ."

"I don't think she's ready for anything serious, but she

can't convince our mother. Weren't you aware that there were two single men, other than you, at dinner today? Mama would like to fix me up with Raymond, and she had high hopes of putting Robyn with the new preacher, but it seems my little sister is more interested in you." Bernie snapped her head around and looked right at Jim. "And apparently the interest is mutual."

"Then you wouldn't have a problem with my asking your sister out?"

"No, why should I?"

"Conflict of interest. My being your chief deputy and her being your sister."

"Captain Norton, you are free to date anyone you choose and that includes my sister."

Richie Lowery was short and stocky with curly brown hair. His voice was slightly high pitched, and at the moment the guy was more than a little agitated. He clenched and un-clenched his hands as he stared at the sketches laid out on the table in front of him and a fine sheen of perspiration moistened his upper lip. Of course, it was July in Alabama and everyone sweated in this oppressive heat.

"You think I drew these?" He chuckled nervously. "I can't draw a damn stick figure. Ask anybody who knows me. I don't have a bit of artistic talent."

"If that's the case, then why did Stephanie Preston think you sent them to her?" Jim posed the question from where he stood on the other side of the table. Charlie Patterson sat at the end of the table and Bernie stood in the corner, observing.

"How should I know? Besides, you just got her husband's word for it that Stephie thought I was the one sending her all that stuff."

"Are you saying you think Kyle Preston is lying?" Jim asked.

"Hey, I don't know. All I know is that I didn't draw them damn lewd pictures or take snapshots of Stephie or send her notes and little presents." Richie faced Jim boldly. "I haven't been pining away for her or nothing like that. I've got a girl-friend. She lives in South Pittsburgh. That's where I was yes-terday and last night. If you don't believe me, you can ask her."

"If that's the case, then why didn't your parents or any of your buddies know where you were?" Charlie asked.

Richie focused on the ABI agent. "Look, my folks wouldn't approve of my girlfriend. She's . . . well . . . she's not white, and my old man would beat the shit out of me if he knew I was dating a black girl."

Jim cleared his throat. "Where were you the night Stephanie was kidnapped? And where were you the day she was killed?"

"When was she kidnapped exactly?"

Jim told him the dates.

"I was at work the night she was kidnapped. Swear to God. I work swing shift at the poultry plant and I was on evening shift then. I didn't get off until midnight. And that's a good thirty-five-minute drive from the college."

"What about the day she was murdered?" Charlie asked.

"Same thing. I was at work. Day shift. You can check with my boss and with the people I work with. They can vouch for me. I was at work. Honest to God."

Bernie noticed Jim and Charlie exchange knowing looks and realized they were agreeing on something—probably the fact that it didn't appear that Richie Lowery was their killer.

"Mr. Lowery, we appreciate your coming in to answer our questions," Jim said. "We'll check out your alibis and if we find you've been straight with us, then that's that. But if you've lied to us—"

"I haven't lied. Everything I've told you is the gospel truth."

Jim nodded.

"Can I go now?" Richie asked, almost pleadingly.

"Yeah, you can go," Jim told him. Richie scooted back his chair. "But first, I've got one more question: Do you know of anybody who might have had a reason to harm Stephanie? Somebody with a grudge against her or her husband or her father?"

Richie thought for several minutes, then said, "Nah, nothing like that, but . . . what about guys who were interested in her? You know, guys she fooled around with."

"Was there someone else?" Jim asked.

"Yeah, there was this one guy who kind of had a thing for her and when we broke up, I think she might have seen him a couple of times before she hooked up with Kyle."

"This guy got a name?"

"Yeah, yeah. Kelley. Brandon Kelley. He's a professor or something over at the junior college where she took night classes."

"Thanks, Mr. Lowery."

"Can I go now?"

"Yes, you can go."

As soon as Richie closed the door behind himself, Charlie stood and stretched. "Think he's telling us the truth?"

"Yeah, I think he is," Jim replied.

"I know Dr. Brandon Kelley," Bernie said. "He's got quite a reputation with the ladies. Word is that he's dated more than one of his students."

"Interesting."

"You know what's even more interesting? Brandon Kelley is the art director at Adams County Junior College." She glanced at the charcoal and ink sketches lying on the table. "The man's an artist and from what I hear, a damn good one."

Chapter 8

The bottles of pink nail polish and tubes of matching lipstick peeked at him through the sheer plastic gift bag he'd bought at Wal-Mart. He'd placed the bag on the desk, directly in front of his sketch pad. His first gift to a new lover was always the pearls, perhaps because that was the one item above all others that he associated with—

His hand holding the ink pen quivered ever so slightly.

Cursing himself for allowing her memory to still have such a hold on him, he laid down the pen and grabbed his hand to steady it. She was the past. She was insignificant. Unimportant. She could never hurt him again. Never laugh at him. Never ridicule him in front of her friends.

Unwanted memories flooded his mind. He pressed his fingers against either side of his head, at the temples, and closed his eyes. Don't remember that afternoon. Don't think about it. Don't, damn you, don't.

Vivid images of her appeared inside his head. Her long dark hair. Her big, expressive brown eyes. Her beautiful face. And her incredible body. He had dreamed of her, worshipped her from afar, wanted her as he had never wanted anything before or since.

He beat the sides and top of his head with his open palms. "Get out of my head, damn you, you vicious little bitch!"

Darkness appeared behind his closed eyelids, then swirls of deep red and flashes of white.

There, that's better. She's gone now. You don't have to think about her. Concentrate on your new love. Think about Thomasina. Move forward with your courtship. You have to finish the drawing so you can put it in the bag with the lipstick and nail polish for her next gift.

Before picking up his pen, he looked at the unfinished sketch and smiled. He hadn't had the privilege of seeing Thomasina naked. Not yet. But he knew her body, every lush curve. Her slender neck; her long, shapely legs; her full, high breasts.

His semierect penis twitched with anticipation.

He wished they were already lovers, wished she was lying beneath him, telling him she loved him, begging him to make love to her.

Soon, my beautiful Thomasina. Soon.

He lifted the pen and added the subtle nuances to the drawing that brought it to life. Just the right shading to make the nipples appear puckered. And then he moved on, completing the fingers on her right hand that demurely tried to cover her pubic hair.

Brandon Kelley lived outside Adams Landing, in a rock and cedar house built on the banks of the Tennessee River sometime back in the fifties. Brandon had paid five hundred thousand for the place, a fact Bernie knew because her sister, Robyn, had dated the man and he'd bragged to her about how much the house had cost, as well as what his antique Aston Martin was worth. Actually, Bernie knew more about the man and his house than she'd ever wanted to know because her sister was the type who did kiss and tell. Robyn had a penchant for regaling Bernie with stories about her exciting love life. She knew Brandon Kelley liked to give and receive oral sex, that he was a talker during the act and that Robyn, who'd bedded more than her fair share of men, had been impressed with the size of his cock.

"You're awfully quiet," Jim said as he drove along the bumpy dirt road leading to Brandon's house.

"Just thinking."

"About the case? About whether or not Kelley might be our man?"

"Mmm . . ."

"What are your gut instincts telling you?"

"Nothing really," she replied. "I'd never consider Brandon as a suspect if it wasn't for the fact that he's a talented artist, which our guy apparently is."

"You referred to him by his given name. How well do you know him?"

"Not well. Robyn's the one who knows him."

"Oh." Jim tightened his hands on the steering wheel, a fact that Bernie noted and took as a sign of aggravation.

"They dated for a while. Nothing serious."

"Who broke things off: him or her?"

"What difference does it make? It has no bearing on our case." Bernie mentally counted to ten, then said, "Unless you're asking for personal reasons, because you want to make sure she's not carrying a torch for another guy before you ask her out."

"Forget I asked."

"Take the turnoff up there on the left. You can see a glimpse of Brandon's house from here."

Jim nodded, took her directions and within a couple minutes pulled his old Chevy truck to a halt in the driveway beside the house.

"Robyn broke things off," Bernie said. "My sister's never been dumped in her entire life."

Jim grunted.

"Well, let's get this over with." Bernie opened her door and got out, not waiting for Jim to assist her. He could save his gentlemanly manners for her sister. All she wanted from him was his respect.

Yeah, sure, that's all you want. You can lie to the whole freaking world, Bernadette Granger, but you shouldn't lie to yourself.

Jim got in step with her quickly as they approached the wide, sprawling porch that circled three fourths of the house and faced the river. Before they reached the front door, the porch lights came on and the door opened to reveal Brandon standing there waiting for them. Bernie had telephoned half an hour ago and explained that they had a few questions for him about his relationship with Stephanie Preston, and he'd invited them to come to his house this evening. He'd acted charming and cooperative, as if he had nothing to hide.

Maybe he didn't. She'd know after they talked to him. She'd always had a sixth sense about these things, had always been good at figuring out when somebody was lying to her. That sixth sense had been what alerted her to the fact that her husband had been cheating on her. The only problem was she had chosen to ignore that inner voice for years. And dear God, how she had lived to regret not listening. She had never made that mistake again.

"Come on in," Brandon said. "Or would y'all prefer to sit out here on the porch? It's turning out to be a fairly pleasant night, but I'm afraid we'll get rain before morning."

"Out here will be fine," Bernie said.

"Would y'all care for something to drink? I just made a pitcher of iced tea."

"No, thanks," Jim said.

"Nothing for me either," Bernie added.

"Well, then, come on over and sit down." He indicated the rattan settee and chairs to his right. "I don't know what I can tell you about Stephanie, poor little thing, but if there's anything I can do to help y'all find the person who killed her, I'll be more than happy to."

"We appreciate your cooperation," Bernie told him as she sat in one of the chairs, while Jim took the other.

Brandon sat on the settee, crossed his legs and leaned back, looking perfectly at ease as he glanced from Bernie to Jim.

"We were told that you and Stephanie were involved at one time," Jim said. "Is that correct?"

Brandon smiled and Bernie thought how very attractive he was, very smooth and debonair, almost too sophisticated for a rural area like Adams County, Alabama.

"We had a brief—very brief—fling." Brandon accentuated his speech with hand mannerisms. "She was a pretty little thing and deliciously eager. But I soon realized that she was taking things a little too seriously, so I ended our relationship quickly."

"Do you make a habit of dating your students?" Jim narrowed his gaze, giving Brandon what Bernie thought of as "the evil eye."

Brandon laughed. "I make a habit of dating beautiful young women. Some are students, a few are colleagues"—he looked pointedly at Bernie—"and some are gorgeous fitness instructors with fabulously toned bodies."

The guy was a sleaze. He might be handsome, cultured, well educated and talented, but he was a sleaze nonetheless. If there was one thing Bernie hated, it was men who bragged about their conquests.

"Did you ever sketch Stephanie?" Bernie asked.

"What?"

"Did you ever—"

"No, I never sketched her. Why do you ask?"

"Just curious," Bernie told him. "You're an artist. She was, as you say, a beautiful young woman. I just thought maybe you liked to sketch or paint your lovers."

"Have you ever sketched or painted any of your lovers?" Jim asked.

"Yes," Brandon replied. "But not Stephanie. As I told you, our relationship was short-lived."

"Were you teaching a class the night Stephanie came up missing?" Jim studied Brandon. Bernie guessed that he, too, had a knack for sensing when someone was lying.

"I don't teach night classes," Brandon replied with an air of superiority.

"Then where were you the night Stephanie disappeared?" Jim asked.

"And where were you the day she was killed?" Bernie kept her gaze on Brandon's face, searching for any sign that might tell her if he was lying.

"You can't seriously believe that I had anything to do with Stephanie's disappearance and murder, can you?" An outraged expression marred Brandon's classically handsome features.

Bernie told him the dates and approximate times of the disappearance and the murder and watched him as he thought about the information. He didn't appear to be the least bit nervous. Either he was completely innocent or he had simply perfected the art of being "cool."

"I was here, at home, the night Stephanie disappeared." He held up a restraining hand. "And before you ask—yes, I have someone who can corroborate that fact. Her name is Holly Burcham. Deputy Holly Burcham."

Bernie clamped her teeth together tightly, then swallowed hard. Why was she not surprised to discover that one of her few female deputies was banging Brandon Kelley? Could it possibly be because ever since they were high school cheerleaders together, Holly had considered Robyn her rival. Whatever Robyn had, Holly wanted.

"What time did Holly arrive and what time did she leave?" Bernie glared at Brandon, doing her best to disguise the disgust she felt. And yes, the fact that his lack of morals reminded her of her ex did affect her opinion of the man.

"She got here around seven and stayed all night. We went to bed early, but didn't go to sleep until around midnight." Brandon clicked his tongue and winked at Bernie.

Sleaze. Irritating, arrogant sleaze. Bernie groaned internally, longing to reach out and slap that silly, honey-I'm-so-good-in-bed smile off his face.

"What about the day Stephanie was killed?" Jim asked totally deadpan, without any expression whatsoever, not on his face or in his voice.

"I was at the college all day. My first class was at eight and my last one ended at five. And no, I did not leave the campus and there should be dozens of witnesses to that fact." Brandon twined his fingers together and leisurely rested one elbow against the settee arm as he leaned his body comfortably in that direction.

"If everything you've told us checks out, you're in the clear," Jim said.

"Is that all?" Brandon asked.

Jim stood and looked down at Brandon. "Only one more question tonight: Do you know of anyone who might have wanted to harm Stephanie? Anyone who held a grudge against her, her husband or her family?"

Brandon shrugged. "No, sorry. I'm afraid I didn't know much about Stephanie's personal life. We weren't friends. We were simply lovers for a couple of weeks and my interest in her didn't go beyond a mutual sexual attraction."

Bernie rose to her feet, forced herself to shake hands with Brandon and said, "Thank you for your cooperation."

He held her hand a moment too long and said, "Tell Robyn I said hello."

Bernie plastered a weak half smile on her lips, then turned and headed off the porch, wanting to get away from this guy as quickly as possible before she acted in an unprofessional manner.

She made it back to the truck ahead of Jim, and by the time he opened the driver's door, she was already inside the cab and had her seatbelt fastened. Jim got in, inserted the key in the ignition switch and started the engine; then he spread his arm out across the back of the seat, his big hand resting behind her head.

"Nice fellow," Jim said.

"Isn't he?" Bernie replied sarcastically.

"So, is he the type of guy your sister likes?"

That was it—the straw that broke the camel's back. The tension that had built up inside her at having to deal with a bastard like Brandon Kelley had brought her to the very edge, but she had managed to remain in control. But now this! She'd thought she could handle Jim's interest in Robyn, that even if the two dated, she would not get upset. After all, Jim Norton was nothing more to her than any other deputy.

Yeah, right. He's just the man she'd had a teenage crush on, the man she had idolized from afar like so many other teenage girls had done a couple of decades ago. And he was just the first man in only God knew how long who had stirred back to life something uniquely feminine and sexual within her. That's all Jim Norton was to her.

"Robyn doesn't actually have a specific type," Bernie said, doing her best to keep her voice calm. "So if you're thinking that she might not date you because you're nothing like Brandon, don't worry. My sister loves to sample a variety. She has very eclectic tastes in bed partners. Although I have to admit that given the choice between a nice guy and a real sleaze, she usually tends to choose the sleaze."

Jim sucked in his cheeks, then huffed out a boy-did-I-step-in-it breath and said, "Okay, thanks for clearing that up for me."

"You're welcome," Bernie said much too loudly.

But Jim appeared to ignore her. He backed his truck out of the driveway and onto the dirt road without saying another word or glancing her way. They drove in silence all the way back to town, which made Bernie feel rather foolish. She kept wondering if Jim realized the real reason she had overreacted to his perfectly normal question about her sister's preference in men. Did he realize that she was jealous of the fact that he was interested in her sister and not in her? God, she hoped not.

Jim couldn't figure out what was wrong with Bernie, why she seemed to be angry with him. Or did he have nothing to do with her attitude? Maybe she was mad at her sister for apparently sleeping around and choosing the wrong kind of guy time and again.

Just like Mary Lee. Another thing Robyn Granger had in common with his ex-wife. If this similarity didn't warn him off, nothing would. Hadn't he sworn that if he ever got seriously involved with another woman, he would listen to his brain and not his dick? Yeah, but who said that if he and Robyn became involved, it would turn into something serious. He got the idea that she wasn't interested in settling down. So what would be the harm in getting to know the lady a little better, in getting himself laid?

"You'll have to give me directions to your house," Jim said. "I don't know where you live."

"Huh?"

"You want me to take you home, don't you? Or should I drop you off to pick up your Jeep? I assume you don't still live at home with your parents."

"No, I have my own place and my folks probably took my Jeep to my house for me. I live on East Jefferson Street. That's two blocks down from Washington. One-oh-four. It's the third house on the right, an old twenties bungalow. Pale yellow with dark green shutters."

Jim nodded and continued driving. He had kept silent because Bernie seemed to prefer it that way; besides, he really didn't know of anything to talk about other than the case they were working on together. He had immediately sensed the tension between them and wished he knew if he'd done something to create the problem. Too bad Charlie Patterson had gotten a call from his headquarters in Huntsville and had to drive back there overnight; otherwise, Charlie would have gone with them to question Brandon Kelley, and maybe his presence would have diffused whatever had set Bernie off. It wasn't as if she'd screamed or chewed him out or told him that she was totally pissed. But it didn't take a genius to figure out that something had ruffled her feathers.

"This is it, right?" he asked as soon as he spotted the house. He knew it had to be the right one since the street numbers had been painted on the curb and glowed in the dark. And with the porch light on, the large brass numbers attached to the door frame were visible.

"Yes, this is it."

He pulled into the drive and stopped at the brick sidewalk that led from the drive to the porch. As soon as he killed the motor, he opened his door, but before he got out, she said, "You don't have to go to the trouble of seeing me to my door."

He hesitated for half a second, then got out anyway and replied, "No trouble." By the time he made it around to the passenger side, she'd already opened her door and gotten out on her own. They stood there and stared at each other for just a minute; then she started walking. He fell into step beside her, and together they rounded the truck's hood, walked up the sidewalk and stepped up on the porch.

When they reached her front door, she stopped and turned to face him. "Thanks."

"Yeah, sure."

"Good night."

"Good night." He made it halfway down the sidewalk before he turned around and called to her. "Do you want to go somewhere and get a bite to eat? We didn't have any supper and I don't know about you, but my stomach's growling."

She paused in the middle of opening her front door, squared her shoulders and glanced at him. "There is absolutely nothing open in Adams Landing this late on a Sunday night."

"You're kidding? Surely one of the fast-food places stays open past nine."

"Not on Sunday nights."

"Great. I guess I'll have to settle for some peanut butter and crackers when I get to the house."

When he walked away, she called, "Jim?"

He halted. "Yeah?"

"Want to come in and eat supper with me? I'm sure my mother brought some leftovers from dinner and put them in my refrigerator. She always loads me down with leftovers since she knows I seldom cook just for myself."

"Lady, if you think I'm going to turn down an offer like that, you don't know me." He hurried up the sidewalk and was right behind her by the time she opened her front door.

She flipped on the overhead light as she entered the house, and Jim scanned the large, square-shaped living room as he came inside behind her. He wasn't sure what he'd been expecting to find—maybe a plain, colorless decor with functional furniture—but this warm, homey room filled with comfortable-looking chairs and a sofa and what he figured were several antique pieces surprised him. The walls were pale yellow, with wide crown molding at the top and old-fashioned mopboard at the bottom. Floral silk curtains hung over plantation blinds at the windows. Standing there in the middle of the room, Jim got the oddest feeling. He felt at home, and God knew he hadn't felt at home anywhere in ages. What was it about Bernie's house that made him react like this?

It's because this house, even this room, reminds you of your grandmother Norton's house in Mississippi.

"Sit down and relax," Bernie told him. "Turn on the TV or the radio or put on a CD while I go warm us up some supper. Do you prefer ham or fried chicken? Since Mama served both today, I'm sure there's some of both in my refrigerator."

"I'm not picky. Either is just fine with me." But he didn't sit down; instead, he followed her through the house and toward the kitchen.

She glanced over her shoulder and stared at him. "What?"

"I'm coming out to the kitchen to help you," he said.

"Oh."

Her kitchen was small, no more than twelve by twelve, and a set of long windows commanded most of the space on the back wall. The room had been wallpapered in tiny, navy blue gingham checks and white curtains hung at the windows and on the half-glass backdoor. The cabinets and appliances were all white, as were the small table and two chairs situated in front of the windows.

"So, what can I do to help?" he asked.

"Get us a couple of plates and some glasses." She pointed to the top center cabinet. "And the silverware is in the drawer directly below." Again, she pointed. "You set the table and I'll see what I can find in the refrigerator."

"Okay."

Twenty minutes later, they sat across from each other at the table, two wiped-clean plates in front of them, along with two empty iced tea glasses and a couple of crumb-covered dessert plates.

Jim leaned back, rubbed his belly and sighed. "Your mother is a great cook. If possible, that food tasted better the second time around."

Bernie groaned. "I ate too much. I shouldn't have eaten dessert, but I cannot resist my mother's Mississippi mud pie."

Jim chuckled.

"What's funny?"

"You are," he told her, then added, "in a good way."

When she stared at him quizzically, he explained, "It's just that most women won't eat like you did in front of a man. They pretend they have these delicate little appetites and nibble at their food."

"You'll learn soon enough that I'm not like most women."

"What I said, I meant as a compliment, not an insult."

"I didn't take it as an insult."

"Good."

"I can put on some decaf coffee, if you'd like."

Jim shook his head. "As tempting as that is, I'll pass." He scooted back his chair, stood and stretched. "After I help you clean up, I'd better head on home. Six o'clock will roll around in a hurry."

She stood, picked up his plate and stacked it on top of hers. "You don't have to stay and help me clean up. It won't take a minute to put these things in the dishwasher. You go on and get a good night's rest. We've still got a murder case to solve."

"If you're sure you don't need my help."

"I'm sure."

She walked him to the front porch, then stood there and watched him as he got in his old truck. He paused, looked back at her and waved before he started the engine. She lifted her hand and waved, a soft smile on her lips. All of a sudden, Jim didn't want to leave. He didn't want to go back to his cold, lonely duplex. He wanted to stay here in this warm, inviting home . . . with Bernie.

Hellfire, what was wrong with him? He wasn't attracted to Bernie, didn't feel "that way" about her, so why was it that he didn't want to leave her?

Because you felt comfortable with her, as if you'd known her all your life.

He rolled down the window and called to her, "See you in the morning, boss."

Laughing, she shook her head and called back to him, "That's Sheriff Granger to you, deputy."

"Thanks for supper."

"You're welcome."

"And thanks for the good company."

"Same here."

"Sleep tight."

"You, too."

Damn it, Norton, go home, will you? If you keep hanging around, she's going to think you don't want to leave.

I don't.

Go home. You can't stay here and sleep on Bernie's couch, even if you want to and she might actually let you. What would the neighbors think? Chuckling to himself, Jim put the truck's gears into reverse and backed out of the driveway, then headed down Jefferson. Halfway to his duplex apartment an odd thought hit him. Not once while he'd been with Bernie had he thought about her beautiful sister.

Chapter 9

Thomasina had worn a dress today instead of her usual slacks and blouse. Wanting to get into the old-fashioned romantic mood Brandon was setting for their relationship, she felt a dress was appropriate. Besides, she had great legs and she could showcase them in a just-above-the-knee hemline. Nothing too sexy, just slightly alluring. Of course, she'd had to contend with a few lascivious stares from her young male students, but she had simply ignored them.

Fingering the pearls around her neck, she thought about what Brandon might say or do when he saw that she was wearing his gift. Would he simply smile at her or would he tell her how pleased he was to see her wearing the pearls? Surely he would understand that her wearing the pearls was a sign of her willingness to begin a meaningful relationship.

She had arrived early this morning, hoping to meet up with Brandon in the faculty lounge since he, too, had an eight o'clock class, but he'd been a no-show. Her disappointment must have shown on her face because Marianne Clark had asked her if something was wrong. She'd lied to the middle-aged busybody who was teaching basic biology for the summer quarter.

"I'm fine," Thomasina had said. "Just thinking about how to motivate my students. Not too many of them are actually interested in history."

And today during the morning classes, she had been as disinterested in the rise and fall of the Roman Empire as her students had been. She'd caught herself daydreaming more than once, and for the past thirty minutes, she had practically counted the minutes until her midday break. When the class ended, she grabbed the sack lunch she'd brought, rushed out of her building and headed straight toward the arts department. If she didn't catch a glimpse of Brandon, she could walk casually by his office, which was adjacent to the art studio. And if anyone asked her what she was doing there, she had the perfect excuse. The students' artwork was on display for the entire month of July. Sketches, paintings, sculptures.

As nervous as a thirteen-year-old on her first date, Thomasina made her way down the corridor toward the studio. The door stood wide open, so she simply paused and glanced inside, doing her best to act nonchalantly. The studio was empty. A couple of students passed by and spoke. She smiled at them, nodded and walked past Brandon's office. The door was closed. Approaching the door cautiously, not wanting anyone to realize that she was checking to see if Dr. Kelley was in, she eased over to the closed door and listened. Nothing. Not a sound. But he could be in there, eating quietly or reading or just resting.

Why don't you knock on the door and say hello? Tell him you came over to look at the students' artwork. But if she did that, would she appear too eager? Would her making the next move be appropriate or would he prefer for her to wait for him to take things to the next level?

But she didn't want to wait, was tired of waiting. She

wanted to hurry things up just a little, to at least reach the point where they acknowledged the fact that they had a relationship.

Garnering all her courage, Thomasina curled her hand into a fist, reached up and knocked on the door. Her heartbeat thundered maddeningly in her ears.

No response.

She knocked again. A little harder and for twice as long.

"He's not there," a familiar male voice said.

Sucking in a deep breath, Thomasina turned and faced Scotty Joe Walters with a smile. The handsome young deputy was in charge of the D.A.R.E. programs in the Adams County schools and assisted with the neighborhood watch programs and the senior citizens programs such as T.R.I.A.D. The junior college provided the sheriff's department with a storage area for books, booklets, pamphlets, and other items used with the various programs and they also allowed the sheriff's department to use their auditorium facilities for various group meetings and events. Scotty Joe was such a familiar face around Adams County Junior College that he seemed like a member of the staff. Everyone liked the good-looking deputy. The guy was always friendly and cordial, and he had the kind of gentlemanly manners every mother wished her son had. She wasn't sure how old he was. Mid-to-late twenties would be her guess.

"I beg your pardon?" Thomasina acted innocent, as if she had no idea what he'd meant.

"Dr. Kelley. He's not in his office," Scotty Joe said. "You were looking for him, weren't you?"

"Well, actually, I came over to take a look at the student art that's being displayed this month and I just thought I'd say hi to Brandon while I'm in his building."

"You just missed him. Robyn Granger picked him up in her snazzy little yellow sports car. I figure they're headed out somewhere for lunch."

"Oh." *Please, dear God, don't let what I'm feeling show on my face. Don't let Scotty Joe figure out that I'm hurt and disappointed and on the verge of bursting into tears.*

"Hey, you okay, Thomasina? You look sort of green or something."

"It's nothing. I didn't eat breakfast and I guess I'm just hungry," she lied as she held the tears at bay.

"Is that your lunch you've got with you?" He eyed the small brown paper bag she held so tightly that her nails bit into the flesh of her palm.

Easing her death grip on the bag, she nodded, but heaven help her, she couldn't respond verbally because she was choking down her on-the-verge-of-erupting tears.

"I brought my lunch, too," he said. "Bologna sandwich, dill pickles, a bag of chips, and a couple of brownies from Cummings Bakery." He held up his brown paper bag, which was twice the size of hers since hers contained only a banana and a bag filled with carrot sticks, raw broccoli, and raw cauliflower. "Want to join me? We could get a couple of Cokes from the machine down the hall, then go out to the gazebo and share our lunches."

The tears Thomasina had been struggling to control suddenly broke free and trickled from her eyes and down her cheeks.

"Hey, gal, don't do that." He reached out as if he was going to touch her, but let his hand hang there in midair. "Don't waste your tears on him. He's not worth it."

As the tears seeped into the edges of her mouth, she sucked in a deep breath, then bit down on her bottom lip to keep from crying out loud.

Scotty Joe opened his lunch sack and pulled out a paper napkin, then held it out to her. "Here, dry your eyes. You don't want somebody seeing you like this. It would be all over school by the end of the day."

She grabbed the napkin and dried her eyes. "What—what

would be all over school?" she asked as she looked right at him and saw pity and concern in his big blue eyes.

He shook his head. "Nothing. Don't pay any attention to me."

"It's not what you think." She patted her damp face, then crushed the napkin into her fist and searched Scotty Joe's face again. "I'm not one of Brandon's girls, one of his women."

Scotty Joe grinned from ear to ear. "Good. I'm glad to hear it. You're far too good for him, if you don't mind my saying so."

"You don't like Brandon?"

"It's not that I don't like him." Scotty Joe's tanned cheeks flushed. "I guess it's just that I think it's downright wrong of him to take advantage of the girls he teaches and of women in general." Scotty Joe hung his head shyly.

"If that offer to share our lunches is still open, I'd like to take you up on it." Thomasina managed a weak smile.

"You bet it is," Scotty Joe told her. "And the Cokes are on me."

Charlie Patterson laid the preliminary reports down on Jim's desk, then took a seat in one of the old vinyl and metal chairs in front of the desk. Looking like a man who hadn't gotten much sleep last night, Charlie had arrived from Huntsville fifteen minutes ago, while Jim had been out for lunch. He'd gone with Ron Hensley and John Downs to Methel's for the Monday special—meatloaf, creamed potatoes, green peas, and homemade rolls—topped off with banana pudding, which was almost as popular as the restaurant's peach cobbler. When they arrived back at the office, he'd found Charlie sharing coffee and chocolate chip muffins from Cummings Bakery with Lieutenant Hoyt Moses.

"I called Bernie's office and left a message for her to

come on over," Charlie said. "No point in going over every-thing now and then again with her."

"Wish I could hang around," Downs said. "But I'm due in court at one-thirty. I have to testify in the trial about that big marijuana bust we made back last fall."

Jim nodded, then glanced at Hensley. "Bring in another chair. We'll be one short when Bernie gets here."

"She's here," Bernie said from the doorway.

Jim looked up from where he sat behind his desk and motioned for her to come into his office. Downs paused to say hello to Bernie on his way out and Hensley spoke to her as he headed off to commandeer another chair.

"What have I missed?" she asked.

"Nothing," Jim told her. "We're just getting started."

She glanced at Charlie. "Rough night?"

"Does it show?" he replied.

She grinned at him. "Only around the edges."

He grunted. "Our ten-year-old kept us up all night with a stomach virus. When I left this morning, she was finally resting and had been able to keep down some 7-Up and crackers."

"How many children do you have?" Bernie asked.

"Three girls. Eight, ten, and thirteen." Charlie chuckled as he got up and offered Bernie his chair by pointing to her and then to the chair. "Lucky for them, they all look more like their mother than they do me."

"I guess your wife will be glad for you to wind things up here and come home to stay." Bernie accepted the offered seat.

"I think I miss her and the girls more than they miss me."

"I doubt that." Bernie smiled. "Take it from somebody who was a daddy's girl, at the ages your daughters are, there's no other man in their lives as important as their fa-ther."

Hensley brought in a folding chair, opened it and sat; then he reared back and placed his hands on his thighs. The guy swaggered when he walked, his every action proclaiming his cocky attitude, and there he was sitting back like he owned the world. Jim studied his deputy, but when the guy's gaze met his, Jim focused on Bernie. She looked today as she looked every day. Neat and orderly. Brown slacks, white blouse, minimum of makeup, simple gold jewelry, her hair pulled back in a loose ponytail.

As if sensing that he was staring at her, she turned and looked right at him. Their gazes connected and held. He smiled. She smiled. Jim figured they had the makings of a firm friendship. The more he got to know Bernie, the better he liked her.

Charlie tapped his fingers on the file folder lying on Jim's desk. "I brought the preliminary report on Stephanie Preston. As we all know, her death was caused when the carotid arteries were severed when her attacker slit her throat, pretty much from ear to ear. Her throat was cut from left to right in a manner indicating the killer was behind her, probably on top of her, and that he jerked her neck backward and brought the knife down and across. There were no signs of defensive wounds, so it's unlikely she tried to fight him. The knife had a smooth blade, which means no distinctive marks from the blade on the neck. And the knife was very sharp. The murderer probably made sure it was sharp because his intent was to end her life quickly and relatively painlessly."

"I thought we had decided he had tortured her, so why would he care if her death was quick and painless?" Hensley asked.

"Good question." Charlie glanced at Jim.

"He'd gotten whatever it was he had wanted from her, from raping her and torturing her," Jim said. "When it came time to end things, he was through with her. All he wanted was to get rid of her quickly. I'd say he thought of the way he killed her as a reward to her for having given him what he'd needed from her."

"What sort of sick mind would look at it that way, would believe that she'd given him anything?" Bernie frowned. "She didn't give. He just took everything from her, even her life."

"Our boy is not only one sick puppy, but he's smart," Charlie said. "He trimmed her fingernails and toenails and cleaned out from under the nails, leaving no trace evidence. And he washed her hair and her body before he dropped her off in the middle of nowhere."

"Then he's no run-of-the-mill nut case." Bernie draped her right arm across her waist, then propped her left elbow atop her right fist and rested her chin atop her tilted left hand.

"You're right—he is a nut case and definitely not run of the mill," Charlie agreed. "Whoever he is, he likes rough sex, he likes to make his victim suffer and he's smart enough to remove any evidence on the body."

"What about any evidence from where her body was found?" Hensley asked.

Charlie shook his head. "Nada, at least so far."

"And that's about what we've got," Jim said. "Nada. We've ruled out our three most likely suspects—the husband and two former lovers."

"Yeah, their alibis checked out," Hensley said. "So that leaves us back at square one."

"If only someone had seen something the night Stephanie was kidnapped." Bernie rubbed her thumb across her lips. "The last anyone saw of her, she had just exited the building and was heading toward her car. So what happened between the building and her car? There is no evidence she made it to her car, but then again there's no evidence to indicate she didn't."

"Y'all didn't find anything that belonged to her in the

parking lot, did you? Not a notebook or scattered papers or her handbag or—"

"Nothing," Bernie said. "And her purse and books weren't inside her car either, which we figured meant she'd taken them with her."

"Unless the guy who abducted her gathered up all her belongings after he nabbed her." Jim tapped his fingers against the desktop as he mulled things over in his mind. "If she took the items with her, then I have one question. Why, if she was being abducted, would she have hung on to her purse and other items instead of trying to fight this guy off?"

"She didn't fight him, did she?" Bernie tightened her left hand into a fist and huffed under her breath as she figured out Jim's theory. "Damn it, she knew him. And for some reason, she went with him willingly." Bernie looked straight at Jim. "Am I right? Is that what you're thinking?"

Jim nodded. "Where is her car?"

"We had our wrecker pick it up and bring it in," Hensley said. "We went over it with a fine-tooth comb and found nothing unusual, so we turned it over to Taylor's Wrecker Service. Last I heard, no one in the family has come to pick it up yet."

"Did y'all have a mechanic check the car?" Jim asked.

Hensley looked questioningly at Jim. "Why would we have had a mechanic check it? The car had nothing to do with Stephanie's disappearance."

"Call over to Taylor's Wrecker Service," Jim said. "Have them see if the car will start, and if not, why not?"

"Oh shit," Bernie cursed under her breath.

"What is it, Sheriff?" Charlie asked, a hint of a smile curving the corners of his mouth.

"You know damn well what it is." She glared from Charlie to Jim. "Why would a woman not drive her own car? Why would she accept a ride from someone else? Because her car wouldn't start."

"Yep." Charlie's smile widened.

"Our guy deliberately put Stephanie's car out of commission, then he waited around to play Good Samaritan when her car wouldn't start." Bernie gritted her teeth and groaned. "Ooh . . . She knew him. Whoever he is, Stephanie knew him and trusted him enough to accept a ride with him."

"That narrows down our field of suspects to probably at least a fourth of all the men in Adams and Jackson counties," Hensley said.

"Maybe so, but it also means our guy is probably still around, that he either lives in Adams County or in one of the neighboring counties, that he's probably a native." Jim tapped his fingers against the desktop again. "And if he enjoyed what he did to Stephanie, it's probably only a matter of time before he chooses a second victim."

"I agree," Charlie told him. "But that's assuming Stephanie Preston was his first victim."

"Are we back to the serial killer theory?" Hensley asked.

"Yeah," Jim said. "So Lieutenant, I'd like for you to put in a call to the sheriff's departments of all the neighboring counties within a hundred-mile radius and find out if there's been another murder similar to Stephanie's within the past six months. No, make that the past year."

When Thomasina arrived home, she called out to her mother, who was in the kitchen. "Mom, I've got a headache. I'm going to my room to lie down for a while. I don't think I'll want any supper."

As she headed toward her room, she heard the kitchen door open. *Please, don't let her follow me and try to talk to me.*

"You got a package," her mother said. "I found it in the mailbox with today's mail, but there wasn't any postage on it. That's odd, don't you think?"

A package? Another present from Brandon? "What did you do with it?"

"I put it on your dresser."

"Thanks, Mom."

"Want me to bring you some aspirin?"

"No, I'll get some if lying down doesn't help."

Thomasina rushed into her room, closed the door behind herself quickly and went straight over to her dresser. The package, about twelve inches square and four inches deep, had been wrapped in plain brown paper and sealed with clear, wide tape. She moved close enough so that she could see her name printed in large black block letters across the top. No return address, and no postage. He had brought the gift by and left it sometime today. But when? Was it possible that Scotty Joe had been wrong about Brandon leaving with Robyn Granger at lunchtime today?

No, it's not possible. Scotty Joe wouldn't have lied to me.

She knew Brandon and Robyn had indulged in an on-gain, off-again affair, but she'd assumed it was over, that Brandon was now ready for real love. Had she been wrong? Had he and Robyn made love this afternoon?

Was he simply playing her for a fool, sending her love notes and presents, luring her to him, when all she meant to him was just another conquest?

When had he made the time to drive all the way over here to Verona? Or had he gotten someone else to drop off this new gift? She skimmed the top of the package with nervous fingers. What had he sent her this time?

Open it and find out.

She'd need a pair of scissors.

As if it were fragile, perhaps even explosive, Thomasina picked up the parcel and carried it with her to her bed. She sat on the edge, deposited the package in her lap, and then rummaged in her nightstand drawer for a pair of scissors. For several minutes, she sat there, the wrapped box in her lap and the scissors in her hand, and thought about what a miserable afternoon she'd had. It had been all she could do to get through the two classes without crying. If it hadn't been for Scotty Joe's kindness at lunchtime, she wasn't sure she could have made it through the rest of the day. He hadn't mentioned Brandon again; instead, he'd entertained her with jokes and cute stories about the kids he met through his work with the D.A.R.E. program. And he'd insisted she eat one of the scrumptious but fattening brownies from Cummings Bakery.

"You don't need to worry about calories," he'd told her. "You're just the right size."

She had eaten every morsel of the delicious brownie and enjoyed it immensely. By the time she had washed down the last bite with her cola, she had been able to smile. Of course, once lunch ended and she and Scotty Joe went their separate ways, all the jealous thoughts about Brandon and Robyn came rushing back, flooding her mind with images of the two of them making love.

You cannot assume Brandon is guilty. Not without proof. You have to give him the benefit of the doubt.

Grasping the scissors in her right hand, she cut the tape holding the brown paper in place; then she removed the paper to reveal a white box. She tossed the paper aside and lifted the lid on the box. Inside she found white tissue paper covering the contents, which she promptly removed. She picked up the first two items—a bottle of pink nail polish and a tube of matching lipstick. Holding one item in each hand, she inspected them. Revlon items that could be purchased at Wal-Mart or Kmart or the local drugstore.

Thomasina laid the nail polish and lipstick on her pillow, then searched deeper into the box. She removed two envelopes. She felt certain the smaller one contained a note and the larger one possibly held another sketch.

She opened the note and read it. Then read it again.

You're more beautiful in pink than in any other color. Will you wear pink for me, my darling Thomasina?

Tears lodged in her throat.

She placed the note alongside the nail polish and lipstick, then ripped open the large white envelope and pulled out the sketch.

"Oh my God!"

It's me, and yet it's not me. It's my face and the body is similar to mine, but—

She stared at the ink sketch of her standing in a very sensual pose, her hair falling over one shoulder and almost touching the top of her naked breast. Her nipples were tight. Thomasina's gaze moved from the obviously tight nipples down over her navel to the hand that covered her mound.

He's drawn me naked and aroused.

Oh, Brandon, what kind of game are you playing? If I'm the woman you want, why did you go off with Robyn today? Why didn't you come looking for me to see if I was wearing your pearls?

Tears streamed down Thomasina's face as she curled up in a fetal ball in the middle of her bed, the ink sketch crushed in her tight fist.

Bernie rubbed the back of her neck as she stretched her other arm over her head. Ron had already left for the day and Charlie had just said he was going to head back to the Adams Landing Hotel down the street.

"I need to call Jen and check on the girls, see if anybody else has come down with that stomach virus," Charlie said. "If Jen's gotten it, I'll head on home tonight. Otherwise, I'll stay in town and try to get a good night's rest."

"See you in the morning," Jim said.

"Yeah, let's make it eight o'clock tomorrow, okay?"

"Sure thing."

Charlie patted Bernie on the back as he headed for the door. She offered him a smile and then turned to Jim. "It's been a long day."

"Yes, it has."

She wanted to ask him if he had plans for supper tonight, but she wasn't willing to risk making a fool of herself. After all, she figured Jim Norton was the type who did the asking—if he wanted to spend time with a woman.

"Guess I'll head on home," she said.

"Would you be interested in catching a quick bite over at Methel's first?" he asked.

He'd taken her off guard with his invitation. *Don't act too eager or overly pleased.* "Uh . . . sure. That would be fine."

"I figure we'd both be eating alone otherwise . . . or am I wrong? If you've got other plans—"

"My only plans are with a hot shower and a good book," she told him.

"Then you're one up on me," he said. "I don't even have a good book to read."

She was having dinner with Jim and he had been the one to ask, not her.

But this is not a date, Bernie, she reminded herself. *It's just two colleagues grabbing a bite. He could just as easily have asked Charlie or Ron. Do not make a big deal out of this.*

"Methel's has great food," she said as they walked out into the hallway together. "The dinner menu is about the same as the lunch menu. But if you want something different—juicy burgers and fries and ice cream sundaes—then we should go over to the King Kone on North Adams."

"A burger and fries sounds good to me." Jim closed the door, then placed his hand in the center of her back. "And instead of ice cream sundaes, how about a couple of banana splits?"

The moment he touched her, her stomach did a silly, girlish flip-flop. "Oh, Captain Norton, you are a man after my own heart. I love banana splits."

"Somehow I figured you did." He winked at her.

Her stomach did another crazy flip-flop.

Just as they reached the entrance that opened onto Washington Street, the door flew open and in pranced Robyn, wearing a hot pink cotton skirt that was so short it barely covered her butt. And her white blouse was completely sheer, showing off the hot pink lace camisole beneath.

"Hey, I'm glad I caught you before you left," Robyn said, looking directly at Jim.

"Who are you talking to?" Bernie asked. "Jim or me?"

Robyn giggled. "Jim, of course, silly. Why would I be asking my sister out to dinner when I could go with her handsome new deputy?"

"You're here to ask me out?" Jim grinned.

Bernie wanted to knock that stupid grin off his face.

"I'm sorry I didn't call first, but it's been wild over at the fitness center." Robyn insinuated herself between Bernie and Jim, then laced her arm through his. "I'm running a two-for-one special this week and—"

"Bernie and I were just heading over to the King Kone for burgers," Jim said. "You could join us."

"Yuck, the King Kone. They serve nothing but junk food." Robyn ran an appreciative eye over her own body and sighed dramatically. "I couldn't keep this figure if I ate burgers and fries, now could I?"

Jim glanced over at Bernie and shrugged. "What about Methel's?"

"Absolutely not," Robyn said. "River's End has great seafood and wonderful salads."

"And it costs an arm and a leg," Bernie said.

"So, if price is a problem"—she batted her eyelashes at Jim—"we'll go Dutch treat."

"Is this place fancy?" Jim asked. "I'm not dressed for fancy and neither is Bernie."

"It's not that fancy," Robyn replied.

"Look, why don't you two go on out to River's End and have a great seafood dinner. I think I'll just head on home and scramble myself some eggs."

"Eggs are bad for you," Robyn said.

Bernie forced a smile, then gave Jim a quick glance. "See you in the morning, Jim."

Before he had a chance to say anything, Bernie rushed out the front door and walked hurriedly down the street. Her Jeep was parked at the courthouse, so she had no choice but to walk along the sidewalk, meeting and greeting people as they were leaving the antique shop and the library.

Just keep that phony smile in place, she told herself, *and keep walking. You are not going to cry because you have nothing to cry about. Okay, so your feelings are hurt just a little because you know Jim would much rather have dinner with Robyn than with you. And you're a teensy bit upset with your sister because it never entered her pretty little head that Jim might have asked you to dinner and that his invitation had thrilled you beyond all reason.*

Bernie made it to the area of the courthouse parking lot reserved for her and her deputies and was forced to face and speak to several deputies who were leaving for the day. By the time she got in her Jeep, started the engine and pulled out onto Washington Street, tears clouded her vision. Lifting one hand, she swiped the tears away and called herself all kinds of a fool.

Stop acting like a girl. You are not a sissy. You're better than that.

Chapter 10

Thomasina had been staring at the large manila envelope for endless minutes, wanting to open it and yet afraid to see what surprise "gift" might be waiting inside for her. One of her students in the last afternoon class had found the envelope, with her name printed on it in bold black letters, lying on the floor at the back of the classroom, as if someone had accidentally dropped it there. She had thanked the student, laid the envelope on her desk and waited until the room was clear before she burst into tears. What had started out less than a week ago as an exciting romantic adventure had now turned into an unnerving nightmare. After allowing herself a good cry, she'd gathered up her things, including the unopened envelope, and driven home. Often when she had to teach a night class, as she did tonight, she didn't bother going home; instead, she either stayed at the school and caught up on work or she drove into Adams Landing to shop and have an early dinner. But today, she had wanted—no, she had needed—to come home where she felt safe.

She'd found a note on the refrigerator from her mother, telling her that she'd gone to Huntsville with her best friend,

Rose Johnson, for a shopping spree at Parkway City Mall,
and they wouldn't be home until late. In a way, she was glad
her mother wasn't here to question her about her odd mood
again, which she'd been doing all week. But a part of her
wished her mother was here so she could tell her what had
been going on for the past week and ask her advice.

Thomasina had placed the envelope in the middle of the
kitchen table, poured herself a glass of iced tea, sat down
and studied the damn thing as if she could figure out what
was inside without opening it.

Monday's gift would have been sweet, even endearing, if
she hadn't thought that Brandon was playing her for a fool,
stringing her along while he kept seeing other women. But
the gift that she'd received on Wednesday, an envelope con-
taining sketches and a small box, had been stuffed in her P.O.
box at the college. She'd questioned the secretary, asking if
she had any idea who'd put the envelope in her box.

"No, I'm sorry," Kerrianne Gipson had said. "It's been
one of those days. I've been in and out of the office all day
long. I'm afraid just about anybody could have left it. Why?
Is there a problem?"

"No, no problem. I was just curious. I'm sure there's a
note or something inside."

But the note hadn't been signed.

She'd waited only until she'd reached her car before ripping open the envelope and dumping the small box out into
her hand. Inside the box she'd found a small bottle of perfume. White Shoulders. She didn't know that particular scent
was still being manufactured. It was such an old-fashioned
fragrance. Her mother had used it for a couple of years nearly
twenty years ago.

She'd read the note before looking at the sketches.

*I dream of you this way. Of our being together. Of your
loving everything I do to you.*

She'd found three sketches inside the envelope, each one

more graphic and sickening than the one before, and all three depicting her naked and aroused in various S&M scenes. Her being whipped—the hand holding the whip large and menacing. Her on all fours, a dog collar around her neck attached to a leash. And her lying chained to a metal bed, a large dildo in her mouth and the tip of another one sticking out between her clenched thighs.

She had ripped the sketches and the note into pieces, then had shoved them and the perfume bottle back into the envelope and gotten out of her car. Without even thinking about what she was doing, she'd marched straight across the parking lot to the large, green Dumpster, opened the heavy lid and thrown the envelope on top of the other trash.

When she'd gotten home yesterday evening, she'd gone straight to her room; then she'd taken the pearl necklace, the lipstick, the nail polish, all the photos, notes, and sketches from the top of her closet where she'd stored them, stuck the nonpaper items in her slacks pocket and shoved the notes, photos, and sketches under her arm and carried them with her through the kitchen. She had taken a handful of matches from the box her mother kept in the drawer beside the sink, then had gone outside. She'd placed all the paper items inside the large brick outdoor barbeque grill and struck one match after another, placing each lit flame to various edges of the papers. After that, she had tossed the other things into the outdoor garbage container.

Brandon Kelley was no dream lover. No old-fashioned gentleman. He was a sicko. A pervert. And she wanted nothing to do with him. Robyn Granger could have him, if she wanted him. If Robyn was "into" Brandon's kind of sex.

This morning, Thomasina had written Brandon a succinct letter warning him that if he ever sent her another package of any kind, she would call the police. She had thought that would be the end of it. She'd been wrong. So very wrong.

She kept staring at the manila envelope lying in the middle of the table. Wishing it would go away. Wishing she had the guts to open it. Knowing that if it contained what she thought it did, she'd have no choice but to contact the local authorities.

Enough was enough.

Allen Clark drove a late-model Mercedes, dressed in suits and ties and when he had moved Mary Lee and Kevin to Huntsville, he'd moved them into a three-hundred and fifty-thousand dollar house in the southeast area. The guy was in his late forties, had been divorced for eight years when he met Mary Lee and had no children of his own. As much as Jim wanted to hate the guy, he couldn't. From what he could tell, Allen really loved Mary Lee and seemed to genuinely care about Kevin. And for the first time in a long time, Mary Lee acted as if she was truly happy. Of course, her taking Kevin away from Memphis had screwed up Jim's life and he resented the hell out of her attitude that Allen would make Kevin a better father. Okay, so Allen had more money. Big deal. And with Kevin living under his roof, Allen spent more time with him. But Goddamn it, Allen was not Kevin's father. He was. And he loved his son, would do anything for him—anything short of giving him up for another man to raise.

Jim hadn't seen Kevin in nearly two months, although he called him a couple of times a week. When they talked, Kevin raved about his new room, his new computer, his fabulous dirt bike, and his great new stepdad. Unless another guy had gone through the same experience, he wouldn't be able to understand how Jim felt, how worthless and insignificant. When the only really good thing in your life is your child and suddenly you're no longer the primary man in his world, it's like having your heart ripped from your chest without the benefit of any painkillers.

Despite his heavy workload at the office, Jim had taken off early to accommodate Allen's schedule. Allen had explained that he wanted to drop Kevin off at four and be home by five-thirty to have dinner with Mary Lee.

"She needs me," Allen had said. "She's scared out of her mind and if I'm not with her, she panics."

Yeah, that sounded like Mary Lee. For as long as Jim had known her, she'd been self-centered, her needs coming before anyone else's. In Mary Lee's world, everything revolved around her. So why, when she was facing major surgery for cancer, would anything be different? He didn't envy Allen in the least for having to play nursemaid to a woman who could never be satisfied. It wasn't that Jim didn't wish Mary Lee the best—he did. He prayed she'd come through the surgery with flying colors, have a complete recovery and live to be ninety.

It had taken him a long time to stop hating her. And even longer to stop loving her.

Jim stood on the small front porch of his duplex and watched as Allen pulled his Mercedes into the driveway. By the time Allen opened his door, Jim was at the end of the sidewalk meeting him. They shook hands cordially; then Jim glanced across the hood of the car and saw Kevin's dark head. His twelve-year-old son was already five-eight. Jim figured by the time he was eighteen he'd be as tall as Jim, at six-three.

Allen popped the car's trunk and Kevin joined him to retrieve a couple of suitcases and a laptop computer. For a minute there, Jim halfway expected Kevin to pull his dirt bike from the trunk.

"Is that everything?" Jim asked. "Need any help?"

Allen handed Jim one of the suitcases. "He should have enough to do him for several weeks," Allen said. "If not, buy whatever he needs and send me the bill."

Jim growled under his breath and said in a low, rough

voice, "I think I can manage to buy my son whatever he needs."

Allen's craggy face turned pink. "Sorry. I didn't mean anything. It's just . . . Well, okay then." He turned to Kevin who'd walked over and now stood between his father and stepfather. Allen smiled at Kevin. "I'll call you tomorrow as soon as your mom comes out of surgery, and she'll call you herself as soon as she can."

Kevin nodded.

"She's going to be all right." Allen's smile wavered. "And you'll be home with us before school starts."

"Yeah, sure." Kevin shrugged.

"If you need anything . . ." Allen left his sentence unfinished.

"I'll be fine," Kevin replied. "You take care of Mom and don't worry about me."

Jim and Kevin, each with a suitcase in hand, stood on the small front porch of Jim's duplex and watched Allen Clark back out of the driveway and head off down the street.

"Come on in and I'll show you your bedroom." Jim opened the door and waited for Kevin to enter first. He wanted to reach out and hug his son, to tell him how glad he was that they were going to be living together, at least temporarily, for the first time since Kevin was six. But a boy of twelve-going-on-twenty probably didn't want his dad hugging him.

Kevin hoisted his suitcase and laptop onto the bed and looked around at the room. Jim dropped the other suitcase on the floor beside the closet and tried to assess the room through his son's eyes.

"It's probably nowhere near as nice as your room in Huntsville," Jim said.

"It's okay, Dad. Really."

"Hey, at least here you've got a room of your own. Back in Memphis, you had to bunk in with me in that tiny apartment I had."

"Yeah, this is better."

"Look, Kevin, I know this isn't going to be easy for you, staying with me for several weeks when we haven't spent more than a few days together since you were little. And I know you're worried about your mom. I'm concerned about her, too. But if anybody on earth can lick cancer, Mary Lee can. She's a real scrapper. Always has been. It was one of the things I always love—liked about her."

"It's just not fair, you know."

Kevin looked as if the weight of the world was sitting heavily on his slender shoulders and Jim would give anything if he could lift that burden and carry it for him.

"I know," Jim said.

"She's really happy with Allen. And she's different, you know. She stays at home more and she laughs a lot and—" Kevin choked up.

"Your mother's going to come through the surgery just fine."

"But it's cancer. Cancer! She could come through the surgery okay and still die."

"That's not going to happen."

"How can you be so sure? Besides, I know you hate Mom. Why do you care if she lives or dies?"

Jim reached out and grabbed Kevin by the shoulders and looked him square in the eyes. "I don't hate your mother." No point in admitting to his son that he *had* hated her for years. "And I care because she's your mother, because she was once my wife . . ."

Tears pooled in Kevin's blue eyes. Norton eyes. Eyes like Jim's. Eyes like Jim's father's.

Jim squeezed Kevin's shoulders affectionately, doing his best to comfort his son. "You can call and talk to her every day. She'll want to hear from you and know you're doing okay."

Kevin swallowed hard. "I can unpack and put everything away by myself."

"Yeah, sure." Jim understood that his son needed to be alone for a little while, that he needed to cry without his father watching him. "You unpack and get settled in while I make a few phone calls, then later we'll go out for supper. How does that sound?"

"Fine."

Jim nodded, gave Kevin a keep-your-chin-up look and made a quick exit. After closing the door behind him, he stood there in the small, square hallway between the two bedrooms and said a prayer, something he hadn't done in a long time. He prayed for Mary Lee. And he prayed that he wouldn't screw up this chance to be a real father to his son.

Knowing she couldn't keep her terrible secret to herself any longer, Thomasina had called her sister and asked her to come over as quickly as possible. And when Amanda arrived, she had told her everything, starting with that first "love note" and ending by showing her the unopened manila envelope lying in the middle of the kitchen table.

"You shouldn't have gotten rid of the other stuff," Amanda told her. "You should have saved it for the police. They'll need all the evidence they can get if they're going to arrest Brandon Kelley."

"I—I wasn't thinking," Thomasina admitted. "I just wanted all of it gone, out of the house, out of my sight forever."

"Want me to open it?" Amanda indicated the manila envelope.

"No, I'll do it. I just wanted you here with me before I did it."

"Go ahead." Amanda stood behind Thomasina's chair and clamped her hands down reassuringly on her shoulders. "I'm right here."

Her hands shook so badly that she paused for a couple of

minutes after she picked up the envelope. "I'm a nervous wreck. This is what he's done to me, and I let him do it. I've been so stupid." Fueled with anger and indignation, she ripped open the envelope, turned it upside down and watched as two small envelopes and three pieces of art paper drifted out and floated down onto the table. She noticed that one of the small envelopes was flat and the other was puffy, as if it contained bubble wrap.

"He always sends a message." Thomasina reached for the flat envelope first.

"Maybe you should open the other one first and look at the sketches, then read the note."

Thomasina shook her head, ripped open the flat envelope and removed the note.

She read it to herself first.

I know that you love me and want to please me. Soon, very soon, we'll be together and you'll be able to show me just how much you care.

She handed the note to her sister. "Should we be wearing gloves or something? If there are any fingerprints—"

"Just read the damn note, will you?" Tears swam in Thomasina's eyes.

Amanda took the note, being careful to hold it by the edges, then read it. "Open the other envelope."

Thomasina opened the puffy envelope and removed a small square of bubble wrap. She tore apart the padding to reveal a gold ankle bracelet. She dropped it on the table as if the touch of it burned her fingers.

"Now the sketches," Amanda told her.

Thomasina turned them over and looked at them one at a time, then handed them to her sister. Just looking at the sketches made her sick to her stomach.

"Oh, Thomasina, these are awful," Amanda said. "If

Brandon Kelley drew these, he's crazy. And if he wants to do these things to you, he's dangerous." She waved the third sketch in the air. "This picture shows you with your throat slit and blood dripping down on your breasts." Amanda tossed the sketch aside, then rushed across the kitchen, picked up the telephone and said, "I'm calling Chief Nichols right now. If he can't arrest Brandon Kelley on any other charges, he can arrest him for harassing you."

"Wait," Thomasina called to her sister.

"No, I'm not waiting. I'm calling the police. It's something you should have already done."

"We'll call the police and tell them everything," Thomasina said. "But . . . but I have no way to prove that Brandon is the one who sent me the notes and gifts and sketches."

"Who else could it be? He's an artist and it would have taken a very talented artist to have drawn those wicked, sickening pictures. And he's flirted with you for months now, hasn't he? And when he got your message today, he didn't come to you and deny he'd been the one sending you this stuff, did he?"

"No, he didn't, but—"

"We'll call Chief Nichols, tell him everything and let him take it from there. Just tell him that you think these things are from Brandon Kelley, but you can't be sure."

"That's just it, Amanda. I'm not sure. Not now. What if it was someone else all along?"

"Then the police will find out who."

"Will they? How? How will they find out? What if he keeps sending these things? What if—"

"First things first. Let's get the police involved and go from there."

Thomasina nodded. "I have to be back at school by seven." She glanced at her watch. "It's already after six. Maybe I should wait until tomorrow to call the police."

"No, you will not wait. Call and cancel your class tonight."

"I can't. I'm giving a major test tonight. I have to be there."

"Okay. We'll go to the police station first. You take your car and I'll follow you in mine. We will talk to the police, tell them what's happened, leave this stuff"—she glowered at the envelope's contents lying on the table—"then whatever paperwork needs filling out, you can do tomorrow. But the sooner the police know, the better for you."

Thomasina gathered up the items, shoved them back into the ripped envelope and said, "Let's go."

Bernie arrived at Robyn's new apartment, located on Main Street in downtown Adams Landing directly above the town's only bookstore. Many of the second levels of the downtown buildings had been converted into apartments over the past ten years, and since living so close to her fitness center was ideal for Robyn, she'd jumped at the first available apartment. After getting out of her Jeep, Bernie walked across the sidewalk and opened the street-level door that led up the stairs to the second floor of the building. As soon as she headed up the stairs, she heard voices and recognized two of them—her sister's and her mother's. Both women were talking at the same time, both issuing orders. Then she heard the shuffle of feet, several pairs of feet, and the sound of furniture being dragged. There was no telling who all was up there. Between the two of them, her mother and sister had probably invited half the people they knew to "come over and help us."

If it wasn't for the fact that she'd never hear the end of it if she didn't show up this evening, Bernie would have gone straight home. She was physically and mentally exhausted, having put in a ten-hour day. Despite the evidence the ABI had collected, they were no closer to discovering the identity of Stephanie Preston's killer than they had been nearly a week ago when her body had been discovered. Everyone working on the case was becoming frustrated, and frustration led to squabbling among her deputies—especially between Ron and Jim. Charlie had refereed several sparring matches between them in the past few days, but after tomorrow Charlie would be gone, back in Huntsville at the ABI substation. He'd done all he could do here in Adams County and although he would continue to be in charge of the case, he'd simply drive back and forth whenever necessary, instead of staying in town. After all, it would probably be several months before all the DNA evidence was processed and unless new evidence came to light before then, they had hit a dead end in their investigation.

When Bernie reached the top of the stairs and moved down the hallway to the first apartment, she found the front door open, making it unnecessary for her to knock. She glanced inside and saw a crowd of people, along with her immediate family. Paul Landon lounged on a bright yellow leather sofa. Yellow was Robyn's favorite color. The others were working like little solider ants, each one following the queen's and the princess's instructions. Brandon Kelley was in there and at this precise moment he was helping her mother hang a painting over the fireplace. Raymond Long and his mother, Helen, were also inside the apartment, along with Reverend Donaldson, Ron Hensley, and Scotty Joe Walters.

Bernie released an exasperated huff and shook her head. She was surprised that Jim hadn't come over and brought his son with him. It seemed that most of the good-looking, single men in Adams Landing were in her sister's apartment.

Her father came toward her, stepped outside into the hallway and closed the door behind him. "If I don't get out of there for a few minutes, I'm going to have to shoot somebody and I don't want it to be your mother or your sister."

Bernie chuckled, then rose on tiptoe and kissed her father's cheek. "Rough day, Dad?"

"If your sister ever wants to move again, I'll hire professionals to move her." He motioned to the apartment. "There are half a dozen men in there and each one of them is showing off for Robyn. Hell, they're like a bunch of little boys wanting to be chosen for a team. They might as well be screaming, 'Choose me! Choose me!'"

"Robyn has that effect on men." Bernie shrugged. "She can't help it because she's beautiful like Mama and men find her irresistible."

"Yeah, but she could put a stop to all of that nonsense if she'd narrow the field down to one man at a time. Your mother never dated half a dozen guys at the same time, I'll tell you that."

"Things were different when Mama was dating."

"If you're about to tell me anything about your sister's love life, don't."

Bernie put her arm around her father's waist and hugged him. "She'll eventually settle down, find herself a husband and give you and Mama some grandkids."

Her dad hugged her. "What about you, honey?"

"What about me?"

"When are you going to find yourself a nice guy, get married and have some kids? You're not getting any younger, you know."

Bernie sighed. "I'm thirty-two, Dad, not fifty-two."

"What do you think of Jim Norton?" R.B. asked.

Bernie eyed her father skeptically. "What's Jim Norton got to do with—"

"I like him, Bernie. Don't you?"

"Well, yes, I like him. But I've only known him for a week."

"So, get to know him better. Ask him out. Women do the asking now, don't they?"

"He's not interested in me. Besides, Robyn already asked him out. They went to dinner at River's End this past Monday."

Brenda Granger opened the door from inside Robyn's apartment, stuck her head out and called to them. "There you are, R.B. And Bernie . . . when did you get here? You two come on in. We've just about got everything finished and I've unloaded all three picnic baskets and put out paper plates so everybody can start eating."

"We'll be there in a minute," R.B. said. "I'm sure you won't run out of food. You brought enough to feed a small army."

"Well, we are feeding a bunch of strapping young men and I'm sure they all have healthy appetites." Brenda slipped out into the hall and pulled the door almost closed. "Bernie, Raymond is here. He was asking about you. You should go in and make a point of talking to him."

Bernie groaned. "Mama, Raymond Long did not come here tonight to see me or talk to me. He's here for the same reason all those other men are here—because of Robyn."

"Nonsense. I've told Robyn quite specifically that Raymond is yours and she's to keep her hands off him."

"Mother, you didn't!" Bernie wished a hole would open up in the floor and swallow her.

"Brenda, for goodness' sake." R.B. glanced sympathetically at Bernie.

"I have two unmarried daughters and no grandchildren," Brenda said. "Robyn has too many men in her life and Bernie has none. I have to do something, don't I?"

"You can stop playing matchmaker," Bernie told her mother. "Stop interfering in our lives. Robyn likes being single and playing the field. She loves being the belle of the ball and keeping half a dozen guys dangling on a string. And I like my life just the way it is, too, so butt out!"

Bernie turned around and headed down the hall.

"Bernadette Granger, you come back here," her mother called after her.

Bernie paused when she reached the stairs, glanced over

her shoulder and said, "Tell Robyn I'll stop by this weekend and see her new place."

As she headed down the stairs, she heard her mother say, "R.B., go after her. Talk to her."

When Bernie reached the bottom of the stairs, she heard her father's footsteps behind her. She opened the door, walked outside and waited for him on the sidewalk. When he caught up with her, he grinned sheepishly.

"I guess I'm as guilty as your mama, aren't I? I was trying to hook you up with Jim Norton."

"It's okay, Dad. And you can tell Mama later that I'm sorry I lost my temper with her."

"It's this Stephanie Preston murder case, isn't it? It's got you all tied in knots."

"It's bad," Bernie said. "It's not just having no real leads in the Preston case that has me so concerned, it's the fact that I'm worried sick the murderer will kill again."

R.B. glanced up and down the sidewalk, then said, "Let's go into the bookstore and sit in the coffee shop and get ourselves something to drink."

Bernie glanced upward toward the second story of the building. "You'll be missed."

"Your mother told me to come talk to you and that's what I'm doing, aren't I?"

"She meant talk sense to me about Raymond Long, not discuss business with me."

"I won't tell her if you won't." R.B. put his arm around Bernie and led her to the front entrance of the bookstore.

Once they were seated at a table in the back, they ordered two decaf coffees and a couple of cheese Danishes. The coffee shop was empty except for the cashier cum waiter, so they had plenty of privacy.

"Want to tell me what's going on?" R.B. asked. "Why are you concerned there will be another murder?"

"Because Jim thinks we may have a serial rapist/murderer on our hands."

"And he thinks this because . . ."

"Because we found out that there was another woman, Jacque Reeves, over in DeKalb County who was raped and murdered about three months ago."

"And?"

"And her physical description was similar to Stephanie Preston's. Long dark hair, slender, young, pretty. She came up missing and sixteen days later, her body was found out on a lonely country road. Her throat had been slit and her body posed, with one hand covering her . . . down there . . . and her other arm draped over her breasts."

"What about sketches, photos, gifts, notes?"

Bernie shook her head. "If there were any, they weren't found."

"So maybe it's just a coincidence that there are some similarities. Maybe it was two different guys who killed Stephanie and the Reeves woman."

"And what if it's the same guy? He could kill again and soon. How am I going to stop him if I have no idea who he is?"

"What does Jim think? And what about Charlie Patterson's opinion?"

"Charlie is going to look into the case over in DeKalb, check all the records, interview Jacque Reeves's parents and siblings and ex-husband," Bernie said. "And Jim thinks we need to start treating our case as a potential serial killer case."

"And you don't?"

"I do not want to jump the gun and create panic in town. And you know word of this would leak out no matter what precautions I took. People are upset and worried enough as it is, but what if Jim's right? My God, Dad—"

R.B. reached out across the table, grabbed Bernie's hands

and held them in his. "Now, you listen to me, Bernie Granger, you're the sheriff and you have all the right stuff in you to handle this job. Follow your Granger instincts. They won't let you down."

"Dad, I—" Her cell phone rang. Her father released her hands. She yanked her phone from the belt clip and answered it. "Sheriff Granger."

"Sheriff, this is Roy Lee Nichols. You remember me, don't you?"

"You're the police chief in Verona."

"Yeah, that's right. And I've got some information I think you might find interesting."

"Do you? And just what would that be?"

"Well, it's not that I know all that much about the Stephanie Preston case, since y'all have kept most of the info confidential, but word gets around within the law enforcement community and I've heard things."

"Chief, I don't mean to be rude, but could you get to the point?"

He chuckled. "Sorry, I tend to go on and on. My wife's always fussing at me about it." He cleared his throat. "We got us a stalking case over here in Verona. Seems somebody's been sending notes and gifts and some ugly drawings to one of our nice young ladies."

"Gifts and notes and—what kind of ugly drawings?"

"Sexual drawings," the chief said. "Pretty rough stuff."

A chill raced up Bernie's spine. "The gifts—what kind of gifts?"

"She brought in an ankle bracelet, but said she threw away the other things."

"Did she say what they were?"

"Yeah, just a minute. I wrote it all down."

R.B. looked inquisitively at Bernie. "I think we may have gotten our first real break on the Preston murder case," she told her father.

"Sheriff?" Roy Lee Nichols said. "Those other gifts were a pearl necklace, a bottle of perfume, a tube of lipstick, and a bottle of fingernail polish."

"Do you have the young lady there with you now?" Bernie asked.

"No, ma'am. She and her sister came in and told us what was going on and she's coming back in tomorrow to file a formal complaint against a guy she works with over at the community college."

"What's the woman's name and who is the man she works with who she believes sent her those items?"

"Her name is Thomasina Hardy. She's a teacher over at the college. And the guy's name is Dr. Brandon Kelley. He's not a real doctor, just a fellow with one of those PhDs."

Chapter 11

God knows she had tried her best to forget about Brandon Kelley, the notes, the gifts, and the sketches. But on the way to her Thursday night class, Thomasina had been able to think of little else. It didn't help that it was getting dark early this evening, because of the gray storm clouds, or that more than half the trip from downtown Verona to the college was on lonely stretches of country roads. Music on the radio helped a little. It kept her from feeling totally alone and isolated. But nothing could erase from her mind the images of the sketches he had sent her today, especially not the one of her throat slit, with blood dripping from the wound onto her naked breasts. What kind of sick mind could produce such heinous artwork?

If Brandon Kelley was her so-called secret admirer, then the man needed to be in a mental institution, not teaching art at the community college.

But what if it isn't Brandon? What if I've spent a week indulging in a fantasy that wasn't even remotely possible? What if the police can't find this guy? What if he continues stalking me?

With a country-rock tune blasting away on the radio, the words and music nothing more than background noise, Thomasina gasped when she saw the heat lightning flash through the gray evening sky off in the distance. A shudder rippled up her spine. She was as nervous as a cat. Thank goodness she had listened to Amanda and gone to the local police. If she hadn't allowed the foolishly romantic side of her nature to build castles in the air when she'd received the first note, she wouldn't be in this position now. But there was no point looking back, regretting what she had or had not done. She had already canceled her first class in the morning so that she could go back to the Verona police station and file a formal complaint. Chief Nichols had advised her to keep someone with her whenever possible until the authorities had a chance to investigate. If Brandon was her stalker, then perhaps just receiving a visit from a policeman would end his pursuit of her.

And if it's not Brandon?

A loud boom of thunder rocked the car. Thomasina cried out and grasped the steering wheel with white-knuckled tension. Her nerves were frayed, the least little thing unsettling her.

What was she so nervous about anyway? She was inside her car, with the doors locked, driving a familiar route on a safe road. She had a cell phone in her purse, as well as a can of pepper spray.

She glanced at the lighted digital clock on the control panel. Twelve minutes till seven. She was running late, but being less than fifteen minutes from the college, she should make it there in plenty of time to give her students their test.

Suddenly, without warning, her car pulled to the right. Simultaneously she heard the rumbling and felt the bumpiness that warned her of a tire going flat. No! This couldn't be happening. Of all times, why this evening?

Heaven help me!

Knowing she had no other choice but to stop, she slowed down and searched the area for a place where she could safely pull off the road. Naturally, she'd had a flat tire in the middle of nowhere, not a house in sight. The houses out here in the country were spaced far apart, often separated by ten to twenty acres and even the new subdivisions had been constructed off the main road. All she could see to the right and left, ahead of her and behind her, were patches of woods and acres of cleared farmland.

There's a spot, she told herself when she saw a patch of level ground that had probably once been an old dirt road, but was now partially covered by grass and weeds. Acting quickly, she veered to the right, taking her car off the road and pulling to a standstill. Leaving the motor running and the lights on, she put the gear into park. As she lifted her hands from the steering wheel, she took a deep breath. *Stay calm. You're not in any danger. You can call for help.*

She picked up her handbag from the passenger seat, opened it and retrieved her cell phone; then she hit the instant dial for her home phone. When her mother answered on the third ring, Thomasina released a relieved breath and reached out to turn down the volume on the radio. Just now she remembered that her mother had gone to Huntsville and shouldn't be at home.

"Mom? Oh, thank God. Why aren't you still in Huntsville?"

"Rose got to feeling poorly, so we came home early. She thinks she's coming down with that summer cold thing that's going around."

"I'm sorry about Rose, but I'm so glad you're home."

"Thomasina, are you all right? You sound odd."

"I'm okay. But I've had a flat tire and I need Tommy to come fix it for me."

"Oh dear. Your brother's not home. I think he went out with some of his buddies after work. And you know how that is. He might not be home for another hour or two. But I'll call over to Amanda's and get Mike to come find you. Exactly where are you?"

"I'm about fifteen minutes from the college," she told her mother. "About a mile past Sunflower Creek."

"I'll get Mike out there to you just as soon as possible, honey. You keep your doors locked, you hear me?"

"Yes, ma'am, I will."

"Do you have that pepper spray with you?"

"Yes, I do."

"Don't you dare get out of the car for any reason until Mike gets there."

"I won't." Thank goodness her mother didn't know anything about the notes and gifts and sketches from her secret admirer. If she knew, she'd be out of her mind with worry.

"I'll call you back when Mike heads out, if you want me to."

"Just call if for any reason he can't come right away."

"Okay. Do you want to keep talking to me for a while?" her mother asked. "You must be nervous, out there all alone. But don't you think about anything bad happening. After all, Adams County is one of the safest places on earth, despite that poor Preston girl getting murdered."

Oh, great. Leave it to her mother to remind her of the recent murder of a young woman about her age and general physical description. It wasn't like she wasn't already scared. But then her mother didn't know anything about what had been happening to her recently, about the idiotic fantasy she had built around a man who could well not even be the one who'd been seducing her with notes and gifts and—

"Thomasina, are you still there?"

"Yes, Mom. I'm going to hang up now. I have to contact the college so someone can let my class know that I'll be running late. Just call me if Mike can't leave right away."

Not even waiting for her mother's response, Thomasina closed her cell phone, effectively ending the conversation. She immediately called the college and informed them of her situation; then she slipped the phone back into her purse. She sat there, alone in the shadowy stillness of the backcountry road, distant thunder rumbling and streaks of lightning zigzagging through the sky. She hoped that Mike got here soon. It wasn't that she didn't know the basics of changing a flat tire, but the simple fact was that neither she nor a lot of other women had the physical strength to remove the wheel's lug nuts. And if you couldn't do that, you couldn't change the tire.

Glancing at her gasoline gauge, she smiled when she saw that she had more than half a tank. She'd just keep the motor running, the lights on and the radio playing. She turned up the volume and patted her fingertips against the steering wheel to the beat of the rocking country tune. Then she sang along, the words familiar, and soon the tension eased from her muscles and she relaxed. Leaning her head back and closing her eyes, she concentrated on the music.

Several minutes later, as she sang along with a classic tearjerker, she saw a set of bright headlights bearing down on her from the opposite direction. Well, it couldn't be Mike—for two reasons. First of all, this car was coming from the wrong direction. And second, it hadn't been five minutes since she had phoned her mother.

Don't panic. Stay calm.

The vehicle came up alongside her and slowed to a stop. Her heartbeat accelerated. But when the driver looked toward her, smiled warmly and waved, she gasped with relief when she recognized him.

The car pulled off the road directly in front of her. The driver parked, opened the door and got out. When he came over to her window and tapped on it, she looked up at him and smiled, then rolled down the window.

"Hey there," she said. "You don't know how glad I am it's you."

"I see you've got a flat tire." He glanced around the area. "Heck of a place for it."

"My brother-in-law is on his way here," Thomasina said. "Would you mind waiting with me until he gets here?"

"If you want, I can change the tire for you."

"Oh, that would be great. How can I ever thank you? I was already running late for my night class before the tire blew."

"Hey, I've got a better idea. Just leave your car here and let me drive you over to the college," he suggested. "I'm sure Mike and I can figure out a way to bring your car over to the college later."

"That's a great idea. You're a lifesaver." Thomasina turned off the lights, the radio, and the car's engine, then grabbed her purse before opening the door and getting out. After she locked the car, she handed her rescuer the keys. "You and Mike will need these."

He placed his hand in the small of her back and escorted her to his vehicle. Before she got in, he lifted the mini-cooler and small grocery sack from the passenger's side floorboard and carried them with him around to the other side. As soon as she was seated, he tossed the sack in the back before opening the cooler.

"Coke or Dr. Pepper?" he asked. "I've got both."

"Oh, thanks. A Coke's fine."

"It's pretty warm in here," he said. "It'll take a couple of minutes for the air to cool things off." He inserted his key into the ignition and started the engine.

"I'm just so glad you came along when you did. I was already as nervous as I could be before I called Mom, and then she reminded me about that Preston girl who was murdered recently. I started imagining all kinds of things."

He removed a canned Coke from the cooler, popped the

tab and handed the can to her. "I hope you know you're safe with me."

"Of course I know that." Feeling completely secure, Thomasina accepted the cola, lifted it to her lips and took several sips.

"Just sit back and relax. I'll have you at the college in no time flat." He winked at her.

She smiled at him, grateful that there were some truly good men left in the world.

He set the cooler between them, shifted the gears into DRIVE, and pulled out onto the road.

Bernie had picked up Jim and Kevin at his rental duplex, then dropped Kevin by her parents' house where her folks had been waiting. She wasn't sure how her father had persuaded her mother to leave Robyn's apartment and go home with him. Perhaps it had been the prospect of playing grandmother that convinced her.

Bernie and Jim had driven over to Verona together to talk to Roy Lee Nichols. The more information the local police chief had shared with them about his conversation with Thomasina Hardy and her sister, the tighter the knots in Bernie's stomach got. She and Jim had exchanged several oh-God! glances, each of them fearing the worst—that whoever had killed Stephanie Preston and Jacque Reeves was the same person who was now stalking a new victim. If that was the case, then it might be possible to catch this guy, to stop him before he killed again.

"Did Ms. Hardy and her sister go home when they left here?" Jim had asked.

"I don't think so. I believe she went on in to work. She teaches over at the junior college and said she couldn't miss tonight's class. That's why she's coming in again tomorrow," Chief Nichols said. "I cautioned Ms. Hardy to make sure she had somebody with her all the time until we'd had a chance to talk to this Dr. Kelley and see if he's the guy stalking her or not."

"Did Ms. Hardy leave a number where she can be reached?" Bernie asked.

"Yep. A home number, work number, and cell number. I wrote all three down right here." He tapped the notepad lying atop his desk. "Want me to jot them down for you?"

Bernie nodded, then waited while he wrote the numbers on a piece of paper and handed it to her. "I want to speak to Ms. Hardy tonight," Bernie said. "Why don't each of us take a number right now and one of us should be able to find out exactly where she is."

"I'll call her home number." Chief Nichols picked up the phone on his desk.

Bernie memorized the cell number, then handed the piece of paper to Jim. "I'll call her cell. You try the college."

Jim took the paper, nodded and walked to the other side of the chief's office. Bernie stepped outside into the station's central hub and dialed the cell number. It rang repeatedly, then went to voice mail.

"Thomasina, this is Sheriff Bernie Granger. Please give me a call as soon a possible." Bernie stated her cell number, then repeated it.

When she returned to his office, Chief Nichols's gaze met hers. "Any luck?" he asked.

She shook her head. "No, I got her voice mail."

"I got an answering machine," the chief said. "I left a message."

They both glanced at Jim, who was talking quietly into his phone, but Bernie couldn't make out exactly what he was saying. As he clipped his phone to his belt, he looked directly at her. She didn't like the concerned expression on his face.

"I spoke to a Ms. Everett at the college. She said that Ms. Hardy phoned about half an hour ago to tell them she'd had a flat tire and would be running late for her Thursday evening class. They're expecting her at any time."

"Was she alone?" Chief Nichols asked.

"I have no idea," Jim said. "Ms. Everett didn't know any details."

"Let's go." Bernie headed for the door, then paused and spoke to the chief. "To get to the college from here, she'd probably have taken County Road One-fifty-seven, right?"

"Yeah, it's the way I'd go. It takes you across Sunflower Creek and then you turn left onto Forty-four. You can get from here to the college in less than thirty minutes if you take that route."

Jim followed her outside and straight to her Jeep. Once inside and securely belted, they paused momentarily and looked at each other, a silent understanding passing between them, before Bernie revved the engine.

"Call Ron and have him track down Brandon Kelley," Bernie said.

Jim nodded, then made the call while Bernie zipped through downtown Verona, which consisted of a couple of blocks that crisscrossed each other. Since they rolled up the streets in Verona around seven, there wasn't any traffic. When she stopped at the railroad tracks that intersected with the main road, she looked both ways before preceding. In her peripheral vision she saw Jim punching in a number on his cell phone, then heard him call Ron's name before filling the deputy in on what was going on.

"We're heading toward the college now. Give us a call as soon as you track down Dr. Kelley. If you find him." Jim clipped the phone to his belt.

"I don't like this." After crossing the railroad tracks, Bernie took a right onto County Road 157. "We're pretty sure that Stephanie Preston had car trouble the night she was abducted and now Thomasina Hardy has a flat tire. If she's alone . . ."

Jim grunted.

"If we have a serial killer on our hands—"

"If?" Jim growled the word. "You keep saying if."

"I'm saying if because we're not sure of anything. Yes, there are similarities between the gifts Stephanie received and the things Thomasina said this guy sent her, but maybe it's just some terrible coincidence."

"You don't believe that any more than I do."

Thoughts of what that psychopath had done to Stephanie Preston raced through Bernie's mind. What if he already had Thomasina Hardy? What if they were too late to save her? Bernie's stomach churned and salty bile burned her esophagus. For half a minute, she thought she might actually be sick.

"Are you okay?" Jim asked.

"Yeah, I'm okay. Why did you ask?"

"You look kind of funny, like you might throw up."

"I said I'm okay." She practically bit his head off. "Sorry. I'm taking my frustration out on you. It's just the thought that we are probably dealing with a serial killer scares the crap out of me. And just between the two of us, I'm not sure I'm equipped to handle a situation like this."

"Take a couple of deep breaths," he told her. "Then listen to what I'm going to tell you."

As she sped along County Road 157, Bernie hazarded a quick glance at Jim. He gave her a stern look. She took the deep breaths.

"No law enforcement officer is ever ready for something like this," Jim said. "Even if he—or she—has experience with this type of killer. There's no shame in admitting that you're worried, that you're concerned, even that you're scared."

Jim's voice soothed her. *Odd,* she thought. A minute ago, she'd felt as if she were going to jump out of her own skin. Now, her heartbeat had slowed almost to normal and the queasiness she'd experienced subsided. All because of Jim's calm, even voice and his no-nonsense words.

"You don't know how difficult it is for me. Not only am I the first female sheriff in Adams County, I'm also the youngest. And—ta-da, drum roll, please—I'm R.B. Granger's daughter. There's no way I can live up to my dad's reputation."

That's it, Bernie, admit all your insecurities to your chief deputy. That's the way to earn his respect.

"When you ran for sheriff, how much of that decision was because it's what you wanted and how much was because it was what your dad wanted?"

Jim had hit the nail on the head. He had voiced the question she had never dared ask herself. Did everyone see through her so easily or did most people not suspect the truth?

"Truthfully, I don't know."

"What about now? You've been the sheriff for several years. Do you like your job? Are you glad you're the sheriff?"

"Yes, I like my job. At least most of the time. And yes, I'm glad I'm the sheriff. Just not tonight. Not right now." She kept the speed at fifty-five, even when the speed limit lowered to forty-five as they passed over Sunflower Creek. "I'm afraid my insecurities are showing. I certainly never thought I'd have to deal with a serial killer. Not here in Adams County."

When Jim didn't respond, she instinctively cut her eyes to catch a quick glimpse of his face. He was looking straight ahead, not at her. All of a sudden, she felt vulnerable and even stupid. She had opened up to her chief deputy in a way that surprised her. Why was it that she'd gotten diarrhea of the mouth tonight and with, of all people, Jim Norton?

The silence between them dragged on for several minutes, but those three or four minutes seemed more like hours to Bernie.

"TMI?" she asked.

"Huh?"

"Too much information?"

"No, that's not it. I just got to thinking that maybe I was being too nosey, that your relationship with your father is really none of my business."

"Oh."

Sharing sensitive personal information would change their relationship from strictly professional to more intimate. Bernie cringed. Wrong word. Intimacy implied a strong emotional attachment, romance, even sex. The best she could expect to share with Jim was friendship.

"Hey, look up ahead." Jim motioned to the right-hand side of the road. "There's a parked car over there. Maybe it's Thomasina Hardy's car."

Bernie pulled off the road directly behind the Grand Am. She and Jim cautiously exited her Jeep and took a look at the abandoned car.

"Flat tire." Jim pointed to the tire.

"You look things over while I go back and call this in to make sure it's Thomasina's car."

Jim nodded in agreement.

By the time she'd called in and had verified the tag number, Jim had finished his inspection and they met at the hood of her Jeep.

"It's Thomasina Hardy's car," Bernie said.

"No sign of foul play. The car's locked."

"I don't like the feeling this gives me."

"Don't jump to conclusions."

"I've got a couple of deputies coming out to secure the scene," Bernie said. "In the meantime, we'll contact the college to see if Thomasina ever showed up."

Once back in the Jeep, waiting for the deputies to arrive, Bernie placed a second call to the school.

"No, Sheriff Granger, Ms. Hardy isn't here, but her mother and brother-in-law are. They're terribly worried," Ms. Everett said. "They found her car on County Road One-fifty-seven, but Thomasina was nowhere to be seen."

"May I speak to the brother-in-law?"

"Sure, he's right here."

"Yeah, this is Mike Anderson. Have you found Thomasina?"

"No, sorry," Bernie said. "We're here where she left her car parked on One-fifty-seven. I've called in deputies to secure the scene."

"You think something bad has happened to her, don't you?"

"I don't know." *Don't get emotionally involved. Act in a professional manner.* "Once the scene is secure, my chief deputy and I would like to talk to Thomasina's family, especially her sister."

"Which sister? She has two."

"The one who went with her to speak to Chief Nichols this evening."

"That would be my wife," Mike said. "Amanda." He lowered his voice to little more than a whisper. "Look, Inez, Thomasina's mom, doesn't know anything about the stalker. Thomasina had just told Amanda this afternoon, and Amanda told me this evening. Is there any way we can keep this from Inez? She's worried enough as it is."

"Mr. Anderson, I'd like for you and Mrs. Hardy to go home to your house, tell your wife what's happened and wait for us. I'm afraid we can't keep the facts a secret from your mother-in-law. Thomasina was being stalked and now she's missing. One and one usually adds up to two."

"I understand. We . . ." He gulped. "We'll go home and wait for you. And please, Sheriff, find Thomasina."

"We will do our best."

When she hung up, she turned to Jim. "If we formed a search party, we'd have no idea where to look. It seems apparent that somebody came along and gave Thomasina a ride. She could be in Tennessee by now or right under our noses close by."

"Professor Kelley had better have a damn good alibi," Jim said.

"You don't like Dr. Kelley any more than I do, do you?"

"Nope, I detest his type. But just because he's a cocky, womanizing jerk doesn't mean he's a kidnapper or rapist or killer."

A foreboding chill rippled along her nerve endings. Bernie shivered. "God, I hope Thomasina shows up safe and sound, with some logical explanation of what happened to her."

"Yeah, that would be nice, but we both know the odds are against a happy ending."

"You think whoever killed Stephanie and Jacque has abducted Thomasina, don't you?"

He nodded. "First thing in the morning, I'll fill out a VICAP form with the info about Stephanie's and Jacque's murders. We need to find out if there are more cases similar to Stephanie's and Jacque's. If there are, they could be related."

The department had a special computer program that generated a request form with all pertinent information about a crime that linked to the FBI's Violent Crime Apprehension Program. During her father's last term in office, he'd been determined to bring the Adams County Sheriff's Department into the twenty-first century.

"But I thought we agreed that this guy is local, that Stephanie knew him and trusted him. And that's probably what happened tonight with Thomasina. She got in a car with a man she knew and trusted. If that's the case, how is using the FBI's VICAP going to help us figure out anything about our killer?"

"Yeah, we did agree that both Stephanie and Thomasina knew the guy who abducted them, but using the VICAP might help us figure out if this guy has lived in the area all his life and whether Jacque was his first victim. Or if he's killed before, somewhere else, and moved here in the past year or so."

"The county is going to be in an uproar," Bernie said. "Unless Thomasina miraculously reappears, I'll have no choice but to hold a press conference tomorrow. And I'm torn between cautioning women to contact us if they receive notes and presents and sketches from a secret admirer and knowing I can't reveal too much info without jeopardizing our cases."

Jim reached over, clamped his hand down on Bernie's shoulder and looked right at her. "If this guy stays true to his MO and repeats the sequence of events he did with Jacque and Stephanie, we'll have two weeks tops to find Thomasina before he kills her."

Bernie closed her eyes and said a quick, silent prayer, pleading with the Almighty to help them. And to help Thomasina Hardy, wherever she was tonight.

Thomasina came to in a semidark room, her head pounding, her mind fuzzy.

What had happened to her? Why was she here?

Where was "here"?

She lifted her head from the pillow and at that moment realized she was lying on a bed of some kind. She tried to sit up and couldn't.

Why couldn't she?

She tried to lift her arms, but found that her wrists were bound together over her head. She opened her mouth to scream, but couldn't. It was then that she knew someone had bound and gagged her, that she was totally helpless and . . .

she turned her head to one side and looked around the small, shadowy room, lit only by the glow of what she thought was a nightlight.

She was alone. All alone.

Think, Thomasina, think!

She had been on her way to teach her Thursday evening class at the college when she'd had a flat tire. She had called her mother, who'd said she'd send Mike to fix the tire. But before Mike showed up—

Oh, God! No!

He had come along and offered to take her to the college and then go back and help Mike fix the flat. She'd had no reason to distrust him and every reason to believe she was safe with him.

He'd given her a Coke and she'd drank nearly all of it while they drove along County Road 157. All the while, she'd thought he was taking her to Adams County Junior College. They'd talked and laughed and she'd felt so completely secure and at ease with him.

But what had happened next?

She vaguely remembered feeling sleepy.

Had he put something in the cola? But how could he have? She'd seen him pop the tab on the can, hadn't she?

She hadn't really been paying close attention. He could have easily slipped something into the drink. He'd probably drugged her. But why?

Was he the man who'd been sending her the notes, the gifts, the sketches? Was he her secret admirer?

A surge of sheer, unadulterated fear consumed Thomasina as she lay there on the bed, in the semidarkness of a damp, silent room. Alone.

Where was he? When would he come back? What was he going to do to her?

Chapter 12

Dead on her feet, frustrated and worried sick, Bernie pulled her Jeep into her driveway at three-thirty on Friday morning. Jim sat quietly at her side, so quietly that she wondered if he'd fallen asleep on their ride back from Verona. Jim had agreed that it was best to let Kevin stay with her parents until he could pick him up this evening; he'd also readily accepted Bernie's offer to fix breakfast for them at her house. Charlie Patterson would drive over from Huntsville and be in Jim's office by seven, which gave Jim and her a little over three hours to rest for a while, grab a bite to eat and freshen up.

Bernie reached out, intending to gently shake Jim, but before her hand made contact with his shoulder, he grunted and turned to face her.

Her hand paused midair. "I thought you were asleep."

"Just had my eyes closed."

"It's been a long night."

He nodded.

Bernie opened the driver's door and got out of the Jeep. She waited on the sidewalk for Jim to join her. Even this early in the morning, there wasn't a hint of a breeze and the temperature probably hadn't dropped below the high eighties. Alabama's sweltering July humidity made it feel hotter than it actually was, something the weather forecasters referred to as heat indexes. When it was ninety, it often felt like a hundred.

Once inside her house, the cool air-conditioned atmosphere surrounding them the minute they entered, Bernie sighed deeply, then removed her belt and hung it on the hall tree just inside the entrance. Jim hung his belt beside hers and followed her into the living room.

"Sofa or recliner?" she asked.

"Either."

"You take the recliner," she told him. "My feet hit the sofa arm when I lie down, so there's no way you can get comfortable on it."

He sat down in the recliner, released the footrest latch on the side of the chair and propped up his big feet. "Damn, this feels good."

Bernie kicked off her brown loafers, stacked one decorative throw pillow on top of another and laid her weary bones down on the sofa, stretching out all the way and resting her heels on the sofa arm.

"I can't begin to imagine what Thomasina Hardy's family is going through right now." Bernie glanced over at Jim, who had his eyes closed. His arms rested on either side of the chair's cushioned back, his hands cupping his head.

"Mmm . . . They're wondering if they'll ever see her alive again."

"What do you think?"

"I think it's too soon to make any predictions." Jim yawned.

"Want me to shut up so you can take a nap?"

He opened his eyes, lifted his head and looked at her. "I doubt either of us can sleep. We're too tired. Plus, we know we have to be at the office in a little over three hours."

"I wish we had some idea where Thomasina is, where he took her. If we just had a clue of some kind, something—anything—that could help us."

"If Ron can't track down Professor Kelley, we might have ourselves a real suspect." Jim yawned again. "The guy could be with Thomasina right now, hiding her away."

"If only it could be as simple as finding him and making him talk. But we both know that just because Brandon Kelley wasn't at home when Ron checked on him and apparently hasn't come home yet, it doesn't mean he abducted Thomasina or that he's the man who's been stalking her."

"True. But according to her family, there hasn't been any special guy in her life since she broke up with Ron. They have no idea who her secret admirer might be if it's not Kelley."

"I'm concerned about Ron," Bernie said. "I know her sister said that he's the one who broke off things with Thomasina, but he must still have some feelings for her. I mean, wouldn't you think that even if he doesn't love her now—"

"I'm sure that knowing a former girlfriend's life might be in jeopardy makes this case a bit more personal for him. But just because they dated and, as her sister implied, had a sexual relationship, doesn't mean they were in love."

"No, of course not."

"Too bad Thomasina disposed of everything except that final batch of sketches and the ankle bracelet." Groaning contentedly, Jim burrowed his head into the cushioned softness of the recliner. "Of course, I doubt the guy was stupid enough to leave fingerprints. And like with the stuff we found at Stephanie's, the ankle bracelet, the artist paper, and the envelopes are all probably items that could be purchased just about anywhere by anybody."

"Why on earth didn't she go to the police as soon as she started receiving those notes and presents?" Bernie flipped over onto her side and curled her legs at the knees. "What would make her think that any of it was romantic, that the notes and gifts and sketches were from some guy playing secret lover?"

"You'd have to ask her," Jim said. "I'm the last man on earth you should ask about why women think the way they do. I never could figure out my ex-wife's thought processes."

"You shouldn't assume that all women think alike." Bernie felt an odd twinge of something in her gut. Jealousy? *Get a grip, girl.* She had absolutely no right to feel anything even remotely related to jealousy where Jim Norton was concerned, certainly not because he was talking to her about his ex-wife.

"Yeah, you're right. Mary Lee was—is one of a kind."

She wanted to ask if he meant one of a kind in a good way or a bad way, but it was really none of her business. If he wanted to elaborate, he would. If not . . .

"You've never been married, have you, Bernie?" Jim asked.

"What makes you think that?"

"Well, your last name is still Granger and—"

"I married my high school sweetheart before we left for college and I divorced him seven years later." She had been nuts about Ryan, had twisted herself like a pretzel, every which way, to please him. And in the end he'd thanked her for being a good wife by not contesting the divorce. "I haven't seen Ryan in years. I heard from one of his cousins over in Pine Bluff that he remarried about five years ago, has a couple of kids and is living in Nashville." Remembering her two miscarriages still hurt, still made her feel inadequate. "I took my maiden name back after the divorce."

"Mary Lee and I got married right after I graduated from UT. Seems like a lifetime ago. Hell, even the divorce seems like a lifetime ago. Kevin was only six when his mother and I split and now he's fixing to turn thirteen."

"At least you have a kid." Bernie hadn't meant to say that out loud. It had just slipped out, gone straight from her thoughts to her tongue.

"Did you want kids?"

She knew he was looking at her, but she couldn't face him, not when she had tears in her eyes. Had she wanted children? God, yes, she'd wanted them. At least three, maybe four. But apparently it just hadn't been in the cards for her to be a mother.

Glancing down at the floor, she swallowed, then said, "Yes, I wanted kids. It just didn't happen."

"Guess we'd better get a little rest," Jim told her, as if sensing her discomfort in answering his question. "I'll help you with breakfast before we head over to the office. Seven o'clock will roll around before we know it."

She took his comments as a cue that he wanted peace and quiet, a little downtime to rest and regroup before they returned to work and dealt with the horrible fact that another Adams County woman had been abducted.

Bernie closed her eyes, took a deep breath and tried to relax. But her brain wouldn't shut off, wouldn't allow her any peace. Various thoughts flickered through her mind, everything from who might have abducted Thomasina Hardy to what her life could have been like if Ryan had never cheated on her and if one of her babies had lived.

Stop thinking, damn it.

She hummed silently, a repetitive tune that was soon overpowered by her thoughts. Then she tried counting. That, too, didn't work. It never did, but she kept trying it anyway. Finally, she gave up the effort to switch off her mind and allowed the thoughts to take over, which they always did anyway.

Wonder about what Jim's marriage had been like. Wonder whether he still cared about his ex-wife. Mary Lee was probably gorgeous, the way Robyn was. Guys like Jim always went for the obviously sexy types. Hey, who was she kidding—all men went for the sexy types. So why had a jock like Ryan married someone like her, someone who'd been an athlete in high school?

He married you because you worshipped the ground he walked on. He liked having his own little groveling slave. She had given in to Ryan's wishes in a way she'd never given in to anyone else, not even her dad. In her teens and early twenties, she'd had some major self-esteem issues, and it wasn't until after her divorce that she'd come into her own. Well, as much as it was possible for a people-pleaser to choose her own path in life.

Had Jim's ex-wife adored him, tried to please him, loved him beyond all reason? Had he broken Mary Lee's heart? Or had it been the other way around? Something instinctive within her sensed that Jim had been the one who'd gotten his heart broken and that maybe he still carried a torch for this ex-wife. Mary Lee, who'd remarried. Mary Lee, who was now facing a battle with breast cancer.

Stop thinking about Jim Norton. He's not interested in you.

Concentrate on something else, someone else. What can you do to find Thomasina Hardy before she becomes another murder victim? She was doing all that could be done, wasn't she? Her chief deputy was a top-notch detective who'd proven himself on the Memphis PD. And Charlie Patterson was an experienced ABI agent. It wasn't as if she was in this all alone, so why was it that she felt an overwhelming need to call her father and ask for his help?

Your lack of self-confidence is showing, Bernadette.

Her mind continued jumping from one thought to another, asking her questions she couldn't answer, posing problems she couldn't solve, demanding that she listen instead of sleep. But finally, exhaustion claimed her and she dozed off for a few minutes.

When she woke fifteen minutes later, her house was quiet and still. All she heard was the tick of the mantel clock and the hum of Jim's hard, steady breathing. She sat up, put her feet on the floor and stretched. A sudden chill hit her, making her wonder if Jim might be too cool sitting there in his short-sleeved shirt. She removed the cream knit afghan from the back of the sofa, got up and walked over to him. For a couple of seconds, she stood by the recliner and watched him as he slept. She liked the way he looked, the way he talked, the way he moved. He appealed to her on so many different levels, including the physical. He was a big, tall man with an athlete's body. And he was good looking in a rough, rugged sort of way.

Bernie unwrapped the afghan and laid it over Jim, spreading it out from his chest to his ankles. He grumbled and turned onto his side.

That's when several almost irresistible urges hit her—the urge to touch him, to caress his face, to lean down and kiss his slightly parted lips. She moved back toward the sofa, putting distance between them.

Damn it! Why is it that you bring out all my female instincts, Jimmy Norton? All those nurturing, loving, sexual instincts that I work so hard to control?

Charlie Patterson was waiting for them when they arrived at the jail promptly at seven A.M. And he wasn't alone. Ron Hensley had also come in early, and from the looks of him, he hadn't gotten any more rest than they had. Bloodshot eyes, a heavy five o'clock shadow and a wrinkled shirt said it all. The guy had probably been up most, if not all, of the night.

R.B. Granger sat behind Jim's desk, drinking coffee and talking to Ron and Charlie. Jim glanced at Bernie as they stood side by side, just a few feet over the threshold. When she saw her father, she stopped dead in her tracks. Jim noted her reaction change from what he thought was gladness in seeing her dad, knowing he was here to help, to a sense of disappointment, as if she understood that her father didn't trust her to handle this case without him.

"Good morning." Charlie saluted them with his cup.

"Are we late?" Bernie asked, her tone tense.

"We just got here," R.B. said. "I met up with Charlie outside a few minutes ago. Ron was already here and had put on a fresh pot of coffee."

Jim walked over to R.B. and asked, "How's Kevin this morning?"

"He was still asleep when I left," R.B. replied. "Brenda's planning on making him blueberry pancakes this morning."

"I really appreciate you and your wife looking after him for me."

"It's our pleasure. He's a great kid. Smart and friendly. Has really good manners, too."

Jim grinned like the proud papa he was, even though it was a bittersweet pride. Kevin was his son, flesh of his flesh and all, but Mary Lee had been the one who'd raised him.

"How long have you been here?" Bernie asked Ron.

"About fifteen minutes," he replied. "I came straight here from"—he glanced at R.B. and grimaced—"from where I found Brandon Kelley."

"You finally found him?" Bernie focused on her deputy.

Ron nodded.

"Where? Was Thomasina—"

Ron shook his head. "The guy has an alibi. He was with a young lady from yesterday evening until I tracked him down around four-thirty this morning."

"And this young lady will swear that he was with her all evening and night?" Jim asked.

"Yep." Ron looked down at his feet, as if deliberately avoiding eye contact with anyone in the room.

Jim noticed Bernie and R.B. exchange odd glances.

"Was he with Robyn?" R.B. asked.

"Yep." Ron walked over to the coffeemaker and refilled his half-full cup.

"Damn that girl." R.B. growled the words. "She's turning my hair white. And what she's doing to her mother's nerves . . ."

"Okay, so that rules out Brandon." Bernie gave her father a stern glare, then followed Ron to the coffeemaker, picked up a clean cup and filled it with hot coffee.

Jim wondered why, if he was actually interested in Robyn Granger, the knowledge that she'd spent the night with Brandon Kelley didn't bother him in the least. He'd had exactly one date with Robyn—dinner at the River's End restaurant—and if she'd offered him sex on that first date, he wouldn't have turned her down. But she hadn't offered, although he'd gotten the feeling from the way she'd been all over him that she'd have made the offer on their second date. And until just this minute, he'd believed there would be a second date.

Now he knew that he had no intention of asking Robyn out, and if she asked him out, he'd turn her down. And it had nothing to do with the fact that she'd spent the night with Dr. Kelley. But it did have everything to do with the fact that the more he learned about Robyn, the more she reminded him of Mary Lee. The truth had just hit him like a sledgehammer right between the eyes. If he got involved with Robyn, she would be a substitute for his ex-wife. And that wouldn't be fair to Robyn or to him.

With her coffee mug in hand, Bernie turned around and

faced the others. "We knew Dr. Kelley being our assailant was a long shot. So now we're back to no suspects and no clues." She looked at Charlie. "Jim's going to run a check using VICAP this morning. That's a start anyway. I don't suppose you have anything from your people yet, do you? Any evidence left in or around Thomasina's car?"

"It's too soon for results," Charlie replied. "But if this guy was never in her car . . ."

"I know, I know," Bernie said.

"And that stretch of One-fifty-seven is pretty isolated, not much traffic, so I doubt anybody saw anything," Ron added. "But we're going to ask around, just in case. We might get lucky and find someone who saw something."

"Are we convinced that this has all the same earmarks as the Stephanie Preston abduction?" R.B. asked. He looked directly at Jim. "Have we got ourselves a serial killer?"

"Possibly," Jim replied. "Probably."

R.B. cursed under his breath. "How long will he keep her before he kills her?"

"Stephanie Preston was murdered fourteen days after she disappeared," Jim said. "And Jacque Reeves over in Fort Payne was missing for sixteen days before she was killed."

"Approximately two weeks." R.B. grunted. "He rapes and tortures them for two weeks, then kills them." He looked right at Bernie. "We've got two weeks, gal, to find this guy and stop him before he kills again."

"Yes, sir, I know that." Bernie's cheeks flushed.

Jim had the craziest urge to step in between Bernie and her dad, to tell R.B. that Bernie was the sheriff, a very capable sheriff, and she didn't need his badgering. But he kept quiet, knowing full well that neither Bernie nor R.B. would appreciate his interference in what was obviously a father/daughter thing.

R.B. turned back to Charlie. "So what's our next step?"

Charlie glanced at Bernie. "Well, since this isn't officially an ABI case yet, the next step is up to the sheriff."

Jim wanted to slap Charlie on the back, shake his hand and thank him for figuratively reinstating Bernie to her elected position, for finding a way of tactfully putting R.B. in his place.

R.B. grunted. "Ball's in your court, gal."

Bernie gripped her coffee cup with both hands. "Unless someone comes forward to say they know something, that they saw something, there is no point in searching for Thomasina, is there? We'd have no idea where to look." Bernie sipped on her coffee, then placed the mug on Jim's desk. "If we had a profile of this guy, something to give us an idea of what kind of man we're looking for, of who might be a suspect—"

"I think I know somebody who could help us with that," Jim said, remembering the former FBI profiler Griffin Powell had hired on the Quinn Cortez case. He glanced at Charlie. "Unless you can get—"

"I could put in a request, but with the backlog at the FBI, I have no idea how long it might take." Charlie grimaced. "If you've got an 'in' with an independent profiler, then I say go with it."

Jim checked with Bernie. "Sheriff, do I have your authorization to make some phone calls and ask for this profiler's assistance?"

Bernie hesitated for a split second; then she and her father spoke at once, both saying yes. Jim glowered at R.B.

"Sorry, honey," R.B. told his daughter. "I forget sometimes that I'm no longer the sheriff."

Bernie forced a smile, then said, "Go ahead, Jim, make your phone calls." Her gaze traveled around the room, settling momentarily on each man. "Why don't we vacate Jim's office so he can make those calls?"

The other three men nodded, mumbled agreement and cleared out of Jim's office. Just before exiting, Bernie paused in the doorway. "I'm going to take Dad back to my office with me. I have a press conference to prepare for and he enjoys giving me pointers on how to handle the press.

"If I line up this profiler, I'll give you a call. No, scratch that. I'll come over to your office. As your chief deputy and the lead detective on this case, I should be there when you give the press conference."

"Of course."

Bernie closed the door behind herself. Jim stood there and watched her through the half glass as she walked up to her father, laced her arm through his and smiled at him with love and adoration in her eyes.

Shaking off an odd feeling, Jim sat down behind his desk, removed a small black notepad from his shirt pocket and looked up Griffin Powell's private number. After memorizing the Knoxville number, he glanced into the outer office and saw that it was empty. Ron Hensley must have walked out with the others. He couldn't help wondering about Bernie and her father. Didn't R.B. have any idea that by constantly 'helping' his daughter, he was undermining her confidence? Probably not. Although she was a grown woman and the duly elected sheriff of Adams County, R.B. undoubtedly still saw her as his little girl. And what man wouldn't want to help and protect his child?

Jim envied R.B. He wished his son loved and admired him half as much as Bernie did her father.

Jim cleared the stray cobwebs from his mind, lifted the telephone receiver and dialed Griff's number. His old college buddy was now a very wealthy man who owned a prestigious private security and investigation firm based in Knoxville, Tennessee. They had worked together on a high-profile case in Memphis not long ago, a case involving a serial killer.

Sanders, Griffin's personal assistant, answered on the fourth ring. "Powell residence."

"Sanders, this is Jim Norton. Is Griffin there?"

"Yes, sir, he's here."

"I need to talk to him. It's important."

"If you'll wait, I'll let him know you're on the line, Lieutenant Norton."

"Captain Norton," Jim corrected in an offhand manner, not really thinking about what he'd said.

"Congratulations, sir, on your promotion."

Jim chuckled. "Thanks." No need to explain to Sanders that the so-called promotion had meant a job change, a move from one state to another and a demotion in pay.

"I'll see if Mr. Powell can come to the phone," Sanders said.

While Jim waited, he eyed the coffeemaker. Just as he rose from his chair, intending to get himself a cup of coffee, Griffin came on the line.

"Jim?"

"Yeah, Griff. I . . . uh . . . need a favor."

"All right."

"I left the Memphis PD recently." He went on to explain about Mary Lee's remarriage, his subsequent move to Adams Landing and his new job as chief deputy. "We have a possible serial killer on our hands here in Adams County. Two women have been kidnapped and murdered and, as of last night, a third has come up missing. We have very few clues and our only suspect in this latest case has an iron-tight alibi."

"What can I do to help?"

"You can put me in touch with the profiler you used on the Quinn Cortez case."

"Derek Lawrence doesn't work cheap," Griffin said.

"Yeah, I figured as much. I'm not sure the Adams County Sheriff's Department can afford him, but we need him. Any chance you might intervene and see if he'll give us a discount?"

Griffin laughed. "Is that a subtle way of asking me if I'll pick up the tab?"

"I wouldn't dream of asking you to—"

"Derek owes me a favor. I'll call in his IOU. But if I do, that means you'll owe me one."

"Deal," Jim said."

"Derek will be in touch with you by noon today."

"Thanks, Griff."

The dial tone hummed in Jim's ear.

There had been a time when he and Griffin Powell were best friends and teammates. They'd both had big dreams of turning pro after they graduated from UT. A couple of bad knees had ended any hopes of that pro career for Jim. But nobody knew what had happened to destroy Griffin's plans. Shortly after graduation, he had disappeared off the face of the earth, then reappeared ten years later, a very rich man. A rich mystery man. Only Griffin could answer the questions of where he'd been and what had happened to him during those missing ten years. Griffin and possibly Sanders, the man who had returned with him from only God knew where.

Chapter 13

Jim took his lunch break at eleven-thirty, exactly five minutes after Allen Clark phoned with the news that Mary Lee had come through the surgery just fine. When Jim pulled up in front of the Granger house, he sat inside his old pickup for several minutes, pulling his thoughts together, figuring out exactly what he was going to say to his son.

Be honest, but optimistic.

As he emerged from his truck and walked up the sidewalk to the front door, his mind wandered back a dozen years to when Kevin had been a baby. And Mary Lee had been his wife. They'd been happy then, hadn't they? He and Mary Lee had still been in love. They'd been proud parents planning a future for their son. A future that they'd believed would include the two of them raising Kevin and giving him a brother or a sister at some point down the line.

Then everything had gone wrong. Little things at first. His obsession with his job. Mary Lee's boredom and restlessness. The arguments. The accusations. And then his partner had been murdered and for a while, Jim had nearly lost his mind. After that, nothing had ever been the same again. Not with his marriage. Not with his life.

Just as Jim reached out to ring the Grangers' doorbell, he heard loud laughter and splashing water, the sounds coming from the back of the house. He vaguely remembered R.B. telling him to make sure Kevin brought along some swim trunks because they had a backyard pool. Jim stepped down off the porch, rounded the side of the house and opened the black wrought-iron gate. He stopped a good fifteen feet away and watched Kevin and R.B. in the pool. They tossed a huge beach ball back and forth, the boy and the man laughing. Brenda Granger, in a pair of yellow capri pants and a short-sleeved white blouse, stood on the patio watching the two, a wide smile on her face. As if sensing Jim's presence, she turned and waved, then called to him.

"Hello there. You're just in time for lunch. We're having hot dogs, potato chips, and chocolate pie," Brenda said.

Kevin tossed the ball out onto the patio, then swam across the pool and pulled himself out and onto his feet. "Hey, Dad. Any word on Mom?"

Jim nodded. "Allen just phoned."

"How is your ex-wife?" Brenda asked in a hushed tone as she approached Jim. "We've been trying to keep Kevin occupied so he wouldn't worry."

"Thank you, Mrs. Granger. I can't tell you how much I appreciate everything y'all have done for Kevin and me."

"It's our pleasure. And please, remember to call me Brenda."

Kevin rushed up to Jim and looked him square in the eyes. "How is she? She's all right, isn't she?"

"Allen said she came through surgery just fine. She's still asleep. He'll call us tonight and then if she feels up to it, your mother will call you tomorrow." Jim glanced at Brenda. "I gave him your number. I hope that's all right."

"Yes, of course, it is." Brenda reached down and picked

up a large beach towel from a nearby chaise lounge and handed it to Kevin, then turned to R.B., who had just emerged from the pool. "Come inside and help me get lunch on the table."

"Let me dry off first."

"Well, hurry up. I'm sure Jim needs a few minutes alone with Kevin," Brenda said.

As soon as the Grangers went into the house, Jim put his hand on Kevin's back. "Let's go sit on the deck and I'll tell you what Allen told me."

They walked over to the deck that separated the patio area around the pool from the back of the house. As soon as they sat in a couple of cushioned, brown wicker chairs, Jim faced his son.

"They removed your mother's left breast. They're testing the lymph nodes they removed during surgery, and they should know in a few days whether the cancer has spread. Either way, she's looking at chemotherapy, which means she'll lose her hair and the treatments will make her tired, sick and very weak."

"Mom will hate losing her hair." Tears pooled in Kevin's eyes.

Jim wanted to pull the boy into his arms and hug him. He wished he could promise his son that everything would be all right, that there was no chance his mom would die. *Be optimistic,* he reminded himself, *but be honest.*

"Your mom's a tough lady. She's a fighter. She won't let this thing beat her."

Kevin glanced down at the deck floor. "She's not going to want me to see her sick."

"Probably not."

"It'll be a good while before I get to see her again, won't it?"

"I know it'll be rough on you not seeing her, but we've got to think about her right now. What she wants and needs."

Kevin lifted his head and blinked. Teardrops clung to his eyelashes. "Allen will take good care of her. He loves her."

Jim swallowed hard. He heard his son's unspoken words: *You didn't take care of her. You don't love her.* All the old guilt resurfaced. He could have stayed with Mary Lee. He could have forgiven her for sleeping with other men. If he'd swallowed his pride. But how did a man erase the image of his wife screwing another man in their bed? Jim had walked in on them in the middle of the act and he'd come very close to killing both of them. Even now, he could still feel a little of that old rage.

But Kevin didn't know what his mother had done, would never know if it was up to Jim to tell him. Besides, he was too young to understand then and now. All Kevin knew was that his dad had divorced his mom. And felt that his dad had divorced him, too.

"She's not going to die, is she?" Kevin almost choked on his tears.

Clenching his teeth, praying he would say and do the right thing, Jim reached over and laid his hand on Kevin's damp knee.

"I don't think so," Jim said.

Brenda Granger opened the back door and called to them, "Lunch is ready, you two."

"Come on, son." Jim stood. "Let's go eat."

When Kevin got up, Jim placed his arm around his son's shoulders. Kevin shrank away from Jim, but stayed in step at his side as they headed for the house.

Jim sat at his desk and studied the information he'd gotten when he ran their killer's MO through VICAP. There were numerous women who'd been raped, tortured and murdered, many of them killed by having their throats slit. But there were only four murder cases that were practically identical to what they knew about Stephanie Preston's and Jacque Reeves's abductions and murders. And there was a fifth murder case that had some similarities. All five women had been killed in the Southeastern part of the United States, all within the past five years. Two in Georgia—Julie Patton and Michelle McMahon; one in Tennessee—Courtney Pettus; one in North Carolina—Sara Hayes; and one in South Carolina—Shannon Elmore. Jim had no idea if these women had anything in common other than the fact they were all victims of brutal rapes and murders, their killer's MO practically identical to the killer now stalking women in northeastern Alabama. But did that mean all these women had been murdered by the same man?

Thanks to this FBI program, Jim had access to the names of the lead detectives on all of the murder cases. He intended to get in touch with each of them in order to obtain as much information as he could. The more he learned about these similar cases, the better able he'd be to judge whether their northeastern Alabama killer was or was not the same man.

Although Bernie had given him free rein as the lead detective in the Preston murder case and the Hardy missing person's case, she had asked him to make sure she was included in everything.

"I think I can learn a lot from you, Jim," she'd told him. "And I'm not too proud to admit that fact. You're probably better qualified to be sheriff than I am, but this is Adams County and my last name *is* Granger."

He admired her honesty, admired her for having the guts to speak so bluntly. But he thought maybe she was selling herself short because she kept comparing herself to her father.

As if thinking about her had brought her to him, Jim heard Bernie's voice in the outer office. She was talking to John Downs, asking him for an update on the Thomasina Hardy case.

"Have you and Ron questioned everybody you know of who traveled County Road One-fifty-seven between six and seven-thirty last night?"

"Yeah, there were only half a dozen people that we could find," John said. "And none of them remembers seeing Thomasina, except old man Hammonds remembers meeting a car fitting that description around six-forty, right before he crossed the Sunflower Creek bridge. He said that the best he could tell the woman driving was alone."

"Where's Ron now?" Bernie asked.

"He's over at Taylor's Wrecker Service, waiting around for those crime scene fellows Charlie Patterson sent over from Huntsville to finish up with Thomasina's car."

Jim shoved back his chair, stood and walked across the room. When he opened the door, Bernie and John turned around and looked at him.

"Afternoon," Bernie said.

Jim glanced at the wall clock above the outer door. Five-thirty-five. "It's nearly evening."

"I'm sorry I couldn't get over here sooner, but my day has been wild. After this morning's press conference, I had to meet with Jerry Dale; then Lisa has been fending calls all day from local citizens concerned about the fact we've had two abductions in such a short time span. And just when I thought I might escape and come over here, Robyn breezed in with the invitations to Mom and Dad's fortieth wedding anniversary party, which she was supposed to have sent out a week ago."

"Your folks have been married forty years?" Jim's own parents hadn't made it to their fortieth anniversary. His dad had died a month shy of their thirty-fourth.

"Is the party a surprise?" John asked.

"Yes, they've been married forty years," she replied to Jim. "And they're still very much in love. Imagine that." She glanced at John. "No, the party is not a surprise. You don't honestly think we could keep a secret like that from Brenda Granger, do you? My mother expects something special, and if she didn't know for sure that Robyn and I were planning an extravaganza for her and Dad, she'd suspect something and start searching for answers."

John laughed, but before he could lead Bernie off into some idle chitchat, something Jim had learned John was very good at doing, he motioned to Bernie with a nod of his head, indicating for her to come into his office. He backed up the nonverbal invitation by saying, "If we're going to leave here before midnight tonight, we should get started on that profile we need to work up as soon as possible. The sooner we send it off, the sooner we'll see results."

"Oh, sure thing." Bernie patted John on the arm as she passed him. "Tell Cathy not to make any plans for two weeks from Saturday. Y'all will be getting your invitations to the big bash tomorrow."

"We'll be there." John grinned. "You know Cathy and I wouldn't miss it for the world."

As soon as Bernie entered Jim's office, he closed the door behind her. "I have the VICAP report, and it looks like there were four almost identical abduction and murder cases, with a possible fifth."

"In Alabama?"

Jim shook his head. "Two in Georgia, one in Tennessee, one in North Carolina and another in South Carolina. All within the past five years."

"I've never done a profile matrix before," Bernie said. "Except in theory at the class I took at Quantico."

Jim pulled a chair around the side of his desk and aligned it next to his, then indicated for Bernie to sit. "You take my chair."

After she sat in the big swivel chair, he sat and scooted his chair closer to hers, then picked up the yellow legal pad lying on his desk. "As you know, it's a matter of developing a picture of the criminal and his crimes, connecting the dots to see what fits together."

"Okay."

"We start with asking and answering those six all-important questions."

Bernie's eyes widened. "Who, what, when, where, how and why?"

He clicked his tongue and grinned at her. "I knew you were a smart girl."

Shaking her head, she laughed.

"What?" he asked guilelessly. "Ah . . . it's not politically correct to call you a girl, huh?"

"I don't mind, but some female officers do."

"I'll try to remember that. But I'm glad you don't have a thin skin."

Bernie cleared her throat. "So we start with the question of who."

"Yeah, who are the victims?" Jim asked.

"Our three are all young, attractive women in their mid-to-late twenties."

"Hmm . . . And what else did they have in common?"

"Thomasina Hardy teaches at Adams County Junior College, Stephanie Preston was a student there, and Jacque Reeves had been a student several years ago."

"It could be a coincidence that they all had a connection to the college, but we won't rule out that fact being important." Jim glanced down at the legal pad. "Were you aware of the fact that all three women had dark hair and brown eyes?"

"No, not really. So, they were all young, attractive brunettes."

"Young, attractive, popular brunettes."

Bernie snapped her head around and looked directly at Jim. "Popular?"

"Translated that means women who have dated a lot of different men."

"Okay. The answer to our who question is young, attractive, popular brunettes." Bernie counted off each adjective on her fingers. "We need to find out if that description fits those four or five women you came up with through VICAP."

"I've put in calls to two of the lead detectives, starting with the ones in Georgia, since they were the most recent. I expect to hear from them no later than tomorrow sometime. In the morning, I'll contact the ones in the other states, too."

Bernie nodded.

"There are two parts to the who question," Jim said. "Who are the victims was part one."

"And who is our killer is part two."

"What type of killer is he?" Jim looked directly into Bernie's brown eyes. Brown eyes flecked with dark gold. Odd that he'd never noticed her eyes weren't a true brown the way Robyn's were. But then again, he'd never been this physically close to Bernie.

"Our guy plans out the details," she said. "He stalks the woman, which he probably sees as courting her. Then he kidnaps her, rapes her and kills her. Since rape is a crime of power and control and not one of passion, I'd say that is what motivates him."

"I agree."

"He's an organized, power/control-oriented killer."

"That leads us to the question of what," Jim said. "What was the cause of death in our two murders? Was there any deviant sexual behavior? Is there anything unusual about the murders?"

"He slit both women's throats. He tortured and raped them repeatedly. And as for anything unusual—I'd say the courtship is unusual, the gifts and notes. But what really sets Stephanie's and Thomasina's cases apart from the norm are those frightening S&M sketches."

Jim wrote hurriedly, jotting down all the information as he and Bernie continued discussing the case. When did the crime occur? Were the dates significant? And where did the crimes occur?

"All three victims were abducted, but it doesn't seem any of them put up a fight, so that indicates they knew and trusted their abductor," Jim said.

"Well, the how and why of the actual killings are simple. The how is that he slit their throats with a sharp knife, and if we can't find Thomasina soon, that will be her fate." Bernie sighed heavily. "As for the why—only God knows."

"We've got enough information here for me to go ahead and send it to Derek Lawrence," Jim said. "I'll fax everything to him before we leave this evening."

"How did you manage to get a former FBI profiler, who now works independently, to do a profile for us for free?" Bernie leaned back in the swivel chair, crossed her arms under her breasts—her full, nicely rounded breasts, Jim noticed—and pinned Jim with her questioning gaze.

"I have an influential, wealthy friend who has used Derek Lawrence on other cases and he just called the guy and asked him to do me a favor."

"Hmm . . . Must be nice to have a friend like that. Mind telling me who he is?"

Jim shrugged. "Griffin Powell."

"Your old teammate, *the* Griffin Powell?"

Jim groaned. "No, please don't tell me that you had a major crush on Griff the way ninety percent of the girls and women in the South did when we were playing ball at UT."

Bernie smirked. "As a matter of fact . . ." She laughed. "I did *not* have a crush on Griffin Powell. But I'm as curious as everyone else about where he went and what happened to him during those ten missing years of his life. All the newspapers and magazines, as well as every radio and TV station in the South, have all speculated about him, about why he disappeared and how he earned his fortune." Bernie leaned toward Jim. "Do you know?"

Jim noted a distinctly sweet, flowery smell and realized Bernie must be wearing perfume. That was something else he'd never noticed about her. She didn't seem the type to wear perfume.

"Nope. I've never asked him and he's never volunteered the information," Jim replied.

"Oh, I see."

"What's that perfume you're wearing?" He suddenly realized he'd spoken his thoughts aloud. Damn!

"Ah . . . er . . . I'm not wearing perfume." Bernie seemed startled and confused by his inappropriate question.

Jim forced himself to laugh, hoping humor would get him out of the situation his stupidity had gotten him into. What on earth had possessed him to notice gold flecks in Bernie's eyes or to ask her about her sweet scent? "Hey, somebody in this room smells like flowers and it's not me."

"Flowers?" Bernie's eyes widened; then she smiled. "Oh, I know what it is. It's this new hand lotion that Mom bought for me." She held her right hand under Jim's nose. "Is this what you smell? It's something called Vanilla Jasmine."

He grasped her wrist and held her hand in place, took a whiff, and grinned at her. "Yep, that's it. You know, that hand lotion is some mighty powerful stuff. You'd better not use too much of it the next time you're around Raymond or he's liable to sweep you off your feet."

Bernie's smile vanished. "I'll have you know that I am not the least bit interested in Raymond Long. He's a very nice man, and I've known him all my life, but there is nothing between us. Not in the past before he married and moved away from Adams Landing. Not now that he's divorced and back home running his father's hardware store. And not in the future. Not ever. Besides, he's gaga over Robyn, just like all you men are."

"Are you lumping me in with all men?"

Narrowing her gaze, she looked right at Jim. "Only when it comes to what type of woman interests you."

"And you think you know what kind of woman interests me, do you?"

"You can't help yourself. Robyn has that effect on all men, and you are a man."

"Guilty as charged. I am a man. I appreciate a good-looking woman as well as the next guy. And Robyn is a looker. But I don't like sharing my woman. I tend to be the possessive type. And your sister seems to enjoy playing the field."

"Robyn will eventually settle down when the right man comes along."

"Yeah, she probably will." He thought about Mary Lee, who was now married to her Mr. Right, Allen Clark. "But I'm not that man. Not for Robyn."

Bernie grinned. "Don't tell her that. There's nothing she likes better than a challenge. If she hasn't already seduced you, then finding out you're not interested . . . Shit. I can't believe I'm sitting here warning you about my own sister. Whatever's going on between the two of you is none of my business." Bernie scooted the chair back and stood. "I'm going to get a cup of coffee. Want one?"

"I've got a better idea," Jim said. "Why don't we finish up here, then go over to your folks' house and pick up Kevin. I'll take you two out for dinner. My treat. You name the place."

Bernie's smile widened. "I have an even better idea. Why don't you pick up Kevin and you two come over to my house for dinner? I'm not as good a cook as my mother, but I can grill some steaks and pop some potatoes in the microwave."

"Well, come on, woman, let's fax that profile to Derek

Lawrence and close up shop for the evening." When he stood, she moved away from him as if she thought he was going to touch her and didn't want him to. He lowered his arm, realizing that he had intended to put his hand on the small of her back.

Okay, Sheriff Granger, I get the message. And you don't have anything to worry about from me. I'm not going to hit on you. I want us to be friends. That's all. Just good friends.

He had stripped off her clothes and then bathed her. She hadn't fought him, and now she wondered if maybe she should have, but she'd been too terrified at the time. Too disoriented. Too confused. She had no idea where she was and saw no means of escape. He had told her that he loved her, that he knew she loved him and wanted to please him. Not knowing what he wanted to hear, she had neither agreed nor disagreed.

"I'm taking care of your personal hygiene for you this time," he said as he brushed her hair. "But from now on, I'll expect you to do it. Do you understand?"

She nodded her head weakly, every muscle in her body taut, every nerve rioting, as she sat quietly—obediently—in the wooden chair.

He reached down, clamped his hand around her jaw, his fingers and thumb biting into her cheeks, and glared directly into her eyes. "When I ask you a question, I expect a verbal answer. Do you understand?"

"Yes, I . . . understand." Her voice trembled.

He smiled and went back to brushing her hair. "You have beautiful hair, Thomasina. Long and lustrous and so dark it's almost black. Your hair was the first thing I noticed about you. And then as I studied you, I realized how truly lovely you are."

Fear ate away at her like an insidious poison, building

gradually, increasing with each passing moment of bondage. And despite the fact that he had unbound her feet in order to undress her and take her to the shower to bathe her, she was his prisoner in every sense of the word. Trapped not only in this tomblike room, but by her own terror.

When he bathed her, he had touched her intimately. He'd lingered over her breasts, scrubbing her nipples until they were almost raw. And when he'd washed between her legs, he had slipped his fingers inside her.

"Please," she'd begged him. "Don't. Don't do this."

"Oh, Thomasina. I promise I won't tease you too much before I give you what you really want." He had then concentrated on her clitoris, rubbing the washcloth over the sensitive nub until she thought she would scream.

"No . . . no . . ."

"What's the matter, darling? Can't you come without my being inside you?"

He had laughed and moved on to finish her bath.

Thomasina had no idea what time it was, but she felt fairly certain that it was Friday, the day after she'd been abducted. He had left her here overnight—wherever here was. Left her alone in the semidarkness of what she believed to be a subterranean room, a basement of some sort. There was a bed, a table, a chair, and what appeared to be an unfinished bathroom, with a shower, sink, and commode, surrounded by a four-foot-high concrete block wall. The wall separated the bath from the room, but provided no privacy whatsoever.

"There, all finished," he said. "You're ready now." He held out his hand to her.

She stared at his hand, which seemed large and powerful and frightening.

He frowned. "Never hesitate, Thomasina. If you do, I will see it as a rejection and be forced to punish you."

Her hand shot up and into his of its own accord, prompted

by her innate survival instincts. She had to do whatever was necessary in order to survive.

He smiled. "Come with me."

She stood and followed him as he led her to the small bed in the corner. *Please, God, help me. Help me!*

"Lie down," he told her.

She obeyed his command.

You could fight him. You could hit him and scream and scratch him. You could hurt him. But you can't stop him. He's larger and stronger. And you have no weapon.

And you can't escape. There is no way out.

Do as he says. Obey him. Pacify him. And maybe . . .

"What did I tell you about hesitating?" He growled the words through clenched teeth.

She hurriedly lay down on the bed.

"You're learning," he told her. "But that's twice you've hesitated."

Lying there, her mind crying out silently, her heart pleading for mercy, Thomasina closed her eyes and waited for her punishment. She heard him grunting, moving about, and wondered what he was doing, why he hadn't acted immediately. She had expected a slap or even a hard punch of some kind.

Then she felt the side of the bed give and sensed him hovering over her. He was going to rape her and there was nothing she could do to stop him.

"Open your eyes, darling."

She opened her eyes instantly and stared up into the handsome face of a madman.

With a swift, subtle survey, she scanned his body. He was naked, but not aroused. His penis hung limply, the tip brushing her left thigh.

"I'm not quite ready," he said. "But there's no need for you to worry. I'll be hard as a rock very soon."

She swallowed the knot of fear in her throat.

His big hands roamed over her shoulders, her breasts, and her belly. Then he lowered his head and licked a trail from her navel to her throat. Her heartbeat accelerated. Sweat dotted her forehead.

His mouth played with her breasts, tormenting her nipples. And suddenly, without warning, he bit the side of her breast. She cried out in pain. He bit her again and again, covering her right breast before pausing at the nipple.

Weeping profusely, she tried to push his head away, but he captured her hands and held them over her head. With his powerful body holding her in place, she could barely breathe. His erect penis probed between her thighs. Then he bit down on her nipple and thrust into her simultaneously.

Thomasina screamed with agony as he viciously raped her.

Chapter 14

"You really played basketball and softball and soccer?" Kevin stared at the framed photos on the walls and the shelves filled with trophies in Bernie's small den. "You must have been really good to have won all those trophies." Kevin turned and surveyed Bernie from the top of her head to the bottom of her feet. "I guess you were good because you're so big and tall. Not many girls are your size."

"Kevin, I don't think—" Jim corrected his son.

"No, no, it's all right," Bernie said. "I am bigger and taller than most women." She smiled warmly at Kevin. "Yes, my size was definitely an asset when I played sports in school. And it works to my advantage as the sheriff. I'm as tall as many of my deputies, so I can look them right in the eye when I issue orders."

Kevin laughed. "You can't look my dad in the eye. He's taller than you."

"So he is." When she glanced at Jim, he squared his shoulders and stood tall and straight. She chuckled at his antics.

"My mom's not very tall." Kevin's smile vanished. "I'm

taller than she is. She told me just a couple of weeks ago that I wasn't her little boy anymore, that I'm her—" Kevin's voice cracked.

"Hey, you two had better go check those steaks," Bernie said. "You like yours medium well, right? Just like your dad does. We don't want them to get overdone." She nodded her head toward the door. "While y'all are doing that, I'll put the salad together and set the table in the kitchen."

Jim laid his hand on Kevin's shoulder. "Come on, son."

"Wait up a minute," Bernie called to them as they headed out of the den.

Father and son paused in the hallway and glanced over their shoulders, their mannerisms identical. Not for the first time, Jim thought how much Kevin was like he'd been at that age. Minus the happy home life, with parents devoted to each other and a pesky little sister. Jim had wanted all those good things for his son, but had failed to give them to him.

"I'm making homemade ice cream," Bernie said. "Kevin, what's your favorite flavor?"

With unshed tears glistening in his eyes, Kevin swallowed and then said, "I like just plain old vanilla."

"So do I. And I use my mom's recipe that calls for half a dozen eggs, so it's super rich."

"Yum." A fragile smile lifted the corners of Kevin's mouth.

Jim herded his son down the hall, through the kitchen and onto the open back porch. He lifted the lid on the barbeque grill, then picked up a two-pronged fork from the side shelf and quickly flipped the three T-bone steaks.

"Five more minutes, tops," Jim said.

"What can I do to help?"

"Go inside and get a platter from Bernie to put these beauties on."

"Okay."

"Kevin?"

"Huh?"

"It's okay to be worried about your mother. And if you need to talk about her surgery or—"

"I just want her to be all right. I don't want her to die."

"I understand. I want that, too."

"Why did she have to get cancer? Why now, when she's happy with Allen and—" Kevin clamped his teeth together tightly.

Jim ached inside, his gut tightening painfully. He couldn't bear to see his son suffering this way. As a parent, he had learned that nothing hurt you the way seeing your child in pain did, especially when you knew there wasn't a damn thing you could do about it.

"I don't know why she got cancer or why it had to happen now. But you have to believe that she'll be all right, that she'll get well."

"Do you believe it?"

Tell him what he needs to hear. "Yeah, I believe your mother will be all right."

Kevin sighed heavily. "Dad?"

"Hmm . . . ?"

"I like Sheriff Granger. She's a real nice person, just like her mom and dad are."

"You're right, Bernie is a nice person, just like her folks."

"Do you like her, too?"

Jim hesitated for a moment before replying, not quite sure if there was more than the obvious to his son's question. "Yes, of course I like her."

"How much do you like her?" Kevin asked.

Jim narrowed his gaze and studied his son's expression. "I like her a lot, as a friend."

"Oh." Kevin turned around, opened the back door and walked into the kitchen.

Jim stood there and stared through the half-glass door, watching as Kevin went over to Bernie and started talking to her. He couldn't hear what they were saying, but within a couple of minutes, Kevin smiled and then laughed.

Thanks, Bernie. Thanks for knowing what to say and do to put a smile on my kid's face.

Bernie reached up into a top cabinet for a platter. Jim's gaze zeroed in on her butt when the material of her brown slacks tightened across each cheek. She had a nice rear end. High, rounded, and firm. A twinge of sexual awareness reminded Jim that he was ogling his boss.

Jerking his gaze away and focusing on the sizzling steaks, Jim sucked in a deep breath, then blew it out in a loud whoosh. What the hell was the matter with him, looking at Bernie's rear end and actually getting aroused? Not only was she his boss, she was also definitely not interested in him as a man. *And you're not interested in her. She's not your type. Her sister, Robyn, is your type.*

But that was another problem. He'd had one date with Robyn, and despite the fact she was a gorgeous woman, he had discovered that she was far too much like his ex-wife to suit him. One Mary Lee in a lifetime was more than enough for any man.

"Here's the platter." Kevin held out the large oval plate as he emerged from the kitchen. "Bernie set the ice cream maker in the sink and plugged it in. She said the ice cream would be frozen by the time we get through eating our steaks. Are they ready yet?"

"Yep, they're ready." Jim took the plate and set it on the shelf on the side of the grill, then using the large fork, he lifted each steak and placed them one by one on the platter.

"It is okay for me to call her Bernie, isn't it?" Kevin asked. "She said friends should call each other by their first names, and she wants us to be friends."

"Sure, it's okay."

Bernie opened the back door and called to them. "Everything's set. Bring those steaks in here and let's dig in."

Within thirty minutes the three of them had finished off their salads, steaks, and baked potatoes. Then they ate huge bowls of vanilla ice cream, the best Jim had eaten since he'd been a kid. After supper, Jim went outside and cleaned the grill while Kevin helped Bernie clear away the table and load the dishwasher. When Jim finished up and headed back in, he paused for a couple of minutes at the closed door and watched his son with Bernie, the two of them talking and smiling and working side by side. An odd sensation hit Jim in the gut. A warm and familiar feeling, reminding him of his own childhood when he'd helped his mom in the kitchen.

Jim opened the door. "If you two are all squared away in here, Kevin and I had better head for home."

"Ah, Dad, can't we stay for a while longer?" Kevin gazed pleadingly at his father. "Bernie's neighbor's dog just had puppies, and she's already called to see if we can go over and take a look at them tonight."

"They're Boston terriers," Bernie said. "I've bought one of them from the Nolans. I thought maybe Kevin might like to take a look at my puppy and help me decide on a name for him."

"Please, Dad."

"Sure, why not." Jim shrugged. He'd do just about anything to make Kevin happy, to keep his mind off of Mary Lee for a little while.

"Bernie said that Brenda and R.B. are going to babysit her puppy, so that means I'll get to spend a lot of time with him, and Bernie said I could help her folks train him."

Jim glanced at Bernie and they exchanged a brief moment of understanding without either of them saying a word. Kevin needed a distraction, something to keep him from worrying himself sick about his mother.

"The Nolans are expecting us, right?" Jim asked.

"Yes, they are." Bernie placed her hand on Kevin's shoulder and gave it a gentle squeeze. "Are you ready?"

Kevin glanced at Jim. "Are you going with us?"

"Yeah. Yeah, sure."

"Chuck and Diane Nolan keep the mama and her babies in the laundry room." Bernie led the way outside and across her backyard to the gate. "They said just come around to the backdoor and knock."

Jim followed behind Bernie and Kevin as they entered her neighbor's backyard. The sun had set nearly an hour ago, leaving behind a colorful twilight that was fading fast into darkness. Jim glanced down at his lighted digital watch. Eight-fifty-two.

"My puppy is the runt of the litter. His face is almost solid white," Bernie said. "You'll know him the minute you see him."

"How old is he?" Kevin asked.

"Six weeks old."

"That's old enough for you to bring him home, isn't it?"

"Yes, it is. And I'm getting him very soon. First, I'll have to buy all the stuff he'll need. Maybe your dad will let you go shopping with me tomorrow. The local Feed & Seed carries a whole line of supplies for dogs."

Jim listened to Kevin and Bernie as they discussed the puppy, the supplies and how Bernie was counting on Kevin to help her folks with her new pet. Once again that strange notion of Bernie and Kevin reminding him of a mother and son came over Jim. It was then that Jim realized Bernadette Granger was a natural. Mothering was simply a part of her basic nature.

All Kevin talked about on the way home was Boomer, the name he had chosen for Bernie's black and white puppy. Jim wondered why he'd never realized how much his son had always wanted a dog. Maybe because he'd been too damned busy fighting with Mary Lee. And he could admit now that all those arguments hadn't been his ex-wife's fault. There was more than enough blame to go around, even if he could never forgive her for cheating on him or for deliberately trying to drive a wedge between Kevin and him. For years after their divorce, he expected the worst from his ex-wife and somehow just couldn't give her the benefit of the doubt.

As soon as they entered his duplex apartment, Jim sent Kevin off to the bathroom. "Go take a shower, brush your teeth and then hit the sack. You can sleep late tomorrow because I'm going to be working from home most of the day." His plan was to speak to the lead detectives on the four, possibly five, murder cases in various southeastern states that were eerily similar to the two here in northeast Alabama. He could do that from home as easily as he could from his office.

Kevin paused before leaving the living room. "Don't forget that Bernie's picking me up at two tomorrow to go shopping for Boomer."

"I won't forget." Jim grinned. "And if I did, you'd remind me."

"Do you think I'll get to talk to Mom tomorrow?"

"I don't know. Maybe."

"I have my own cell phone, you know. Allen got one for me. She can call me even if I'm not here at your place or not over at the Grangers' house."

A twinge of parental jealousy zapped Jim and he instantly felt like a heel for resenting Allen's ability to provide special things for Kevin that he couldn't afford. But the truth of the matter was that he wasn't sure he approved of a twelve-year-old having his own cell phone. "If Mary Lee doesn't call tomorrow, she'll call you soon."

"Yeah, if not tomorrow, then Sunday for sure."

No matter how many times his ex-wife had bad-mouthed him to his son, he would not say anything against Mary Lee to Kevin, especially not now. But he knew his ex-wife for the selfish bitch she had always been, even in the early days of their relationship. Back then he'd been too in love and in lust to see her for what she was. God, what a fool he'd been. The worst thing about it all was that Kevin had to pay the price for his mistake. Jim realized he should cut Mary Lee some slack because of what she was going through, but if this near-death experience didn't alter her basic nature, then she would simply continue to put her needs above everyone else's, including Kevin's.

"Go on, get ready for bed," Jim said.

Kevin hesitated.

"Something wrong?" Jim asked.

"Could I invite Bernie to have supper with us tomorrow?"

Jim nodded. "Yeah, sure, ask her."

"Can we take her to the King Kone for burgers and fries?"

"If that's what you want."

"Thanks, Dad."

Jim stood in the middle of the living room in his duplex rental and savored the moment. *Thanks, Dad.* Two simple little words that meant the world to Jim. Did a lot of other divorced dads endure the same guilt and anger that plagued him? Did these other weekend fathers cherish every minute with their kids the way he did?

Enjoy this time with Kevin. It'll come to an end soon enough, once Mary Lee recovers and sends for him. The selfish side of Jim's nature wished Mary Lee would decide she couldn't deal with being a cancer survivor and handle a soon-to-be-teenage son. If only she would allow Kevin to stay here with him. Yeah, and that would happen about the same time he'd be able to go ice skating in hell.

The "what-if" game was a waste of time. "What if" and "if only" were Jim's old friends. He'd spent too much time with them over the years. What if he'd been able to play pro ball? If only he hadn't married Mary Lee. What if his partner on the Memphis PD hadn't been murdered? If only Mary Lee hadn't cheated on him.

Jim walked into his bedroom, flipped on the bedside lamp, undid his belt, and jerked out his shirttail. He went over to the chest of drawers, opened the top drawer and removed a bottle of Jack Daniel's. After unscrewing the cap, he lifted the bottle to his lips and took a swig, blew out a hot breath and then wiped his mouth. His knees ached, but then they always ached. The pain had become a part of him. If Kevin wasn't staying with him, he'd be tempted to down the whole bottle of whiskey tonight. Getting drunk would not only ease the continuous ache in his knees, but it would erase the memories of all his failures. As a football hero, as a partner, as a husband, as a father, as a man.

Jim took a second swig, then recapped the bottle and returned it to the top drawer. He sat on the edge of his bed and rubbed the back of his neck.

Don't look back. Don't think about past failures. Think about the opportunities you have now to be a good father and a top-notch chief deputy.

After removing his shoes and socks, he lay down atop his unmade bed and rested his head on his pillow. He stared up at the ceiling, then closed his eyes.

"Dad? Dad?"

Jim heard Kevin's voice, but couldn't quite come out of the sleepy fog.

"Huh?" Jim managed to open his eyes and search for his son.

Kevin stood in the doorway. "Dad, are you okay?"

"Yeah, fine. I just dozed off for a couple of minutes."

"I'm going to bed now. See you in the morning."

Jim sat up and lifted his hand in a wave. "Sleep tight."

"Yeah, you, too."

After Kevin went to his room, Jim turned and sat on the edge of the bed for a couple of minutes, then got up and headed to the bathroom. He'd shave and shower in the morning, but he should brush his teeth tonight. And he needed to piss.

Just as he finished up in the bathroom and lathered his hands with soap, he heard the doorbell. *Who the hell?* It had to be past eleven. He and Kevin hadn't left Bernie's until ten o'clock.

After rinsing his hands quickly, Jim shook them dry as he headed through the house to the front door. He peered through the viewfinder and did a double take. What on earth was she doing here, especially at this time of night?

He unlocked the door and eased it halfway open.

She smiled at him, showing her perfect, straight white teeth. "Aren't you going to invite me in?"

"It's kind of late to be visiting, isn't it?"

"I've just had the most boring date of my life." Robyn Granger sighed, heaving her breasts, which were covered with a very tight white T-shirt. Her peaked nipples pushed against the cotton fabric. "But if you'll invite me in, the night won't be a total waste."

Jim hesitated. Robyn pushed the door open just enough to squeeze inside, then wrapped her arms around Jim's neck and pressed her body against his.

He grasped her wrists and untangled her arms from around him, then closed the front door. "Who was the unlucky guy?" Jim asked.

"Unlucky?"

"Unlucky because he bored you."

Robyn laughed. "I should have known better than to go out on a date with a minister."

"Your date tonight was with Reverend Donaldson?"

She laced her arm through Jim's. "Let's not waste our time talking about him." She cuddled against Jim and whispered in his ear. "I'm horny as hell and you're just the man who can fix that."

Under different circumstances, Jim probably wouldn't turn down what she was offering. After all, he hadn't gotten laid in quite a while, and Robyn was one sweet piece of ass. But his son was here, possibly still awake in his room. No way was Jim going to screw Robyn or any other woman with his son just across the hall.

When Robyn slid her hand beneath Jim's shirt and caressed his chest, he grabbed her hand. "Look, honey, it's the wrong time and this is the wrong place. Did you forget that my son is staying with me?"

"Oh, that's right. The cute kid Mom and Dad are baby-sitting. Keith? Kirk?"

"Kevin."

"Yeah, like I said, cute kid." Robyn leaned into Jim and kissed him on the lips.

He grabbed her shoulders. She smiled and sighed.

"Why don't we go to your bedroom? We'll be very quiet. Keith won't even know I'm here. And I promise I'll leave before he gets up in the morning."

Jim tightened his hold on her shoulders. "Go home, Robyn. Take a cold shower. Or make good use of your vibrator."

She puckered her lips and frowned. "Are you really going to send me away?"

He nodded. "Yeah, honey, I'm afraid so."

She pulled away from him, stepped back and threw her arms out in a take-me gesture. "Think about what you're turning down." Robyn lifted her T-shirt to show him that she wasn't wearing a bra.

Jim swallowed hard. His penis twitched. *Down boy. You aren't getting any of that. Not tonight. And if I'm really smart, not ever.*

"It's my loss," he told her.

Huffing, she lowered her T-shirt. "Well, this is a first for me. Turned down by two men in one night."

"You propositioned the preacher?" Jim chuckled.

Robyn grinned. "Well, not exactly. But by a couple of hours into the date it was obvious that he didn't fuck on a first date. Hell, he didn't even kiss on a first date. I think something's wrong with the guy."

"He's a minister. My guess is he thinks fornicating is a sin."

Robyn tiptoed her fingers up Jim's chest. "Are you sure you don't want to do a little fornicating tonight?"

"Not tonight." Jim turned Robyn around and marched her to the front door.

"Want a rain check?" She winked at him.

Jim didn't respond immediately.

"Who is she?" Robyn asked.

"What?"

"You wouldn't have hesitated in answering if you weren't either getting it or planning on getting it from some other woman. Who is she?"

"There is no other woman," Jim told her. And just to prove to her that there wasn't, he said, "I'll take the rain check."

She gave him a tongue-thrusting kiss, then breezed through the door. Pausing on the sidewalk, she turned and waved at him. "Call me. Okay?"

"Okay."

Jim watched her get in her little yellow sports car and drive away. He had the hard-on from hell. His body wanted a woman in the worst way. Not Robyn Granger in particular, just a woman. Any woman.

Chapter 15

He had left Thomasina weeping. The stupid cunt. She thought that by being compliant and meek, she could fool him. But he wasn't fooled, not in the least. She didn't love him the way he needed to be loved, the way he deserved to be loved. She was like all the others, nothing more than a beautiful whore who lied as easily as she breathed. She told him she loved him and begged him to make love to her, but she was as big a disappointment as Stephanie had been. And Jacque. And . . .

Why was he doomed to suffer, to believe he'd found true love, only to have his hopes dashed? But he wouldn't give up. He couldn't. He was more determined now than ever to find the perfect woman, his perfect mate.

He had found her once, years ago, his perfect girl.

Even now, her name was like music to his ears. Soft and sweet and beautiful. He had loved her, been obsessed with her, would have died for her. She had promised him her heart and her body.

No! Stop thinking about her. Don't remember what hap-

pened. Remembering hurts too much. It will rip you apart all over again.

He had to forget the past and concentrate on the here and now. For her sake and his, he had to set Thomasina free. And he had to do it soon. In the beginning, he'd had such high hopes, such fabulous dreams of what it would be like for them. He had wanted her to be "the one." Everything about her had seemed so right. She was young and pretty, with lustrous dark hair and a bewitching smile. And she was very popular. All the guys liked her, wanted her, dreamed of fucking her. But she didn't want any of them. Not the way she wanted him. She'd been waiting for him, longing to be with him, had accepted all of his little gifts, each a special token of his affection.

She loved him.

But she didn't love him enough to give him everything he needed. She tried, but she had failed over and over again. Maybe it wasn't her fault that she couldn't satisfy him, even though he satisfied her completely. He knew he did. She told him so. She liked all the things he did to her and always begged him for more.

Lies. All lies!

They had lied to him. Every single one of them. They had promised him everything, but never gave him enough. They'd always held something back.

But next time would be different. Wouldn't it?

He parked, got out and locked his vehicle. She lived only a few blocks away, a quick and easy walk, especially if he went down the back alleys. At this time of morning when it was still dark outside, no one would see him. She didn't have a security alarm, didn't even have deadbolt locks. Getting inside her house should be easy. She would still be asleep. If he was very quiet and very careful, he could go inside, find her bedroom and watch her while she slept.

Maybe she sleeps in the raw.

His dick twitched.

As he hurried up the alley, he imagined what it would be like with her. She wouldn't disappoint him. He felt sure that she would know how to please him in ways none of the others had. She had flirted with him, teased him, made him silent promises with those sultry looks she gave him.

You can watch her, but you can't touch her. Not yet.

No, he wouldn't touch her, wouldn't begin their courtship until he ended things with Thomasina. He wasn't the kind of man who betrayed one woman with another. With the others, he had known within a couple of weeks that their relationship wasn't going to work out the way he had hoped. He and Thomasina had been lovers for nine days and already he knew he could never care for her the way he had his first love. And that's what he wanted—to love and be loved with equal passion and devotion, to once again share what he had shared with *her.*

But she didn't really love—

He hummed inside his mind, blotting out any negative thoughts about the past, shutting out the agony.

Just as he came up alongside the chain-link fence that ran the length of her property, separating her yard from the alley, he heard voices. Who was awake and outside at four-thirty in the morning? Stopping dead in his tracks, he looked and listened.

The shadows cast across her back porch, created by the blending of illumination from the moon overhead and the streetlight in front of her house, revealed the two dark silhouettes embracing.

She was giggling. He knew her laughter, recognized it instantly. But who was the man? It couldn't be her husband. He was in the Middle East.

When he saw her kissing the man on her back porch, every muscle in his body tautened. She was his. How dare she give herself to another man!

But she's lonely with her husband away. And she doesn't know that you want her, that you can offer her a love that is true. A love that could be forever.

He crept out of the alley and into her neighbor's backyard, being careful to keep hidden behind the trees and tall shrubbery.

"I wish you could stay," she said, clinging to the man.

"You know I can't. If anyone saw me . . ."

"I know. I know. But damn it, Ron, I'm sick and tired of sneaking around this way."

Ron? She'd called the man Ron.

He moved in closer, as close as he could get to the fence separating her yard from her neighbors' without revealing his presence.

Ron Hensley? Deputy Ron Hensley.

He should have known. That guy couldn't keep his pants zipped. He'd screwed every willing woman in Adams County. He'd even been one of Thomasina's lovers.

She kissed Ron again before he left her standing on the back porch. The country-bumpkin Lothario sneaked around the house and disappeared down the street. Ron had probably parked several streets up.

When she went back inside her house, he waited there for several minutes and watched in the darkness. He desperately wanted to go to her, to tell her that she didn't have to waste her time on a guy like Ron Hensley. She was too good for that womanizing deputy, far too good. She deserved better.

"Soon, my darling Abby. Soon we'll be together and you can show me how much you love me."

Bernie stood in front of the mirror—naked. She was far from slender. Although not fat, she didn't possess a lean, exercise-toned body. Her wide hips and big butt stubbornly held on to those extra ten pounds Bernie's mother constantly reminded her she needed to lose. Well, actually, to be in fashion, she'd have to lose at least twenty-five pounds to achieve that waif-thin physique, have her C-cup breasts enlarged to double-D and undergo liposuction on her inner and outer thighs.

Her hair was okay, she supposed. Thick, shiny and shoulder length. But the color wasn't anything special. Just a plain old medium brown. And her eyes were nondescript. Except for the gold flecks.

She studied her facial features. It was a pleasant face, her features all medium in size, working quite well together. Just a hint of her mother's glamorous beauty softened a face that greatly resembled her father's.

Bernie heaved a deep sigh, turned from the mirror and walked over to her closet. It wasn't often that she took the time to scrutinize her physical attributes and deficiencies. Usually she considered it a waste of valuable time. But for the past week, she'd been more concerned about her appearance than she had in years. And it was all Jim Norton's fault. Damn the man!

Despite her best efforts not to let her emotions overrule her common sense where her chief deputy was concerned, she was falling for the guy. Yeah, sure, she'd had a major crush on him when she'd been a teenager—one of those hero-worshipping-from-afar deals. But it wasn't memories of star athlete Jimmy Norton that put butterflies in her tummy or made her cream her pants. No, that would be world-weary, rode-hard-and-away-wet, devoted father, all-around good-guy, forty-year-old Captain Jim Norton.

For the first time in years, Bernie had planned ahead. Last night she had chosen what she would wear today—Saturday. Jeans, just a tad too tight. A red tank top that clung to her breasts, and a short-sleeved, oversize red and white shirt that hung down to just below her hips. Her wide hips.

After taking out the items of clothing from her closet, she

laid them across the foot of her bed, then retrieved her underwear from her dresser drawer. She didn't own anything except plain white cotton panties and bras. What was the point of investing in beautiful lingerie if she was the only one who ever saw it?

When she sat down on the edge of the bed, Boomer wriggled free from beneath his small blanket atop the king-size pillow and came over to her. His little wet nose nuzzled her naked hip. She reached out and picked him up, hugged him to herself and mumbled nonsensical baby talk to him. He licked her face, which made her laugh. He was such an adorable mutt, with his funny white face, his big, black bug-eyes, and his loving disposition. It amazed her how attached she'd become to him in a week's time. And she wasn't the only one. Kevin Norton had become Boomer's best buddy, the two practically inseparable when her parents acted as baby-sitters for boy and puppy.

"Do you need to go out again?" Bernie asked. She'd taken him outside first thing this morning when she woke at her usual five-thirty and he'd done his job, but he was just a pup and not housebroken yet, so better safe than sorry.

He looked up at her with those soulful eyes and wagged his cropped tail. "Okay, okay. Give me a couple of minutes to put on my clothes and we'll go."

She dressed hurriedly. She'd do her makeup and hair when they came back inside.

A few minutes later, as she raced through the kitchen to the back door, Boomer in her arms, she glanced at the wall clock. Twenty till eight. She had twenty minutes to tend to Boomer, do her hair and makeup and put on a fresh pot of coffee before Jim and Kevin arrived. Although it was Saturday, she and Jim had to work half a day and had decided to meet at her house so he could bring Kevin with him. While they worked, Kevin could spend the morning with his new best friend.

Bernie opened the back door and made it out onto the porch before she felt something wet and warm spreading out over her arm. She groaned.

"Boomer! Couldn't you wait another minute?"

So much for color-coordinating her tank top and blouse. The red and white blouse now had a large yellow stain on one sleeve. She took Boomer out into the yard, set him down, and then removed her shirt. She hoped this incident wasn't an indication of how the rest of her day would go.

"That's it. Fuck me harder . . . faster." *Oh, Jim . . . Jim . . .* "God, you're good, baby. So good. Mmm . . ."

Trembling and crying out, Robyn came. While she spiraled back to earth, the man on top of her came a couple of minutes after she did. He jetted into the condom he wore, groaning as he clutched her hips.

When he fell to her side and flopped onto his back, she nuzzled his shoulder and sighed. He lay there for several minutes, breathing hard, his big hand idly caressing her thigh; then without saying a word, he got up and headed for the bathroom. Robyn opened her eyes and looked at his naked backside. Sleek, slender, firm. A real pretty boy. And a damn good lay.

But he wasn't Jim Norton. And she wanted Jim Norton. But Jim hadn't called her, hadn't taken her up on the rain check she'd given him—so to hell with the guy. Robyn knew herself well enough to realize that the main fascination with Jim was the fact that he was playing hard to get. She wasn't used to a man turning her down, not for any reason.

Maybe he's not playing hard to get. Maybe he's really not interested.

But she didn't intend to give up without one more try. Tonight, at her parents' anniversary party, she'd give Jim one final chance.

"Hey, babe, where's your shampoo?" Paul Landon called from the bathroom doorway.

Robyn glanced at him and smiled. "It's in the caddy hanging inside the shower stall."

He grinned at her. "Want to join me? I could scrub yours and you could scrub mine."

Robyn stretched like a cat warming herself in the sun, then languidly crawled out of bed and sauntered toward the bathroom. Paul—rich, handsome, attentive—held out his hand to her, and when she put her hand in his, he drew her close and kissed her.

Robyn clung to Paul, all the while pretending he was another man. An older, tougher, stronger man. A man she intended to seduce, somehow, someway. Maybe tonight.

"Can I take Boomer with me and watch TV in the den?" Kevin asked as he dumped the remnants of his breakfast into the garbage can under the sink.

"Would you mind taking him out first?" Bernie asked.

"Sure," Kevin replied. "Hey, Bernie, what are you going to do with Boomer tonight while we're all at your parents' big party?"

"I've got that covered," she told him. "I've hired a babysitter for him."

Kevin grinned as he picked up the puppy from where he lay beneath Bernie's feet under the kitchen table. "You're a lucky dog, Boomer. You know that, don't you? You've got Bernie for a mom." Kevin headed for the back door, Boomer tucked securely under his arm.

Bernie sensed Jim staring at her, and although she tried her best to not look his way, she couldn't stop herself from hazarding a quick glance. A shiver danced up her spine when their gazes met and locked for a split second. Was she imagining things, seeing what she wanted to see, or was Jim actually aware of her as a woman? The way he was looking at her made her go weak in the knees.

"Kevin really likes you," Jim said.

Bernie cleared her throat. "I really like him. He's a great kid. Smart and funny and kind and . . ." When Jim laughed, she frowned. "What is it?"

"You should hear Kevin singing your praises. He thinks you're a really special lady. You and my son seem to have formed your own mutual admiration society."

"What can I say other than that Kevin and I both have great taste and good judgment?"

"I agree." Jim kept looking at her, studying her, as if he was trying to figure out what it was about her that made her so special to his son.

When Bernie felt a warm blush creeping up her neck, she hurriedly looked away, and then she gathered up the discarded paper wrap from her biscuit and sausage. Jim had told her yesterday afternoon when they'd made plans to work at her house this morning that he'd stop by the King Kone and pick up breakfast for the two of them and Kevin. In the past week, she had spent five of the seven evenings with Jim and his son. They'd stayed for dinner at her parents' house twice, had eaten out twice, and had ordered takeout and eaten at Jim's duplex one night. She wanted to think Jim enjoyed her company, that he was actually interested in her the way she was interested in him, but more than likely he was spending so much time with her because of Kevin.

She and Jim's son had formed an almost instant friendship, partly thanks to Boomer, but partly because they simply liked each other. She saw so much of Jim in Kevin, more than just a strong physical resemblance. She didn't think Jim realized how much alike he and his son were.

"Finished?" Bernie asked Jim.

"Yeah, I'm finished."

She cleared away the table and dumped everything in the

garbage, then glanced over her shoulder. "Since Kevin's going to take Boomer and watch TV in the den when they come back in, we can work in here if you'd like."

Jim scooted his chair out from the table and stood. "Why don't you sit down and I'll pour us both another cup of coffee before we get started."

"You sit," she told him. "I'll get the coffee."

Jim stretched his arms over his head and twisted from side to side, then picked up his vinyl carryall from where he'd laid it on the counter when he'd entered the kitchen earlier. After sitting down, he unzipped the case, pulled out a notepad and several file folders and spread them on top of the table.

Bernie placed their refilled coffee cups on the table and took her seat catercorner from Jim. "Did you get in touch with Derek Lawrence last night?"

Jim shook his head. "I talked to his wife. Lawrence got called in on an urgent case in Louisiana, but he told her to let me know he'd have the profile for us no later than Monday. It seems he wants the info we've compiled on the victims from the other states so he can compare the two and see if he thinks we're dealing with the same guy."

"What do you think?"

"I think it's possible, maybe even probable, but I'm withholding making a final judgment until you and I go over everything. I want your opinion."

Bernie nodded. "Were you able to get in touch with the lead detective from the murder case in South Carolina yesterday after we last talked?"

"Yep, I finally tracked down former Captain Hal Shepard last night. After he retired a couple of years ago, he moved to Louisville. And to make it even more difficult to find him, he'd gone off on a fishing trip with his son and grandson."

"So, what did he have to say?"

"Pretty much what I expected." Jim grimaced. "The victim, Shannon Elmore, was like all the other victims—young, pretty, dark haired, and popular. And when I explained about the other murders and described the killer's MO, he agreed that there were similarities, but several inconsistencies."

"Such as?"

"Shannon Elmore was abducted, raped and brutalized before her killer slit her throat," Jim said. "But she was missing only three days before her body was discovered, naked and posed. And there's no record of her receiving any gifts, except a few S and M sketches done in ink."

"Do you think she was the first victim and that's why there were no gifts, no real seduction before he grabbed her?"

"That's exactly what I thought until Shepard mentioned another case he'd worked on approximately a year before the Elmore case."

Bernie lifted her eyebrows. "Another similar case?"

"Sort of, but not exactly."

"Meaning?"

"A year before Shannon Elmore was murdered in Greenville, South Carolina, another young woman in that city was killed in the same way—her throat was slit. Heather Stevens had been raped and brutalized and her body left on a lonely stretch of road. But Heather had been missing for less than twelve hours. And she hadn't been completely naked." Jim paused for effect. "She was wearing a string of pearls."

Bernie blew out a whistling breath. "How many of the victims received a gift of pearls?"

"We know for sure that Stephanie and Thomasina did and both Georgia victims did, but none of the lead detectives in the other cases mentioned anything about pearls as one of the gifts."

"Did both Shannon Elmore and Heather Stevens fit the description of all the other victims?"

Jim nodded. "Young, pretty, brunette, and popular. All

eight women. Eight if we count Heather, and nine if we lump Thomasina Hardy in with the others."

"You believe, despite the lack of consistent similarities, that Heather Stevens was killed by the same man, don't you?"

"Yes, I do. And my gut tells me that Heather was probably the first, not Shannon."

"Then are we to assume this killer simply chooses a certain type of woman at random? Our three Alabama victims, counting Thomasina, lived within easy driving distance of one another, but they didn't know each other and the only connection they had to one another was that two of them had attended Adams County Junior College and one was a teacher there." Bernie looked directly at Jim. "What about the other victims? Were they connected in any way?"

"I don't know about anybody else, other than Heather and Shannon. Hal Shepard told me that the two women had gone to private school together, that they'd been close friends."

"Is that fact significant? Could it mean that they knew the killer, that he chose his first two victims for a specific reason, other than the obvious?"

The backdoor flew open. Kevin came running inside and chased Boomer through the kitchen. As he skidded to a halt by the refrigerator, he asked, "May I have a cola?"

"Help yourself," Bernie replied.

Kevin glanced at the notepad and papers scattered about on the table. "You two have already started working, huh?" Boomer jumped up on Kevin, pawing his leg. "We'll get out of here pronto and you won't hear a peep out of us until lunchtime."

"Thank you for taking care of Boomer for me this morning," Bernie said.

"You're welcome." Kevin grinned broadly, then retrieved a canned cola from the refrigerator, picked up Boomer and jaunted out of the kitchen.

Jim turned his attention back to business. "Let's assume that the same man killed all eight women, beginning with Heather nearly seven years ago."

"Okay, we'll work with that premise. We have a man who, for reasons unknown, targets young, pretty, popular brunettes. As far as we know there are only eight victims, not counting Thomasina, and I refuse to give up hope on her. But he apparently isn't killing within a certain time frame. He has murdered two women in our area within the past six months and in a little over a week after Stephanie's body was discovered, he abducted Thomasina."

Jim rummaged through the papers on the table, picking up one, scanning it, and then repeating the process again and again. "Son of a bitch."

"What did you find?"

"Probably nothing," Jim said. "Heather Stevens was killed seven years ago, and then the next three murders occurred the following year, all within a six-month time span." He lifted a couple of sheets of paper and fanned them back and forth. "The two Georgia murders didn't occur until three years later." He glanced at one report, and then another. "The first Georgia murder took place in September in Gainsville and the second occurred in December in Rome. That was two and a half years ago."

"There really is no time frame. He's killed sporadically. One murder, then three, then two, then one, and now two, three if you count Thomasina."

"There is one thing we're overlooking," Jim said. "We assumed that Jacque Reeves and Stephanie Hardy knew their killer and trusted him enough to get into his car. But if our guy is the same man who committed the other murders, that means he is not an Alabama native or if he is, he's moved around or traveled quite a bit. He has either recently moved to this area or moved back to this area."

"You don't actually think we can come up with a list of

suspects from those facts, do you? This guy could live any-where in northeast Alabama."

"He could, but what if he lives in Adams County?"

"What if he doesn't?"

"Come on, Bernie, we're putting together a hypothesis. We're playing a game of what if. What if this guy lives in Adams County? What if he's either new to the area or has moved back here in the past year? You know just about everybody in the county, don't you?"

"Oh shit. You want me to name names?"

"Yeah, I do."

"I can't just accuse somebody—"

"You're not accusing anybody," he told her. "But we have to start somewhere in compiling a list of possible suspects, and I'd say this is as good a place as any."

Bernie nodded, hating the idea of pointing fingers un-justly at anyone. Absentmindedly, she tapped her fingernails on the table as she thought. "Well, the first person who comes to mind is Reverend Donaldson. He's our most recent new-comer."

"A minister who's a serial killer. Hmm . . . unlikely, but not impossible."

Bernie chuckled. "Matthew is a pussycat."

"And you know this how?" Jim asked. "From personal experience? I thought your mom had picked out Matthew for Robyn. You haven't been homing in on your sister's territory, have you?"

Bernie laughed nervously, the sound odd to her own ears. "Don't be silly." *If I were going after one of Robyn's men, it wouldn't be Matthew Donaldson. It would be you, Jim Norton. It would damn well be you.* "Robyn isn't interested in Matthew. She told me that she was bored to tears on their one and only date. And as far as how I know, Matthew really is a pussycat. That's Mom's opinion and Dad's, and the few times I've been around him I sensed that he's a kind, gentle man."

"Serial killers wear masks," Jim told her. "They have been known to masquerade as charming, gentle men when, in reality, they're monsters."

"You don't honestly think that Reverend Donaldson could be—"

"Where was his last church? Where did he come from?"

"I don't know. I could ask—No, wait a minute. I think I remember Mom saying something about how Matthew's first preaching assignment straight out of the seminary was in Carrollton, Georgia. Mom's got some cousins who live there and they attended the church where Matthew was the assistant minister."

"Georgia, huh?"

"Oh my goodness. He's not the only person I know who has lived in Georgia. Raymond Long and his ex-wife lived in Atlanta for several years, and Paul Landon lived in Savannah for a while, and Scotty Joe Walters came to us from the Canton police department, and if I'm not mistaken, I believe Robyn said something about Brandon Kelley visiting his parents just outside Chattanooga in Rossville, Georgia."

"Okay, you've made your point." Jim held up his hands in an I-surrender gesture. "There are probably dozens of men in Adams County who have connections to the state of Georgia, but that doesn't make any one of them our serial killer."

"Our DA Jerry Dale's sister lives in Georgia and his family visits over there several times a year. And Ron Hensley inherited a time-share in a condo on St. Simons on the Georgia coast from his uncle and—"

Jim reached over and placed his open palm over Bernie's mouth. "Hush up, woman. Don't you know it's not polite to make fun of your chief deputy?"

The moment Jim's hand touched her lips, Bernie's breath caught in her throat. She clamped her teeth together tightly to trap her tongue so that it wouldn't act on impulse and lick Jim's hand. Her heartbeat drummed an excited rat-a-tat-tat.

They stared at each other for one endless moment.

Mumbling beneath his hand in an effort to diffuse the tense moment, Bernie pulled away from him. He eased his arm down to his side and diverted his gaze.

"What did you say?" he asked.

"I said doing something like that is a good way to get your hand bitten," Bernie told him jokingly.

Jim grinned.

His cell phone rang.

He removed it from the belt clip and flipped it open. "Captain Norton here."

Bernie watched and listened as Jim nodded a couple of times, and then said, "Yeah, yeah. We'll head on over there right away."

"What is it?"

"That was Sheriff Mays," Jim said. "A couple of hikers found a woman's body out in the woods over in Jackson County, just across the county line. He's on his way out there now. He thought we'd want to know."

"Is it Thomasina Hardy?"

"He doesn't know for sure, but he said it could be."

"Damn! It's been only nine days."

"It might not be her."

"And if it is?"

"Then our killer is speeding things up, changing his MO a little and has probably already chosen his next victim."

Chapter 16

Filled to overflowing with well-wishers, the Adams Landing Country Club sparkled with candlelight and champagne. The tinkling of glasses blended with conversations and laughter, with light jazz music creating a subtle undertone for all the other sounds. Men in suits, some like R.B. Granger in tuxedos, escorted wives, sweethearts, and dates. Ladies of all ages were decked out in silk and satin and sequins. And none was more beautiful than Brenda Granger in her white satin, floor-length gown that caressed her slender curves. Not even her younger daughter, Robyn, who wore a skintight, hot pink little number that scooped to her waist in the back and sported a slit that ended mid-thigh, outshined her. And all the children in attendance looked as if they had stepped out of the pages of a kiddie fashion magazine.

As Bernie and Jim entered the fray, half an hour late, she caught a glimpse of her parents in a far corner of the grand ballroom, Robyn and her date chitchatting with them. Her sister lifted a hand and waved, a predatory smile on her face. Bernie wondered how long it would take Robyn to zero in on Jim. It didn't matter that Paul Landon was her official date for this evening. It wouldn't be the first time her sister had arrived at a party with one man and left with another.

"I feel downright underdressed." Jim glanced around the main ballroom at all the elegantly attired guests. "I've had this old blue suit for years." He twisted the knot in his blue-and-white-striped tie. "And this is the only tie I own."

"You look fine," Bernie assured him. *You're the best looking man here.*

"I'm sorry you're late for your parents' fortieth wedding anniversary. Will your mom be upset?"

"If she is, she won't let me know. She was a sheriff's wife for nearly thirty years. She understands that sometimes work comes first and that it often interferes with family events."

Bernie glanced around, searching again for her parents, who seemed to have disappeared; but she figured the two were on the dance floor, which was set up in the smaller of the two ballrooms. She could remember when she'd been a little girl, she and Robyn sitting at the top of the stairs and watching their parents in each other's arms downstairs in the living room, the two of them dancing to old tunes from the sixties. As she grew older, she realized how much in love her parents were and knew that one day she wanted that kind of love. She wanted a man to look at her the way her dad looked at her mom.

"Mom and Dad must be on the dance floor. I don't see them anywhere."

"They hired a live band to play tonight?"

"They sure did. It's a jazz band from Huntsville."

"This is some shindig," Jim said. "I hate that your folks had to keep an eye on Kevin on their big day."

"I'm sure he wasn't any trouble. After all, Kevin's nearly thirteen, not three. It's not as if he can't look after himself."

"Hmm . . ." Jim nodded. "I wonder what he found to wear tonight. I think he brought one pair of dress slacks and a sport coat with him when he came from Mary Lee's."

"If I know my mom, she probably rented him a tux."

"What!"

Before she could reply to Jim's outraged expression, Deputies Scotty Joe Walters and Holly Burcham, looking like models out of a physical fitness catalogue with their buffed, tanned bodies, approached Bernie and Jim.

Ken and Barbie, Bernie thought.

"Evening, Sheriff." Scotty Joe smiled, showing a set of perfect white teeth that practically glistened against his leather brown face.

Not for the first time, Bernie thought what a handsome guy he was. Tall and muscular, with bright blue eyes and golden blond hair. And to add to his good looks, the young deputy had a warm, outgoing personality. Everyone who knew him liked him.

"Hello there, Captain Norton." Holly flirted quite openly with Jim, smiling up at him as she stroked his arm.

Scotty Joe didn't seem to mind in the least that his date was ogling another man, but why should he? It wasn't as if he and Holly were an item. They both played the field, apparently neither of them interested in a serious relationship with each other or with anyone else.

"We heard y'all went over to Jackson County today," Scotty Joe said. "I sure was relieved that the body those hikers found in the woods wasn't Thomasina. She's such a sweet lady. Nice and friendly. I still can't believe that anybody would want to hurt her. Not even Dr. Kelley, even if he did break her heart."

"You know Dr. Kelley didn't send those gifts to Thomasina," Jim said. "She just thought he was leading her on when, in reality, it was whoever stalked her and later abducted her."

"Did y'all find out who the woman was that the hikers found?" Holly asked.

"We have no idea," Bernie said. "They've sent her badly

decomposed body to Huntsville. The Jackson County coroner said she'd probably been dead at least a year."

"Could she be another victim of our serial killer?" Scotty Joe asked in a hushed tone, knowing the sheriff's department didn't want the term *serial killer* used publicly in reference to the recent murders.

Bernie shook her head. "We don't think so. This woman wasn't naked and her body had been buried in a very shallow grave out in the woods, not posed in an open area where it could be easily found."

Robyn sauntered up behind them and slipped between Scotty Joe and Jim, then placed her arms around their shoulders. "Can't you lawmen stop talking about murder and mayhem, even at a gala event like this?"

"Well, hello, beautiful," Scotty Joe said. "Aren't you looking especially sexy tonight."

Robyn giggled softly. She loved for men to notice her. She lived off of attention and praise. Bernie figured most extremely beautiful women were like that. Robyn always had been, even as a little girl. Odd thing was Bernie thought of her sister's narcissism as part of her charm, a large part of who and what Robyn was. A beautiful woman who knew she was beautiful. What was wrong with that? Nothing. Absolutely nothing.

"Aren't you just the sweetest thing." Robyn leaned over and kissed Scotty Joe on the cheek, then raked her gaze over Jim. "Hello, Captain Norton. I'm a little disappointed." She puckered her lips in a seductive pout. "I was hoping to see you in a tuxedo."

"I don't own one," Jim said.

Robyn tsk-tsked and wagged her index finger at him. "You could have rented one."

"Jim's been busy," Bernie said. "He's had more important things on his mind than tuxedos."

"Why didn't you just ask Dad to pick one up for you

when he got his?" Robyn removed her arm from around Scotty Joe's shoulders and clung to Jim's arm with both hands. "He got your son one today and you should see the kid. He's a doll. One of these days, Keith will be a real heart-breaker . . . just like his dad."

Frowning, Jim glanced down at his feet and cleared his throat. "Where is *Kevin*?"

"Oh, right, his name is Kevin. But then Kevin and Keith are practically the same name, aren't they? He's somewhere around," Robyn said. "Probably with Dad. Those two have certainly become great pals."

"If y'all will excuse me, I'm going to find Kevin." Jim glanced at Bernie as he dragged Robyn's hands down his arm and broke free. "Don't forget to save me a dance, Sheriff Granger."

Bernie's heart did a wild flutter. *Idiot!* She offered him a fragile, closed-mouth smile before he wandered off in search of his son.

"And you save me a dance, Miss Robyn." Scotty Joe winked at Robyn, then led Holly off toward the buffet tables.

Robyn huffed. "I'm going to have that man if it's the last thing I do."

"I assume you are not referring to Scotty Joe," Bernie said.

Robyn guffawed. "Hell no. I could have him by snapping my fingers. I meant Jim Norton. That man is playing hard to get for some reason. I even asked him if there was another woman in his life and he said there wasn't."

Bernie's stomach tightened. "Why don't you just leave him alone? If he's not interested—"

"Oh, stop playing mother hen. Just because he's your new chief deputy doesn't mean you have to look out for him and protect him from your wicked little sister. Jim's a *big* boy. He can take care of himself."

"You've got every single man in town panting after you

and a few married ones, too," Bernie said. "You just want Jim because, for once in your life, you're having to do the pursuing instead of the other way around. If he had hit on you first thing—"

"We'd be lovers by now."

Bernie's stomach muscle knotted painfully. "Look, I'm going to find Mom and Dad and wish them a happy anniversary."

"I suppose I should find Paul and play nice with him," Robyn said. "Just in case."

"Just in case?"

"Just in case I can't persuade Jim to take me home tonight."

For the first time in her life, Bernie actually hated Robyn. *Damn it, I'm jealous of my own sister. And all because of Jim Norton. I'm a fool. Jim and I are friends. He's not the least bit interested in me as a woman.*

"Hmm . . ." Bernie couldn't manage to say anything else. At the moment, it took all her strength to keep the emotion lodged in her throat from bursting free into tears. If she knew her sister—and she did—Robyn would get what she wanted. Jim Norton in her bed. Tonight.

Bernie found her parents, but wished she hadn't when her mom hauled Raymond Long away from his mother, Helen, and practically threw Bernie into the man's arms.

"You two young folks get out there and dance," Brenda said.

"Don't they look wonderful together?" Helen Long smiled as she gazed proudly at her son, who stood stiffly at Bernie's side.

Bernie glanced pleadingly at her father, who gave her an I'm-sorry-honey-but-what-can-I-do? look.

"Would you care to dance, Bernie?" Raymond asked, in a tone that implied he'd rather have a root canal.

"Yes, thank you. That would be nice."

He didn't take her hand as they walked side by side onto the dance floor. When he put his arm around her waist and she placed her left hand on his shoulder and her other hand in his, she tried to smile.

"I'm sorry about this, Bernie," he said.

"It's okay, Raymond. Really. Our mothers mean well."

He led her into the dance, his movements slow and steady, as if he was afraid he'd step on her toes.

"It's not that I don't like you," he told her. "Heck, we've known each other all our lives and we used to be friends, back in high school. But I've never thought of you as . . . well, you know . . . a girl."

Bernie laughed. "Yeah, I know." She looked at Raymond briefly, not wanting to stare and embarrass him. He hadn't changed much since high school, except he'd filled out from a tall, skinny teenager into a broad-shouldered man. He still wore his black hair short and neat, and instead of correcting his farsightedness with contacts, he still wore glasses. "You're not interested in me and I'm not interested in you. But we can be friends, right?"

He heaved a sigh of relief and Bernie almost laughed in his face. Did Raymond actually think she wanted him?

"Hey, I know you've got a thing for Robyn," Bernie said.

Raymond's face turned beet red.

"Oh, look, I didn't mean to embarrass or upset you."

"I'm not upset." His muscles tensed. "I'd just rather Robyn didn't know how I feel, that I'm nuts about her and always have been."

Oh, get real. Robyn knew. Heck, everybody in Adams Landing knew.

"Mums the word," Bernie assured him.

"Is she serious about Paul Landon?"

Robyn serious about a guy? He had to be kidding, right?
"No, I'm pretty sure she's not serious about him."

"Would you laugh if I told you that I've been in love with
your sister for as long as I can remember?" Raymond looked
directly at Bernie, sincerity and hopelessness in his expression.

"No, I'd never laugh at you or anyone else about something as serious as being in love."

Shrugging, Raymond forced a rather pitiful smile and
paused, doing little more than shuffling his feet. "I married
someone else and moved away from Adams Landing because I knew I didn't have a chance with Robyn. But she's
older now and sooner or later she'll settle down. Why not
with me?"

Bernie widened her eyes. "Ah . . ."

"You think I'm crazy?"

"No, that's not it."

"Robyn needs a man who'll put her up on a pedestal and
worship her. She needs a man who'd be totally devoted to
her." Raymond jerked his hand out of Bernie's and laid his
open palm over his heart. "I'm that man."

"Oh, Raymond . . . I . . . I . . ."

He released her and stepped back, his sad brown eyes
glistening with tears. "God, I don't know why I told you all
this. I feel like such a fool. But you said we could be friends
and I thought . . . if you could put in a good word for me
with Robyn . . ."

Bernie reached out and grasped Raymond's arm. "Let me
give you some advice about my sister."

He looked at her, hope in his eyes.

"Play hard to get."

"What?"

"Robyn loves a challenge. Pretend you're not interested
in her."

"I—I don't know if I can do that."

Bernie patted him on the arm. "I'll tell Robyn that I think you're a great guy and a real catch for some lucky girl, but not for me."

Raymond nodded. "Thanks, Bernie. I'm sorry I went all emotional on you."

"Why don't you go ask Holly Burcham or Renee Michaels to dance? Show Robyn that you aren't pining away for her. Consider it a first step in proving to her that you're not the least bit interested in her."

"I guess I can do that. You're her sister. You should know what would work with her."

Bernie stood there alone on the dance floor for several minutes and watched Raymond Long make a beeline to Renee Michaels, who had been dancing with her date for the evening, Ron Hensley. Holding her breath, Bernie prayed that Renee wouldn't reject Raymond. The poor guy needed something to boost his sagging ego. When Renee slipped her arm through Raymond's and led him onto the dance floor, Bernie sighed with relief and turned to go to the buffet table. She hadn't eaten a bite since breakfast and she was hungry.

When she turned around, she ran right into Jim, who grabbed her shoulders and shoved her backward to keep them from colliding.

"I thought you said you weren't interested in Raymond Long," Jim said teasingly.

"Ha-ha. Very funny."

"I was headed this way to rescue you, but you two looked awfully chummy."

"I was giving him pointers on how to deal with my sister. The poor guy is so crazy about her that he's downright piti-ful."

"What did you advise him to do?"

She looked Jim right in the eyes. "I told him to do what you're doing—play hard to get."

Frowning, Jim released his hold on Bernie's shoulders. "Do you think I'm playing games with Robyn?"

"Aren't you? You have to know that the more you resist her, the more she'll want you."

"Hmm . . . I take it that she hasn't been turned down very often."

"Make that never."

"There's a first time for everything." Jim grasped Bernie's hand. "Let's dance."

With her head spinning and butterflies doing a mating dance in her belly, Bernie stared wide eyed at Jim. "What?"

"You promised to save me a dance," he told her. "So do you or don't you want to dance with me?"

Yes, I want to dance with you. I want you to take me in your arms, hold me close, whisper sweet nothings in my ear. And when you leave here tonight, I want it to be with me, not my baby sister.

"Well, actually, I was thinking about heading to the buffet tables. My stomach's on the verge of making some very unseemly noises."

Jim chuckled. "One dance, then we'll hit the buffet tables together."

She nodded and didn't hesitate when Jim slid his arm around her and pulled her into his arms. For an entire minute, she couldn't breathe. He was so close she could smell him. Just a whiff of a light citrus aftershave, a mint mouthwash, and an underlying masculine scent that was as individual to Jim Norton as his fingerprints. She was sure that she could pick him out from a dozen other men simply by his smell.

"Don't be surprised if Kevin asks you for a dance later," Jim said.

"What?"

"My son has a crush on you. He asked me if I thought it would be all right if he asked you for a dance."

"I'm flattered."

"Kevin's a smart kid. He knows when someone genuinely likes him."

Is his dad as smart as he is?

"Does he know how much you love him?" Bernie gasped. "Oh, God, Jim, I'm sorry. That just popped out. Your relationship with your son is none of my business."

"It's okay. You and I are friends, aren't we? At least I feel like we are. You've spent a lot of time with Kevin and me the past week or so and I know you weren't asking just to be nosy."

"I'd like to think that you and I are friends and that Kevin and I are, too. But friendship doesn't give me the right to—"

Jim tightened his hold around Bernie, drawing her so close that her breasts pressed against his chest. "I want to be a good father more than anything, but I've made such a mess of my life. I've got a real chance with Kevin now and I don't want to blow it. I think he knows how much he means to me, but I'm not sure. My relationship with my ex-wife has been volatile, to say the least, and she's used Kevin to get back at me. For over six years, she's undermined my relationship with Kevin."

"I don't understand why she would do that. Doesn't she know that by driving a wedge between you and Kevin, she's hurting him just as much as she's hurting you?"

"I'll give Mary Lee the benefit of the doubt and say she doesn't know, but you'd have to know my ex-wife to understand the way she operates. She loves Kevin, and in many ways she's been a good mother. But she doesn't love him as much as she loves herself. If it came to a choice between what she wanted and what Kevin needed—Damn, would you listen to me bad-mouthing a woman who's battling breast cancer and could die. You must think I'm a real jerk."

Bernie lifted her hand from Jim's shoulder and without thinking about what she was doing, caressed his cheek. "I think you're human. Your ex-wife hurt you, then undermined your relationship with your son. You have every right to resent the way she's treated you."

"I want you to know that I've never said anything against Mary Lee to Kevin. I wouldn't do that."

"No, you wouldn't, because you love your son."

Jim cleared his throat. Bernie laid her hand back on Jim's shoulder.

"You know what, Sheriff Granger? I'm beginning to agree with what my son said about you."

Her heartbeat accelerated with excitement. "What did he say?"

"He said, 'Bernie's a really super lady.' He was right. You are."

Oh, God. Oh, God. How should she respond? Don't gush and goo and go all fluttering female on him. "Well, for the record—I think you and Kevin are pretty super, too."

The band ended one romantic jazz number and began another. Jim released Bernie in the interval. "Ready to hit the buffet tables?"

She placed her open palms over her stomach. "I am so ready I may eat a gallon of boiled shrimp all by myself."

Jim slipped his arm around her waist and escorted her off the dance floor. Bernie felt as if she were floating on air. The words to an old song flitted through her mind. Something about this being *the* night and him being *the* one.

Jim hated big parties like this one. He hated wearing a tie and being sociable. He was a blue jeans, beer and chips, kicking-back-with-his-buddies kind of guy. He'd much rather be over at the King Kone wolfing down burgers and fries with Kevin and Bernie than eating gourmet food and drinking champagne with hundreds of people, most of whom he didn't know. But putting in an appearance tonight had been mandatory. After all, Bernie was not only his friend, but his boss. And God knew he owed Brenda and R.B. Granger big time for the way they'd practically adopted Kevin as their grandson.

Jim flushed the urinal, then went over to the sink, turned on the faucets and lathered his hands. He had escaped the music, laughter, loud chatter, and requests to dance from countless women by taking the back stairs to use the second floor men's restroom. The second floor was practically deserted and there had been only one man in the restroom when he arrived. He was alone now and a part of him wished he could hide out in here until it was time to leave. After drying his hands, he checked his watch. Ten till ten. He'd promised himself that he'd stay until eleven, then use Kevin as an excuse to leave.

After dancing with Amy Simms, the DA's wife, and with Deputy Holly Burcham, he'd lost track of Bernie. Then just as he headed out of the ballroom, he'd caught a glimpse of her talking to Reverend Donaldson and couldn't help wondering if Bernie found the new minister more interesting than her sister had. Surely not. The good reverend wasn't the right guy for Bernie any more than Raymond Long was.

When Jim reached out to open the restroom door, it flew open, nearly knocking him down. On the verge of saying something rude and crude to the numbskull coming into the restroom, Jim did a double take when he got a good look at the person.

"This is the men's room," he told Robyn Granger.

She grinned from ear to ear. "I know that, silly." She pointed her index finger into the center of his chest and eased into the room, closing the door behind her. "I followed you up here. I've been trying to get a minute alone with you all evening."

"This is hardly the place for a private conversation."

"The door's closed and we're all alone."

He eyed the door. "Somebody could walk in at any minute. How would you explain being in the men's room?"

She shrugged. "I like to take chances. Live dangerously."

"I don't."

She wrapped her arms around his neck and pressed herself intimately against him.

"Liar." She kissed him.

He clamped his hands down on her shoulders, then put some distance between them by pushing her back a few inches. "Why me? You can have your pick of just about any guy here tonight."

"Then aren't you lucky." She gave him a sultry, I-want-to-fuck-you look.

"Robyn . . ."

Brenda Granger grabbed Bernie's arm and led her out of the ballroom and into a quiet corner in the massive foyer.

"What's going on?" Bernie asked, startled by her mother's sudden request of "We need to talk" seconds before she grabbed her.

"Tell me something," Brenda said. "And I want the truth."

Bernie nodded.

"Are you involved with Jim Norton?"

"What?"

"I said are you—?"

"Jim and I are friends."

"Nothing more?"

Bernie shook her head.

"Oh, sweetie, you've fallen for the guy, haven't you?" Brenda gazed sympathetically at Bernie. "You should have told me. You should have told Robyn."

"My personal relationships aren't any of your business. Besides, you're wrong. I'm not—"

"Bernadette Granger, do not lie to me. I've watched you with Jim all evening. The way you look at him . . . Oh, my sweet girl, it's obvious that you adore him."

"Jim and I are friends. That's all."

"But you want more."

"Mom!"

"We have to tell Robyn how you feel. She's set her sights on Jim and she's determined to . . . well, you know. But if she had any idea that you were in love with him, she'd back off in a heartbeat."

"Don't you dare say anything to Robyn!"

"But if she doesn't know how you feel, she won't realize that if she and Jim become"—Brenda struggled for the correct word—"close, it will break your heart."

"You're being melodramatic, Mother."

"Your father and I have become very fond of Kevin and we both like Jim very much. We approve of him as potential son-in-law material." Brenda patted Bernie's cheek. "You and he looked so good together on the dance floor. You were practically glowing, and I couldn't help noticing how close he held you."

"Jim and I are just friends."

Brenda opened her mouth to respond, but before she uttered a word, another voice interrupted them.

"Hey, Bernie," Kevin called to her from across the foyer. "Have you seen my dad?"

"No, not recently," Bernie told him as he came toward her and her mother.

"I overheard him ask R.B. if there was a men's room upstairs," Brenda said.

"Oh, okay, thanks, Miss Brenda. Can you tell me exactly where the bathroom is?" Kevin asked.

"I'm sure he'll be back down any minute," Brenda said. "It isn't urgent that you find him, is it?"

"Not exactly urgent. It's just that J.D. Simms asked me to sleep over tonight. Since he's been coming over to your house nearly every afternoon and horsing around in the pool with me, we've become buddies. Mr. and Mrs. Simms are leaving any minute now and I need to ask Dad if it's okay for me to go with them."

"Come on, Kevin. I'll show you where the upstairs men's room is," Bernie said.

"Bernie?" Brenda called when Bernie led Kevin toward the staircase.

Bernie glanced over her shoulder. "Yes, Mom?"

"We'll talk later."

Bernie nodded. *No, we will not talk later.*

She and Kevin climbed the spiral staircase; then he followed her down the long hallway toward the men's restroom.

"This is some place," Kevin said. "It's like a mansion out of a movie or something."

"This used to be a private residence, back a hundred years ago. It's been the Adams Landing Country Club all my life. My parents held their wedding reception here forty years ago and the celebration for their twenty-fifth anniversary."

"When you get married, you should have your reception here," Kevin said. "It would be carrying on a family tradition, like your being the sheriff after your dad and granddad were."

"I'll keep that in mind." Bernie paused outside the closed door to the restroom. "Here we are."

"Would you wait around just in case I need somebody to help me talk Dad into letting me spend the night with J.D.?"

"Sure, I'll wait."

"You're the best, Bernie. The best."

Kevin opened the bathroom door, then stopped dead in his tracks.

"What's wrong?" Bernie asked as she came up behind a frozen-to-the-spot Kevin.

When he didn't respond, she followed his gaze, looking directly into the men's restroom.

"Oh, God." Bernie groaned.

Jim had Robyn backed up against the wall. She had her arms around him, her hands cupping his butt. And they were kissing, hot and heavy.

"Dad, what are you doing!"

Jim and Robyn broke apart instantly.

"You're not supposed to be kissing her," Kevin said. "What's Bernie going to think, catching you kissing another woman?"

Jim's startled gaze jumped from Kevin to Bernie. "Kevin, son, I can—"

"Why did you have to go and ruin things?" Kevin screamed at his father. "You ruined things with Mom, and now you've ruined things with Bernie."

Kevin turned and ran down the hall.

Jim rushed to the door. "Kevin. Wait. Please, wait."

Bernie felt numb, as if a sudden violent winter storm had frozen her solid. She glared at her sister, who grinned sheepishly.

"Damn." Jim rubbed his forehead, then glared at Bernie. "Why the hell did you bring him up here?"

Bernie bristled. "Don't you dare take this out on me, Jim Norton. Kevin wanted to find you to ask you if he could spend the night with J.D. Simms. My mother said she thought you'd come up here. I had no idea you hadn't *come* alone."

"I've got to find him and talk to him, to explain." Jim grasped Bernie's shoulders. "I'm sorry. This isn't your fault. It's mine."

"I think I should go with you," Bernie said. "He's awfully upset with you."

"Yeah, I'd appreciate that. I think he's gotten the notion in his head that you and I are more than friends."

"I'll make him understand that he's wrong." *You certainly*

proved to me how wrong I was to hope that tonight might be the beginning of something special between the two of us.

"Want me to go along, too?" Robyn asked.

"No!" Jim and Bernie responded in unison.

Chapter 17

The past three days had been a guilt-ridden exercise in hindsight torment for Jim. If he had it to do over again . . . But what was done, was done. He couldn't change the fact that his son and his boss had caught him making out with his boss's sister. Well, *making out* might be too strong a phrase. He'd tried to turn down Robyn's advances, but she hadn't taken no for an answer. When she'd rubbed herself all over him and practically thrust her tongue down his throat, he had reacted like any normal man would have. He'd kissed her back, even though he knew the woman was trouble and not somebody he wanted to get mixed up with. But to be totally honest, he wasn't sure how far things would have gone if he and Robyn hadn't been interrupted.

Kevin hadn't spoken more than half a dozen words to him since Saturday night and here it was Tuesday afternoon. It didn't help that Mary Lee hadn't called Kevin since her surgery, and when he'd telephoned her, Allen had interceded and said she was resting and couldn't be disturbed. If it hadn't been for Bernie and her parents, Jim wasn't sure what he would have done. When he and Bernie had caught up with

Kevin Saturday night at the country club, they'd taken him outside and tried to explain things to him.

"Your dad and I are just friends," Bernie had said. "He didn't do anything to betray me or you. You know, it's not against the law for a man to kiss a pretty woman."

But no matter how much he and Bernie had tried to explain the situation, Kevin didn't respond, except to finally ask if he could spend the night with J.D. Reluctantly, Jim had agreed. When he'd picked Kevin up at the Simms's house Sunday afternoon, his son had made it perfectly clear that he was still pissed at him.

"I talked to Miss Brenda and asked if I could stay overnight with them for a few nights and she said it would be okay." Kevin had refused to make eye contact with Jim.

He had wanted to tell Kevin no, that they should work things out at home, but he reconsidered, figuring a few days apart might help Kevin come to terms with his anger and disappointment. Once again, Jim felt like a total failure as a father.

And as if his problems with his son weren't bad enough, things between him and Bernie were strained, to say the least. She'd been decidedly cool around him at work and seemed to be deliberately avoiding him. He'd seen her once since they had parted company Saturday night. He wasn't sure if she was pissed at him on Kevin's behalf or if she just didn't like the idea of him fooling around with her sister. The bottom line was that he was in the dog house with the two people he most did not want to disappoint—his son, who meant everything to him, and his boss and newfound friend, whose opinion truly mattered to him.

Robyn had called him a couple of times on Sunday, both times on the pretense that she was concerned about him. Maybe she was. He didn't know, didn't care. He was attracted to Robyn the way he'd be attracted to any good-looking woman, but he didn't have any real feelings for her and he seriously doubted that she had any for him.

Jim had woken up with a headache this morning. He'd drank a little too much Jack Daniel's last night, so the headache was his own damn fault. As he sat behind his desk, rubbing his temples and berating himself for overindulging, his phone rang.

He grabbed the receiver off the base. "Captain Norton here."

"Captain Norton, this is Derek Lawrence. I have the profile of your killer ready. Do you prefer that I fax it or e-mail it?"

"Whichever you'd rather do. And thanks. I appreciate this."

"Thank your friend Griffin Powell."

"Yeah, I'll do that."

"Captain Norton?"

"Yes?"

"I believe the man who has killed the two women in your area and kidnapped a third is more than likely the same man who committed the similar murders in the other southeastern states over the past six years," Derek said. "There's a good chance that Heather Stevens was his first victim, and either all the other women have reminded him of her or she and the others all remind him of someone from his past."

"I figured as much."

"There's one other thing . . ." Derek paused. "It's apparent that he's killing more frequently now, and that's not likely to change. He will continue killing until he's caught, and he's probably not going to put much, if any, time between the murder of one woman and the abduction of another."

"Not what I wanted to hear, but what I expected."

"I'll fax my report to you." He called out the fax number

Jim had given him to confirm it was correct, then said good-bye.

Jim hit the OFF button on the phone, then dialed the sheriff's office. Lisa Wiley answered on the third ring. "This is Jim Norton. I need to speak to the sheriff on official business."

He'd added the bit about official business because he wasn't sure Bernie would take his call otherwise. Not that he'd called her since Saturday night, but all things considered, he didn't know how she would react.

"Jim, what's up?" Bernie asked.

Well, at least she'd called him Jim and not Captain Norton. "Derek Lawrence is faxing our killer's profile to me and I thought you might want to come over so we can take a look at it together."

"I'll be over in about five minutes. Put on a fresh pot of coffee."

"I'll go do that now. See you in five minutes." When she hung up, he smiled. She'd sounded like her old self, not angry or upset. *But don't assume you two can go back to where you were before the Robyn incident. You'll have to rebuild her trust in you, just as you'll have to rebuild it with Kevin.*

Both Ron and John were working other assignments today and were out and about, so when Jim walked into the outer office, he expected to find it empty. Instead, he found Robyn Granger standing there in skintight jeans, a tank top, and sandals. She offered him a let's-be-friends smile.

"What are you doing here?" he asked on his way to the coffeemaker.

"I came by to apologize. Again."

"That's not necessary." He lifted the nearly empty coffeepot and took it into the adjacent bathroom.

"I talked to Kevin this morning over at Mom and Dad's,"

Robyn said. "I told him that what happened between us Saturday night was all my fault."

Jim dumped the black liquid into the sink and rinsed out the pot and then the sink. "You didn't have to do that."

"Oh, yes, I did. I had orders from Mom to do what I could to make things right between you and Kevin."

"Did you do any good?" Jim refilled the pot with fresh, cool water and came back into the outer office.

"I think so. Well, maybe. A little."

"Thanks." Jim put a new filter in the coffeemaker and measured the ground coffee, then poured the water into the reservoir.

"Mind if I ask you a question?"

"Depends." Jim turned to face Robyn.

"Did you leave your ex-wife or did she leave you?"

"I left her."

"And you filed for divorce?"

"Yeah, why do you ask?"

"My bet is that you wouldn't have left her and filed for divorce without a really good reason. Right?"

Jim narrowed his gaze. "What's this all about?"

"It's about the fact that your son blames you for the divorce. He thinks it's all your fault. If that's not true, why haven't you told him?"

"Because I will not bad-mouth his mother. She is his mother and he loves her."

Smiling, Robyn shook her head. "Jim Norton, you're a good man. Much too good for the likes of me." She walked over and kissed his cheek.

Naturally, Bernie chose that moment to arrive—earlier than the five minutes she'd told him. When she saw Robyn kissing Jim, she halted in the open doorway.

"Excuse me. I didn't mean to—"

"It's not what you think." Robyn turned to face her sister,

a pleasant smile on her face. "Not this time." She glanced at Jim and sighed. "If you ever change your mind about the two of us, give me a call."

Jim didn't respond; he was too busy studying Bernie's face, trying to discern her reaction. Other than the fact she wasn't smiling, he couldn't tell if she was upset, disappointed, concerned or what.

"See you later, big sister," Robyn said as she headed for the door.

"Yeah, later." Bernie spoke to her sister, but kept her gaze on Jim.

As soon as Robyn left, Bernie closed the door and walked into the outer office.

"Have you received the fax from Derek Lawrence?" she asked.

"Not yet, but it should be coming through soon." Jim nodded to the coffeemaker. "It's perking. Why don't you go on into my office and I'll bring us both a cup as soon as it's ready."

A phone rang twice, then the fax machine clicked in and began processing the message.

"You get the coffee," Bernie said. "And I'll get the fax."

Jim nodded. "Bernie?"

With her back to him as she walked toward the fax machine positioned on a small stand between John's and Ron's desks, she paused. "Hmm . . . ?"

"About Robyn and me . . ."

Bernie's shoulders tensed as she continued walking toward the fax machine. "You and Robyn are none of my business."

"That's just it—there is no Robyn and me. There really never was."

Bernie stood over the fax machine as the report from Derek Lawrence printed out.

When she didn't respond to his declaration, Jim wondered if he should elaborate or just let it drop. He watched the coffeemaker as the liquid dripped into the glass pot. *Come on, will you, fill up as quick as you can.*

The fax machine clicked off just about the time the coffee-pot filled almost to the rim. Jim glanced over at Bernie and saw her collecting the faxed pages. He turned over two clean cups, lifted the pot and poured the coffee.

He and Bernie met at the partially open door to his office. He stood back and waited for her to enter.

"Take my chair," he told her.

When she sat in his chair and laid the thin stack of papers on the desk, he placed both cups of coffee on his desk, side by side, then dragged up another chair. He sat down beside Bernie and picked up his cup.

She eased her cup to her lips, took a couple of sips, and then set down the cup before focusing on the profile. After she scanned the first page, she handed it to Jim.

"Mr. Lawrence has pegged our serial killer as an orga-nized, violent offender," Bernie said. "No surprise there. Highly intelligent, socially and sexually competent."

Jim read the first page. "Controlled moods. Maintains a stereotypical masculine image, is charming. Possibly an only child who suffered some type of abuse as a child or teenager."

Bernie read aloud. "This type usually moves the body from the murder scene and disposes of the body to advertise the crime." Bernie continued reading, then handed Jim the second page. "He's got our guy down pat. It all fits." She gave Jim the third and final page of the report.

Jim read over the listing of other characteristics. Plans the offense. Personalizes the victim. Controls the crime scene. Requires the victim to be submissive. Uses restraints. Acts aggressively. Moves body. Removes weapon. Leaves little evidence.

"Our guy is definitely power/control oriented," Jim said.

"Lawrence believes he tells his victims what to say during the assaults in order to recreate previously fantasized scenarios with idealized partners."

"Lawrence also theorizes that our killer keeps records— writings, drawings, photographs." Bernie closed her eyes and shivered. "Thomasina Hardy has been missing for thirteen days and we're no closer to finding her than we were the night she disappeared."

"Our boy's smart. He's out there laughing at us. He thinks he's invincible."

"What good is this profile if we don't have even one suspect?" Bernie wrapped her hands around her coffee cup.

"It can help us rule out quite a lot of men," Jim said. "Lawrence thinks our guy is young, under thirty-five, highly intelligent, possibly with some college or even a degree, and that he's a mobile killer, that he moves around."

"So what do we do—interview every man in Adams County under thirty-five who is intelligent, educated, and charming?"

"I think we need to find out more about the victims in the other states, starting with Heather Stevens and Shannon Elmore."

"You've already talked to the lead detective on those cases, what more can you do?"

"I can talk to him again, ask him more questions. My guess is he knows more than he realizes. Things that might shed some light on who our killer is."

"So call him."

"I did first thing this morning. I'm just waiting for him to return my call."

Bernie lifted the cup to her lips and drank. "You make good coffee."

Jim grinned. "You make a good friend. One that I don't want to lose."

When she didn't look at him or respond, he clamped his hand down on her shoulder. She tensed. "Bernie?"

She lifted her head and looked at him. "You haven't lost me. We're still friends."

"Good friends?" he asked.

"I think we're headed in that direction."

"I'm not going to be dating your sister, so if you're worried about me chasing after Robyn, don't be. I know you were concerned about my using her and—"

Bernie laughed and shook her head.

"What's so funny?" he asked as he lifted his hand from her shoulder.

"You are. I was never concerned about your using Robyn. Don't you think I know that my sister is the user and not the usee in each of her relationships. I was worried that she'd break your heart."

"Were you now?"

"I was. I worry about my friends."

"That's good to know."

"Dad tells me that Kevin is still upset with you. What are you going to do about mending fences with your son?"

Jim raked his hand through his hair and reared back in his chair. "Damned if I know. I love that boy more than anything on earth, and yet all I seem to do is hurt and disappoint him. I can't believe he walked in on Robyn and me. What were the odds of that happening? And I don't know where he got the idea that there was something going on between you and me."

"The three of us have spent a great deal of time together lately and we've had a lot of fun. Kevin and I have a marvelous rapport. I believe he liked the idea that if his dad was going to have a girlfriend, she'd be somebody he genuinely liked and someone who felt the same way about him."

"It makes sense. You're the kind of woman most kids would like to have for a mother."

"Well, thank you, Captain Norton."

Jim chuckled. "So, should we return to the way things were—you and Kevin and me? Or would the three of us spending more time together feed this fantasy he has of you and me as a couple?"

"That's a difficult question. I don't know. Maybe we should both talk to him again. Together."

"Tonight?"

"Tonight's fine with me. Why don't I call Mom and tell her that you and I are coming to dinner, and that afterward we plan to talk to Kevin about our relationship."

"Thanks."

"For what?" she asked.

"For being my friend."

He couldn't go to her until tonight. They would make love for the final time, and then he would say good-bye. She'd be heartbroken when he told her that he no longer loved her, but she wouldn't be surprised. She had to know what a disappointment she'd been to him. Poor Thomasina. She had tried so hard, done everything he'd asked her to do, and yet she hadn't measured up. None of them had measured up to his ideal. To his perfect woman.

Perhaps Abby would be different. She wasn't classically beautiful the way some of the others had been, but she was lovely in a sultry, earthy way. And she was older, already thirty, but still young enough. And she had the kind of body that men had wet dreams about. He fantasized about sucking on her big tits. Licking, sucking, biting. Just the thought of her whimpering with pleasure and pain excited him. She was the type who would enjoy variety. Ass fucking. Blow jobs.

But he couldn't begin his courtship, his seduction of Abby Miller, until he ended his relationship with Thomasina.

He sat and watched the students as they walked from the building, some preparing for another class, others heading for their vehicles. It was such a delicious little coincidence that Jacque and Stephanie had both attended the community college and that Thomasina had taught here. And now there was Abby, another night school student, who'd signed up for classes she seldom attended as a smoke screen to cover up her illicit affair.

He smiled, thinking about how the sheriff's department was wasting time trying to figure out what it meant that all the victims were somehow connected to the college. He hadn't deliberately set out to choose women who were students or even teachers at the school. But it had worked out to his advantage, giving the authorities a red herring.

If only Sheriff Granger and her hotshot chief deputy knew that there was a far more important reason they should be looking at Adams County Junior College than the obvious.

He would outsmart the local law just as he'd outsmarted the others—in Georgia, in Tennessee, in North Carolina, and in South Carolina. He was a smart man. He'd been a smart boy. But women didn't appreciate men with brains, not any more than girls appreciated boys with brains.

Don't go back there. Don't remember what happened.

She had been the prettiest, most popular girl in school and he had worshipped her when she hadn't even known he was alive. The first time she smiled at him, he'd nearly died on the spot. And when she spoke to him one day, he'd been speechless at first, and then tongue-tied. She'd been so sweet, so friendly, so nice.

He could see her clearly in his mind's eye—slender and dark haired, with big brown eyes and a smile so warm that it could have melted the polar ice caps. She always wore pink lipstick and nail polish, not a gaudy hot pink, but a pale, lady-like shade. Even now, he could still smell her delicate perfume, a flowery gardenia fragrance. And he'd never forget the delicate gold ankle bracelet she wore every day, whether she was in slacks, shorts, or a skirt. Her parents had given her a string of real pearls for her sixteenth birthday, and whenever there was a special event at school where everyone had to dress up, she wore her pearls.

He had loved her with all the innocence and adolescent passion of an inexperienced sixteen-year-old boy. A virgin. A nerd. A bookworm.

Emotion tightened his throat. The memories were bittersweet. Ecstasy in the beginning, and then a torment beyond bearing in the end. Tears clouded his vision.

Her laughter echoed inside his mind. No matter how many years had passed, how hard he'd tried to forget, he could never escape that mocking laughter.

Thomasina lay beside him, as silent and still as death. After raping her in the anus with the wooden phallus until she'd wept from the pain, he had turned her over and taken her with brutal force. No matter how much she tried to please him, he was never satisfied. He punished her if she fought him and yet he punished her even when she obeyed his every command. He enjoyed tormenting her, derived some sadistic pleasure from hurting her.

In the quiet stillness, with her abductor asleep at her side, the sound of her own pleading voice echoed inside her head. She had told him repeatedly what he demanded to hear.

"I love you. I love you more than anything or anyone. Please make love to me."

Cutting her gaze in his direction, she noted that his eyes were closed and his mouth was open. Lifting her head a few inches, she dared a closer glance at his handsome face.

Thomasina's heartbeat accelerated. He was asleep. She was awake. Lifting up her arms, she stared at her unbound wrists; then she arched first one foot and then the other, reminding herself that she was not shackled.

Rising to a sitting position, she paused, took a deep, steadying breath, then gazed at his naked body. A perfect male body.

After easing her legs off the side of the bed, she placed her feet on the floor and sat there, her arms wrapped in a comforting hug around her bruised breasts. She had lost count of how many days he had held her prisoner in this underground hellhole. There was no way to tell day from night. Time had no meaning to her. She counted her life not by minutes and hours, but by the number of times he visited her. And with each subsequent visit, she lost more and more of herself to the fear of waiting and wondering when he would return. If only she could get away from this madman.

She rose to her feet and took a few tentative steps away from the bed.

He made an odd, snorting noise.

Her heart leapt to her throat. Terror zinged along her nerve endings. She glanced over her shoulder. He was snoring. Relief spread through her, relaxing her taut muscles.

Tiptoeing, she crept to the foot of the bed, then rounded it, her gaze fixed on the stairs that led to the only door, the only means of escape. But he kept the door locked, so what good would it do her to climb those stairs?

Suddenly she stepped on something lying on the floor. When she glanced down in the semidarkness, she saw his shirt and slacks crumpled in a heap where he'd discarded them. She lifted her foot, leaned over and stared at the small metallic object shining there on the cool concrete floor.

It's a key.

Oh my God, the door key must have fallen out of his pants pocket when he took off his clothes.

Listening to the sound of his soft snoring, she assured herself that he was still asleep. Bending her knees, she crouched down, reached out and pinched the key between her thumb and forefinger. Her heartbeat drummed in her ears; perspiration coated her palms.

Her captor was sound asleep. She had the key to the door. If she could manage to climb the steps and unlock the door without waking him, she could escape.

For the first time since she had awakened in this dark, dank prison—days ago? weeks ago?—Thomasina felt that there was actually a chance she might get away, that she might live.

With the key in her hand and hope in her heart, she made her way across the room to the stairs. Before taking that first step upward, she paused and looked back at the snoring man. Lifting her foot, she hesitated; then when the stairs didn't creak, she followed one cautious step with another, increasing her speed until she practically ran up the last few steps to the door. Trembling and sweating profusely, she narrowed her gaze on the door lock, then aimed the key at the lock. Her fingers quivered so badly that she almost dropped the key. Clasping it tightly, she shoved the key into the lock. Her chest ached. Her breathing came in ragged gulps. She smelled her own sweat mixed with the heavy odor of sex.

All she heard was her own breathing. All she saw was the key in her hand.

Turn the key, unlock the door and open it to the outside world. Then run like hell.

She turned the key and twisted the knob. The lock didn't budge.

She turned the key in the opposite direction.

Click.

She emitted a whooshing breath of relief as she grasped the doorknob and turned it.

The door creaked as she opened it.

Damn!

Instinctively turning around to check and make sure the

noise hadn't awakened him, Thomasina gasped when she came face to face with her captor.

"Where are you going, darling?" he asked.

She whirled around and yanked open the door, trying her best to get away from him before he grabbed her. Thomasina stepped forward as she shoved on the door and managed to open it halfway before he grabbed her, flung one arm around her waist and pressed her back against his chest.

Screaming and crying, her instinct for survival strong, she fought him like a wildcat when he jerked her backward and slammed the door shut. There at the top of the stairs, he held her so tightly that she could barely breathe, held her as she wriggled and squirmed and clawed at him.

She'd been so close, had almost escaped.

Tears streamed down her cheeks.

Finally, when all the fight had gone out of her, he bent his head and kissed her shoulder. Then he bit her neck. She yelped in pain.

"You failed the test," he whispered in her ear.

"What?"

"You've told me again and again how much you love me, but I've had my doubts from the very beginning. So I devised a plan to test you, to allow you to prove your love."

Sobbing, trembling, immobilized by fear, Thomasina realized that he hadn't been asleep at all, that he had been faking. "The key?" she asked.

"When I took off my clothes, I placed it right where you could find it," he told her. "If you'd left the key lying on the floor, if you hadn't tried to escape, I would have known you truly loved me."

A test? The whole thing had been a test! And she had failed.

There would be no escape. She was trapped.

"There can't be a happily ever after for us," he said. "You've ruined any chance we might have had."

Icy fear chilled Thomasina. The certainty of her own death confronted her.

"Please . . ."

"Please what?" With his fingers threaded in her hair, he yanked her head back and kissed her cheek. "Do you want me to set you free, my darling?"

"Yes," she replied, knowing that there was only one way she could ever escape from this madman.

Chapter 18

Abby Miller noticed the plastic bag hanging on the door-knob of the back entrance to the Kut and Kurl as soon as she arrived at her beauty shop on Wednesday morning. She and the other operators parked in the back, leaving the front parking slots available for customers. Only on Wednesdays did Abby arrive before the others, one of the perks of being the owner. But Amy Simms had a standing appointment at eight-thirty every Wednesday for a nail fill-in and a pedi-cure. The D.A.'s wife was a busy lady and couldn't drop by just any old time, so since Amy was a regular customer who gave generous tips, Abby did her best to always accommo-date her.

When she reached the door, she studied the bag curiously, wondering if one of her sales reps had come by after closing last night and left the bag. It was just a plain white plastic sack, no logo or print of any kind on it. *Odd.*

Changing her key ring from her right hand to her left, she lifted the bag from the knob, slipped it over her hand and onto her wrist, then put the key ring back in her right hand and inserted a key into the lock. Once inside, she closed and locked the door from within, then headed for the kitchenette/ lounge, one of two rooms in the beauty shop that were off limits to the customers, the other being the crowded store-room. After dropping her key chain in her purse and deposit-ing her purse and the plastic bag on the small dining table, she went about her Wednesday morning routine—making a fresh pot of coffee, checking the air-conditioning tempera-ture and resetting it for the day, then unlocking the front door and removing the CLOSED sign. While the coffee brewed, she took a diet cola from the small, compact fridge, snapped the pop-up lid and took a deep swallow of the sweet liquid. In the winter, she drank coffee, but not in the summer. She pre-ferred to get her caffeine from colas when the temperatures rose to about eighty. But she knew that Amy Simms expected fresh brewed coffee to be waiting for her when she arrived.

As Abby sat down in one of the comfy vinyl chairs and took another sip of cola, she eyed the plastic sack on the table. She reached over, grabbed it, placed it in her lap, and then opened it. There were two items inside—a small square envelope and a larger manila envelope. She removed the small envelope first. Her name graced the front, printed in large black letters—Abby. She opened the envelope, slipped the one-page note out and unfolded it.

I worship you from afar, my beautiful Abby.

A nervous tickle fluttered in her belly. How sweet. Did she have a secret admirer? It wasn't unreasonable to assume that she did, was it? Ron Hensley wasn't the only man in town interested in her. Guys flirted with her all the time. A few had even propositioned her since Ricky Wayne's unit had been deployed to the Middle East. And doing her best to be the faithful wife, she had turned down every one of them—everybody except Ron.

She read the note again and wondered who had written it.

Definitely someone with a romantic flair. After dropping the note and envelope back into the bag, she pulled the larger envelope out and ripped off one end. When she turned the envelope upside down and shook it several times, a single sheet floated out. She grabbed it before it hit the floor, then turned the blank side over and gasped when she saw the sketch on the other side. An ink sketch of her. A talented artist had captured everything about her, from the slight crook in her nose to the sultry way she smiled. Whoever had created the sketch was someone who knew her, had observed her, even studied her.

A gentle wave of apprehension washed over Abby, making her extremely curious about the author of the note—the artist. Her feminine instincts told her that this guy was no ordinary redneck good old boy, so that narrowed down the field considerably here in Adams County.

Abby folded the sketch and stuffed it and the ripped manila envelope back in the white plastic sack; then she opened her purse and put the sack inside, shoving it to the bottom of her large carryall shoulder bag. She took another sip of cola, then checked the wall clock. Eight-twenty-seven. Amy should be here any minute. Abby removed a lavender nylon work jacket from the pile of clean, protective shirts/ jackets, snapped it from midchest to just below her waist, and then picked up her cola and headed out into the shop to her workstation.

The telephone rang. Abby jumped.

Get hold of yourself. It's just the telephone. Don't let your imagination go haywire. Just because the unexpected note and sketch unnerved you as much as it flattered you, that's no reason to be so nervous.

"Kut and Kurl. Abby speaking."

"Hello, Abby."

She didn't recognize the voice and thought it sounded odd. "Hello. How may I help you?"

"Did you get my note?" The deep, muted baritone voice asked.

Abby's heartbeat went wild. "Yes, I did. And the sketch, too."

"Did you like the sketch?"

"Yes, it's wonderful. You're very talented."

"Thank you, but I had the perfect subject."

A man who knows the right thing to say.

"Who are you?" Abby asked.

"I'm your secret admirer."

Abby giggled. "I figured that out. But why? If you're interested, then you should make yourself known. Stop by the shop today around six and introduce yourself. Or do I already know you?"

"I will reveal my identity to you when the time is right. But for now . . . think about me and about what I long to do—touch you, whisper love sonnets in your ear, fulfill your every fantasy."

Abby's mouth gaped wide. She'd never had a man talk to her this way—romantically seductive. Guys usually talked dirty to her, told her they wanted to fuck her in no uncertain terms, but this guy—her secret admirer—was good. Hell, he was great. She'd be thinking about him all day.

"I wish I knew who you were," she said.

"You will, very soon, my beautiful Abby."

The dial tone hummed in her ear. Sighing, she returned the receiver to the base. Standing there daydreaming about her fantasy lover, she didn't hear Amy Simms enter the shop. When Amy called her name, Abby jumped as if she'd been shot.

"What's wrong?" Amy asked. "You're awfully jumpy."

"Sorry. Nothing's wrong. I was just thinking about a very special man."

"Ricky Wayne, no doubt. You must miss him something

awful. I know if my Jerry Dale was off a world away fighting in some horrible war, I'd be half out of my mind."

"Hmm . . . I do miss Ricky Wayne."

But there is no law that says I have to be miserable while he's away. And if I can keep his mama from finding out about my affair with Ron, maybe I can juggle having two lovers at the same time.

Bernie sat on the side of her parents' backyard pool, Kevin at her side, both of them drinking her mom's delicious raspberry tea and absorbing the last rays of the early evening sunlight. Here in northeastern Alabama in July, it didn't get good and dark until nearly eight-thirty, and it was just now six-thirty.

She remembered when her folks had put in the pool; it was the summer she'd turned eight and Robyn was a babe of barely four. She'd grown up swimming like a fish, getting brown as gingerbread in the summer, and she and Robyn being the envy of the other kids in the neighborhood. Almost every year, her mother had given her and Robyn a joint swim party for their birthdays. Bernie's was May thirtieth and Robyn's was June fifth.

"My dad's got a date tonight," Kevin said, his gaze fixed on his feet submerged in the water on the shallow end of the pool. "It's not with your sister, Robyn. It's with that woman deputy, Holly Burcham."

"Yes, I know. Holly's a lot of fun. Jim should have a good time." *A real good time.* Holly had never met a man she didn't like and she had a thing for her fellow officers. She'd been through just about all the single guys in the department and a few married ones, too. Lucky for Holly, none of the married men's wives had complained. Either they didn't know or had chosen to look the other way.

More than once, Bernie had wondered if she'd been able to just look the other way when Ryan had been unfaithful, would they still be married? Would they have a child or two by now? But there was no point in wasting time wondering about what might have been. She wasn't the type to forgive and forget infidelity. She took marriage vows seriously and expected her husband to do the same. As for having children, that might not ever happen for her even if she did remarry one of these days. She'd had two miscarriages and the doctors couldn't promise her that if she got pregnant again she could carry a baby to full-term.

"Bernie?"

"Huh?"

"I wish my dad had a date with you tonight."

Bernie forced a smile. "Kevin, we've tried to explain—your dad and I are just friends."

"Friends date sometimes, don't they?"

"Sometimes."

"I liked it when the three of us were spending time together. Didn't you like being with us?" Kevin glanced at her, then looked away quickly.

Bernie set her iced tea glass down on the tiled patio floor behind herself and put her arm around Kevin's shoulders. "If I didn't like being with you, I wouldn't be here right now. And I can't think of any place I'd rather be."

"Honest?" Kevin lifted his head, looked right at her and smiled as if she'd just given him the greatest present on earth.

She hugged him to herself. "Honest."

Kevin jumped up, bouncing with enthusiasm. "I'll race you to the other end of the pool."

Bernie leaped to her feet. "You're on. But what does the winner get?"

"Hmm . . . What do you want if you win?"

She wasn't sure exactly how to word her request. "I want you to stop being angry with your father. He loves you and he'd do anything for you. He'd be spending all his free time with you if you'd just stop pouting and go home."

"Dad can be a real dope," Kevin said. "If he prefers your sister or that Holly woman to you, he's nuts. But what could I expect from him since he left my mom and she's a wonderful . . ." Kevin swallowed and looked away.

Bernie knew he was on the verge of tears and would be terribly embarrassed if she saw him crying. "Your mom will call you when she feels better. She just doesn't want you to hear her sounding weak and sick. That's the way moms are." Bernie was lying, of course. She had no idea why Mary Lee hadn't spoken to Kevin since her surgery, which Jim had told them had been successful and the doctors had explained to Mary Lee's husband that her cancer hadn't spread. Despite how physically weak Mary Lee might be or how emotionally devastated she was at losing a breast and facing months of treatment, she was still a mother, with a son who needed her reassurance that everything would be all right. As far as Bernie was concerned, it wasn't too much to ask that Kevin's mother give him that reassurance.

Kevin cleared his throat. "Yeah, I know Mom will call. She's got to take care of herself right now and not worry about me or anybody else."

"And if you need anything, all you have to do is ask your dad. You know what—I love my mother very much and she's the greatest mom ever," Bernie said. "But I'm a daddy's girl. My dad is my best friend. Your dad could be your best friend if you'd give him the chance."

Kevin grunted. "Yeah, I guess so." He glanced at Bernie and grinned. "Are you ready for our race?"

"I'm ready if you are. So, if I win this swim meet, you'll go home and give your dad a chance to prove to you how important you are to him?"

"Yeah, okay. And if I win, I want you to ask me and Dad over to your house for supper again."

Bernie blew out a deep breath in an exaggerated expression. "Well, I suppose I can agree to that, but you're asking for an awful lot. It will be sheer misery to spend a whole evening with you and Jim."

Kevin laughed and so did Bernie. "If it's a tie, we'll both be winners." She winked at him, then dove into the pool, Kevin a millisecond behind her.

Bernie deliberately slowed when they reached the far end of the pool, just enough so that she and Kevin ended their race neck and neck. Without a photo finish, no one could say who came in first. Bernie lifted herself out of the pool and sat on the edge. Kevin came out right alongside her, smiling as if he'd won the race.

"It was a tie, wasn't it?" Kevin said.

"I believe it was."

"That means we both have to pay off on the bet. So I'll go home with Dad tomorrow evening, and then you'll invite us over to your house this weekend, right?"

"Right."

Bernie ruffled Kevin's dark, wet hair and had to restrain herself from encompassing him in a motherly bear hug. She had discovered one more thing Jim and Kevin had in common: Both Norton men were very easy to love.

Wearing a pair of khaki pants and a short-sleeved, navy blue polo shirt that he'd put on for his date with Holly Burcham, Jim stood on the Grangers' porch and rang the doorbell. When no one answered, he walked around to the side gate, opened it and entered the backyard. He saw Kevin first, sitting at the wicker and glass table under the huge umbrella. Before Kevin noticed him, Bernie called out from the back steps. Jim glanced her way and did a double take. She was coming out the backdoor and was carrying a tray laden

with food. Jim couldn't take his eyes off her—off every incredible inch of her five-nine body. She wore a red one-piece
bathing suit that did absolutely nothing to disguise her
knockout figure. She was a tall, large woman, with curves in
all the right places. Long legs that went on forever. Full thighs
and hips, narrow waist, and high, round breasts.

"Jim!" Bernie gasped. "What are you doing here? I
thought you had a date with Holly."

Jim swallowed hard. "Uh, I did. But I had to call her and
cancel. Something's come up. Sheriff's department business." *Yeah, and something else is going to come up if I don't
stop staring at Bernie's body.*

She walked over, set the tray down on the table and
glanced from Jim to Kevin. "It must be something . . . Oh,
God, please don't tell me that it's about Thomasina."

Jim nodded. "Kevin, maybe you'd better go inside for a
few minutes."

Kevin frowned. "Do I have to?"

"Please go inside and call my father's cell phone and tell
him to come home right away. Jim and I are going to have to
leave in a few minutes." Bernie looked from Kevin to Jim.
"Right?"

Jim nodded. "Yeah, I'm afraid so."

Kevin responded immediately to her request, and as soon
as he went inside the house, she turned to Jim. "Did someone find Thomasina?"

"Yeah, a motorist crossing Sunflower Creek just happened to notice a body lying on the bank, about ten feet from
the water's edge. The deputy who took the call got in touch
with me a few minutes after he arrived on the scene. He says
he's pretty sure it's Thomasina Hardy, says she looks like the
picture her mother gave us. She's naked. Posed. Her throat's
been slit."

Bernie clenched her jaw. "Give me five minutes to get on

some clothes. Dad should be home by then. He dropped Mom by Wednesday night church services on his way to play pool with some of his buddies."

Just as she started to walk away, Jim grabbed her arm to halt her. She spun around and gave him a questioning look.

"If this guy holds true to form since he killed Stephanie Preston, he'll start a new courtship soon," Jim said. "He might have already chosen his next victim."

"Oh, God, I know." Bernie closed her eyes, absorbing the knowledge that another woman had been murdered and yet another unknown woman was in mortal danger. "I'm the sheriff. It's my job to protect the people of Adams County. I'm doing a hell of a job, aren't I?"

"Stop beating yourself up, honey. Nobody could do a better job." Instinctively, without thinking about what he was doing, Jim slipped his hand around Bernie's waist and pulled her into his arms. She went willingly and even allowed him to hug her for a few seconds before she pulled away from him.

"Come on in and talk to Kevin while I get out of this bathing suit."

"I'm not sure Kevin will talk to me. He wasn't very responsive when we tried to talk to him last night." Jim followed Bernie, appreciating the view from behind. He'd never noticed how her hips swayed, how her butt moved up and down, how downright sexy she was.

But she's not interested in you as anything other than a friend. She's made that perfectly clear. A few minutes ago, when you had her in your arms, she could have stayed there a while longer, but she couldn't wait to get away from you. Face it, Norton, you couldn't get to first base with Bernie if you wanted to.

And strangely enough, he suddenly realized that he wanted to.

*   *   *

County coroner, Morris Claunch, confirmed what Jim and Bernie already suspected—Thomasina Hardy had been raped, tortured and ultimately murdered. The killer's MO seemed identical to Stephanie Preston's murderer. No surprise there.

Bernie had called in six deputies to protect the crime scene and keep onlookers at bay. Word had spread quickly in Adams County, and by the time the ABI Crime Scene Response Unit arrived, Bernie estimated that the crowd on and around the bridge crossing Sunflower Creek had grown from half a dozen when she and Jim had arrived to probably forty people now. After this, there would be no way to keep the general public from knowing that there was a serial killer loose in northeast Alabama.

Charlie Patterson drove up around eight-forty and officially took over the investigation. R.B. Granger showed up around nine.

"You've got a real circus on your hands, gal," her dad told her. "You might ought to call in a few more deputies for crowd control."

"I will, if I think we need them. But right now, we have everything under control."

"Just making a suggestion." R.B. turned from her and shook hands with Agent Patterson. "We've been seeing way too much of you lately, Charlie."

Charlie grimaced. "Yeah, it's bad, R.B. No way we can deny the facts. We've got ourselves a psychopath on our hands."

Bernie suddenly felt insignificant, as if she were nothing more than R.B.'s kid and he was still the sheriff. Her father didn't mean to undermine her authority, or by his mere presence here at the crime scene imply to everyone that his daughter couldn't handle the situation without his help. He thought he was helping, that he was being supportive. After all, why shouldn't she appreciate him sharing his vast knowledge and years of experience with her on a major case such as this?

"Sheriff," Deputy Dennison called.

"Yeah?" R.B. and Bernie responded simultaneously.

"Over here." Bernie motioned to the deputy who was bouncing his gaze back and forth between her and her dad.

"Sorry." R.B. chuckled. "I keep forgetting my kid's now the sheriff."

Deputy Dennison smiled and nodded at R.B., then made his way straight to where Bernie and Jim stood with Ron Hensley, the three of them watching the ABI Crime Unit at work.

"What's up?" Bernie asked.

"There's a reporter and a photographer here from the *Daily Reporter* and crews from two Huntsville TV stations have shown up. How are we supposed to handle them? What do you want us to do?"

"Great, just great," Bernie mumbled under her breath. "Don't let any of them get beyond the barricade, and do not answer any questions."

"Yes, ma'am." Deputy Dennison stood there fidgeting, apparently not knowing whether to stay or go.

"And tell them that the sheriff's department will make a statement at"—she glanced at her watch—"I'll brief the press no later than eleven o'clock, before then if possible."

"Yes, ma'am."

"That's all, Deputy."

Dennison all but clicked his heels as he turned and headed toward the barricade up above the creek near the roadside. Bernie groaned silently when she looked at the crowd again.

"They'll be coming in by the busloads if we don't do something," she said.

"Why don't you order roadblocks half a mile in each direction?" Jim suggested.

"Good idea." Bernie looked at Ron. "Go up there and announce to all those concerned citizens that we're blocking off a one-mile section of County Road One-fifty-seven immediately, and if anyone doesn't want to get delayed leaving later, they'd better go now."

"Sure thing," Ron said. Then just as he walked off, he stopped dead still and cursed. He turned around and came back over to Bernie and Jim. "Thomasina Hardy's sister and brother-in-law are up there in that crowd. I just saw her sister." Ron gritted his teeth tightly and took a couple of deep breaths. "When I dated Thomasina, I got to know the family pretty well. They're good folks."

"Look, why don't I handle explaining to the crowd about the roadblocks while you make arrangements to get them set up," Jim said to Bernie. "And since Ron knows Thomasina's family, let him talk to her sister and brother-in-law."

Bernie nodded, then as Jim turned to leave, she called, "Wait just a minute, Jim." She looked at Ron. "If the sister wants to speak to me personally, let me know and we'll work out something. We'll need someone to ID the body. See if the brother-in-law will do that."

"I dread talking to her sister. Amanda and Thomasina were really close." Ron cleared his throat. "Thomasina deserved better than this. She was a nice person. Too good for me, that's for sure."

Bernie patted Ron on the shoulder. As soon as he headed up the embankment toward the bridge, she turned to Jim.

"I have to decide what to tell the press. How much information do I release to the public? Where do I draw the line between what the public needs to know and what I need to keep under wraps?"

"Good question." Jim glanced over at R.B., who was dogging every step Charlie Patterson made, then looked at

Bernie. "You're second-guessing yourself because your father is here. Stop doing that. You don't need his opinion or his approval to make a decision. Trust your own gut instincts."

"Can I do that—trust my own instincts?"

"I trust your instincts," Jim told her. "I trust you."

The power behind his statement overwhelmed her. She didn't know how to respond. *Get a grip. He didn't say I love you. He said I trust you.* But she knew, deep in her soul, that trust between two people was the second most powerful emotion. You could love someone, but if you didn't trust them, you had nothing.

Tears threatened the false calm she tried so hard to project, not just to Jim, but to everyone here tonight. "Thanks."

Jim looked at her as if he wanted to touch her, as if he'd like to hold her, comfort her, reassure her. And oddly enough, she felt his caress—the tender touch that he expressed through his gaze.

"I won't share any specific details," Bernie said. "I'll say that we suspect a link in the murders of Jacque Reeves in Jackson County and the murders of Stephanie Preston and Thomasina Hardy. I'll try to avoid the use of the term *serial killer*. I don't think the fact that all three were young, attractive brunettes is a secret, so I'll mention that."

"Reiterate that the ABI is in charge of this investigation."

"Right. And I'll stress that there is no need for panic, but everyone should err on the side of caution."

"They're going to want to know about suspects."

"Of course they are." Bernie felt the beginning of a stress headache. "And all I can tell them is that although we interviewed several people of interest in the Stephanie Preston case, we do not at this time have a suspect and it's too early in this new case to make any other comments."

"I believe you've got it down pat."

"Oh, God . . ." Bernie's stomach churned. She felt like she was going to vomit.

"What's the matter? You look green." Jim held out his hand, as if to grab her arm.

She jerked away. "I'll be okay. I'm just sick to my stomach and I've got a headache coming on, but I don't want to announce to the world that the sheriff is so emotionally wrung out that she can't handle the job she was elected to do. I'll give female law enforcement officers a bad name."

"You're only human," Jim told her. "You haven't eaten since lunch, have you? That's part of what's wrong. And just a little while ago, you had to take a look at a pretty young woman who was brutalized and murdered. The second woman in your county this month. There's a serial killer out there, probably getting ready to strike again, and we don't have a clue who he is or how to stop him. And I said *we*. Both Charlie Patterson and I have had experience with serial killers before, but neither of us can come up with a suspect."

When she tasted the salty bile that rose up her esophagus, she forced it down and read herself the riot act. *You're not going to get sick. You're not going to cry. You're not going to act like an emotional female. Remember, you are the sheriff. You're strong and tough and in control.*

A hundred tiny drummers beat a fast-paced tune inside her head.

"I'm okay," she said. "You go up there and handle the crowd while I get the roadblocks set up."

He gave her another one of those tender, concerned looks that made her feel as if he'd wrapped his arms around her. She turned and all but ran from him, knowing that if she didn't get away from Jim Norton, she was liable to fall smack-dab into his big, strong arms.

Chapter 19

Robyn locked the backdoor of her fitness center, dropped the keys in her shoulder bag and headed up the back alley toward the side street. She liked having her own apartment within walking distance of her job, but more than anything, she loved the privacy living on her own afforded her. It wasn't that she didn't enjoy being around her parents. She did. They were great and she loved them to pieces. But at twenty-eight, she neither wanted nor needed her parents' supervision or protection.

When Robyn reached the end of the alley, she noticed that the traffic along Main Street had slowed to a trickle. There usually wasn't much going on downtown on a Monday evening. That's why she didn't keep the fitness center open past six on Mondays. As she passed Adams Federal Savings and Loan, she noted the digital time and temperature displayed on their billboard: six-thirty-seven, ninety-four degrees. Damn, it was hot. But this was the first week of August in Alabama, so she could expect nothing less than hot and humid. You'd think by six-thirty the temps would have dropped below ninety, but even when they did drop later tonight, the humidity would make it feel like a sweltering steam bath.

Pausing on the sidewalk to adjust her left sandal, that had picked up a piece of gravel in the alley, she caught a glimpse of Scotty Joe Walters driving by. He threw up his hand and waved. She waved back at him. *Now, there's a prime piece of horseflesh.* Sooner or later, she'd have to get around to sampling it. But at present, she was juggling two lovers—Paul and Brandon. Things were winding down between Brandon and her. They were more off than on these days, which suited them both just fine. Neither of them liked being exclusive. But Paul was becoming a little too possessive to suit her. She didn't see them still dating two months from now. Although Paul was rich and handsome—two things that appealed to her in a man—he wasn't all that good in the sack. He was far more concerned with his own satisfaction than hers and kept wanting her to tell him how great he was. What a bore!

If she was honest with herself, she'd have to admit that she kind of missed Ron Hensley. He was the best lover she'd had since coming back to Adams Landing, but he liked to play the field as much as she did. She'd heard a rumor that he was having an affair with a married woman and several names had been mentioned, including Amber Claunch, the coroner's wife, and Abby Miller, who owned the Kut and Kurl beauty salon. She knew both women well enough to know that neither was a faithful wife.

When Robyn neared the bookstore, she decided to go inside for a frozen coffee and to pick up the latest issue of *Glamour* magazine. The moment she entered the building, she sighed as delicious, cool air enveloped her. She paused several steps from the coffee bar when she saw Reverend Matthew Donaldson sitting at one of the tables placed along the row of windows facing the street. But before she could turn around and hurry toward the back of the store, he saw her, smiled and waved.

"Good evening, Robyn." He rose from his chair.

Oh, God, she didn't want to spend another minute in that man's boring company. In the pulpit, he was all razzle-dazzle, hellfire and brilliance. And just looking at him—curly dark hair, sexy blue-gray eyes, and spectacular bod—you'd never suspect he was such a humdrum stick-in-the-mud.

Smiling, she curled her fingers, lifted her hand and gave him a little, shy wave.

"Won't you join me?" Matthew asked.

Jeeze, how do you turn down a minister's cordial invitation in a public place? Suddenly, Robyn saw her salvation. *Thank you, God.* Sitting at a back table, absorbed in reading a hardback book and sipping on a cup of coffee, was the answer to her prayers. Raymond Long.

Robyn approached Matthew. "Why thank you, Reverend Donaldson. I'd love to join you, but I'm afraid I can't. I'm meeting someone."

She waved toward the back table. Raymond seemed oblivious to her presence, but she didn't let that deter her. Marching purposefully toward her goal, she breezed passed Matthew. When she reached Raymond's table, she paused. He kept reading.

"Raymond, sugar, I'm sorry I'm running late." Robyn curved her fingers over his shoulder and squeezed. "Order me an iced coffee, will you? I'm hot and simply dying of thirst."

As if he'd actually been expecting her, Raymond closed his book, laid it on the table, removed his gold-framed glasses and motioned to the waiter. Raymond removed her hand from his shoulder, brought it to his mouth and kissed her knuckles.

"I never mind waiting for you," he said.

Robyn sat down in the chair beside him, cuddled her

shoulder against his and whispered in his ear. "Thanks so much. I owe you one."

Raymond shrugged. "Any particular flavor?"

"Huh?"

"For your coffee." He nodded to the waiter who stood by their table.

"White chocolate, please."

"You heard the lady." After the waiter scurried off, Raymond turned halfway around in his chair and studied Robyn. "You're going to get cold in here wearing nothing but short-shorts and a halter top."

"If I do, you can order me some hot coffee."

"Staying long, are you?"

"I'm not leaving until Reverend Donaldson is gone." She batted her eyelashes at Raymond in a mockery of blatant flirtation. "Unless you want to walk me upstairs to my apartment."

Raymond chuckled. "What would you do if I took you up on that insincere offer?"

"What makes you think it's insincere?"

He gazed at her, a puzzled expression on his face. She looked at him, really looked at him, and liked what she saw. Raymond was not handsome, but he had a good face. Large, kind brown eyes. A prominent, manly nose. Full, rather sensuous lips. And a strong jawline. His hairline was receding just a bit and she suspected that by forty, he'd be partially bald.

"How old are you?" she asked.

"What?"

"How old are you? I know you're a little bit older than Bernie, but I don't remember how much older."

"I'm thirty-four."

"I'm twenty-eight."

"I know."

"When you got a divorce, why did you move back to

Adams Landing? And why on earth are you living with your mother?"

"Adams Landing is home," he told her. "As you know, my father died last year and Mother's had a difficult time running the business. It just made sense for me to come back here and take over the hardware store." His lips lifted in a quirky, contemplative smile. "As for living with Mother— why not? She cooks my meals, does my laundry, and is doing her best to find me a new wife. The lady wants grandchildren very badly."

Robyn laughed. "Tell me about it. My mom is driving me and Bernie nuts because she wants grandkids so much. You are aware of the fact that our mothers had their hearts set on getting you and Bernie together."

"That's not going to happen."

"Yeah, I know. Bernie feels the same way. She likes you and all, but—"

"Bernie and I understand each other."

The waiter returned with a large iced coffee, placed it in front of Robyn and smiled flirtatiously with her. She reached up, tapped him on the chest and said, "You shouldn't come on to a lady who's on a date with another man. It's bad manners."

The young waiter, probably no older than twenty, turned as red as a clown's nose and said, "Yes, ma'am." Then he hurried off.

"Are we on a date?" Raymond asked.

Robyn twisted the straw in her drink around and around, then grinned at Raymond. "Yes, I think we are."

"Do I get to walk you home afterward?" he asked.

"Do you want to?"

"Yes, I do. Very much."

Raymond might not be rich or handsome, but he was rather charming. And she'd known him forever, since they were kids, knew he was a good guy. She'd bet if she asked him in when he walked her to her apartment, he'd accept the invitation. And she bet that if she came on to him, he wouldn't turn her down the way Matthew Donaldson had.

Abby stroked the strand of cheap pearls as she reread the latest note her secret admirer had sent.

Please accept this small token of my affection. Pearls for a lovely lady.

The first note and sketch had arrived five days ago, last Wednesday. Today, she had received a note, the pearls, and a new sketch.

She knew that quite a few guys in Adams County had a thing for her. Some were bold enough to proposition her outright, the way Ron had done. And others admired her from afar. Knowing she could arouse men's passions did a world of good for her ego. But she'd never been approached by such a romantic man in such a romantic way. She laid the pearls aside and lifted the ink sketch. Whoever had drawn this picture had captured the sexy, sultry side of her nature, one she reserved for the bedroom. Either this man had once been her lover or he instinctively knew how she'd look right after making love.

The only guy she'd ever fucked who had the least bit of artistic talent was back in high school—Tim Burcham, Holly Burcham's cousin. But Tim had gone off to college, had become an architect and now lived somewhere in Virginia.

She really couldn't think of anyone in Adams Landing who was an artist, except that art professor over at the community college, Dr. Brandon Kelley. About six months ago, he'd started coming into her salon for a haircut and a manicure every few weeks. They'd exchanged some harmless sexual banter, but he'd never actually put the moves on her.

Beverly Barton

Could he be her secret admirer? If he was, he just might be able to give Ron Hensley a run for his money.

Just as she gathered up the items lying on her kitchen table, her telephone rang. She hurriedly stuffed everything into the small box they'd come in, stood up and grabbed the receiver from the wall phone.

"Hello."

"Abby?"

Not recognizing the voice and wondering if it might be *him*, Abby shivered with excitement. "Yes, this is Abby. Who are you?"

"Oh, I'm sorry, I didn't identify myself immediately. This is Reverend Donaldson. I was wondering if I might stop by and see you for a few minutes this evening."

Reverend Donaldson? "I—uh—sure, I guess. But why?"

"Your mother-in-law, Glenda Miller, asked me to speak to you."

That old witch! "Speak to me about what?"

"I'd rather not discuss this over the phone."

"Then by all means, come on over and we'll talk face to face."

"Thank you. I can be there in fifteen minutes."

"Make it thirty, will you?"

"Thirty minutes, then."

Fuming, Abby hung up the phone. Just what was her mother-in-law up to? Had Glenda found out about her affair with Ron and was siccing the new minister on her? Or was it something else?

With her gift package under her arm, Abby hurried into her bedroom, tossed the box onto her bed and rummaged through her closet. She wanted to be wearing just the right thing when the good reverend paid her a visit.

*   *   *

Robyn's climax sent off explosions through her whole body. She writhed and moaned and clutched at Raymond's head positioned between her thighs. Her heart raced; her body soared. And her mind turned to mush.

"Oh, God, that was wonderful," she told him.

He worked his mouth up over her mound, across her belly, dipped into her navel, and then ventured upward to her breasts. When he braced himself over her and came down to suckle one breast and then the other, she bucked up off the bed and clung to him.

"I want you inside me," she murmured.

"Not yet."

"Yes, please."

"I need to protect you," he said.

"I'm on the pill."

"I should still wear a condom and I'm afraid I don't have one."

She gazed up into his tortured face and smiled. "It's okay. I have some in the nightstand." She nodded to her right. "Take your pick."

He eased off her, opened the nightstand drawer and stared at the variety. "Do you have a preference?"

"Just a plain old ordinary rubber will do just fine."

He nodded, then sorted through the supply and retrieved a condom. When his trembling fingers couldn't quite manage to rip apart the packet, Robyn got up on her knees, crawled over beside him and took the packet from him.

"Here, let me do it." She ripped the shiny plastic apart, removed the condom and scooted out of bed. "I'll put it on for you."

When she went down on her knees in front of him, he sucked in a deep breath and groaned. She smiled when she saw the look on his face—a combination of fear and hope and disbelief. How fabulous it was to have a man so in awe of her. She loved the feeling of power it gave her.

Robyn reached out and circled his penis. Pumping his erection several times she sighed. "I guess you know that you've got an impressive cock." Before he could respond, she leaned down and covered the bulbous tip with her mouth.

"Oh, God!" Raymond cried.

She pressed her tongue against him and sucked gently. He moaned deep in his throat, then clamped his hands down on her shoulders and held her in place. She sucked him for a while, taking all of him into her mouth, then coming up for air, she licked him from tip to root, repeating the process over and over again.

"Robyn . . . I don't think I can stand much more of that. You're driving me crazy."

She eased off slowly, then took the condom, still in one hand, and fitted it over his rock-hard dick. "Which way? You choose the position."

"I've dreamed of you being on top," he confessed, his cheeks flushed.

She gave him a shove, toppling him back on the bed. "Then lie back, big boy, and let me fulfill your dreams."

She climbed on top of him, situated herself over his erection and impaled herself. He filled her completely. When she dangled her breasts over his mouth as she began a slow, steady rhythm, he wasted no time in sampling her offering.

Within a few minutes, Robyn couldn't hold back because it felt so good to have him inside her, to be on top of him and able to maneuver her body for the greatest sensation. She rode him hard and fast. And when she came, she cried out her satisfaction. A minute later, Raymond came, all the while kissing her like crazy.

"I love you, Robyn. I've always loved you."

As she floated back to reality, the aftershocks of release

rippling through her, she slid off him and cuddled to his side. "Oh, Raymond, you're so sweet."

Abby loved the look on Reverend Donaldson's face when she answered the door in a pair of leave-little-to-the-imagination short pj's.

"I . . . uh . . . I thought you were expecting me." He gulped several times.

She reached out, grabbed him by the lapels of his jacket and dragged him over the threshold. "I was expecting you." She twirled around and threw out her arms. "Like what you see?"

"Mrs. Miller, I—"

"Please, call me Abby." She laid her hand over his heart and smiled wickedly. "It's all right if I call you Matthew, isn't it? Or do you prefer Matt?"

His face splotched an unbecoming reddish pink and sweat dotted his upper lip and forehead. "Matthew is fine. But Mrs.—"

"Abby."

"Yes, well, Abby, I've come here at your mother-in-law's request and obviously none too soon. She's been concerned about you. Glenda is afraid that temptations of the flesh might overpower you while your husband is away fighting for our country."

Abby slowly lowered her hand down over his chest, stopping at his belt. He cleared his throat. She laughed.

"It's so sweet of Glenda to be concerned and wonderfully understanding of her to send you over here to take care of me." Abby eased her hand down over his crotch and grinned when she felt his semihard erection.

He gasped loudly. "You misunderstand, Mrs. Miller . . . Abby. Please, for pity's sake—"

Cupping him, she massaged him with her thumb. When

she stood on tiptoe and pressed her lips against his, she thought he might faint dead away. Instead, he grabbed her shoulders, held her tightly and kissed her. His movements were awkward and rough, exposing him for the novice at lovemaking he obviously was. In a way, she felt sorry for the poor guy and almost regretted having played such a dirty trick on him.

She had to end this before it went any further. But before she called a halt, he released her abruptly, jerked back and gulped down tears.

"Please, forgive me. I—I don't know what came over me. I assure you—"

"It's okay. Really. It was all my fault. I deliberately seduced you. I'm sorry."

"No, no, please, Abby, don't apologize. I'm terribly embarrassed."

"Don't be," she told him. "Look, no harm done. We can both blame my mother-in-law, the nosy, interfering old busybody."

"She's deeply concerned about your cheating on her son. If you could just reassure her that you're being faithful to your husband—"

"If I do that, Reverend, I'd be lying."

"Are you saying that you—"

"We all have our dirty little secrets, don't we?" She winked at him.

He gulped again.

"You keep my secret and I'll keep yours," she said.

"And we'll both burn in hell."

"You think you'll burn in hell because of one little kiss?"

He shook his head. "I lusted after you in my heart. I still lust after you."

"Do you now?"

"Thinking a thing is as bad as doing it."

"Well, if that's the case, then why don't you stay?"

When she tried to touch him, he held up his hands to fend her off. "No."

She reached around him and opened the door. "Then good night, Matthew, and thank you for stopping by. Come back anytime you're in the neighborhood."

He turned and practically ran from her, onto the porch and down the sidewalk. She slammed the door and laughed. Poor fool. He'd probably rush home and jerk off as quick as he could. *Wonder if jerking off is a sin? Probably. But not as big a sin as screwing a married woman.*

Twilight shadows danced across the backyard, over trees and shrubbery, across flowers and grass. As she headed out the kitchen door, balancing three glasses of lemonade on a small plastic tray, Bernie flipped the switch that turned on the back porch light. True to his promise to move back in with Jim, Kevin had returned to his father's duplex apartment four days ago and from what she could tell, the two were getting along okay. Keeping her end of the bargain, she had invited Jim and Kevin to dinner at her house this evening. They'd eaten supper nearly an hour ago, but had just finished cleaning up in the kitchen and feeding Boomer a few minutes ago. Kevin had taken Boomer outside to play, while Jim carried lawn chairs out into the yard, where he and Bernie could sit and talk.

When she approached Jim, he reached over and took the tray from her and placed it on the third chair, which was empty since Kevin was busy chasing Boomer all over the yard.

"Sit down and rest," Jim said. "You have to be tired after putting in a full day at the office, and then cooking us a great supper."

When Bernie sat, Jim picked up one of the glasses off the tray and handed it to her, then took one for himself before sitting.

While watching Kevin frolicking with Boomer, Bernie took a sip of the sweetly tart lemonade. "Kevin needs a dog of his own."

"Kevin needs a lot of things he doesn't have."

"If you're going to blame yourself for everything wrong in Kevin's life, I'm not going to listen."

Jim chuckled. "I can't blame you for being tired of hearing me bellyache about how I've failed my son."

"Stop worrying about how you've failed him in the past and concentrate on how you're going to be a good father now and in the future."

Jim nodded, then sipped on his lemonade.

They sat side by side in silence for a while, watching Kevin and Boomer and the lightning bugs flitting around in the evening sky, listening to the tree frogs and katydids, breathing in the scent of the honeysuckle vine that grew along the fence. Bernie hadn't felt at peace since last Wednesday night when Thomasina Hardy's nude body had been found near Sunflower Creek. She hadn't gotten a good night's sleep since then, had spent every waking minute worrying about who their killer's next victim would be and praying they could find a way to catch him and put a stop to his killing spree.

"Penny for your thoughts," Jim said.

"Just thinking about Derek Lawrence's profile of our killer."

"What about it?"

"He was very specific in certain areas and yet so much of the profile was too general to help us. There were things that he listed as possible traits that might be true of numerous men."

"Such as?"

"Mr. Lawrence believes that sometime in his past, someone who looked like all the victims played a part in some traumatic event in our killer's life, so traumatic that it triggered his need to kill."

"Revenge. It's a powerful motive."

"A pretty, young, popular brunette did something terrible to him—"

"Or someone did something terrible to this young woman, someone important to our killer."

"See, you just proved my point. There are too many ways to interpret Lawrence's findings. How many men over the age of twenty-five haven't had their hearts broken at least once? They don't turn into killers. And what might be traumatic for one person might not be for another."

"Often profiles are as good for ruling out suspects as they are in pinpointing a specific person."

"The problem is, we don't have any suspects."

"Hey, Dad, Bernie, watch this," Kevin called. "I've taught Boomer to fetch." Kevin threw a small stick and Boomer chased after it; then he grabbed it in his mouth, laid down on the ground and chewed the stick to pieces.

Jim and Bernie couldn't stop themselves from laughing at the puppy's antics and at the funny expression on Kevin's face.

"Ah, Boomer, you messed up our trick." Kevin hurried across the yard to Boomer, who jumped like a jackrabbit and ran away, thinking Kevin wanted to play some more.

Instead, Kevin came over to where Jim and Bernie were. He picked up his glass of lemonade, set the tray on the ground and dropped down into the chair. "Tonight's been really nice, hasn't it, Dad?"

Jim glanced at Bernie and grinned, then looked at Kevin. "It sure has."

"Bernie's a pretty good cook," Kevin said.

"Yes, she is." Jim saluted his son with his glass. "And she makes delicious lemonade."

"Aw, shucks, 't'weren't nothing," she said jokingly. "Just squeeze a few lemons and add sugar and water."

Kevin laughed. It was so good to hear him laughing, to see him smiling, to listen to him kidding around with his father again. Bernie wished she could save this night, like recording a TV show on video, something she could play back over and over again, savoring every minute. If she could have anything she wanted, anything in the whole wide world, she'd ask for Jim and Kevin. To be Jim's wife and a mother to his son.

Boomer came racing across the yard and jumped up in Kevin's lap, almost knocking his glass out of his hand. At the same time, Jim's cell phone rang. Bernie's stomach knotted. *Please, God, don't let it be news that another woman has been abducted.*

Jim jerked his phone off the belt hook, flipped it open, and said, "Captain Norton here." After pausing to listen, he cut his eyes toward Kevin. "Yeah. Un-huh. How's Mary Lee?"

Kevin's eyes widened in surprise. He grabbed Jim's sleeve and yanked.

"Is it Allen?" Kevin asked. "Tell him that I want to talk to Mom. Please."

"Kevin would like to speak to his mother," Jim said.

Bernie could tell by the expression on Jim's face that he hadn't liked the response from Allen Clark. "Yeah, I understand and I'll deal with it the best I can."

Bernie sensed something was wrong—something that was going to hurt Kevin. Her maternal instincts came into play, urging her to protect Kevin.

Jim listened for a few minutes, his expression growing colder and more tense by the second.

"I want to talk to Mom," Kevin repeated.

"Look, Allen, tell Mary Lee that—" Jim cursed under his breath and Bernie instinctively knew that Allen Clark had hung up on him.

"What's wrong?" Kevin asked. "Is Mom okay?" Boomer licked Kevin's face.

Jim closed his cell phone, clipped it back to his belt and hesitated for a full minute before facing his son. Kevin placed a squirming Boomer on the ground.

"Your mother is all right," Jim said. "But she's not dealing with the treatments very well. They're making her very sick and she doesn't want you to see her so sick."

"I don't understand." Kevin looked at Jim pleadingly. "School starts the end of next week, and I'll go home then and—"

"Would it be so bad if you stayed here in Adams Landing with me for a while longer, maybe even started school here?" Jim turned and held out his hand to Kevin.

Tears clouded Bernie's vision, her heart breaking for father and son.

"I can't stay here with you." Kevin jumped up, spilling his lemonade all over his shorts and bare legs. "I have to go home. My mom needs me. She wants me with her."

Kevin threw his glass on the ground and went running into the house.

"What did Allen Clark say?" Bernie asked.

"He said just what I told Kevin—that Mary Lee's treatments make her deathly sick. She wants Kevin to stay here with me."

"For how long?"

"Indefinitely."

"Oh, Jim."

"I cannot tell him that his mother doesn't want him, that she can't deal with an almost teenage son while she's battling cancer. He won't understand." Jim got up and walked away toward the far side of the yard.

Bernie followed, caught up with him and placed her hand on his back.

He tensed. "What am I going to do?"

"You're going to be tactfully honest with Kevin. He'll be angry and hurt, and he just might take it out on you. But you're going to love him and support him and be there for him. And I'll do anything I can to help you."

Jim turned, looked at Bernie for half a second, then grabbed her and kissed her. Taken off guard by his actions, she froze at first, then when she felt his tongue probing, she opened her mouth and returned his kiss with all the passion she'd been keeping bottled up inside her.

Chapter 20

Matthew Donaldson knelt in front of the altar in the sanctuary of his church on this sweltering hot summer night. Alone, just he and his God. With guilt and remorse in his heart, he begged for forgiveness. More than anything, he wanted to serve the Lord, here in Adams Landing. His church. His people.

Having served as an assistant at two other churches, one in Georgia and one in North Carolina, he felt an overwhelming sense of pride that this was his church. He was the minister, the one to whom the congregation looked for guidance, expecting him to lead by example. He had the opportunity to prove himself, to overcome his weaknesses and become the dedicated and influential disciple of the Lord he aspired to be.

With his hands folded in a prayerful gesture and his eyes focused upward, toward heaven, he beseeched the Heavenly Father.

"Forgive me, dear Lord. I have sinned grievously. I have lusted after a woman—a married woman. I was tempted almost beyond reason."

And this was not the first time since coming to Adams Landing that the Devil had tested him, putting temptation in his path. It had taken every ounce of his willpower to resist Robyn Granger. She was one of the most beautiful, desirable women he had ever known. If she were a different type of woman, he might have pursued a chaste relationship with her, perhaps even chosen her for his wife. But Robyn was not the type of woman suited to being a minister's wife. Knowing that fact did not stop him from wanting her, from desiring her in the most sinful way possible.

It was Robyn's fault that tonight when he had gone to counsel Glenda Miller's wayward daughter-in-law, he had been sorely tempted by her luscious body and wicked seduction. For endless days and nights, he had been tormented by his desire for Robyn, tormented almost beyond reason.

"Help me, merciful God. I am a sinner. I have evil thoughts, and I have done terrible things. But you and you alone know the agony I have experienced, the torture I have endured in my efforts to be a good man, a man worthy of the position I hold."

Tears of remorse trickled down Matthew's cheeks. Overcome by his guilt and remorse, he fell prostrate on the floor. Sobbing as he prayed, he wept until he was spent, until he was unable to utter a single word. With the soft carpet pressing against his cheek, he closed his eyes and sighed deeply.

Images of Abby Miller appeared in his mind. Abby naked, holding her arms open, begging him to make love to her.

His eyelids flew open. "Damn you, Abby. Damn you, Robyn. You will be punished for your wickedness. If you do not change your evil ways, you will both burn in hellfire for all eternity."

Robyn busied herself in her small apartment kitchen, placing the sandwiches she'd just made onto plates, setting the plates on the bar, and then pouring two glasses of iced tea. Raymond was still in the bathroom, which gave her a few more minutes to figure out what she was going to say to him. It wasn't as if he was the first man who'd ever told her he loved her, but he just might be the first man who'd ever said it and meant it.

She liked Raymond. She'd always liked him, even when she was a kid. He'd been a sweet boy who had grown up to be a very nice man.

Robyn laughed. She didn't make a habit of dating nice men. She usually preferred bad boys. Good-for-nothings like Paul Landon—rich, handsome, and worthless. Or cocky, self-confident studs like Ron Hensley and Brandon Kelley. And then there was the rare breed—the unobtainable, like Jim Norton.

The last thing she wanted to do was hurt Raymond Long. But she wouldn't lie to him and tell him she loved him. She didn't love him, certainly not the way he proclaimed to love her. But she liked him a lot. And the guy was a skillful, ardent lover, who, during their lovemaking, had concentrated more on her satisfaction than his own. That alone was a real turn-on for her. Probably for most women. After all, what woman wouldn't want to be adored. Worshipped. Cherished.

"You didn't have to fix me something to eat," Raymond said as he emerged from the bathroom, neatly dressed and a hopeful expression on his face. "I would understand if you wanted me to go now."

"Don't be silly." She pulled the satin lapels of her mid-thigh-length robe closer together and stepped out from behind the bar that separated the kitchen from the living room. "I haven't had supper and figured you hadn't either."

"That's very nice of you." He offered her a shy, closed-mouth grin.

He's adorable. It wasn't often she met a thirty-four-year-old guy who was shy and sweet after the lovemaking.

Robyn pulled out one of the bar stools, patted the cushioned seat and motioned to Raymond. "Come on, let's eat." As he approached her, she smiled warmly. "And maybe we should talk, too."

Pausing, appearing to be greatly concerned by her suggestion that they talk, Raymond frowned. "Look, I know I probably made a fool of myself tonight. I shouldn't have blurted out that I love you. And believe me, I don't expect you to—"

Robyn rushed over to him, threw her arms around his neck and kissed him. When she lifted her head, she saw that his eyes were closed, almost as if he was praying. "Open your eyes and look at me."

He obeyed her request.

"You have great eyes," she said, then eased her hands downward and cupped his buttocks. "And you're a wonderful lover."

His face flushed scarlet.

Robyn laughed. "Hasn't any woman ever told you that before?"

He stared at her, speechless, everything he felt there in his eyes for her to see.

Robyn lifted her hands upward and pulled her arms from around his body, then entwined her fingers behind his neck again. "I'm not in love with you."

Suddenly, unexpectedly, as if somehow they were emotionally connected, Robyn felt his disappointment and subsequent acceptance of what he perceived as her rejection.

"But you know what, Raymond Long? You're the kind of man I'd like to fall in love with."

"What does that mean . . . exactly?" he asked. His body was rigid, his voice tense.

"It means I don't want tonight to be a one-night stand." She pulled away from him, locked her gaze with his and stated emphatically, "I'd like for us to start dating."

He swallowed hard. "Do you mean that?"

Smiling encouragingly, she nodded. "Yes, I mean it. I'm not saying we should date each other exclusively. At least not right away."

"I understand. Whatever you want, however you want it is fine with me."

"You are the dearest, sweetest man."

He grabbed her. Gently. Tentatively.

"I worship the ground you walk on, Robyn. I always have. I'd do anything for you. If you were mine—really mine—I'd spend every day of the rest of my life trying to make you happy."

"Oh, Raymond." Emotion tightened her throat.

"No one could ever love you as much as I do."

Clearing her throat and keeping her smile intact, she clasped his hand in hers. "Let's eat supper, then why don't you spend the night?"

"You want me"—he gulped nervously—"to spend the night?"

She squeezed his hand. "Oh, yes. I most certainly do."

Bernie ended the kiss, pulled away from Jim and sucked in several deep, hard breaths. Dear God, what had just happened?

Jim Norton kissed you. Kissed you the way you've dreamed he would kiss you. Passionately. Forcefully. As if he wanted you desperately.

And you kissed him back. Hell, you practically devoured him.

"What . . . what was that all about?" Bernie asked breathlessly.

Jim looked stunned, as if he was as surprised by his actions as she'd been. "I don't know. I'm not sure."

"Well, I think we'd better figure it out, don't you?"

Jim nodded.

"You were upset about Kevin's reaction to his mother's request that he stay here with you and start school in Adams Landing." Bernie tried to think logically, despite the fact that her hormones had kicked into overdrive and she was still aroused.

"And you advised me how to handle Kevin, then said you'd do anything you could to help me."

"And I meant it. I will do anything to—"

Jim grabbed her by the shoulders. Gasping, Bernie's eyes widened as she fixed her gaze on his.

"You and your family have befriended Kevin and me. You've gone out of your way to help me and I'm grateful," Jim said. "I like you, Bernie. I respect you . . . admire you."

Please stop talking. Don't say anything else. Don't tell me you kissed me out of gratitude. If you do, I think I'll die.

"I feel the same way about you," she told him. *Yeah, only I just happen to be in love with you, too.*

"I think I kissed you because . . . well, because . . ."

Don't say it. Don't say because you're so grateful to me.

"Because you make me feel good about myself," Jim said. "You make me feel strong and capable. You make me feel like I can be the kind of man I want to be, the kind of father Kevin deserves."

Bernie drew in and released a phantom relieved breath, a mental and emotional aah.

"What are friends for?" Bernie tried her best to sound jovial.

Jim tightened his hold on her shoulders. "Is that all we are—friends?"

How should she respond? What did he want her to say? She didn't feel confident enough to risk making a fool of herself. "I suppose . . . I—"

Jim released her abruptly, but stood so close she could

feel his breath on her face as he watched her, studying her for a reaction. "Yeah, you're right. We don't want to do something we'll regret, do we? After all, we've both been pretty badly burned by past relationships and neither of us is looking for anything permanent and—"

"And why let unbridled passion screw up a friendship." Bernie turned around and walked away from him.

Don't cry. Don't you dare cry. Don't let him see you vulnerable. Don't let him figure out how you really feel about him.

"Bernie!" Jim called after her.

"I'm going inside to check on Kevin," she said. "Give me a few minutes alone with him before you come into the house. Okay?"

"Okay."

Bernie hurried across the yard, onto the back porch and through the open kitchen door. Once inside, she paused for half a second, sighed, keened softly and then squared her shoulders.

Let it go. Whatever is going on between you and Jim, don't dwell on it. He doesn't feel what you feel, doesn't want what you want.

Right now isn't about you or Jim. It's about Kevin and how you can help him. The poor kid's whole world is falling apart. He's angry with Jim, probably even blames him for everything. It's up to you to do something—anything—to put father and son together.

She found Kevin and Boomer, who had apparently followed Kevin into the house, in the den. Curled up on the sofa, his knees drawn up to his chest and his face buried between his clasped knees, Kevin ignored Boomer's whimpers. The puppy so obviously wanted to comfort the boy.

"Kevin?"

"Huh?" he replied, his body tensing, his reply muffled.

"May I come in and talk to you?"

"Yeah, I guess." He raised his head, but didn't look at her. Instead, he focused on Boomer, as if he'd suddenly realized the puppy was there. He picked Boomer up and cradled him in his arms between his chest and propped-up knees.

"You're going into seventh grade, right?" she asked.

"Yeah, my birthday is in December, so Mom held me back."

"Adams Landing has a great middle school."

"Hmm . . ."

Bernie ventured into the den. "Mind if I sit down with you and Boomer?"

Still holding Boomer, Kevin scooted around, unbent his knees and made room for her on the small sofa.

Bernie sat, placed her hands in her lap and glanced at Kevin, who averted his gaze. Staring down at the floor, he stroked Boomer's back.

"Your stepdad suggesting that you stay with your dad and start school here doesn't mean your mother doesn't love you and want you."

"Yeah, I know."

"And none of this is your dad's fault."

Kevin's head snapped up. He glared at Bernie. "Yes, it is his fault."

"How do you figure that?"

"He left us a long time ago when I was just a little kid. He divorced my mom."

"He left your mother," Bernie said calmly. "He divorced her. He didn't divorce you. You're his son. You're the most important person in the world to him."

"Yeah, well, he's got a funny way of showing it."

"What do you mean by that? Do you mean spending every moment with you that he was allowed to since the divorce is showing you the way he feels? Do you mean living for the weekends you two were together is showing you how he feels? Do you mean never saying one word against your mother because he knows how much you love her—"

"Stop saying those things!" Kevin shouted. Boomer jerked out of his arms and bounded onto the floor. "They're not true."

Bernie looked Kevin square in the eyes and said, "Yes, they are true. Why do you think your father gave up his job as a Memphis police detective and accepted a lesser paying job here in Adams County? He did it so he could be close to you."

"He did?" Kevin's eyes widened.

"Yes, he did. And he rented a two-bedroom duplex so you could have your own bedroom when you visited."

Kevin nodded.

"He was very sorry to hear about your mom's breast cancer," Bernie said. "But he was thrilled that you'd be living with him for several weeks. All he thought about was how he could do his job and spend as much time with you as possible."

"You like my dad a lot, don't you?"

"Yes, I do."

"You think he's a good guy?"

"I think he's a very good guy."

"My mom doesn't think so."

Okay, tread carefully here. Defend Jim without defaming Mary Lee.

"Sometimes when people get a divorce, they're angry and hurt and say things they don't mean about each other. If your mother ever said anything against your father, that's probably the reason."

Kevin thought for several minutes. "I think she used to hate him. Before she married Allen."

"Maybe she did. And hate makes us say and do things we shouldn't."

"I always felt like I couldn't love my dad—you know, really love him—if I love my mom. But that's not true, is it?"

Bernie inched closer to Kevin, longing to wrap the boy in her arms and comfort him. "No matter how your parents feel about each other or what either of them might have said about the other, you can love both of them without betraying either of them."

What on earth had Mary Lee done to her son by poisoning his mind against his father? Try as Bernie might to feel compassion and concern for a woman struggling to overcome a deadly disease, she could feel little but contempt for anyone who would so shamefully use their child in a battle against their ex-spouse.

"My dad really wants me to live with him?" Kevin asked. "He's glad I'll be staying here and going to school?"

Bernie eased her arm around Kevin's shoulders. A loose, casual hug, nothing to make him feel like a little kid being smothered by an adult. "Yes to both questions."

"Bernie?"

"Hmm . . . ?

"Where's my dad?"

"Outside. Waiting."

"I don't really feel like talking to him tonight," Kevin said. "I mean, I'll go home with him and all, but I don't want to talk about my mom or about my staying here in Adams Landing to start school. Couldn't that wait until later?"

"I'm sure it can." Bernie removed her arm from around Kevin's shoulders, stood, and being careful not to step on Boomer who had curled up at Kevin's feet, headed for the door.

"I'll let your dad know you're ready to go home now."

When she exited through the kitchen, she found Jim pacing back and forth on the porch. The minute he saw her, he stopped and looked at her, his gaze cautiously optimistic.

"Will he talk to me?" Jim asked.

"He doesn't want to talk to you tonight about his mother or his staying on in Adams Landing."

Jim's hopeful expression altered to one of dismay.

"But he's ready to go home with you," Bernie said. "And I think in a day or two, he might be ready to talk."

Jim huffed loudly, then grasped Bernie by the shoulders. "Damn, woman, you're a miracle worker. What did you say to him? You didn't—"

"No, I didn't say one word against your ex-wife. I simply pointed out to Kevin that you're a good man and that you love him more than anyone on earth."

Jim swallowed. "Thanks, Bernie. I owe you—"

"You don't owe me anything. We're friends, remember?"

"Yeah, and I'm one lucky bastard to have a friend like you."

When he pulled her into his arms and hugged her, Bernie thought she'd die from the pleasure . . . and from the pain.

The dream came again, as it so often did. Sweet and pro-mising, reminding him of the greatest joy he'd ever known. But soon the dream turned cold and cruel, ripping out his heart, leaving him humiliated and longing to die. His sub-conscious mind replayed the dream over and over again, never letting him forget, constantly reminding him.

She was the most beautiful, desirable creature on earth, and he loved her madly. Although he had worshipped her from afar for such a long time, he'd never dared to dream that one day she would speak to him. He hadn't realized that she even knew who he was.

"Hi, there," she said in that kitten-soft, syrupy-sweet Southern drawl.

"She's talking to you." His friend Marcus punched him in the ribs.

"Huh?"

She curled her index finger and wiggled it at him. He nearly peed in his pants.

"Come here, silly," she said.

He moved toward her like a robot.

"Can't you even say hi?" When she smiled at him, his heart went wild.

"Hi." He croaked the one word.

She giggled. "Since we both have Mr. Higgins for American history next, want to carry my books for me?"

"You want me to carry your books?"

She batted those long black eyelashes at him. "Of course I do, or I wouldn't have asked."

In his effort to take her books and stack them on his, he clumsily dropped all their books on the floor. Red faced and trembling, he went down on his knees and picked up every book, praying she wouldn't laugh at him. But when he stood up again, she slipped her slender arm through his skinny arm and smiled at him.

He'd been a goner from that moment on. He was hers to command, to do with as she willed.

He fought with his subconscious, struggling to end the dream before it turned deadly.

Wake up! Damn it, wake up!

But the dream wouldn't stop. The memories washed over him like a tidal wave, drowning him in shame and torment.

With her laughter ringing in his ears, he cried out, struggling against the soul-wrenching anguish. His eyes flew open. He woke in a cold sweat. Lying there in the darkness, he listened to the loud, racing beat of his heart.

Don't think about the past. Think about the future. Concentrate on the woman who may make all your dreams come true.

Tomorrow I'll send her another gift. Pink lipstick and nail polish. And I'll sketch her, partially nude this time.

He sighed as one thought filled his mind—the thought of making love to Abby.

Chapter 21

Abby Miller laid out all the notes, sketches, and gifts on her bed, then stood there and looked over the treasure trove of items from her mystery lover. In the beginning, she had been flattered and mildly curious as to who this romantic secret admirer might be. But the sketches included with the most recent gift—a gold-plated ankle bracelet—had unnerved her, to say the least. It wasn't that she hadn't tried a few sexually kinky things with various partners, but she wasn't really into S&M, other than enjoying an occasional spanking. She sure as hell didn't find seeing herself depicted as a brutalized sex slave appealing in any way. Staring at the trilogy of sketches that had arrived this afternoon, she shivered. In one she was totally naked and had been impaled, vaginally and anally, by enormous dildos. The expression on her face was one of terror and agony.

Her stomach churned. Just looking at these ink sketches made her sick. The second one was just as revolting. She lay on a bed of flames, her mouth open in a silent scream. But the third was the most menacing of all. Her throat had been sliced open and droplets of blood splattered her chest and dripped off each nipple.

Nausea overcame her just as the doorbell rang. She rushed into the bathroom and retched, emptying her stomach. How could she have been foolish enough to think her mystery man was simply too shy to approach her, or that he had a strong romantic nature and wanted to woo her gradually? She should have suspected, from the moment she had received that first gift, that some nutcase was stalking her.

As she rinsed out her mouth, she heard Ron's voice calling her name.

"Abby? Abby! Where are you? Are you all right?"

After wiping off her damp mouth, she hung the towel on the rack and turned to leave the bathroom. When she did, she ran right into Ron, who apparently had used the key she'd given him weeks ago to let himself into her house.

"Damn it, why didn't you answer me?" He glared at her.

"I was too busy throwing up," she told him.

He narrowed his gaze, glowering at her questioningly. "Are you pregnant?"

"Hell, no!"

"Thank God." The relief showed plainly on his face. "So what's the big emergency? When you called, you said to get over here as fast as I could."

"Did you see the stuff lying on my bed?"

"Not really. I didn't stop to look at anything when I came through the house. I was hunting for you." He grasped her shoulders. "I was worried about you."

She sighed deeply. "I think I'm in big trouble."

He eyed her speculatively. "What kind of trouble?"

She grabbed his hand, then led him into her bedroom and over to her bed. "Look at these things. I've been receiving these items, a few at a time, for the past two weeks."

Ron walked around her bed slowly, studying the items intently, but not touching them.

"Good God Almighty! I don't believe this!"

"What? What is it?" She grabbed his arm and tugged on it.

He turned slowly, then reached out and cupped her face with both hands. "This is bad, baby. Really bad."

"I'm already scared enough," she told him. "You don't have to frighten me any more than I already am."

He squinted his eyes and grimaced. "Why didn't you tell me when you got the first note and gift?"

When he opened his eyes wide and looked right at her, she saw fear—raw, unchecked fear. "What . . . what is it? Tell me?"

After releasing his hold on her face, he took both of her hands into his. "This guy—the one who sent you all these gifts and notes"—he glanced at the bed—"and those sketches—he's the one who killed Stephanie Preston and Thomasina Hardy."

"Wh . . . a . . . t?" Her voice quivered. She'd heard what Ron said, understood the words, but her mind simply could not wrap itself around the meaning. "No, that's not . . . No, you're wrong. You have to be wrong."

She fell apart in Ron's strong arms. He stroked her back and allowed her to cry for a couple of minutes before he grabbed her shoulders, shoved her back and said, "I have to call Bernie and Jim. They need to see these things." He nodded to the bed. "And we need to make sure you have twenty-four-hour-a-day protection."

"You—you think this man—this murderer—is going to come after me?"

Ron nodded. "The last gifts Thomasina Hardy received before her abduction was a gold ankle bracelet and a sketch of her like that one." Ron pointed to the rendering of Abby with her throat cut and blood dripping from her nipples.

"I think I'm going to be sick again." She jerked away from Ron and ran into the bathroom.

As she threw up a second time, she heard Ron on his cell phone. "Jim, it's Ron. Look, get hold of Bernie and you two get over here to Abby Miller's house right away." He recited her address to his boss. "Our serial killer has chosen his next victim."

Ron agreed to spend every night at Abby Miller's house, which didn't surprise Bernie since she'd suspected for months now that the two were having an affair. During the remaining sixteen hours of each day, four other deputies would take four-hour shifts and do it on their own time, to keep the killer's next potential victim safe. Charlie Patterson had shown up with the ABI Crime Scene Unit and they'd whisked away all the evidence—everything Abby had put on display across her satin comforter. The fact that Abby had not only finally notified Ron about the gifts from her mystery man, but that she'd kept all the items her stalker had sent her was the first real break they'd gotten in their Secret Admirer serial killer case.

Bernie played with the Caesar salad that Jim had bought for her when he'd picked up his chicken fingers and fries for lunch. They had been holed up in her office for the past forty-five minutes and Jim had already finished his lunch, including his chocolate pie. Bernie had been talking and thinking and had eaten very little, but she had downed her tall Styrofoam cup of iced tea.

"I think I should fly to Greenville and talk to people who knew Heather and Shannon, the first two victims." Jim gathered up the debris from his lunch and dumped it all in the wastebasket beside Bernie's desk.

"What's the point in doing that?" Bernie tossed the plastic fork down into her salad and closed the lid on the Styrofoam takeout plate. "You talked to Captain Shepard again and he told you that Heather and Shannon were close friends in high school, that they lived only a couple of blocks from each other, and they were both pretty, popular brunettes. What more do you think you'll find out if you go to Greenville? And what makes you think that if you find out anything, it will help us catch this guy?"

Jim huffed. "Call it a gut feeling."

"Look, I'm not discounting your gut feelings, but right now, you're needed here."

When Bernie picked up her plate and cup, Jim reached over and took them from her. They exchanged smiles. He tossed her uneaten lunch and empty cup into the trash.

"We can't count on the crime scene guys coming up with anything useful," Jim said. "We're dealing with a very smart man. There won't be any of his fingerprints on the items he sent Abby Miller. And I'll guarantee you that every gift, every piece of sketch paper, and everything else will all be items that you could purchase just about anywhere, making them pretty much untraceable."

"So you're saying that the fact Abby saved everything really won't help us at all."

"It could help us, but not the way you think."

She eyed him curiously.

"I believe it's time we release a little more information to the press," Jim said. "Just enough so that if any other woman starts receiving strange little gifts and sketches, she'll come to us right away."

"Oh, God, do you know what you're implying? This guy takes one hostage at a time and he doesn't start pursuing another woman until he's killed—"

"Abby's being watched twenty-four/seven. I'm hoping our guy will realize he can't get to her and move on to someone else. Or . . ."

"Or what?"

"Or make a move and get caught."

"How likely is that?"

Jim pursed his lips. "Hmm . . . unlikely, but you never know. He may get so pissed about not being able to grab Abby easily that he'll make a mistake. That's what we have to pray for—that he'll make a mistake, slip up somehow and give himself away."

"Are you saying that's the only way we'll ever catch him?"

"Probably. Sooner or later, most of these guys make a mistake. Sometimes just a small mistake, but it's usually enough to give the officers involved the break they'd been hoping for. Despite how smart our guy thinks he is, it's just a matter of time until he screws up. And he may not even know when he does it."

"Okay, I understand, and you're probably right. But in the meantime, my primary concern is keeping Abby Miller safe." Contemplating, Bernie rubbed her bottom lip over her top lip. "I'm depending on you to help me keep Ron in check. He's emotionally involved with Abby." When she glanced at Jim, he nodded. "You'd already figured that out, hadn't you?"

"Yeah, I think he pretty much gave himself away when he threatened to take apart Dr. Kelley and Reverend Donaldson piece by piece when Abby mentioned them as two men who'd shown an interest in her recently. That's why I ordered Ron to stay away from Brandon Kelley and the reverend and sent John to interview both men."

"Dr. Kelley has alibis for the approximate times Stephanie and Thomasina were murdered," Bernie said. "And I refuse to believe a man as sweet and gentle as Matthew could possibly be a killer."

"Dr. Kelley's alibis are from two of his lovers, women who might lie for him. And it's possible that the good reverend is not what he seems."

"Anything is possible," Bernie agreed. "As for Dr. Kelley's alibis—are you forgetting that my sister was one of those women?"

"And Robyn would never lie?"

"Not to protect a murderer. Not intentionally."

"Hmm . . . Yeah, you're right. She wouldn't."

For the past week and a half—ever since the hot kiss they'd shared in her backyard—Bernie and Jim had been acting as if nothing had happened between them. They were friends—good friends—working together, trying to solve a deadly mystery, trying to catch a ruthless killer. They had shared meals together in the evenings, usually at her house, sometimes at her parents' home. They had assisted Kevin with his homework every night, had taken him to the movies twice, had been enjoying the last days of summer with him at her parents' pool, and had been helping him adjust to his new school and his new life with his father.

But during this time, two subjects had been taboo: the kiss they'd shared and Bernie's sister, Robyn.

"Did you know that Robyn is dating Raymond?" Bernie watched Jim's face for a reaction.

Surprisingly enough, he grinned. "Yeah, I hear those two are quite an item."

"Even my folks think they're an odd couple. Sort of beauty and the beast."

Jim chuckled. "I wouldn't exactly call Raymond a beast."

She stared at Jim, dumbfounded. "You really don't care, do you?"

"That your sister has found someone who'll gladly worship at her feet? Hell, no. I think old Raymond is just what Robyn needs."

Bernie reared back in her chair and crossed her arms over her chest. "You don't have any feelings for Robyn? None at all?"

"I wouldn't say that. I like Robyn. I appreciate the fact

that she's a beautiful woman. And because she's your sister, I care about her."

A silly, totally female reaction fluttered inside Bernie's stomach. "You care about Robyn because she's my sister?"

"Yeah, you know, kind of like any friend of yours . . . or my casa is your casa."

Bernie laughed. "I'm trying to figure that one out."

"You know what I meant. I care about you." He looked right at her. "A lot."

He had rendered her speechless. She sat there and stared at him.

"Heck, you're the first woman, other than relatives, of course, I've ever cared about that I wasn't banging."

Bernie burst into laughter. Jim gave her an odd look. She laughed so hard that her sides hurt and tears dampened her eyes. God love him, he was such an honest man. Bluntly honest, totally macho and about as politically incorrect as a guy could be.

"What's so all-fired funny?"

"You are, Jim Norton. You say something sweet, tell a woman you care about her, and then you go and spoil it by saying something so blatantly macho."

"I warned you that I'm not into political correctness." He reached across her desk and grasped her hand. "I didn't hurt your feelings, did I? The last thing I'd ever want to do is—"

"Ruin our friendship by banging me." She snatched her hand away from him.

Jim's face flushed. She had actually embarrassed him.

"You don't mind cutting a man off at the knees, do you, honey?"

"That's one way to cut you down to my size." She grinned, reminding herself and letting him know that he hadn't seriously offended her, that she neither wanted nor expected more than friendship from him.

He stared at her for one long, rather peculiar moment;

then he slapped his hands on his thighs and said, "Back to business. I should head over to my office and check in with John, see how the interviews with Dr. Kelley and Reverend Donaldson went."

"If anything significant came out of either interview, let me know."

Jim scooted back his chair and stood. "Want to grill steaks tonight?"

"Actually, Dad's Masonic lodge is hosting a fish fry. Catfish, hush puppies, slaw, and fries. All the proceeds go to charity. I bought several tickets. Why don't I pick up three meals and bring them over to your place around six-thirty?"

Jim frowned.

"Something wrong?" she asked.

"You know, I have no idea whether Kevin likes catfish."

"He does. I mentioned the fish fry to him last night and he said he loves catfish."

"What kind of a father doesn't know something like that about his own kid?"

Bernie got up, rounded her desk and put her hand on Jim's shoulder. "A father who hasn't been allowed to spend much time with his son."

"You always know the right thing to say to make me feel better." He leaned over and kissed her cheek. "Just a friendly kiss. Okay?"

"Okay."

"See you around six-thirty."

She stood there and watched him as he left her office, wishing she had the guts to say what she really wanted to say. *Come back here, Jim Norton, and really kiss me. Kiss me the way you did two weeks ago. And as for being the only woman you've ever cared about that you weren't banging— well, screw that. Hell, screw me. Bang me. I want you so much I break out in a cold sweat just thinking about what it would be like.*

* * *

So Abby had kept all his little gifts. That pleased him. But she had shown the items he had so carefully chosen for her to the police. To her lover, Ron Hensley. To Sheriff Granger and Chief Deputy Jim Norton. Why did she have to go and share such precious, intimate items with other people?

Because she doesn't understand. Not yet. She isn't sure who her secret lover is. Once she knows for sure and is certain that I'm the man who adores her, that knowledge will change everything. After all, she's fallen in love with me already. She wants me as much as I want her.

When I go to her and take her away, she'll be happy. I'll make her happy. I'll allow her to prove to me how much she loves me. She won't be like the others. She won't disappoint me.

Abby will give me what I want . . . what I need.

Won't you, my darling?

He watched her house through the binoculars as Deputy Mitchell left and Deputy Hensley entered through the front door. They were guarding her around the clock, protecting her from her destiny, trying to keep them apart. But no power on earth could stop him from claiming what was rightfully his. And Abby was his. Or she soon would be. He simply had to think of a way to outsmart the deputies.

He laughed. Outsmarting these local yokels shouldn't be all that difficult.

Soon, Abby. Soon my love.

Chapter 22

At precisely three o'clock, Jim pulled up at Adams Landing Middle School, which served grades six through eight. R.B. or Brenda had been picking Kevin up every day since school started last week, but Jim had taken off early from work today after promising Kevin they'd go fishing. R.B. had given Jim permission to use his pontoon boat, which he kept moored at the Adams Landing Marina, located in the Tennessee River backwaters, halfway between Adams Landing and Pine Bluff. Jim had invited Bernie to go along with them, but she'd declined.

"I think you two should spend some quality father and son time alone together," she'd told him. And she'd been right. Kevin had been living with him for weeks now, and although they were becoming better acquainted, mostly thanks to Bernie and her folks, he still didn't really know his son. Kevin wouldn't open up and talk to him, not the way he did with Bernie.

Odd thing was, he envied both Kevin and Bernie. He wanted his son to be able to talk to him, to share his worries and concerns, to discuss his hopes and dreams. And sometimes he thought it would be nice if Bernie lavished as much attention on him as she did Kevin. Nutty idea. He was just lonely for female companionship, that's all it was. What he needed was to get laid, and the sooner the better. But except for that one dinner with Robyn and his almost-date with Holly, he hadn't dated anyone since he'd moved to Adams Landing.

Jim opened the driver's door and got out just as the bell rang. Apparently his watch and the school clock weren't synchronized. Either his watch was two minutes fast or the clock was two minutes slow. Within minutes of the bell ringing, front and side doors of the school building flew open and kids of various sizes came barreling outside onto the sidewalks. Kevin had told him that the sixth graders were allowed to leave first; then five minutes later, the seventh and eighth graders were dismissed.

Watching the mad scramble of middle school students, Jim propped up against the side of his truck. He remembered being in middle school, especially eighth grade. He recalled that year for two reasons. He'd gone out for football at the end of that year and had made the team. He'd been big for his age, just like Kevin, who showed no interest whatsoever in the sport Jim loved. And then there was Roseanna Kimball, the prettiest girl in his class. She'd been his first love, the first girl he had French kissed, and the first girl who had let him touch her breasts. He was thirteen, with raging hormones, so whenever he'd just thought about Roseanna, he got a woody. The first time she let him feel her up, he nearly came right on the spot.

"Hey, there's my dad," Kevin called out as he threw up his hand and waved at Jim.

Jim wondered what Kevin was doing coming out of school before his grade had been dismissed; then he saw that Kevin wasn't alone. He was with Deputy Scotty Joe Walters and both of them were loaded down with boxes.

"I'll be there in a minute," Kevin hollered at Jim. "I gotta help Scotty Joe get this stuff to his truck."

Scotty Joe grinned, his teeth bright white against his deeply tanned complexion. Jim wondered if the young deputy got his tan from simply spending a lot of time outdoors or if he used a tanning bed. He was a handsome devil—blue eyed, blond haired, tall and muscular. He'd heard around town that all the young girls had a thing for Scotty Joe. Hell, who could blame them. The guy looked like a cover model out of the latest *GQ* magazine. Or better yet, off the cover of a fitness magazine.

"Kevin helped me with my presentation to the eighth graders today," Scotty Joe said as he headed toward his SUV parked across the street from the line of cars waiting to pick up kids from school. "You've got yourself one great kid there, Captain Norton."

"Yeah, I do." Jim walked over and fell in step with Kevin. "Need some help, son?"

"No, thanks, Dad." Kevin followed Scotty Joe, who hoisted the boxes he carried onto the roof of his vehicle, then unlocked the back hatch and lowered it. He turned to Kevin. "Here, let me take those."

Kevin handed over the boxes. "If you need any help when you come back next week to talk to the seventh graders, just let me know."

Scotty Joe chuckled as he slid the boxes into the back of his SUV. "Smart kid." He winked at Jim. "He's already figuring out ways to cut class without getting into trouble."

"Ah, that's not it and you know it," Kevin said. "I just liked being your assistant today. And I really thought what you had to say was interesting. Besides, you talked to us like . . . well, like we're on your level. You didn't talk down to us like we're a bunch of dumb kids."

Scotty Joe reached out and ruffled Kevin's overly long

hair. Jim realized he needed to get his son an appointment for a haircut pretty soon. He wasn't used to having to worry about things like making sure Kevin got haircuts or him seeing a dentist regularly or dozens of mundane daily things that made up a boy's routine.

"I remember what it was like to be a kid," Scotty Joe said. "It's not easy, especially not when all the grown-ups treat you like you don't have sense enough to come in out of the rain."

Kevin laughed. "You got that right."

"Are you about ready to go, son?" Jim asked.

"Yeah, in just a minute," Kevin replied. "Hey, Scotty Joe, my dad and I are going fishing this afternoon." Kevin glanced back and forth from the young deputy to Jim. "We're borrowing R.B.'s boat. Want to go fishing with us?"

Scotty Joe lifted the other boxes from the roof and looked at Jim, silently asking him how he should respond, whether it was okay to say yes.

"Yeah, why don't you come along with us?" Jim said. "If you have a rod and reel, we can stop by your place and get it."

"If you're sure you don't mind my tagging along, I'd love to go," Scotty Joe shoved the other boxes into place, then turned to Kevin. "Tell y'all what—you two go on and I'll pick up my rod and reel on my way to the community college where we store all our D.A.R.E. stuff, and then I'll meet y'all at the marina. That's where the sheriff keeps his boat, right?" Scotty Joe chuckled. "I guess I should say the former sheriff. But everybody in town still calls R.B. Sheriff Granger."

"Yeah, but Bernie's Sheriff Granger now," Kevin said.

Scotty Joe closed and locked the hatch. "Gets kind of confusing, doesn't it?"

"We're going to pick up some bait and some ice for the cooler," Jim said. "We're drinking colas today. Want any particular kind?"

"Nah, any kind will be fine. And colas are okay with me. I don't drink. Not even beer." He patted his washboard lean belly. "Liquor's not good for the body."

Yeah, probably not when you're young and in prime condition. Just wait till you're forty, got bad knees and ache like the devil. You won't pass up a swig of Jack Daniel's every once in a while.

"We'll see you in about an hour," Jim said.

Scotty Joe nodded, then got in his SUV and started the engine. Kevin followed Jim over to his battered old truck, got in and fastened his seatbelt.

Once Jim was inside, his safety belt secure and his key in the ignition, Kevin asked, "How old do you think Scotty Joe is?"

"I don't know. Late twenties, I guess."

"Do you think he's too young for Bernie?"

"What?" Jim started the engine and knocked the gear into DRIVE.

"Well, if you're not interested in Bernie as a girlfriend, I was thinking maybe Scotty Joe might want to date her."

"What made you think something like that? Scotty Joe is too young for Bernie. Besides, he's not her type."

"What is her type?"

"I don't know. Somebody a little older. A guy who's not such a . . . a . . ."

"A what? I like Scotty Joe. All the guys at my school like him."

"I like him okay, too. It's just that he's not the right guy for Bernie." Jim pulled out into traffic.

"Who is the right guy for Bernie?"

"How should I know?"

"But you said—"

"You shouldn't be playing matchmaker," Jim told his son. "Bernie is perfectly capable of finding herself a boyfriend if she wants one."

"That's not what Miss Brenda says."

Jim groaned.

"I heard Miss Brenda telling R.B. that Bernie didn't know how to get a guy," Kevin said.

"What were you doing eavesdropping?"

"I wasn't. I just happened to overhear them."

"Maybe Bernie doesn't want a boyfriend, ever think of that?"

"I bet if you'd ask her out on a date, she'd go."

"Kevin, I thought we'd settled this issue. Bernie and I are friends. Just friends."

"Yeah, yeah, I know."

Jim reached across the seat and playfully punched Kevin's arm. "Come on, smile. We're going fishing. And your buddy Scotty Joe's going with us."

Kevin offered Jim a tentative smile. "Yeah, we'll have fun." Then he thought for a couple of minutes and added, "But we'd have even more fun if Bernie was coming along, too."

He had been waiting for the right moment. This was the first time he'd ever had to wait longer than he'd originally planned, but Abby had made things more difficult for them by allowing others to become involved in something that should have remained a private matter between the two of them. Although he forgave her, knowing she'd simply made a mistake because she wasn't aware of his identity, he would still have to punish her. She would learn that displeasing him resulted in penalties, often severe, but never unjust. Perhaps Abby would not disappoint him again. Perhaps she would please him from the very first moment they were together.

More than anything on earth, he wanted this time to be the right time, this woman the right woman. He wanted Abby to be more like her. No one could be exactly like her, but he kept searching, kept looking for a duplicate, someone almost as perfect.

Don't think about her. She's gone forever. Resting in peace. Her soul free of earthly torment. You thought when she died that you, too, could find peace, that you would be released from reliving that shameful day again and again.

But her death had not set him free. It had trapped him.

The car pulled into Abby's driveway, alongside the beige Toyota Avalon. Ron Hensley got out and walked to the front door. The door opened and Deputy Downs came outside and talked to Ron a few minutes, then when Ron went inside, John Downs headed for his car.

Changing of the guard.

Abby had police protection twenty-four/seven.

He smiled.

Abby was just the type to want to make him work a little harder to woo and win her. She wanted to see if he would simply give up and go away. She was testing him, forcing him to prove how much he wanted her.

Don't worry, darling. I want you. I want you enough to do whatever I have to do to make you mine.

Abby woke at five-thirty, her head pounding and her heart racing. She sat straight up in bed, gasping for air. She glanced at the other side of the bed. Empty.

"Ron?"

He poked his head out of the bathroom. "I'm here, honey. Just taking a piss before I head for home."

Abby nodded her head in a jerky acknowledgment. "Brett Dennison is relieving you this morning, right?"

"Yep, he should be here any minute." Ron disappeared into the bathroom for a couple of seconds, then reemerged and came over to the bed. He sat down on the edge and pulled Abby into his arms. "Why don't you try to get a couple more hours of sleep? It's Monday and the shop is closed today."

"When I sleep, I dream," Abby said. "I dream about him."

Ron hugged her, then cupped her chin in the curve between his thumb and forefinger. "You're safe, honey. We're not going to let him get anywhere near you. Trust me."

She tried to smile, but wasn't able to do more than lift the corners of her mouth a fraction. "Oh, God, Ron, I'm scared shitless."

He caressed her face tenderly. "Yeah, I know you are."

"You've got to catch this guy." She swallowed a knot of fear. "Soon."

The doorbell rang. Abby jumped as if she'd been shot.

Ron grasped her shoulders and ran his hands down over her arms. "Take it easy. That's just Brett." He forced her to lie back down; then he kissed her forehead. "Try to go back to sleep. I'll see you tonight."

She nodded.

After he left her bedroom, she got up and hurriedly made the bed, then rushed into the bathroom and closed and locked the door. She stripped off her gown, turned on the shower and jumped in while the water was still semicold. Shivering, she stood there, lifted her face and let the spray wash away her tears.

She wasn't sure how long she stayed in the shower— more than five minutes, maybe ten. After she dried off, she ran a comb through her hair, and then searched her closet for something to wear. Shorts and a T-shirt would do since she was staying home all day or at least all morning. Maybe she'd get Brett to take her to the grocery store since Monday was her usual day to hit the Pig and run by Wal-Mart.

Abby's stomach growled, reminding her that she hadn't eaten more than a few bites of supper last night. But the thought of food didn't appeal to her at all. But a cola would hit the spot right about now. She opened the bedroom door and walked down the hall. The least she could do was offer to fix breakfast for Brett. She'd put on a pot of coffee and make him some scrambled eggs and toast. She might be able to keep down some dry toast.

Before entering the living room, she heard the TV and recognized the voices. Brett was watching an early morning show out of Huntsville.

"Hey, I'm up," she called as she walked into the living room. "Would you like some eggs and toast? I thought I'd—"

She stopped dead still. Brett was not in the living room.

He must be in the kitchen or the half bath.

"Brett?"

No response.

"Brett, where are you?"

Silence.

She knocked on the closed door to the powder room. "Deputy Dennison?"

Nothing.

She wiggled the handle, then opened the door. The half bath was empty.

Deputy Dennison had to be here somewhere. Ron would never have left her here alone.

Maybe Brett stepped outside on the front porch.

She rushed to the front door and found it locked and the safety latch in place.

Her heartbeat accelerated.

Don't panic. You are not alone. Brett Dennison is here somewhere. But where? And why doesn't he answer when I call him?

He could be on the back porch. Does Brett smoke? No, I don't think he does. Maybe he's already made coffee and he

*walked out back and . . . Just go see. Reassure yourself that
he's here, that everything is all right.*

When she reached the closed kitchen door, she paused.
What was wrong with her? Why couldn't she just open the
door and go into her own kitchen?

*Because you're allowing your imagination to conjure up
bogeymen where there are none. Deputy Dennison is the
only person beyond that door.*

But what if . . .

Abby turned around and walked across the living room to
where the portable phone lay on the coffee table. She picked
it up and dialed Ron's cell number.

He answered on the third ring.

"Ron?"

"Abby? Honey, what's wrong?"

"You didn't leave me here all alone, did you?"

"What are you talking about?"

"I can't find Brett. The TV's on, but he's not in the living
room and he's not on the front porch."

"Have you checked the kitchen?"

"No, I—I can't. I'm too afraid to open the door."

"Look, honey, just stay calm. I'm heading back to your
place right now. Do you hear me? I'm walking out the door.
Brett's there, probably in the kitchen, fixing some coffee.
Everything is all right. I promise."

"Mmm . . ."

"Abby?"

"What?"

"I'll call Brett on his cell phone and tell him to go into the
living room and let you know everything is fine."

"Yes, please do that. Please."

"I'll be there in ten minutes."

"Ten minutes," she repeated.

With her hand trembling, she tossed the cordless phone

onto the sofa, then turned and stared at the closed kitchen door. After taking a deep breath, she walked straight to the door. When she heard Brett's cell phone ringing, she breathed a sigh of relief. Ron was right. Brett was in her kitchen. Everything *was* all right.

She grasped the doorknob, turned it and opened the kitchen door. Before crossing the threshold, she scanned the room, searching for Brett. The room appeared to be empty. But the backdoor stood wide open. She sighed heavily. He was on the back porch. No wonder he hadn't heard her.

She crossed the room, heading for the back door. But just as she rounded the kitchen table, something blocked her path. It took her brain a couple of seconds to process the information, to realize that what she saw was a body lying on the floor, a small pool of blood around the man's head. The man? Brett Dennison lay facedown on the floor, blood oozing from a wound to the back of his head.

Abby opened her mouth to scream, but before she could utter a sound, someone appeared in the open doorway and entered the kitchen from the back porch.

Trembling, tears clouding her vision, she whimpered, but couldn't move.

"It's all right," he said. "There's nothing to worry about. I'm here now."

She recognized the voice. After wiping the tears from her eyes, she focused on the man coming toward her. He side-stepped Brett Dennison's body.

"Oh, thank God it's you!" she cried. "Something's happened to Brett. Someone hit him on the head. We have to call for help."

"We don't have time to help Brett," he said. "We have to leave now."

"What?"

"Nothing and no one else matters, Abby, except the two of us."

Fear exploded inside Abby as realization dawned. *Dear God in heaven, it couldn't be. It just couldn't be.*

"I've come to take you away," he told her. "So we can be alone, just the two of us."

Chapter 23

Jim handed Bernie a cup of strong, bitter coffee he'd gotten out of the machine in the snack bar downstairs at Adams County General, the county's only hospital. They'd been going nonstop since early this morning, overseeing a massive manhunt for Abby Miller and the person who had almost killed Deputy Dennison. After searching all day and now several hours into the night, using two sets of bloodhounds and the ABI's helicopter unit, they'd found nothing. Nada. Not one damn thing that could lead them to Abby or the madman who had abducted her.

Whoever he was, their Secret Admirer killer, he was a sly devil. Smart. Maybe a little too smart and overly confident. He'd left Brett Dennison for dead. Only thing was, the young deputy hadn't died. His head had been a little harder than his attacker had bargained for. After hours of surgery to relieve the pressure on his brain, Brett was resting in the ICU unit, in critical condition, but hanging on to life.

Bernie took the coffee cup from Jim and set it down on the table at the end of the sofa, then dropped her hands between her spread thighs as she glared down at the floor. Jim was worried about her. The only way he'd gotten her to take a break from the ongoing search was to persuade her that R.B., who was now a reserve inspector for the Adams County Sheriff's Department, could handle things for a couple of hours. He'd had to practically drag her away, despite the fact that she was dead on her feet. But instead of allowing him to take her home for a bite of supper and a short nap, she'd insisted on coming to the hospital to check on Brett.

"I'm concerned about Ron." Bernie nervously tapped the tips of her fingers together. "I've never seen him lose control the way he did this morning. I'd have pulled him off this case if I thought I could have done it without putting him behind bars."

"He'll be okay," Jim said. "Your father will keep him in line."

Bernie rubbed her palms up and down her thighs. "I keep hearing Ron saying, 'I told her she was safe. I told her to trust me.' He's blaming himself. Right now, he honestly thinks that if he'd been with Abby, he could have prevented the kidnapping."

"He might have." Jim sipped on the strong coffee.

Bernie snapped around and glared at Jim. "What are you saying?"

"Nothing against Brett. It's just that our guy picked a time when none of the seasoned deputies were guarding Abby. Not Ron or John or . . . Brett's a novice with only a few months of experience. And our guy chose early morning for the abduction, when there would be very few people up and stirring, and thus few, if any, witnesses to worry about. But there would be enough activity on the roads that no one would pay attention to any specific vehicle."

"You agree with Charlie Patterson, don't you—that Brett knew the guy, that our Secret Admirer killer is a local, a man everybody knows and probably trusts?"

"There was no sign of forced entry at Abby Miller's house.

The backdoor was wide open, so that tells me Dennison actually opened the door for this guy."

Bernie took a deep breath. "Go ahead and say it—tell me what you're thinking."

"Look, honey, let's get out of here. You're not going to be able to see Brett tonight, and the doctors don't know when or if he'll regain consciousness."

"I should talk to his parents again."

"No, you shouldn't. Reverend Donaldson is with them. Let him do his job."

"Then I should be doing mine. Let's drive back out and join one of the search teams."

"Not until you've eaten something and rested for a couple of hours."

"If I were a man, you wouldn't—"

"Stop trying to prove you're invincible," Jim told her. "Damn it, Bernie, we human beings—men and women—can't keep going indefinitely without food and rest. You and I have both been out in the field for a good fifteen hours." He grasped her by the shoulders. "I'm hungry and tired. We need to eat and grab a few hours of sleep."

"Ron is still—"

"Ron's running on guilt and rage. I give him till morning before he burns out and we have to scrape him up off the pavement." Jim eased his hands down Bernie's shoulders, then released his hold on her. He held out his hand. "Come on, let's go."

Bernie sighed loudly. "Okay, you win. We can pick up a bite at the King Kone and—"

"Nope, your mother called me on my cell phone while I was downstairs in the snack bar getting coffee. She has supper waiting for us," Jim told her. "We're going over there to eat and rest. And I can check on Kevin while we're there."

"Oh, damn. I'd forgotten that we were supposed to have

supper with my folks tonight. Mom invited Robyn and Raymond, too. Gee, I hate that I missed that. Robyn and Raymond all lovey-dovey and Mom hearing wedding bells ringing in her head."

Jim stood, reached down and grabbed Bernie's hands, then pulled her to her feet. Standing face to face with her, Jim chuckled. "You just can't bear seeing Robyn and Raymond together, can you, since you had your heart set on snagging him yourself?"

"If I wasn't so damn tired, I'd slap you." Bernie managed a weak grin as she fell into step with Jim as they exited the ICU waiting room. "Maybe you're the one who can't bear seeing those two together."

"Hey, not me. I could care less who Raymond dates."

Bernie emitted a strained chuckle.

Jim paused, reached out and brushed a stray tendril of hair from Bernie's face. His fingertips lingered to caress her cheek. "Raymond was all wrong for you anyway."

"Was he?"

"Hmm . . . You don't need to be worshipped the way Robyn does. You don't want a doormat you can walk all over."

"I don't?"

"Nope, you want an equal. A man who admires you and respects you. Somebody who'll tell you when you're wrong, but stand by your side regardless."

"You don't happen to know somebody like that, do you?"

"I might."

"Well, what if I want more?" Bernie asked as they entered the elevator. "What if I want raw passion and wild sex?"

Jim cleared his throat. "Raw passion and wild sex, huh?"

"Uh-huh."

"I'll see who I can come up with who fits that bill. You

don't mind waiting for the right guy and the right time, do you? I don't think you're quite up to passion and sex tonight, raw and wild or otherwise."

Bernie leaned her head back against the interior elevator wall and closed her eyes. "You're probably right about that. Right now I'd settle for a shower and a thirty-minute nap."

Jim hit the LOBBY button. The elevator doors closed.

"That I can give you tonight," he told her.

"Thank you."

With her eyes still closed, she sighed heavily and crossed her arms over her waist, wrapping herself in a weary hug.

The oddest impulse hit Jim. He wanted to pull Bernie into his arms and hold her. He wanted her to rest her head on his shoulder and let him take care of her.

Instead of acting on that impulse, which he felt certain Bernie wouldn't appreciate, he shuffled his feet a couple of times, looked down at the floor, and stuffed his hands into the pockets of his slacks.

He couldn't go to her. Not yet. It was too dangerous. The local sheriff's department, the ABI, the highway patrol, and police officers from Adams Landing, Pine Bluff, and Verona were still scouring the countryside, searching for Abby Miller and the man who had whisked her away. Reserve officers and local citizens had volunteered to relieve some of the lawmen, allowing them time to eat and rest. It had been easy enough for him to join the search party; actually, it was expected of him.

He'd had a few uneasy moments when the team led by R.B. Granger reported in late this afternoon from the general vicinity of where Abby was waiting for him. Of course, not even the former sheriff was smart enough to figure out his perfect hiding place.

By the time he'd be able to risk going to her—probably

tomorrow night—she would not only be hungry, but she'd probably be filthy. He'd have to change the bed linens, and then bathe her before they made love for the first time. Of course, this morning, when he had deposited her in their little love nest and while she'd still been unconscious from the chloroform, he had touched her and kissed her and . . .

Just thinking about jerking off, his semen spewing out all over her naked belly, aroused him. He had to stop thinking about her, about all the delicious things they would do together, or one of the guys was bound to ask him what he was doing walking around with a hard-on.

Bernie took a quick shower in her mom's bathroom, then slipped into clean jeans and a tank top her mother had laid out for her. Brenda Granger thought of everything. Having a key to both Bernie's house and Jim's duplex had allowed her to send Robyn and Raymond to both places to pick up a change of clothes for each of them. Her mother was nothing if not organized and efficient.

When Bernie entered the kitchen, she found Jim at the round table, wolfing down a plate of summer vegetables and cornbread. Robyn and Raymond sat at the table with him, each of them nursing a glass of sweet iced tea. Brenda, who sat at the bar, and Robyn were chattering back and forth about everything and anything except Abby Miller's disappearance. Raymond remained as quite as a mouse, his dark eyes focused on Robyn.

Poor guy. He's got it bad. And he's actually happy that Robyn is leading him around by the nose. Maybe Jim's right—Raymond just might be the perfect man for my sister.

The moment Brenda saw Bernie, she slid off the bar stool and hurried over to the stove. "I've kept your plate warm. Sit down, dear," she ordered, then glanced at Robyn. "Get your sister a glass of tea."

Robyn obeyed her mother instantly. By the time Bernie sat down across from Jim, her mother had removed her meal from the oven and set the warm plate in front of her. Then Robyn placed a tall glass of iced tea on the table.

Standing behind Bernie, Robyn gripped her sister's tense shoulders. "You need a massage." She kneaded Bernie's neck and shoulders, eliciting a groan from Bernie.

"You're killing me, but don't stop," Bernie said.

"Dad called about ten minutes ago," Robyn said while she continued the massage. "He'll be home by ten. A couple of search teams are going to continue throughout the night, but most of them are calling it quits until daylight." Robyn ended the massage, then gave Bernie's shoulders a hard squeeze.

"Jim's been telling us that Brett Dennison is still unconscious," Brenda said. "That poor boy. His parents are such good people. Brett's engaged, you know, to Melissa Anderson. They're planning a Christmas wedding at the church." Tears flooded Brenda's eyes.

"Mom . . ." Robyn turned and hugged her mother.

"I know. I know." Brenda wiped her eyes with the edge of her lace apron. "I was the sheriff's wife for thirty years and now I'm the sheriff's mother. You'd think that after all these years, I wouldn't allow things like this to upset me so, but I swear, we've never had to face anything like this . . . nothing so horrible. When I think about what might be happening to Abby right this minute—"

"Mother!"

"Oh, Lord, I'm sorry, but this whole Secret Admirer killer stuff has me so nervous. It's got every dark-haired woman in the whole county scared to death."

"We should let Bernie and Jim eat in peace, Mom." Robyn grabbed Brenda's arm and tactfully led her out of the kitchen.

Raymond scooted back his chair and stood. "I'll go see if Robyn needs me."

Alone in the kitchen, Bernie and Jim glanced at each other, but neither of them said anything. What was there to say at this point? They sat there and ate in silence. Despite how much she usually loved her mother's cooking, especially fresh summer vegetables prepared as only Brenda Granger could prepare them, Bernie had to force down every bite. Like her mother, she couldn't stop her mind from wandering into dangerous territory—into the land of imagine the worst. Where was Abby Miller right this minute? And what was happening to her?

Bernie moaned softly as images of Abby's nude body appeared in her mind. Dried blood created a half moon across her neck and droplets of bright red blood dripped from her nipples.

"Don't," Jim said roughly. "Stop it, right now. Do you hear me?"

"He's going to rape her and torture her and then kill her," Bernie said. "And there's not a damn thing we can do to stop him."

Jim shoved back his chair, got up and went over to Bernie. He dropped down on his haunches in front of her, dragged her chair from the table and pulled her into his arms. She went without protest, resting her head on his shoulder and doing her damnedest not to cry. Jim eased her to her feet as she stood up, all the while keeping her wrapped in his embrace.

He rested his chin against her temple. "You need some rest." Without any warning, he scooped her up into his arms and carried her out of the kitchen.

After the initial shock wore off, Bernie draped her arm around Jim's neck. She thought about telling him to put her down, that she didn't need him to take care of her, that she was perfectly capable of walking to her old bedroom up-stairs. But she was too tired, too weak and much too com-fortable in Jim's arms to voice a word of protest.

When Jim passed by the living room as he headed for the staircase, Brenda, Robyn, and Raymond all stared at them with keen interest.

"What's wrong with Bernie?" Brenda cried.

"She's tired," Jim replied. "So I'm taking her upstairs and putting her to bed."

"Oh." Brenda smiled.

Bernie closed her eyes and blocked out everything and everyone as Jim carried her up the stairs. This moment was to be savored, to be enjoyed.

"Which room?" he asked.

"Second one on the right. It's a guest bedroom now."

Jim shoved the door open, carried Bernie over to the bed and deposited her gently on the far side; then he removed her shoes and socks and set them on the floor. She closed her eyes and sighed. A couple of minutes later, she felt the other side of the bed give a little. Her eyes shot open. Jim lay there beside her.

"Go to sleep, honey," he told her. "I'll wake you in a few hours."

"Are you staying here with me?"

"Yeah, if you don't mind."

"I don't mind."

He closed his eyes. They lay there, breathing steadily, not touching, not talking. Then after a few minutes, Jim turned on his side and draped his big arm across Bernie's waist.

Abby had no idea where she was, what time it was or why he had left her alone here in this dark, dismal, underground room.

This is where he'd kept Stephanie Preston before he

killed her. And Thomasina Hardy had probably been shackled to this same bed.

Oh, God, help me!

Had Stephanie begged God for mercy? Had Thomasina
pleaded for her life?

*Damn him. I will not let him kill me. I'll fight him. I'll
claw him and hit him and . . .*

*Ron, where are you? Why haven't you found me? You
promised me that I'd be safe. You told me to trust you.*

This wasn't Ron's fault. He had no way of knowing the
identity of the killer.

No one would ever suspect *him*. He was the last person
on earth she'd have ever thought of as a sadistic killer. She
had trusted him, just as she felt certain Stephanie and
Thomasina had. As everyone in Adams Landing did.

Abby struggled against the ankle chain that bound her,
forcing the metal to dig into her flesh. The pain radiated
from her ankle up and through her whole body. She clamped
her teeth together and endured the pain as she tried harder
and harder to free herself.

Finally exhausted, her ankle bleeding, she accepted the
fact that she could not escape, couldn't move beyond a few
feet from the bed, just far enough to reach the sink, but not
the commode or the shower. She would have to lie here like
a caged animal and wait for her captor's return. She was
hungry and needed to pee. Again. She'd already wet herself
twice, and the stench of her own urine overpowered the
metallic scent of her blood.

*Despite the condition you're in, be thankful. When he
comes back, you don't know what he'll do to you. Prepare
yourself to endure whatever happens, no matter how terrible. Survival is all that matters.*

Chapter 24

Abby Miller's nude body was found by hikers near a campsite at Adams County Park fifteen days after she disappeared from her home. Like the Secret Admirer killer's other victims, she had been repeatedly raped and tortured before her abductor slit her throat, probably with the same knife he'd used at least nine other times. Jim was now convinced, more than ever, that Abby was the madman's tenth victim and twenty-one-year-old Heather Stevens had been his first victim nearly seven years ago.

Jim had spoken to Bernie this morning, shortly before she left home to attend Abby's funeral. The entire town of Adams Landing was in mourning, the whole county shocked and outraged over the third murder that had shattered their quiet, peaceful, safe lives. He wished he could be in two places at once so that he could stand at Bernie's side today. She needed all the moral support she could get. She not only felt overwhelmed by a great sense of responsibility to the citizens who had elected her, but there were rumblings throughout the county that if R.B. was still sheriff, the killer would be behind bars by now. As much as Bernie might need him today, Jim felt certain that what he was doing now would, in the long run, prove more beneficial in solving the case that, up to this point, had proved unsolvable.

As he parked his rental car on the street in front of Hilary Etheridge's home in Greenville, South Carolina, Jim thought about his brief telephone conversation with his boss. Only two months ago, he had dreaded leaving Memphis to live and work in Adams Landing. Now, he realized that making that particular move had probably been the smartest thing he'd ever done. He and Kevin were building a true father/son relationship, and he had formed a friendship with Bernie Granger that meant more to him than he liked to admit.

"I've given Ron a one-month leave of absence," Bernie had said. "He doesn't want to take it, but—"

"You can't let him make that decision. He's in no shape to work. You did the right thing. He needs some time off to mourn and get his head straight."

"I know. It's just I worry that I'll wind up having to put him in jail for interfering in this case. He's sworn he'll keep searching for Abby's killer, whether or not he's officially on the case."

"Have R.B. talk to him. And if that doesn't work, lock his ass up for a few days."

"Ron's not our only problem."

"Are you saying everything's fallen apart since I've been gone? Honey, it's been less than twenty-four hours since I left."

She hadn't laughed, but in his mind's eye, he could see her smiling. "I told you that you were needed here."

"What else is wrong?"

"Brandon Kelley has hired himself a lawyer. He says he's sick and tired of being harassed every time a new body shows up."

"That was to be expected," Jim had told her. "If I'd known all three victims the way Dr. Kelley did, I'd have already hired myself a lawyer."

"Mmm . . . yeah, I know. So, are you going to talk to Heather Stevens's family today?"

"Her father is dead and her mother refused to talk to me. But she has a younger sister. I spoke to her last night and she's agreed to see me this morning."

"Good luck, Jim. I hope you find out something that can help us before our killer chooses his next victim."

Jim didn't know what he'd find out from Heather's sister, if anything. He had no idea what he was looking for, but his gut instincts told him that the answer to all their questions about the Secret Admirer killer were here in Greenville. He felt certain that Heather Stevens was the key to unlocking the mystery.

Hilary Stevens Etheridge had been seventeen when her twenty-one-year-old sister Heather was murdered. The lead detective on Heather's case, Hal Shepard, had met with Jim late yesterday at the police station and had pulled strings to get copies made of the old files. Jim had spent half the night going over those files, reading and rereading the information, hoping something would give him a clue to the identity of Heather's killer. After nearly seven years, the case was still unsolved, as was the murder of Heather's best friend, Shannon Elmore, which occured a year later, here in Greenville.

Jim got out of the rental car, locked it and walked up the sidewalk to the neat two-story brick house in a new, upscale neighborhood. The Stevens family had money and social standing in the community, as did Kyle Etheridge, the man Hilary had married two years ago. If the police could have solved Heather's murder case, they would have. Her family had used all their influence to pressure local law enforcement.

Jim rang the doorbell and waited. Several minutes later, an attractive young woman, obviously very pregnant, opened the door.

"Mrs. Etheridge?"

"Yes." She offered him a fragile smile. "And you're Captain Norton?"

He nodded.

"Please come in."

He followed her from the foyer into the twenty-by-twenty living room and took the seat she indicated on the sleek, modern sofa. She eased her rotund body into a large, over-stuffed chair and placed her hands beneath her protruding belly.

"I appreciate your talking to me," Jim said.

"If what you say is true—that the person who killed Heather has gone on to kill nine more women—" Her voice cracked. She twined her fingers together.

"I've spoken to former police captain Hal Shepard," Jim said. "He's gone over the case with me and I've scoured the records, searching for anything that might help me."

"But you found nothing."

"Yeah."

"In the end, the police concluded that Heather had been kidnapped, raped and murdered by some transient crazy who moved on right after the murder."

"No one in her family, none of her friends or acquaintances knew of anyone who had something against Heather, right?" Jim asked.

"That's right. My sister was very popular in high school and college and well liked by everybody. She was bright and beautiful and—" Hilary swallowed her tears.

"Are you saying she didn't have any enemies, no one who was jealous of her? No old boyfriend who might not have been able to accept that she had someone new in her life?"

Hilary looked directly at Jim. "Of course, there were girls

jealous of her. All the girls envied her. There wasn't a brunette at Leighton Prep who didn't want to be one of the Sable Girls. But a woman didn't rape and murder my sister. And as for old boyfriends . . ." Hilary shook her head. "If you read the police files, you know that Captain Shepard questioned all of Heather's old boyfriends and not one was ever a suspect."

"What's a Sable Girl?" Jim asked.

Hilary smiled. "Oh, that was a very exclusive little club that Heather created, just for her and a few of her best friends who were also brunettes. She formed the group her junior year, when she was sixteen."

Jim's gut tightened. "How many members were there in the Sable Girls club?"

"Oh my, I'm not sure. It was years ago. Not many. Four or five, I think, counting Heather." Hilary laughed. "I did so want to grow up to be a Sable Girl." She ran her fingers through her silky red hair. "But I'm afraid I didn't possess the right color hair."

"Would you mind trying to remember exactly how many members there were and what their names were?" Realizing his tone of voice bordered on badgering, he added, "Please."

"Oh, yes . . . well, let me see. There was Heather and Shannon, of course."

"Shannon Elmore."

Hilary frowned. "She was murdered, too, and for a while we thought . . . The police could never prove the two murders were related. Shannon was killed over a year later, and although there were similarities . . ." Hilary took a deep breath. "But you already know all this, don't you?"

Jim nodded. "Can you recall the names of any of the other girls in Heather's exclusive little club?"

"I'm not sure. You know people from out of state send their kids to Leighton Prep. It's one of the most prestigious private schools in the Southeast."

"Give me a first name, a description . . . anything."

"There was a girl from Tennessee. I can't remember her name. She didn't graduate from Leighton Prep. For some reason, she left at the end of her junior year."

"Was her name Courtney Pettus?"

"It could have been. I only met her once . . . at Heather's birthday party, and there were hundreds of people there."

"Does the name Sara Hayes sound familiar?"

"Hmm . . . Sara Hayes has a familiar ring to it. I'm pretty sure one of the Sable Girls was named Sara, but I'm not sure about the last name. She graduated with Heather, but they went off to different colleges." Hilary pinned him with a sharp glare. "Why are you asking me questions about the Sable Girls?"

"Just curious. Grasping at straws." Jim rose to his feet. "I don't suppose you have a yearbook from Leighton Prep, do you? One from your sister's junior year?"

"No, I'm sorry, I don't, but Mother may have kept Heather's yearbooks."

"Do you think you might be able to get your hands on a copy and send it to me?"

"Why do you—?"

"If you thought it might help to catch your sister's killer, would you send me a copy of that yearbook?"

"Yes. Yes, I would."

"I'll leave you my address and phone number."

"I'll see what I can do, Captain Norton."

"I'd appreciate it."

Abby's funeral had been delayed long enough for her husband to fly home from the Middle East. It was a toss-up as to who was more bereaved—the husband or the boyfriend. Ricky Wayne's mother clung to him, her strength apparently the only thing holding him together. Deputy John Downs and retired sheriff R.B. Granger flanked Ron Hensley through the entire funeral, including the brief graveside service. Just about everybody in Adams Landing showed up and possibly half the county. Being a beautician with lots of satisfied customers, Abby had been well known and well liked.

With such a huge turnout, people would have noticed if he hadn't put in an appearance at the funeral and now at the Miller home. He paid his condolences, spoke to everybody he knew, and made his way outside onto the front lawn, where people milled about in the humid September sunshine.

Abby had been his greatest disappointment. She had fought him to the very end. No matter how many times he punished her, how badly he hurt her, she would never admit that she loved him. Choosing her had been a mistake. Except for her beautiful dark hair, she'd been nothing like Heather. Abby Miller had been a cheap tramp, a stubborn, stupid cunt.

He had agonized over how he could have made such a mistake in choosing Abby. She was the first who had defied him day after day, never accepting the fact that he was her master. He knew he couldn't act hastily in selecting the next woman, possibly the last woman here in northeast Alabama before he'd be forced to move on. His next choice would give him one more chance to find his perfect mate, someone as worthy of him as Heather had been.

She was out there somewhere, just waiting for him. Someone young and lovely. A pretty brunette. A lady desired by many men. She might even be here today in this crowd of mourners.

After leaving Leighton Prep, Jim drove straight to the airport to catch his evening flight. He'd spent most of the after-

noon trying to get in to see the principal, a hoity-toity little
man named Alistair Dueitt, who'd finally agreed to a brief
meeting after Hal Shepard had intervened.

No, he wouldn't reveal the names of any previous Leighton
Prep students, Dr. Dueitt had adamantly declared. It was
against school policy. And no, he would not loan Jim a copy
of the yearbook from Heather Stevens's junior or senior years.
If the Stevens family had not chosen to share Heather's yearbook with Jim, then the school was certainly not at liberty to
do so.

Jim had struck out on all counts. Except one. He'd learned
an interesting bit of information not even mentioned in the
police files. Heather Stevens and Shannon Elmore had belonged to some snobby group of teenage brunettes who'd
called themselves the Sable Girls. And Jim would bet his
pension that Sara Hayes and Courtney Pettus had also been
members of that exclusive little club. But he couldn't travel
from city to city, from state to state, interviewing people, investigating the lives of the killer's victims. He was way out
of his jurisdiction, with absolutely no legal authority. What
he needed was a private investigator. As luck would have it,
he just happened to know one.

Settling in at the busy, bustling airport to wait on his
flight, Jim put in a call to Griffin Powell. He hoped his old
buddy would agree once again to work pro bono. Neither
Jim nor Adams County could afford to pay the kind of fees
the Powell Agency charged.

"What's up, Jim?" his former UT roommate asked.

"I need another favor. Another freebie."

"Something to do with the Secret Admirer killer?"

"Have you been reading Huntsville newspapers, or has
word already spread all the way to Knoxville about what's
going on in northeast Alabama?"

"Let's just say that I've kept informed. So, what do you
need?"

"I need you to do this as a personal favor," Jim said. "The sheriff's department is not hiring you. I am. And you know the state of my financial affairs."

Griffin chuckled. "Like you said, this will be another freebie."

"Okay, thanks. First, I need a list of students who attended Leighton Prep in Greenville, South Carolina, at the same time a young woman named Heather Stevens went there. She graduated eleven years ago."

"Send me what information you have and I'll get right on it."

"I also need a yearbook from that same time, from Heather's junior and senior years."

"Okay."

"And one more thing."

"Just one more."

Jim grunted. "Yeah, I need to find out why a girl named Courtney Pettus left Leighton Prep after her junior year."

When Jim arrived home, he found Bernie waiting up for him and Kevin asleep on the sofa, Boomer resting at his feet. Wearing a pair of faded jeans and a seen-better-days T-shirt, Bernie met him at the door, her hair sleep-tousled, her face void of makeup, and looking better than a woman had a right to at this time of night. His plane had landed forty-five minutes ago, and he'd broken a few speed limits on his drive from Huntsville. Why? Because he'd known Bernie would be waiting for him.

"You look beat," she said.

He dropped his black vinyl overnight bag on the floor, reached out and pulled Bernie into his arms. Her eyes widened in surprise.

"Have you been drinking?" she asked.

"I don't drink and drive." He buried his face in her shoulder and kissed her neck.

She went rigid. "What's gotten into you?"

"Don't get your panties in a wad, Sheriff." He lifted his head and released her. Damn uptight . . . Why did she tense up every time he touched her? "You're not going to have to fight me off."

"Jim, you're acting peculiar."

"Dad?" Kevin roused from his nap, lifting his head from the sofa and waving at his father. Boomer wiggled around, lifted his head and stared at Jim.

"Yeah, it's me, son. I'm home."

"I tried to stay awake," Kevin said.

"You didn't have to. Why don't you go on to bed? I'll see you in the morning."

Yawning, Kevin staggered to his feet, then plodded sleepily to his bedroom; Boomer trotted along behind him. As soon as Kevin was out of earshot, Bernie grabbed Jim's arm.

"What makes you think that if you made a move on me, I'd want to fight you off?"

"Huh?" He was too tired, too frustrated and too horny to play word games.

"Did you meet some sexy little number on the plane, somebody who got you all hot and bothered?" Bernie asked. "Is that why you—?"

He grabbed her, yanked her to him and looked her right in the eyes. "If I'd met a woman on the plane who turned me on, I'd have booked a room, stayed overnight in Huntsville and fucked her brains out until morning."

Bernie stared at him, her eyes wide, her mouth agape.

"But you know what the funny thing is, Sheriff Granger?"

She shook her head.

"The only thing I could think about after I boarded my flight home was you and Kevin and how much I was looking forward to seeing both of you, to coming home to you and my son."

Moisture glistened in Bernie's golden brown eyes.

"And if my son wasn't back there asleep in his bedroom, I'd be all over you right now, because, lady, I've got the hard-on from hell, and you're the one who gave it to me."

"I—I—"

Jim kissed her—deep and hard and long. His tongue in her mouth and his hands on her ass. But less than a minute into the kiss, he ended it. Both of them gasped for air.

"I'd better go home," she said.

"Yeah, you'd better."

She grabbed her shoulder bag off the coffee table and headed for the front door. Jim followed her. After opening the door, she turned and faced him.

"You can give me a full report on your trip to Greenville in the morning," she said.

"I'll do that."

"Boomer can spend the night with Kevin, and he can take Boomer with him over to my parents' house in the morning."

"Okay."

"Good night, then."

"Good night." When she stepped out onto the porch, he followed her. "Oh, by the way, tomorrow night I'm going to take you out on a date, if that's all right with you."

"It's all right with me."

"I'll call your folks in the morning and see if Kevin can sleep over tomorrow night. Is that all right with you, too?"

"Yes, it is."

Jim kissed her again—on both cheeks, then on her lips. When he lifted his head, he grinned. "See you in the morning, honey."

"Uh-huh." She turned and floated down the steps, up the sidewalk and to her Jeep.

Chapter 25

Jim had checked with Bernie before making reservations at River's End, since that was where he'd gone with Robyn on their date. But it was the only really fancy restaurant in the area, unless you drove to Huntsville. It had been a long time since he'd wanted to impress a woman. A long time? Who was he kidding? It had been forever. Not since back when he'd been young and madly in love with Mary Lee. Not that he was in love with Bernie. Not exactly. He wasn't a guy who used the "L" word lightly. Actually, he'd seldom used the word, even when he'd been married. Maybe that was because Mary Lee had said it all the time, to everybody. Said it without any meaning, with no conviction behind it, no actions to support it.

He didn't think much about Mary Lee any longer, except in connection to their son. He didn't hate her. Didn't love her. Didn't care. But for Kevin's sake, he hoped she would regain her health and live to a ripe old age.

After he'd made reservations for seven-thirty at River's End, Jim got to thinking about picking Bernie up in his old truck. One of these days, he'd have to buy something a little newer, but future purchases hadn't solved his problem for tonight. In the end, he'd just told Bernie about his predicament, something he wouldn't have dared do with any other woman. Just one more reason why he liked her so much.

"We'll take my Jeep," she'd said. "No problem."

No problem. No demands. No bitching and complaining. No unreasonable expectations. Bernie was a low-maintenance woman. How lucky could a man get?

Yeah, just how lucky would he get tonight? Jim chuckled nervously as he pulled up in front of Bernie's house, leaving the driveway clear for them to back out in her Jeep. He sure as hell hoped that he and Bernie were on the same page about this date; otherwise, he'd make a complete fool of himself later when he took her back to his place.

Just take things slow and easy. Let her lead and you follow.

When he got out of his truck, he bent down and glanced at himself in the dusty rearview mirror. Maybe he should have worn a tie instead of leaving the button-down shirt open at the neck. But if he'd worn his tie, he'd have had to have worn his suit because the two matched. Would Bernie be disappointed because he'd dressed in khaki pants and a hunter green shirt? He didn't want to disappoint her, but at the same time, if they were going to be dating, she'd just have to take him as he was. Jim Norton was no *GQ* cover model. His sense of style was nil. He dressed for comfort, not fashion.

But what if she's wearing some slinky little dress and maybe bling-bling earrings and—nah, not his Bernie. She wasn't the bling-bling type. But she had mentioned that Robyn was so excited that Bernie had a date, she'd offered to come over and do Bernie's hair and makeup.

The walk to Bernie's front door seemed a mile long. *That's because you're nervous. You'd think you were four-*

teen, not forty. Good God man, your life doesn't depend on how this date turns out.

Then again, maybe it does.

He rang the doorbell.

"Be right there," Bernie called out to him.

Two minutes later, while he shuffled his feet and took some deep breaths to calm his jitters, Bernie opened the door.

"I'm ready."

At first all he saw was her wide, wonderful smile. Then he focused on her entire face. No heavy makeup. No cat-eyes black liner. No red lipstick. Instead, she looked like Bernie always looked, except her skin had a glow to it. The makeup was subtle and suited Bernie perfectly. Pinky peach and subdued.

Jim took a step back so he could scan her from head to toe. "Wow!"

Twirling in a look-at-me spin, she laughed. "Robyn brought over five new outfits for me to try on," Bernie admitted. "And this was the only one that I felt halfway comfortable in. She took the others back to the store."

"You look good, honey."

Good enough to eat.

The dress was simple. He figured it was silk. Light yellow silk. Short sleeves, round neckline that didn't plunge to show off her cleavage and a hem that hit her at the knees. No bling-bling. Just simple little pearl studs in her ears, a gold watch on one wrist, and a single-strand pearl bracelet on the other.

Jim offered her his arm. "Your carriage awaits." He laughed. "And it is *your* carriage."

She turned and locked her front door, then handed him her key ring. "You drive, okay?"

"Okay."

Smiling warmly, with a sly little twinkle in her eyes, she slipped her arm through his. "I haven't looked forward so much to a date in a long time."

That was another thing he liked about Bernie. She was a straight shooter. No games. Just up-front and honest.

"Yeah, me, too," he said, then walked her out to her Jeep.

Raymond had met Robyn at the fitness center and walked her home, something he did almost every day. He was so attentive, so adoring, like a faithful little puppy. At least that's the way she'd thought of him at first, but not so much now. She'd told him when they had started dating that it would not be an exclusive relationship, and at the time she'd meant it. Funny thing was that since the night they'd made love for the first time, she hadn't had sex with anyone else. Why should she? Raymond was a fabulous lover.

So what if everybody in town was referring to them as the odd couple. So what if her own mother had questioned the wisdom of her dating Raymond. And why should she care that Helen Long was disappointed that her son was dating the wrong Granger sister?

"Do you want to drive into Huntsville tonight?" Raymond asked as he took Robyn's key from her and opened the door to her apartment.

She shook her head. "I don't think so. I'm not in the mood to make the club scene tonight. Why don't we stay in and—" She cuddled up to his side, slid her arm around his waist and nuzzled his neck.

Raymond blushed. She loved that she could make him blush. He was such a sweetie.

When Robyn walked into her apartment, she stepped on something that made her foot slide. Tightening her hold around Raymond's waist to steady herself, she halted immediately, then looked down at the floor and saw a small white envelope. *How odd.*

"What is it?" he asked. "What's wrong?"

"I don't know. Nothing, I guess." She pointed to the envelope. "That's not yours, is it?"

"The envelope? No, it's not mine."

Robyn pulled away from him, bent over and picked up the envelope. "Somebody must have slipped it under the door sometime today."

"Maybe it's a message from one of your old boyfriends." Raymond's voice held a hint of jealousy. "Dr. Kelley or Paul Landon or Ron Hensley or—"

She whirled around, envelope in hand, and held it out to him. "Here, you open it."

He stared at her hand for a few seconds, then took the envelope. "It has your name printed on the front. See." He held it up, pinched between his thumb and forefinger.

"Just open the damn thing, will you?"

Raymond ripped it open, removed a single sheet of paper and scanned the page. "I don't think it's from any of your old boyfriends."

"Oh, what does it say?"

He read, "I worship you from afar, my beautiful Robyn."

"That's it?"

"Yes, that's it."

An uneasy feeling rippled along her nerve endings. "It's an odd note, isn't it?"

"Not really all that odd when we both know that most of the men in Adams County are halfway in love with you."

He is jealous. But he has no reason to be. Maybe there are a lot of men in Adams County who have the hots for me, but I'm not interested in any of them. I don't want any of them.

She wrapped her arms around Raymond's neck and gazed

into his eyes. "Well, I'm not halfway in love with any other man. Only with you."

Every muscle in his body tensed. He pulled away from her. "Don't do that. Don't play games with me. Don't say something you don't mean."

"What if I do mean it?" *Yeah, what if I do?*

"Do you?"

She nodded. "Yeah, I think I do." She laughed. "Wow, when did that happen?"

"Robyn?"

"Look, this is all new to me. I wasn't expecting to go and fall for you. The sex is great and all, but . . . oh, jeez, Raymond, you know you're not really my type, so it never entered my head that anything more would come of our relationship."

"Don't get upset, sweetheart." He clamped his hands around her upper arms. "We'll take this one step at a time. I won't try to rush you into anything. Right now, having you halfway in love with me is more than I'd ever dared hope for."

Dinner had been delicious. The wine perfect. The candle-lit atmosphere romantic. So far, this was turning out to be the most wonderful evening of Bernie's life. On the way to River's End, they had made a pact not to discuss business.

"Only personal stuff," Jim had said.

Dinner conversation had included sharing stories of their childhoods, exchanging horrid memories of each of their worst dates ever, and touching on the subject of what had gone wrong in their marriages. They had both been betrayed by cheating spouses whom they had later divorced. She and Jim felt the same way about marriage, about fidelity, about trust.

"Want to dance before we order dessert?" Jim asked.

"I'd love to dance with you." Any excuse to be in his arms.

He stood, came around and pulled out her chair, then took her hand and led her onto the dance floor. The restaurant didn't have a band, just a lone piano player whose repertoire seemed to include every old romantic standard ever written. As Jim eased Bernie into his arms, the pianist began playing a sentimental rendition of "Someone to Watch over Me."

"You know what?" Bernie said.

"What?"

"You're a good dancer."

Jim chuckled.

"A good dancer, a good listener, a good friend, a good father . . ."

Jim tightened his hold around her, pressing her intimately against him as he whispered in her ear. "You're showering me with all these compliments just because later tonight you want to get in my pants."

Bernie giggled. "I can't fool you, can I? You saw right through me, straight to my ulterior motive."

"I think you're pretty special, too, you know."

"Is that right?"

"Uh-huh. And just in case there's any doubt in your mind about my ulterior motive—"

He paused on the dance floor, long enough to pull her closer, close enough so that she felt his erection.

Every nerve in her body tingled. A clutching grip tightened and then released inside her.

"I believe we have the same ulterior motive," she told him.

"Would I be rushing things if I suggested we skip dessert and head over to my place?"

"I'm really not hungry for dessert."

Jim released her, reached down and took her hand, then led her off the dance floor and back to their table. He called the waiter, asked for their check, and paid him immediately, telling the young man not to bother with any change. Hand in hand, Jim and Bernie hurried out of the restaurant. Once inside her Jeep, he leaned across the console, circled her neck with his big hand and pulled her toward him so that he could kiss her.

When he lifted his head, he pulled back and looked at her. "I'm not real good with words, you know. I may not say all the right things. Things you'd like to hear. But . . . I . . . er . . . it won't be just sex for me, for us. I care about you."

"I care about you, too," she said. "And it's all right that you're not good with words. You know what they say—actions speak louder than words. I'm a woman who likes action."

"That I can give you, honey. In spades."

Dear God, if this is a dream, don't let me ever wake up.

Robyn came for the second time. Screaming, shuddering, unraveling completely. As the aftershocks trickled through her, she spread out over Raymond and laid her head on his shoulder. He caressed her naked hip as he kissed her forehead.

"Mm . . . mm." She loved making love with Raymond. Not once had they had sex that she hadn't come, usually more than once.

"Are you hungry?" he asked.

"Ravenous."

"Want me to go out and pick us up something?"

Sighing contentedly, she rubbed her naked body over his, then rolled off him and stretched. "Why don't we just fix sandwiches? I'd rather stay right here and go straight back to bed after we eat."

He grinned sheepishly. "Woman, you're going to be the death of me."

"You think so, huh?"

"Oh, yes. I can see the headlines now: RAYMOND LONG DIES IN THE THROES OF PASSION."

Giggling, Robyn cuddled against him, then kissed his shoulder. "You know what—I really am halfway in love with you."

He came up over her, lowered his head and said, "And I'm completely, totally, madly in love with you." Then he gave her a long, slow, wet kiss.

The phone rang.

"Who the hell?" She rolled over, then reached out and lifted the crystal receiver from the brass and crystal base on her nightstand. "This had better be important because you're interrupting something wonderful."

"Did you get my note?" the male voice asked.

Robyn gripped the telephone tightly as she sat up in bed. "Who is this?"

"I'm your secret admirer."

"What did you say?"

Raymond sat up and put his arm around Robyn. "Who is it? What's wrong?"

"I'm your secret admirer, my darling," the muffled voice repeated. "And when the time is right, I will reveal my identity to you. But for now, sleep well, my beautiful Robyn. And dream of your mystery lover who longs to touch you, longs to whisper love sonnets in your ear, longs to fulfill your every fantasy."

Robyn slammed the phone down on the base, terror racing through her at breakneck speed. "My God. Oh, my God!"

Raymond turned her in his arms, then grasped her chin and forced her to look at him. "Who was that?"

"My—my secret admirer."

"Your what?"

"He said he was my secret admirer, that he'd sent the note

we found on the floor, and that when the time is right, he'll reveal his identity to me."

Raymond wrapped her in his trembling arms. "It'll be all right, sweetheart. It'll be all right. But we need to call Bernie and tell her what's happened."

Robyn shook her head. "No, I can't. Not tonight. Bernie and Jim are on their very first real date. I can't ruin that for her. I won't."

"But, Robyn, if the man who called you is—" Raymond paused, swallowed and then cleared his throat.

"If he's the same man who killed Abby and Thomasina and Stephanie, that means he's chosen me as his next victim."

Raymond held her so tightly that she could barely breathe, but she wanted him to hold her tighter, much tighter, and never let her go.

Chapter 26

Half a second after Jim closed his front door behind them and locked it, he grabbed Bernie and kissed her. His hands went into immediate action, caressing her shoulder blades, her waist, her hips, then sliding over and down to cup her buttocks and lift her so that her mound pressed against his sex. He was hurting something awful. If he'd ever wanted a woman this much, he couldn't remember it. But then his mind wasn't what ruled his actions right now.

As she kissed him back, every bit as hot and hungry as he was, he wadded the back of her dress in his hands. Then he started inching the dress higher and higher until he managed to slide both of his hands underneath the hem. When he stroked the soft, satiny material that covered her butt, she whimpered into his mouth.

While she unbuttoned his shirt, he slipped one hand inside the back of her panties and thought he'd lose it on the spot when he felt her bare skin.

This wasn't the way he'd planned it. He'd wanted their first time to be special, something Bernie would remember with pleasure. Damn, why hadn't he waited a few minutes

Beverly Barton

before pawing her? He'd intended to seduce her slowly, and then lead her into his bedroom. Shit! His bedroom. That's where they should be—the room he'd prepared for their love-making.

Bernie jerked his shirttail from his pants and shoved the shirt off his shoulders and down his arms. Taking over from her, he grasped the cuffs, pulled off his shirt and tossed it aside. The minute his chest was bare, she lowered her head and licked a circle around each of his tight nipples. Then she apparently noticed the scars on his side. With quivering fingertips, she traced the lines of his old battle scars from gunshot wounds he'd received as a Memphis police officer.

Groaning deep in his throat, he reluctantly removed his hands from her panties and searched for the zipper on her dress. As soon as he found the tab, he yanked it down, then peeled the dress to her waist, over her hips, and let it fall to her feet. She kicked the yellow silk aside and stood there in her satin panties and bra, shivering ever so slightly.

"Damn, Bernie . . . damn!"

He'd been more than ready before he got a good look at her, but one glimpse of her nearly naked body sent him beyond ready to got-to-have-it-now.

She reached out and tried to undo his belt buckle. When she fumbled in her attempt, he took over and hurriedly undid the buckle, opened his belt and unzipped his slacks. In no time flat, he divested himself of every stitch of clothes except his white cotton briefs.

With her gaze moving over him appreciatively, Bernie licked her lips. He grasped the back of her head and drew her into another long, hard kiss. She rubbed him through his cotton briefs, her movements agonizingly slow and steady. He was on the verge of coming. Right here. Right now.

Moaning into her ear, he covered her hand with his and lifted it away from his crotch. "I can't take much more of that, honey."

After laying her hand on his chest, he reached around and unhooked her bra. All the while, she kissed his neck and shoulder. He removed her bra, tossed it on the floor, then lifted her breasts in his hands and leaned back away from her just enough to take a good look.

Damn, what a pair of tits! High, firm, round, and a lot more than a handful. He lowered his mouth and suckled her. She tossed back her head and gripped his forearms.

With his mouth sucking on her nipple and his hands kneading her butt, he backed her across the room to the sofa, then toppled her over and came down on top of her. She touched him and kissed him, whimpering and pleading, her body writhing, trying to get closer to him. Barely managing to control her, he lifted her hips and yanked her panties down and off; then before she knew what he intended, he spread her legs apart and positioned himself between her thighs.

She grabbed his head, threading her fingers through his hair. "Jim . . . ?"

He delved his tongue between her wet, swollen lips, seeking her clitoris. When he found the little nub, he pressed his tongue against it. Bernie bucked her hips and tightened her fingers in his hair. Loving the guttural sounds she made, he licked and stroked and sucked. Realizing she was on the verge of coming, he lapped a littler harder, a little faster—and lifted his hands up to cover her breasts. When he pinched both nipples tightly, she fell apart, gushing as she came. Moaning. Shivering.

When he lifted his head, she opened her arms to him.

He eased up and over her, kissing her from mound to navel, from navel to breasts, from breasts to lips. She put her arms around him and licked his ear.

"I want you inside me."

"The condoms are in my bedroom," he told her.

"Then let's go to your bedroom."

He slid off her and stood; then when she sat up, he shoved

his arm beneath her and hoisted her off the sofa and into his arms. She clung to him as he carried her across the living room and into the hall that separated the two bedrooms.

He sat at the desk covered with his art supplies and admired the sketch he had just completed. A portrait of Robyn Granger, a woman almost as beautiful as Heather Stevens. Robyn possessed the same silky black hair, the same dark brown eyes, the same tall, shapely body. Their features weren't identical, of course. No one on earth looked just like Heather. She had been perfect in ways no other woman was or ever could be. Heather had been the ideal woman. She had been destined to be his. But fate had played a cruel hoax on them.

No, no, that's not true, an evil inner voice told him. *Fate didn't play a cruel hoax on the two of you. Heather was the one who played the cruel hoax on you.*

He covered his ears with his open palms. "I won't listen. I won't. Get out of my head and leave me alone. Heather loved me. She told me she did. She promised me—"

She promised you her body, but she never had any intention of keeping that promise. She made a fool of you, that's what she did.

Outraged that he could not control the voice inside his head, could not erase the painful memories, he swept his hand across the table and sent his art supplies flying through the air. Breathing hard, tears threatening to blind him, he went down on all fours and searched for two items—the sketch of Robyn and the string of pearls that would be his first gift to her.

Sitting in the middle of his bedroom, he clutched the portrait and the pearls to his chest. He was sick and tired of being disappointed over and over again by women who swore that they loved him, who enticed him with their sexy bodies and beautiful faces, then in the end begged him to set them free.

They might hurt him, disappoint him, and lie to him, but they did not make the rules of the game. He made the rules. He gave the orders. He snapped his fingers and they obeyed him. He possessed the power, all the power. The power of life and death. He'd shown Heather how strong and powerful he was. He had proved to her that he was not the spineless wimp she had accused him of being.

He was a man who knew how to control his woman.

With an iron fist!

Robyn sat on the sofa, her legs stretched out, her back propped against Raymond. His arms encircled her, criss-crossing over her in a gentle, protective embrace. Neither of them had been able to sleep after the phone call from the man who had referred to himself as her secret admirer. And making love again had been out of the question. Robyn was far too tense. Raymond was understanding, God bless him. She didn't know what she'd ever done to deserve such a wonderful man.

"I think we should call Bernie tonight," he said.

She caressed his arms that cradled her so tenderly. "I will not ruin my sister's big night. Calling her in the morning will be soon enough."

"But if that note and phone call came from the man who has already killed three Adams County women—"

Turning in his arms, she kissed him. Just a quick, let's-not-argue-about-it kiss. "You'll stay with me all night, won't you?"

"Wild horses couldn't drag me away. You know that I'd never leave you alone after—"

"I can't think about it. If I do, I'll go out of my mind."

"Then don't think about it," he told her. "Talk to me about something else."

"Why don't you talk to me?"

"About what?"

"Tell me what you want to do with the rest of your life," she said. "Do you want to get married again? Do you want children? Do you want to stay here in Adams Landing?"

He kissed her temple. "Yes, I want to get married again and I most certainly want to have children. And I'd like to spend the rest of my life in Adams Landing."

"Would you marry someone like me?" she asked.

"No, I wouldn't marry someone like you because there is no one on earth like you, Robyn. But I would marry you in a heartbeat, if you'd agree to be my wife."

A sweet, warm pleasure came alive inside Robyn, overpowering the fear and dread of what tomorrow might bring, temporarily vanquishing the menacing shadows lurking out there somewhere in the night. Raymond made her happy, made her feel safe, made her feel loved and cherished.

"What if one of these days I decide I want to marry you?" The idea of being Raymond's wife was beginning to appeal to her. "Could we have a big, splashy wedding? I've always wanted a dozen bridesmaids. And a white limo and a reception at the country club and a honeymoon in Hawaii—"

"Marry me and you can have any kind of wedding and honeymoon you want."

"You think I'm teasing you, don't you?" She pivoted her head so that she could make eye contact with him. "I'm not. Honest, Raymond, I'm not teasing."

"You're just frightened right now and appreciate having a big, strong man around to hold you."

"No, that's not it. I swear it's not."

When she grasped his face between her open palms, he removed her hands immediately and held them in his. "I'm not walking away from you when you need me, sweetheart. I'll be around for as long as you'll let me stay, for as long as you want me."

Tears clouded her vision. "I think if we get married, we should have a little girl. I'd love to have a daughter. Of course, I know men like to have sons—"

"I can't imagine a greater blessing than having a child with you. A little girl who looks just like her mommy."

Robyn adjusted herself so that she could lie in his arms, her head on his chest. "I'd want her to have your eyes. Have I ever told you what beautiful eyes you have?"

"Yes, you have. Thank you."

He held her with tender comfort, his embrace a protective balm, soothing her rattled nerves, putting a barrier between her and the unknown threat that could take her life. And it was in that moment that Robyn knew, without any doubts whatsoever, that she loved Raymond Long.

Jim's bedroom door stood wide open, so Bernie saw inside as soon as they reached the threshold. The only illumination came from three night-lights that were plugged into three separate outlets around the room. The bed had been neatly made and turned down, the sheets and pillowcases a pale cream. A small bouquet of mixed summer flowers rested on the nightstand. Bernie smiled to herself. Jim Norton had prepared this room for them—for her.

He carried her over to the bed, then paused and asked, "Is everything okay? I know you women like romantic settings and all, but I'm not much of a romantic. I thought about candles, but I couldn't light them earlier and leave them burning. I figured the night-lights would have to do. And I bought new sheets. The salesgirl said that four hundred count were good sheets, whatever that means."

Bernie's smile widened. He'd gone to a lot of trouble, had done his best to make things nice for her, which made her love him all the more.

She lifted her head from his shoulder and kissed his cheek. "It's very nice. Thank you."

He leaned over and deposited her on the bed. Suddenly, she felt vulnerable. She was completely naked, her body with all its flaws completely exposed. When Jim had been busy bringing her to a climax using his very talented tongue, she hadn't given her nudity a thought, nor, she suspected, had Jim. But now he was standing over her, looking at her as if she were his favorite dessert, and all she could think about was, Did he find her beautiful and desirable, or did he think she was fat and ugly and regret getting himself into this situation?

Get real, Bernie. He's a man. He's horny as hell. He doesn't care if your body is perfect or not. He just wants to fuck you.

"I want to say and do all the right things, honey, but I'm not used to . . . usually it's not so important to me that I . . ." Jim rubbed his forehead and chuckled nervously. "Hell, you'd think I'd never had sex before."

"If it helps any . . . it's been a long time for me and I'm pretty rusty." She took a deep breath and slowly eased the top sheet over her legs and hips, up to her waist. She had good boobs—high, round, and firm. He couldn't possibly find anything wrong with them. "And if what you did out in the living room is any indication of your lovemaking techniques, I'd say you don't have anything to worry about."

"Liked the prelude, did you?" He grinned.

Bernie scanned him from head to toe. All six feet three inches of tough, lean man. All eight inches of his impressive erection.

"Oh, I think *liked* might be an understatement." She patted the bed. "How about we get started on the main act?"

His grin widened, a very self-satisfied grin. "Do you want music?"

She shook her head. "Don't need it."

"Want me to take a few of those flowers and scatter them over the bed?"

Smiling, she shook her head again. "All I want in this bed with me is you, Jim Norton."

"Give me a sec, okay?" He sat on the edge of the bed, his back to her, and opened the nightstand drawer.

She scooted to the center of the bed and lay down, resting her head on the big, fluffy pillow. *Wonder if he bought new pillows, too?*

When he turned around, she noticed the condom first thing.

"If I go too fast or do anything you don't like—"

"Stop talking and make love to me."

Jim emitted a huffing laugh, then reached over, yanked the sheet off of her, and came down over her, bracing himself with his knees on either side of her hips and his hands on either side of her shoulders.

"Did anybody ever tell you that you're bossy?" He nuzzled her nose with his.

"Do you have a problem taking orders from a woman?" She lifted her hands to his buttocks and clutched him firmly.

"I'd love to take orders from you, honey. Just tell me what you want and I'll do my best to deliver."

I want you not only to make love to me, I want you to really, truly love me. I want you to be so crazy about me that you can't imagine your life without me.

She looked him in the eyes and said, "All I want is you."

He stared at her for one heart-stopping moment before he swooped down and kissed her, effectively taking her breath away. She kissed him back, putting all her feelings—everything she didn't dare say to him—into that single kiss. Clutching his buttocks, her nails biting into his flesh, she lifted her hips in an invitation. *Take me. Take me now.*

Jim spread her thighs and slipped between them, then eased his hands beneath her and grasped her hips. Bringing her up to meet him, he kissed her again and again, as if the taste of her excited him.

"Bernie . . . I—" He rammed into her. Hard and fast. To the hilt. "God!"

She wrapped herself around him and moved to the rhythm he set, quickly losing herself in him as their bodies joined so perfectly. They went at each other with wild abandon, and a few minutes later, they both came, almost simultaneously, she only seconds before he did. He groaned and trembled and melted down on top of her. She moaned as her second orgasm hit.

Breathing heavily, sweating profusely, their bodies hot and damp, they shared a moment-after kiss that expressed what neither had the energy to say. *It was good. Damn good.*

Eventually he rolled off her, onto his back and rested beside her. She turned onto her side and cuddled up against him. He eased his arm under her head and pulled her close.

"Stay with me tonight," Jim said. "I don't want you to go."

She caressed his chest, then kissed his shoulder. "I'm not going anywhere. I'm right where I want to be." *Now and forever.*

Chapter 27

With only a towel wrapped around his waist and his hair still damp from his shower, Jim grabbed Bernie the minute he walked out of the bathroom. Before she could say a word, he pressed her up against the wall and kissed her.

He had awakened her not long after dawn this morning and they'd made love again. The experience had been slow and lingering, neither of them in a rush, each wanting and needing to explore the other. Being Jim's lover was even better than she'd dreamed it could be. He was passionate, yet considerate. Demanding, but equally giving. How any woman in her right mind could have ever let this man go was beyond her.

While he'd been in the shower, she'd gone into the living room and gathered up their discarded clothes. After slipping on Jim's shirt, she'd laid her garments out on the bed and frowned when she'd seen how wrinkled they were. She was, by nature, a neat, orderly person.

She needed to go home, take a bath and get ready for church services. If she didn't show up, her mother would want to know why not. She could hardly say that she'd spent the entire morning in Jim's bed, could she?

Why not, Bernie? You're a grown woman of thirty-two. Your love life is none of your mother's business and you have every right to tell her so.

Love life? She actually had a love life!

Neither of them had said those three magic words. Not last night. Not this morning. She was in love with Jim, but didn't know how he felt about her.

When he lifted his head after kissing her and then smiled, Bernie's stomach flip-flopped. She was just plain nuts about this guy.

She wrapped her arms around his neck. "I need to go home, take a shower and change clothes, so you'd better hurry up and get dressed," she told him. "If you take me home before eight, I'll have time to fix us some homemade pancakes before I have to dress for church."

"What time is church?"

"Early service is at nine, then Sunday school at ten and late service at eleven."

"You could skip Sunday school and go to the late service. If you do that, we might have time for a quickie after breakfast."

"Jim Norton, you're insatiable." She rubbed herself against him seductively, letting his hunter green shirt gap open in front where she'd closed only a single middle button. "It's one of the many things I lo—like about you."

He studied her expression so seriously that she wondered if he was questioning her near-slip in saying the "L" word.

"What's the matter?" she asked.

"There are a lot of things I *love* about you, Bernie. I could make a mile-long list, starting with just how beautiful you are first thing in the morning."

"Oh, Jim . . ." She felt tears misting her eyes and hated

that she'd reacted in such a silly, girlie-girl way to his compliment. "You must need glasses. I'm an absolute mess."

He clasped her upper arms and looked deeply into her
eyes. "I'm the one who messed you up, and I like my handi-
work." He reached under his shirt that she was wearing to
caress her bare butt.

"No fair," she pleaded as she tried to pull away from him.
"You know how easily I give in to you."

He let her escape, only to yank her back into his arms.
"That's another thing I love about you."

"You love that I'm easy?" Giggling, she yanked off his
towel, leaving him buck naked.

"Yes, ma'am, I do. I love it that you're easy, but easy only
for me."

"Only for you."

Jim undid the single button on his shirt that she was wearing and spread it apart, then walked her backward across the
room, straight to his unkempt bed. Just as he toppled her
over, both of them eager to make love again, Jim's telephone
rang.

"I could just let it ring," he said.

"You can't. It could be Kevin, or it could be business."
She gave him a gentle shove.

He came up off the bed in one fast, fluid motion, then
reached out and grabbed the bedroom extension phone off
its base. "Yeah?"

Bernie rose up on her knees and crawled over to the edge
of the bed, intending to pester him while he was on the
phone. But she noticed the odd expression on his face and
instinctively knew something was wrong.

"Okay. Yeah, you did the right thing calling me," Jim said.
"I'll tell Bernie. You two meet us at her office in about an hour."

Jim replaced the receiver and turned to Bernie. "That was
Raymond Long."

"What's the matter? Has something happened to Robyn?"

Jim sat on the edge of the bed and pulled her over and onto his lap. "Last night when Robyn and Raymond entered her apartment, they found a note that had been shoved under her door." Bernie tensed. Jim rubbed her back soothingly. "Then a little later, Robyn received a phone call from some guy whose voice she didn't recognize."

Bernie shook her head. "No. No, don't say it."

Jim wrapped her in his arms. "This guy told Robyn that he was her secret admirer and that the note she'd found was from him."

Bernie trembled uncontrollably as her brain processed the fact that the Secret Admirer serial killer had chosen her baby sister as his next victim.

Bernie's father arrived at her office while they waited for Robyn and Raymond. When Jim had called her dad before they left Jim's house twenty-five minutes ago, he had simply told R.B. that Bernie needed his help on the case, that some new information had just come to light. There was no way he could tell a man over the phone that one of his daughters had been marked for death by a cold, calculating killer.

R.B. came bustling into the sheriff's department dressed in a suit and tie. He looked right at Bernie. "Okay, girl, this had better be something that couldn't wait, because your mother is none too happy with me for missing church and Sunday school."

"Come on into my office, Dad," Bernie told him. When he followed Jim and her, she added, "Close the door behind you."

After R.B. shut the door, he glanced from Bernie to Jim. "What's going on? I can tell from the looks on your faces that it's bad."

"Dad . . ." Bernie swallowed and tried again. "He's chosen his next victim."

"Who—the Secret Admirer killer?" R.B. asked.

Bernie nodded.

"How do you know? Has someone contacted you about—"

"Yes."

"When?"

"About an hour ago. He slipped a note under her front door last night, and then later he called her and told her he was her secret admirer."

"Son of a bitch." R.B. scratched the back of his head and grimaced. "This just might turn out to be the break we need to catch this bastard. He finally picked a woman smart enough to know to be scared of this guy from the get-go instead of flattered."

"Dad . . ."

Jim knew how difficult this was for Bernie.

"What is it, honey?" R.B. asked. "You're acting mighty peculiar."

"R.B., the woman who received the note and phone call is Robyn," Jim said. "Raymond called me this morning. He was with her last night when she found the note and when the guy called her. Raymond's driving her over to the courthouse. They should be here soon."

"Robyn?" R.B. slumped down into the nearest chair. "He's picked out my baby girl for his next victim?"

"Oh, Daddy." Bernie rushed over to her father, knelt in front of him and grasped his hand. "We're going to protect her. We're going to make sure he doesn't get anywhere near her."

"Damn right about that." R.B. growled the words.

A soft rapping at the closed door alerted them that someone else had arrived. All three of them stared at the door. Bernie rose to her feet as Jim crossed the room and opened the door. Robyn stood in the doorway, Raymond planted protectively behind her, his left hand on her shoulder.

"We're here," Robyn said, then looked beyond Jim to where her father had just turned around in the chair and gazed at her. "Daddy, what are you doing here?" She glared disapprovingly at Bernie. "Why did you call—?"

"Bernie didn't," Jim said. "I did."

"Oh."

Raymond squeezed her shoulder, then looked right at Jim. "When we got down to Robyn's car a few minutes ago, we found a white plastic bag tied to the driver's side door handle." He lifted the sack he held in his right hand. "There's a note, a sketch of Robyn, and a cheap pearl necklace inside. She didn't touch anything, so the only fingerprints on it will be mine . . . and hopefully the man who sent her the package."

R.B. rose to his feet and held open his arms. Robyn flew into her father's embrace and wrapped her arms around him. "It's going to be all right, baby girl."

"Oh, Daddy, I'm so scared."

Raymond handed Jim the white plastic sack.

Jim laid the sack on Bernie's desk. "I doubt our guy left any prints. He's never slipped up and done something that stupid before. He uses supplies that can be purchased just about anywhere, makes phone calls from various phones that can't be traced back to him, and stays one step ahead of us all the time."

"What can we do?" Raymond asked. "You know I'll do anything I can to help keep Robyn safe."

Robyn lifted her head from her father's chest, eased out of his arms and smiled at Raymond. "He doesn't want anything happening to me now that we've decided we might get married."

"What?" R.B. and Bernie asked simultaneously.

Robyn walked over to Raymond and laced her arm

through his. "I would much rather that y'all plan my wedding than plan my funeral."

"Robyn!" Bernie gasped.

"We'll have no such talk. Do you hear me, girl?" R.B. choked up, then cleared his throat loudly.

"Yes, Daddy. But I'm not naive, you know. I'm well aware of just how much danger I'm in from this madman."

"I'll make sure there is a deputy with you around the clock," Bernie said.

"Abby had protection twenty-four/seven," Robyn reminded them.

"We'll make sure every deputy is experienced and that they all know that they can't trust anyone," Jim said. "And I think it might be a good idea for you to move back home with your parents for the time being."

"That goes without saying." R.B. gave his younger daughter a stern look. "Lord knows what this is going to do to your mother."

"If there was any way we could keep this from her, we would," Bernie said. "But we can't."

"Perhaps I should take Robyn away somewhere," Raymond suggested. "If she's not in Adams Landing, then the killer can't get to her. Right?"

"Wrong," R.B. replied. "We don't know who the hell this guy is or how he's able to stay several steps ahead of the law. If you take her away, he could somehow find out where Robyn is and . . ." R.B. looked at Jim. "This Secret Admirer killer has killed before, in other states, right?"

"Right. We're relatively certain that Abby was his tenth victim."

Robyn groaned softly and swayed on her feet. Raymond grabbed her, preventing her from falling.

"Goddamn. Goddamn." R.B. socked his right fist into his open left palm as he paced the floor, cursing all the while. "There's no way to know for sure that if Robyn left Adams

Landing he couldn't find her. No, she's better off here where we can protect her. We won't leave her alone for a minute. Day and night." He narrowed his gaze as he focused on his elder daughter. "We'll post a deputy inside the house, plus Raymond and I will keep a close watch on her and—" R.B. face's contorted with rage. "By God, he's not going to get his hands on her."

Robyn and Bernie went over to their father, a daughter on either side, and put their arms around him.

Jim's cell phone rang. Shit. He glanced at Bernie. "I'll take it out there." Hiking his thumb, he indicated the outer office. She nodded.

After exiting Bernie's private office, he closed the door, then flipped open his cell phone and said, "Captain Norton here," as he sat down on the edge of Lisa Wiley's desk.

"Jim, I've got something for you," Griffin Powell said.

"I hope it's something good because we sure could use it right about now."

"Has something else happened?"

"Bernie's sister Robyn—my boss Sheriff Bernie Granger's younger sister—is the Secret Admirer killer's next intended victim. She's started receiving notes, sketches, and presents. Last night he called her."

"Then this case has become very personal for the sheriff's department, hasn't it?"

"Yeah, it has," Jim said. "And for me, too."

"How's that? Are you involved with the sheriff's sister?"

"No," Jim replied, "I'm involved with the sheriff."

Griffin didn't respond, allowing a full minute of silence before he said, "I've managed to get hold of the list of Leighton Prep students the year Heather Stevens was a senior, along with a yearbook for that year. I'll overnight the yearbook and I've already e-mailed the list to your office computer."

"Resend it to Bernie's e-mail address as soon as we hang up," Jim said, then recited the address.

"Will do."

"I appreciate this," Jim said. "But I really need the year-book and list of students for Heather's junior year, too."

"I'm working on it."

"Thanks. And Griff?"

"Something else you need?"

"Not today, but maybe soon, I might need you to send a couple of your best men down here to Adams Landing to guard Robyn Granger."

"That can be arranged. Just let me know."

Abducting Robyn Granger would be a challenge, one he looked forward to facing. He had no intention of waiting for very long, not now that she had gone to the police with his notes, the pearls, and the sketch he'd drawn of her from memory. He could have given her more time and wooed her more slowly, but she'd taken that choice away from him. The sheriff and her chief deputy would think they had a couple of weeks before he whisked Robyn away to his secret love nest. They'd think that the gifts and sketches would arrive over a period of time, the way he'd sent them in the past. But not this time. He would outsmart them. And he knew just how he'd do it.

Play hard to get, my beautiful Robyn. Pretend you don't want me. Lie to yourself all you want, but in the end, you will admit the truth to me. You'll tell me how much you love me, how desperately you want me, how willing you are to please me.

He opened the front door to his home and walked out of the hot September sunshine and into his cool, air-conditioned living room. As he crossed over into the kitchen, he removed his coat and then his tie, laid them on the bar stool and undid the top button of his white shirt.

Today's sermon had been splendid, the topic well chosen: lusts of the flesh. Every man in the audience must have felt as if he were being singled out personally for chastisement.

We know all about lust, don't we, Robyn?

We know what it's like to be tempted beyond all reason.

You want me the way so many men have wanted you. You lie awake at night and think of me and dream of all the wicked things I'll do to you once we're completely alone.

He removed a jug of tea from his refrigerator, poured himself a glass and took it with him over to his desk. After placing the tea on a sandstone coaster, he opened his sketch pad, then set out a pen and jar of black ink.

He could see her in his mind's eye. Naked. Aroused. Panting.

He began sketching feverishly, creating the image of Robyn burning inside his head. Breasts bared. Nipples peaked. Long black hair flowing down her back. Her eyes closed, her tongue licking her upper lip.

When he finished the sketch, he set it aside, then opened the bottom drawer of the desk and removed a tube of pink lipstick and a bottle of pink nail polish.

"Tomorrow," he whispered. "Tomorrow."

While Bernie walked out to the parking lot with her father, her sister, Raymond, and Deputy Fuller, who would be on guard duty today, Jim sat down behind Bernie's desk and accessed her e-mail. He zeroed in on one message—the e-mail from Griffin Powell—opened it, and began scanning the list of students, fifty-three in all. Their names were in alphabetical order. He scanned the names quickly, searching for one that might sound familiar.

Shannon Elmore.

No surprise there. He already knew that Shannon had graduated with Heather and had belonged to her elite club for snobby little brunettes.

The Sable Girls Club.

Jim stopped on another name.

Sara Hayes.

So the killer's third victim had, as he'd suspected, attended Leighton Prep, had graduated with Heather, and had probably belonged to her exclusive club. Jim would have the yearbook tomorrow and could check Sara Hayes's picture. He'd lay odds that Sara was a pretty, popular brunette. And he'd bet his last dime that whoever killed her—whoever killed all ten women—was somehow connected to Leighton Prep.

Chapter 28

"You damn bitch! How dare you sic your sister and that Neanderthal deputy of hers on me." Brandon Kelley's outrage came through loud and clear over the phone line. "My lawyer is going to sue the Adams County Sheriff's Department for harassment, and we just might sue you, too, for making false accusations!"

"Brandon, I didn't tell Bernie that I suspected you were the Secret Admirer killer," Robyn said. "I swear I didn't. But she and Jim have to question all my former boyfriends . . . just in case."

"I'm neither a boy nor your friend, you brainless little cunt. We were on and off fucking partners and that's all."

Robyn choked up, not so much because Brandon was being such a heartless bastard, but because his cruelty proved to her what a poor judge of character she'd been in the past. Before Raymond. "Brandon, please don't be this way. Don't you have any idea what I'm going through? Why would you—"

Robyn's bodyguard for the evening shift snatched the phone out of her hand. "Dr. Kelley, this is Deputy Scotty Joe

Walters. I don't know what you said to Miss Granger, but I strongly suggest that you do not call her again. As a matter of fact, do not contact her in any way, most certainly not in person."

Robyn wasn't sure what Brandon said in reply, but she smiled when Scotty Joe told him, "In my official capacity as a deputy, I can't respond to that, but unofficially, just as a man, I can say this—you do not want a confrontation with me, Dr. Kelley, because I'd have no problem whipping your sorry ass." Scotty Joe hit the OFF button on her phone and handed it to her. "I don't think he'll bother you again."

Robyn released her held breath. "Thank you."

"My pleasure."

Scotty Joe had been one of the many deputies who had volunteered to act as her bodyguard. Since the county couldn't afford the extra money for overtime, every deputy had taken on the job without pay. Scotty Joe worked the day shift all the time as the only full-time deputy in Adams County's crime prevention division, so he was working the evening shift guard duty for Robyn Granger. He was with her from five until nine, then various other deputies took over for the night shifts. Ron Hensley, who was on a leave of absence from the department, had asked to guard her during the day, from eight until five. At first, Bernie had been reluctant to agree, but when Ron had practically begged her for the chance to do for Robyn what he'd been unable to do for Abby, Bernie had consented. For the past three afternoons— Monday, Tuesday, and today—Scotty Joe had shown up at the fitness center promptly at five to take over from Ron. Since she usually closed the center at eight on Wednesday nights, they'd been just about to leave when her cell phone had rung.

"I'm an idiot for ever having gotten involved with a jerk like Brandon," Robyn said. "The other guys I've dated since coming back to Adams Landing have all been so kind and supportive since they learned that I'm . . . well, that I could be . . ." She couldn't bring herself to put her fears into words. "Paul and Ron have simply been dears. Even Matthew Donaldson has been supportive, but then I suppose that's his job, him being a minister and all. But I'd never survive without Raymond's love and support. He's my rock, you know. I absolutely love him to pieces."

Scotty Joe's cheeks flushed. "I sure never saw that one coming. I mean, Raymond's a fine fellow and all, but since you're really something mighty special, Miss Robyn . . . Well, I guess if you like Raymond that much, then there's more to him than meets the eye." He winked at her.

"That's so sweet of you to say." She patted Scotty Joe's arm. "Raymond is very special to me. And you know what— I'm probably going to marry him, once this nightmare with that crazy Secret Admirer killer is over."

"That's the way to think. Keep your chin up and keep on believing that things will be over soon and you'll get all the happiness you deserve."

Robyn leaned over and kissed Scotty Joe's cheek. "I can't tell you how much I appreciate you and the other deputies volunteering to play nursemaid to me around the clock. And y'all have been very understanding about the way Daddy and Raymond keep dropping by here at the fitness center half a dozen times a day, yesterday and today."

"Your father loves you and he's concerned. There's not a one of us who doesn't understand that. And we don't blame Raymond for checking on you just about as often as your dad does. It's plain to see that the guy's crazy about you."

"Scotty Joe, could I ask you a question?"

"Sure thing. What is it?"

"Do you think y'all will catch him—the Secret Admirer killer—before he . . ." A sob caught in Robyn's throat.

Scotty Joe put his arm around her. "Everybody's doing everything possible to find him. Heck, I heard Agent Patterson was thinking about contacting the FBI about taking over this case. And Captain Norton's got that famous investigator, Griffin Powell, on speed dial so he can bring in private bodyguards for you if necessary. With all that in the works, what kind of chance has that Secret Admirer fellow got? I'd say he's outgunned, wouldn't you?"

"Yeah, I'd say so. And thank you for reassuring me. You can't imagine what it's like to live in fear all the time."

Scotty Joe gave her shoulder a squeeze. "We'd better head out now and get you home; otherwise, your daddy's going to be coming this way, hunting us."

"You're right. I'll shut everything down and then lock up. I'll be ready to go in a couple of minutes."

"I'm ready when you are."

Scotty Joe ran his hand over his hip holster, then nervously knotted his hands into loose fists. It couldn't be easy for him or any of the other deputies guarding her to forget the fact that Brett Dennison was still in the hospital in a coma. These men knew they were putting their lives on the line to protect her.

A few minutes later, when Scotty Joe opened the back door and walked outside, she followed him. She noticed the tension in his muscular body, the way he glanced right and left, back and forth. He kept watch while she locked up. That's when she saw it. Oh, God, not another present!

Apparently she had gasped without realizing it, because Scotty Joe jerked around and asked, "What's wrong?"

"Look." She pointed to the small cardboard box tied to the doorknob. "It's from him."

"Yes, ma'am, it probably is."

She reached for it, then yanked her hand back, afraid to touch it.

"It's all right," he said. "Just leave it right there. I'll call Captain Norton and tell him that gift number three has shown up."

Beverly Barton

"It is number three, isn't it? Just one more and—" Robyn burst into tears.

Scotty Joe wrapped her in his arms. "Don't cry. Everything is going to be all right. You just calm down and I'll get in touch with the captain."

Robyn pulled back, nodded her head and swiped the tears from her face. "I'm okay. Call Jim and tell him to get here as quickly as he can."

The loud thunder woke him. He shot straight up and stared at the lighted digital clock on his beside table. Two-forty-one. The middle of the night. He might as well get up. He couldn't sleep through a thunderstorm. It would be pointless to try to rest.

He could hear the plummeting rain as it hit the roof and beat against the windows. God, how he hated that sound. Sitting in the middle of his bed, he lifted his unsteady hands and covered his ears.

I won't remember. I won't remember.

Fight the memories. Don't let them win. Force them from your mind.

Easier said than done.

The memories claimed him, drew him back into the past. Against his will.

The weather forecasters had predicted rain, so he'd brought his umbrella to school that day. He didn't like Leighton Prep any more than he'd liked his old public school, but his uncle and aunt were paying a lot of money to send him here, so he pretended he was happy with their choice. They were elderly and set in their ways, and the last thing they'd expected was having their teenaged great-nephew foisted on them when his parents died in a car crash.

Those first few months at the new school, nobody had seemed to like him. Then he'd gotten to know a few of the guys on the debate team, who, like he, also took art classes. He couldn't exactly call them his friends, but at least with them around, he didn't feel so alone, birds of a feather and all. But the popular kids didn't like him; some of the jocks even called him a four-eyed freak and an egghead. And the girls laughed at him because he was so skinny and clumsy.

Then one day a couple of weeks ago, everything had changed for him, and all because Heather Stevens had smiled at him and said hello. He'd nearly died on the spot. Heather was the most beautiful girl in the whole wide world and the most popular girl at Leighton Prep. He'd heard that she'd broken up with the senior class president, Blake Powers, and every guy at school was dying to date her.

Heather belonged to an elite group of juniors—all gorgeous brunettes—who called themselves the Sable Girls. There were only four of them—Heather, Shannon Elmore, Sara Hayes, and Courtney Pettus. He'd heard that they'd formed the group recently, and rumor was that each girl would have to undergo an initiation devised by Heather. The Sable Girls were the envy of all the other girls and *the* wet dream for every boy. Until Heather started speaking to him, being so nice and friendly, he'd thought she was a bitchy little snob. Of course, that hadn't stopped him from adoring her like all the other guys did.

She had smiled and said hello to him every day last week; then on Monday of this week, she'd stopped and talked to him in the hallway.

"So, do you have a girlfriend?" she'd asked.

"No, er . . . No, I don't."

"That's good to know."

She'd giggled and walked away, glancing over her shoulder and blowing him a kiss. He'd gotten a hard-on right then and there.

On Tuesday, she'd asked him if he wanted to carry her books to the one class they shared, American history. He'd been dumbfounded, but not so much so that he hadn't grabbed her books, dropping them in the process. She had walked along beside him as they'd gone down the hall, all the while waving and speaking to other students. God, he'd felt ten feet tall that day.

On Wednesday, she had sat by him in the cafeteria and had made him so nervous he couldn't eat a bite. Mostly he'd just sat there and watched her.

He was in love. Madly, passionately, head over heels in love with Heather. He'd do anything—even die—for her.

On Thursday, she'd met him after school.

"Would you like to be my boyfriend?"

"Are you kidding? Am I breathing?"

She'd giggled, then moved in close and kissed him right on the lips. When he'd reached for her, she'd stepped back and held up a restraining hand. "Not now. Not here."

He'd stared at her, his heart beating like crazy and his dick standing at attention.

She had reached down and fondled him, then eased her hand up to rest in the center of his chest. "Tomorrow, after school, I want to show you exactly how I feel about you. Will you meet me downstairs, in the basement, in the room where they store all those old files?"

"You know I will."

"Good. We'll have complete privacy down there. The room's easy to find. Just go down the east wing stairs, take a right, and it's the second room on the right."

"I—I can hardly wait."

"Oh, aren't you just the sweetest thing?"

"You're the sweet one," he'd told her.

"Wait until tomorrow. You'll find out just how sweet I am." She'd licked her lips, then winked at him before walking away to join her giggling girlfriends.

This morning in American history class, she'd slipped him a note.

Meet me at three-thirty. Go into the old file room in the basement and wait for me. I am so excited. It's all I can think about. You are all I can think about.
                    Your Sable Girl, Heather

He'd stored his books in his locker, sprayed spearmint freshener in his mouth and double-checked his pocket for the condom he intended to use. There was no way in this world he'd ever do anything to harm Heather. He wanted to protect the girl he loved.

When he got downstairs, he practically ran to the storage room. His hands trembled as he opened the door. *Take a deep breath and calm down. You don't want to get so excited that you come before you even get inside her.*

There were small, high windows across the top of one wall that let in daylight, but barely enough to illuminate the room, so he searched for the switch, found it and turned on the overhead lights. He realized two things simultaneously. It had begun to rain outside; he could hear the distant rumble of thunder and see the raindrops beating against the closed windows. Also, there was a blanket spread out on the floor, with a bottle of what looked liked wine and two glasses in the center.

He'd never tasted liquor, but if Heather wanted them to share a glass of wine, he'd do it. He'd do anything she wanted him to do. He'd never had sex before either, unless you counted a guy jerking off in the shower as sex. He simply couldn't believe he was lucky enough for his first time to be with Heather.

As the minutes ticked by, his stomach churned and his head throbbed. God, he'd never been so nervous. He checked his watch incessantly, every minute, until he heard footsteps out in the hall.

He held his breath. Then the door opened. There Heather stood, a goddess who was going to give her virginity to him.

"You aren't ready," she said. "I thought you'd be ready when I got here."

"I don't understand. What do you—"

"We can't fool around with our clothes on, silly. I thought you'd be stripped down to the buff when I got here so we wouldn't have to waste time. I took off my bra and panties in the girl's restroom upstairs." She turned and lifted her skirt just enough to give him a glimpse of her bare butt.

He swallowed hard.

"Why don't I watch you undress?" she said. "Then you can watch me."

"Okay."

He'd never been so scared—or so aroused—in his entire life. What if when she saw him naked, she thought he was skinny and ugly and . . .

"Is everything all right?" she asked. "Do you need a little help?"

"Uh . . . I—I'm not sure."

She came over to him and unbuttoned his shirt. White. Oxford cloth. Long sleeved. Part of the school's regulation uniform. "Take it off."

He did.

Then she unbuckled his belt, undid his navy blue slacks and lowered the zipper. "Get out of those."

He did.

"Now, take off your briefs and show me what you've got."

Oh, God, he thought he'd throw up. His hands shook. His heartbeat accelerated. *Don't have a heart attack and die. Not now. Not before you make love to Heather.*

He finally managed to remove his briefs. Standing there in front of her as naked as the day he was born, he looked down at his feet.

"Oh, you're shy. You've never fucked a girl before, have you?"

He shook his head.

Thunder rattled the window panes and rain plummeted against the glass.

"I have a surprise for you," she told him.

He assumed she meant that she was naked and ready to make love, that *she* was his surprise. Then he heard the door open and the sound of giggles alerted him to the fact that he and Heather were not alone.

His head snapped up in time to see Heather, still fully clothed, open the door all the way. Her three fellow Sable Girls stood outside in the hallway, peering in at him, giggling their stupid brunette heads off.

"Bring her in, girls," Heather said.

He didn't know what was going on, what Heather was up to, but suddenly he knew that they weren't going to make love. Not today. Not ever.

Shannon Elmore and Sara Hayes dragged a big, shaggy, mixed-breed dog into the room. With his hands covering his private parts, he looked from the dog and the girls to Heather, who was smiling wickedly.

"I promised you a fuck, didn't I?" she said. "Well, here's the girl for you. She's a real dog, the only kind of female who'd ever let you stick your dick into her."

Heather laughed. They all laughed. Except Courtney, who stared at him with wide eyes, her cheeks flaming red.

Standing there trembling, he looked at Heather and asked, "Why?"

"Why? Can't you figure it out?"

He shook his head.

"This is my initiation into the Sable Girls. I devised this whole plan all by myself. Clever of me, don't you think." She turned around to her friends and said, "Let's go. I'm sure these two want to be alone."

He stood there and stared at the dog, who turned and

wandered out into the hall. Feeling like the biggest fool on earth, he dropped to his knees on the blanket, huddled into a fetal ball and cried.

The sound of the Sable Girls' laughter echoed inside his head long after they left the storage room.

Chapter 29

While Kevin sat in the den watching TV and feeding Boomer tidbits from his breakfast plate, Jim and Bernie found a few minutes alone in her kitchen. Although they'd spent every waking moment together since Sunday morning, working tirelessly on the Secret Admirer serial killer case, along with Charlie Patterson, they hadn't shared another night together. Bernie had spent Sunday night at her parents' home with Robyn. Kevin was in school all day; then he went home with J.D. Simms in the afternoon and Jim picked him up at the DA's house every evening. Between Bernie's concern about and devotion to her sister and Jim's duty as a full-time single parent, there hadn't been any time for the two of them.

Selfishly, he wanted time alone with Bernie. And not just for lovemaking. He enjoyed simply being with her. Listening to her talk and laugh. Watching the subtle changes in her expressions.

Yesterday, the Adams County Sheriff's Department and the ABI had come to a decision. It was time to call in the FBI.

Actually, what Jim had said was, "It's way past time we call in the Feds."

Charlie had agreed with him.

And on behalf of her family, Bernie had told Jim that they wanted Griffin Powell to send in a couple of his agents to re-inforce the contingent of volunteer deputies acting as around-the-clock bodyguards for Robyn. Two agents were scheduled to arrive today and rotate twelve-hour shifts as backup for the local deputies. Everything that could be done to protect Robyn was being done. Jim didn't think there was any possi-ble way the killer could get to her, short of gunning down her guards and alerting half the town to his presence.

Jim came up behind Bernie where she stood at the sink rinsing out the skillets she'd used to prepare their breakfast, pancakes and sausage links. When he wrapped his arms around her, she leaned back into him and sighed contentedly.

He kissed her temple. "I like to start the morning this way. You and Kevin and I together, sharing breakfast. Like a real family."

"Me, too." She lifted her hands from the soapy dishwater, dried them off on her gingham checkered apron and turned in his arms.

"The only thing that I'd add to the scenario to make this morning perfect is for you to have woken up in my arms and for us to have made love before getting out of bed."

She gazed into his eyes. "I thought you told me you weren't a romantic."

"I'm not." He caressed her butt. "But you bring out the best in me. I feel like I can be totally honest with you."

"You can."

He nodded. "When we catch this bastard and Robyn is safe, I think you and I should talk about the future."

"*The* future?"

"Our future. Together."

She grinned. "Are you asking me to go steady?"

Jim chuckled. "Yeah, I guess I am. So, Bernie Granger, do you want to be my girl?"

She lifted her arms up and around his neck, then gave him a quick kiss on the lips. "Yes, I do. Very much."

Kevin cleared his throat. Bernie and Jim jumped apart.

"What are you two doing—making out?" Kevin asked teasingly.

They turned and faced Jim's son, who stood in the doorway, an empty plate in his hand and Boomer at his feet.

"Your father just asked me to be his girlfriend." Bernie eased away from Jim and reached out to take Kevin's plate. "What do you think about that?"

"I think he should ask you to marry him."

Jim cleared his throat. "I . . . uh . . . don't think Bernie and I are ready for marriage yet."

"When do you think you will be ready?" Kevin asked. "Neither of you is getting any younger, and if you plan to give me any brothers and sisters, you might want to get a move on."

Jim glanced at Bernie and rolled his eyes toward the ceiling.

"I think your dad and I will try dating for a while first."

"Yeah." Jim pulled Kevin back against himself, wrapped his arms across Kevin's chest and tickled him playfully. "Don't go putting Bernie and me on Medicare just quite yet. I think we've both got a few more good years left."

Just as father and son started laughing and joking around, Jim's cell phone rang. He immediately released Kevin, who stepped back and stared at the phone clipped to his dad's belt. As Jim removed the phone, his gaze met Bernie's and held for a split second. Then he flipped open the phone.

"Captain Norton here."

"Jim? Jimmy, is that you?"

"Mary Lee?"

"Mom? Is it Mom?" Kevin asked, his eyes round with hopefulness.

"I suppose you're surprised to hear from me," his ex-wife said.

"How are you? Kevin and I have been concerned. We're glad you're feeling up to calling us."

"I'm doing much better." She laughed shakily. "I'm losing my hair. You remember my gorgeous hair, don't you, Jimmy?"

"Yeah, of course, I do." He remembered a lot of things about Mary Lee, but none of them really mattered anymore. Everything he'd shared with her was in the past now, where it should be. Everything except Kevin. Right at this very moment, while he was listening to the sound of Mary Lee's voice, Jim was more certain than he'd ever been that he was completely over his ex-wife. And just as certain that he loved Bernie Granger.

"I want to talk to Kevin," Mary Lee said. "I need to tell him that I love him and . . . well, Jimmy, it's like this . . . I'd like for Kevin to stay on with you. Just until the end of the year. I still have more treatments and I plan on having breast reconstruction soon and—"

"I understand."

"Do you think Kevin will?"

"I believe so. He's a great kid. You've done a good job with him, Mary Lee."

She made an odd little sound, then said, "Thank you, Jimmy. I—I'm sorry that I've kept you two apart so much. In the future, I think we should discuss joint custody."

"I'd like that."

"May I talk to my son now?"

"Sure thing." Jim held out his cell phone to Kevin. "Your mother wants to talk to you."

Kevin grabbed the phone and started jabbering happily,

asking his mother half a dozen questions in rapid succession, then telling her about school, about the new friends he'd made, about Bernie and about Boomer.

"Bernie and Dad make a great team," Kevin said.

Jim walked over, put his arm around Bernie's waist and leaned his head down against hers. "He's right about that, you know. We do make a great team. At work. In life." He whispered in her ear, "And in bed."

They thought Robyn was safe, that they had her adequately protected. But they were wrong. They had no idea just how wrong they were. If they thought posting deputies to watch her around the clock and bringing in professional bodyguards would keep him away from her, then they underestimated him. He had accelerated the rate of his gift giving, sending her his tokens of love on an almost daily basis since Saturday night. She was waiting for that final gift, the one that announced he would soon be coming to get her, to take her away someplace where they could be alone. She had to be as eager as he for that moment. Despite the fact that she was pretending to everyone else that she loved Raymond Long, he knew better. He knew she loved him. Only him. And she wanted him, even more than he wanted her.

Just like Heather.

Don't remember. Don't think about her. Concentrate on the present, on the here and now, on Robyn. You have plans to make and execute.

But the memories never left him alone. They came to haunt him at will. Sometimes the harder he tried to make them go away, the more vividly they played out repeatedly inside his mind. Almost as if they were happening all over again.

He hadn't made any plans to see Heather that night. He hadn't sought her out, had not gone looking for her. And he had not meant to punish her. Despite what she'd done to him, a part of him had still wanted her. At twenty-one, he hadn't been the same pitiful boy she'd so heartlessly duped.

She'd been a senior in college, home for the holidays. He'd been on two weeks' leave from the Army and back in Greenville for Christmas with his aunt, a widow for two years. He hadn't set out to see Heather, but as fate would have it, they had both done last-minute shopping at the mall. He'd recognized her instantly. Beautiful as ever. Maybe even more so.

When their eyes met and she smiled at him, he'd known she didn't recognize him. Who would? He'd changed a great deal, physically and mentally. He was a soldier now. A man, not a boy.

He'd introduced himself to her by his new name. Before he'd joined the Army, he'd had his name legally changed, taking his uncle's last name. They had talked. She'd flirted. Then he'd offered to carry her packages to her car for her. She'd been so busy basking in his attention that she'd never suspected a thing.

After they had sex in her car, he'd told her who he was. She'd freaked out, hitting him, calling him ugly names. That's when he'd lost it. He had strangled her until she passed out; then he'd driven a couple of blocks away, parked in a dark alley, and when she'd come to, they'd had sex again. She'd screamed rape, but he knew better. She'd wanted him.

But because she wouldn't stop screaming, wouldn't stop saying such horrible things to him, he'd had no choice but to silence her. He'd taken out his pocket knife and slit her throat. It had been so easy. Afterward, he'd actually felt good about what he'd done. Satisfied. And powerful. He'd taken the car a few miles out of town, left her there inside and jogged back to the mall parking lot. Then he'd driven home and spent Christmas with his aunt. When he returned to active duty, he'd told himself that now, finally, he could put the past behind himself. Forever. But he'd been wrong. Dead wrong.

"Stop worrying about me," Robyn told Raymond. "I'm fine. Ron just left a few minutes ago and Scotty Joe's here now, along with Mr. Delaine, who is, I swear, six-six and has the most fearsome scowl on his face all the time. That look would scare the devil."

Raymond had called just to say he loved her. And to check on her, as he did several times a day. He took her to lunch, along with her armed guard, every day. And he came for a late supper at her parents' house every evening, along with his mother, Helen, who had done a complete about-face and was treating Robyn as if she were already her beloved daughter-in-law.

"You haven't received another present, have you?" Raymond asked.

"No, I haven't. Besides, you know that Bernie assigned a deputy to watch the backdoor, just in case."

"We couldn't get that lucky, could we? That he'd actually walk up to the back door to leave a gift and a deputy could arrest him."

"Bernie and Jim say he's smart, so he probably won't make that mistake, but they also say it's only a matter of time until he screws up. That's when they'll catch him."

"It can't be too soon to suit me."

"Yeah, me, too."

"You'll be closing up soon and coming home, won't you?"

"Uh-huh. My last aerobics class ended about twenty minutes ago and everybody's gone, except Scotty Joe, Mr. Delaine, and me. I've got about ten minutes of paperwork to do and then we'll be heading out of here."

"Robyn?"

"Hmm . . . ?"

"I love you."

"I love you, too."

Smiling, she laid the receiver on the base atop her desk. Just as she returned to the paperwork she needed to finish tonight, she heard voices beyond her closed door. Scotty Joe and Mr. Delaine? Of course. Who else could it be? Then she heard an odd noise, as if something fell, but she dismissed it as nothing when Scotty Joe knocked on the door and called to her.

"Are you okay, Miss Robyn? We thought we heard a loud bump."

"I'm fine. Maybe it was something outside."

"Mr. Delaine's gone to check around outside and I'm taking a look inside. You sit tight."

"All right."

Sit tight? She could do that. She planned to sit right here and not move a muscle until Scotty Joe gave her the all clear.

What if he's out there, outside the fitness center? What if he was waiting for her? Robyn's heartbeat hammered in her ears. She rubbed her hands together nervously.

You're safe. You have two capable bodyguards and both of them carry big guns.

A dead limb off one of the trees out back might have fallen on the roof. Or a stray cat or dog could have knocked over a trash can in the alley.

Minutes ticked by, each seeming endlessly long. When Scotty Joe finally opened her office door and rushed inside, she jumped as if she'd been shot.

"Sorry, Miss Robyn, I didn't mean to scare you. Everything is okay, except . . ." He pulled the large manila envelope out from where he'd been holding it behind his back. "Looks like our guy has left the final gift."

"Where did he leave it? And why didn't the deputy watching the backdoor see him?"

"He didn't leave it at the back door. When I was looking around to see what that noise was, I found the envelope lying on one of the treadmills. Somebody must have left it there earlier this evening."

"Oh, God!" Robyn covered her mouth with both hands.

Scotty Joe took several steps forward. "Maybe we'd better open it to make sure it's what we think it is."

She nodded.

He undid the clasp, opened the flap and turned the envelope upside down over her desk. The contents dumped out on top of the scattered paperwork—a small envelope with her name printed on it in large black letters, a gold-plated ankle bracelet, and an ink-rendered sketch. She and Scotty Joe stared at the sketch and then at each other.

"It's me," she said. "Look what he's done to me."

"Don't look at it, Miss Robyn. Just leave everything here and let me and Mr. Delaine get you home; then Bernie and Captain Norton can come back here and take care of this stuff."

Robyn nodded. Scotty Joe came around her desk and helped her to her feet.

Robyn had been due home an hour ago. They had tried calling her at work, tried her cell phone and tried contacting Scotty Joe and Griffin Powell's agent Ron Delaine. No one responded. Bernie tried not to think the worst, but horrific doubts kept creeping into her mind. The Secret Admirer killer had outsmarted them, somehow, someway, and had abducted Robyn. They had no idea who he was, so if he had taken Robyn, how would they ever find her?

Bernie had tried to talk her father and Raymond into staying at home with her mother and Helen Long, but they had followed behind her and Jim, in Raymond's car, arriving at the fitness center right behind them. As soon as they got out of her Jeep, John Downs emerged from his car and joined them at the front entrance.

Using the spare set of keys for the fitness center that her parents kept at home, Bernie unlocked the door and shoved it open; then Jim eased her aside and stepped over the threshold. She and John Downs followed Jim into the vestibule, both with their weapons drawn. Illumination from the streetlight cast shadows across the wooden floor. With her free hand, Bernie felt along the wall until her fingers encountered the light switch. She flipped it and light flooded the area.

Carefully, the three of them crept through the vestibule and into the main work room filled with various types of exercise equipment. Bernie turned on the lights. Ron Delaine lay on the floor, facedown, fresh blood circling his head like a sticky red halo.

Bernie gasped, but continued moving forward. Carefully.

"John and I will check things out," Jim said. "You see if Delaine's dead."

She nodded, then knelt down and reached for the bodyguard's arm. "He's been shot in the head." She felt for a pulse. "He's dead."

A couple of minutes later, Jim dragged her to her feet. She stared at him, slightly dazed and far too emotionally involved to do her job properly.

"There's no sign of Robyn or Scotty Joe," Jim said. "But there's a blood trail leading to the back door. It can't be Delaine's blood. He fell where he stood and didn't get up. Someone else was wounded and either was pulled or crawled across the floor."

"He's got Robyn. That bastard has my baby sister." She looked at Jim, her vision blurred with tears. "And he probably shot Scotty Joe. But what did he do with Scotty Joe's body?"

Jim wrapped his arm around her shoulders.

"I'm taking myself off this case officially," Bernie said. "From here on out, you're totally in charge. Do you understand?"

"Yeah, honey. I understand."

Chapter 30

Robyn opened her eyes and screamed. The sound of her terrorized shrieks echoed in the darkness. She couldn't see anything. Dear God, had he buried her alive? Panic overwhelmed her. Then she felt something on her face, covering her eyes. She reached up, grabbed hold of the thick material, yanked it off and tossed it away. It took several minutes for her eyes to adjust to the semidarkness and to focus on the small, faint light in the corner. She tried to sit up, but a sudden dizziness momentarily halted her. She dropped back down onto the bed and rested her head on the pillow.

After taking several deep breaths in an effort to calm her near-hysteria, Robyn surveyed her surroundings.

You have not been buried alive. Thank God.

After her brain absorbed that knowledge, she relaxed a little, enough to think more clearly. Before she could assess her present situation, her mind had to replay her last coherent memories.

Oh, God, no! No, no, it wasn't possible. He had shot—he had killed—blood. So much blood. Blood on him . . . on them. Blood on her. She glanced down at the top of her leotard. The leotard was gone; the blood was gone. She was naked.

She had tried to fight him, but he'd handled her as if she were a helpless child, spinning her around, covering her face with that foul-smelling rag. After that, everything had gone blank.

What had he done to her so that she couldn't remember what happened next? Had he raped her while she'd been unconscious?

It doesn't matter what he did; you're alive and that's what counts.

She vaguely recalled that when she'd realized *he* was the Secret Admirer killer, she'd stared at him in disbelief and said, "You? It can't be you."

Except for her father and Raymond and Jim, he was the last person on earth she would have ever suspected. Was it any wonder that no one had been able to discover his identity? He was liked, trusted, even admired. He was a man who set an example for others.

What was the point of trying to figure out how he'd been able to fool so many people for such a long time? He had managed to abduct her, despite all her so-called protection. What she had to concentrate on now was figuring out a way to get out of here—wherever the hell "here" was.

When she tried again, she managed to sit up. She slid herself around and eased her legs off the side of the bed. That's when she felt something attached to her ankle and heard the clank of metal hitting the concrete floor. Peering down at her feet, she realized that one ankle was shackled. A long, metal chain was attached to the cuff and the other end disappeared under the bed.

Robyn shoved herself up and onto her feet, then tried to take a few steps. One step, two, three, four, five, six . . . jerk! She had gone as far as the chain, which she now realized was connected to the metal bed frame, would allow her. Without dragging the bed with her, she could go no farther than where she now stood, directly beside an old, dirty commode.

There were no windows. No doors. No means of escape. She was trapped.

But he hasn't left you here to die. He'll come back. To rape you and torture you and eventually to kill you.

Robyn dropped to her knees in front of the commode, retched several times, and then threw up again and again until there was nothing left in her stomach except sour, yellow bile.

When the phone rang, Jim answered on line one, hoping it was the call he'd been waiting for all morning. He was temporarily using Bernie's office, per her instructions. Until her sister was found, she was taking a leave of absence to be with her parents. He knew that it had killed her to withdraw from this case, but she was smart enough to realize that she was far too emotionally involved, as was her father. She trusted Jim to take over for her because of his years of experience and because she knew he'd move heaven and earth to save her sister.

Charlie Patterson was in the field, manning the search for Robyn and for Scotty Joe. They were certain that Robyn was still alive and hidden away somewhere, the way Abby and Thomasina and Stephanie had been. They weren't so sure about Scotty Joe. Everybody figured the young deputy was probably dead. If so, where the hell was his body?

"Captain Norton speaking." Jim placed the receiver to his ear.

"Captain Norton, this is Marilyn Ogletree, Courtney Pettus's mother. My husband phoned me here at work and explained that you wanted to talk to me about my daughter."

"Yes, ma'am, I do. But first, let me tell you how terribly sorry I am about what happened to Courtney."

"Thank you, Captain. She was my only daughter . . . my only child from my first marriage. Her father died when Courtney was only five."

"Did your husband tell you about all the other women who we believe were murdered by the same man who killed Courtney?"

"Yes, he told me. And I'm heartbroken for the families of all those other young women. But I can't imagine how I could possibly help you."

"You can help me by simply answering a few questions. Will you do that?"

"Yes, of course. I'll do anything I can to help catch that monster and put him behind bars forever."

"Thank you, Mrs. Ogletree. I was wondering if you were aware of the fact that your daughter belonged to a four-person club called the Sable Girls when she was a junior at Leighton Prep in Greenville, South Carolina."

Mrs. Ogletree gasped softly. "How did you—? You've been investigating my daughter, haven't you?"

"Yes, ma'am."

"I knew about that silly club, but only after the fact."

"Courtney left Leighton Prep after her junior year. Why did she leave?"

"Oh dear. It was such a terrible thing that those girls did to that poor boy. Courtney was so ashamed afterward. She called me in tears and begged me to let her come home but wouldn't explain then why she wanted to leave so desperately. I made her stay a few more months and finish out the year; then when she came home for the summer she told me about what happened."

"What did happen?" Jim asked. "What terrible thing did the Sable Girls do to some poor boy? It was the Sable Girls, wasn't it?"

"Yes, it was the Sable Girls. It was all that Heather Stevens's fault. She was nothing but a rich, spoiled brat. And she must have been mentally disturbed to have concocted such a cruel hoax to play on that poor boy."

"Who was he, and what did they do to him?" Before Mrs. Ogletree explained further, Jim's gut instincts told him that whoever that poor boy was, he had become a serial killer. The Secret Admirer serial killer.

"I believe his first name was Melvin, but I can't remember his last name. I'm not sure Courtney ever mentioned it. This young man was skinny and what the kids referred to as a geek. He wore glasses and was very clumsy. And it seems he had a crush on Heather. She found out about his feelings and . . ." Mrs. Ogletree sighed. "Heather decided to use this boy in some stupid initiation into the Sable Girls. It was a diabolical scheme."

"What was the scheme?"

"When Courtney told me what had happened, I couldn't believe anyone could be so cruel. Heather totally humiliated that boy."

Mrs. Ogletree continued talking, giving Jim all the details that her daughter had shared with her that summer twelve years ago. Jim listened without interruption to the story of how cunning and heartless Heather Stevens had been.

"The janitors found that poor boy the next morning, still naked, huddled on the quilt on the floor and quite out of his mind. His family had called the police when he hadn't come home from school, but no one had any idea he might be in the basement. Courtney heard a few days later that he'd had a complete nervous breakdown and his family had been forced to commit him to a psychiatric hospital. My sweet Courtney felt guilty that she'd played a part in Heather's sick little scheme."

"Do you have any idea what happened to Melvin?"

"No, I'm sorry, I don't."

"Mrs. Ogletree, are you aware that Heather Stevens was murdered a year before your daughter was?"

Silence.

"Mrs. Ogletree?"

"No, I wasn't aware . . . Was her killer ever found?"

"No, ma'am."

"And you think that Melvin killed Heather and Courtney? If he did kill them, why didn't he kill Shannon and Sara, too? The were both Sable Girls."

"He did kill them," Jim said. "And at the time, no one connected their deaths. Shannon was killed in Greenville and Sara Hayes was killed a few months later in the city where she'd moved after college—Asheville, North Carolina."

"Merciful God."

"I'm sorry." Jim couldn't think of anything else to say.

"My husband said you told him this man has murdered other women. If it's Melvin, why is he killing more women? Why didn't he stop with the Sable Girls?"

"Each woman he's killed was a young, pretty, popular brunette."

"He's killing the Sable Girls over and over and over again, isn't he?"

"Yes, ma'am, it would seem he is."

Bernie met Jim at the hospital. He'd waited for her outside and the minute she approached, he pulled her to himself and hugged her.

"Hold me for a few minutes," she told him. "Please just hold me."

He kissed her temple. "How are you holding up, honey? How's Brenda and R.B.?"

"Mom's a basket case. I finally got her to take a sleeping pill and lie down around four this morning. Dad's holed up in his den with a bottle of Jack Daniel's. And me—I'm on the verge of falling apart."

"I'm not sure Scotty Joe's going to be able to help us," Jim said. "John stayed with him in the ambulance and he's waiting for us in the ER. But he said Scotty Joe was pretty incoherent, that he kept saying, 'I couldn't save her. I tried, but I couldn't save her.' They've had to sedate him to calm him down."

"Tell me again where he was found, when, and by whom?" Bernie eased out of Jim's arms, but held on to his hand.

"He was wandering around out on the highway over near the river, blood all over his shirt from the gunshot wound in his arm, and he was blabbering out of his head," Jim said. "He flagged down a guy on his way to work, then promptly passed out."

"How is he? Is he going to be okay?"

"Yeah, as far as I know." He grabbed her hand. "Let's go on in and see if John's talked to the doctor yet."

She nodded, then went with him through the ER entrance, down a long hall, and to the ER waiting room. The minute they entered, John Downs spotted them, threw up his hand, and waved. He headed toward them. They met in the middle of the room.

John pulled them aside. "The doctor just came out. He said the bullet went clean through Scotty Joe's arm, so I figure the bullet is one of the ones we dug out of the wall at the fitness center. Besides the bullet wound, he's got a concussion. Our killer probably knocked him out. I'm just glad he didn't hit Scotty Joe as hard as he did Brett Dennison."

"Have you gotten a chance to question Scotty Joe?" Bernie asked. "Did he get a look at the man who kidnapped Robyn? Can he identify him?"

"We talked on the ride in the ambulance," John said. "He told me that he and Delaine had heard an odd noise and Delaine had gone outside to check on things while he looked around inside. When Scotty Joe went back into the main room that houses all the exercise equipment, he saw Delaine lying there on the floor, and before he knew what was happening, somebody shot at him. Scotty Joe figures the guy must have gotten the drop on Delaine while he was outside and forced him back into the building. Seems this guy was wearing a stocking over his face, so Scotty Joe can't ID him. But he knows the guy was about six feet tall, he was Caucasian, and had dark hair."

"A six-foot white guy with dark hair." Bernie groaned. "That could be at least a sixth or more of the guys in Adams County."

"Scotty Joe said he tried to stop this guy, that he managed to follow him out to his SUV, and that's when the guy forced him to unlock his vehicle. The guy was using Robyn as a shield, so Scotty Joe couldn't get off a clean shot. When Scotty Joe unlocked his vehicle, the guy hit him over the head. That's all he remembers. We figure he must have shoved Scotty Joe inside and drove off, then dumped him down by the river later."

"What about Robyn?" Bernie asked.

"Scotty Joe said the guy must have drugged her, that she was out cold when he carried her outside."

"Oh, Lord . . . Lord. He could have already raped her. He could be hurting her right now. Doing all sorts of—" Bernie choked on her tears.

Jim put his arm around her. "I'm taking you home." He looked at John. "Tell Scotty Joe that we came by and we'll be back. And when he's up to it, see if he can remember anything else."

John nodded, then looked sympathetically at Bernie. "I'm sorry. I wish . . ."

Jim practically dragged Bernie out of the ER. Once in the parking lot, she stopped and dug in her heels, refusing to budge. "I'm okay now. I can drive myself home."

"Are you sure?"

"Yeah, I'm sure. I don't want you wasting your time babysitting me. I want all your time and energy spent on trying to figure out who this guy is and where he's holding Robyn."

Chapter 31

"Honey, you didn't have to bring me supper," Jim said as Bernie placed a large Styrofoam cup and a sack from the Pig Pen down on her desk in front of him.

She came around the desk just as he stood, and then walked into his open arms. They hugged each other and exchanged a brief kiss before she sat down beside him. "Mom's not doing any cooking or eating, not since Robyn was kidnapped. God, I can't believe it's been three whole days."

"We're going to find her . . . alive."

Bernie closed her eyes as if her thoughts were too painful to bear. She shook her head, opened her eyes and said, "I went down on Second Street to the Pig Pen and picked up barbeque plates for all of us. I took Mom's and Dad's home; then I stopped by Jerry Dale and Amy's to check on Kevin. He's doing okay. He talked to his mother again this afternoon."

"How'd that go?"

"He seemed okay about it. He said she told him Allen had

gone out and bought her half a dozen hats and ten scarfs to wear while she's bald."

"You're trying to take care of everybody, aren't you?" Jim told her. "Your parents . . . me . . . and even Kevin."

"It's what I do. It's who I am."

"Yeah, I know and I love you for it."

She started crying and couldn't seem to stop herself.

"Bernie?"

She waved her hands at him and managed to say, "It's okay." Then she sucked in a deep breath, released it and wiped her face with both hands.

The phone rang. Jim looked at her. "Are you sure you're okay?"

Unable to speak because of the tears lodged in her throat, she nodded.

Jim answered the phone. "Captain Norton here."

"I've got the list of students from Leighton Prep you wanted," Griffin Powell said. "I swear you'd think information from that school was top secret, classified government shit."

"You have the list of students from Heather Stevens's junior year?"

"Yep, and I have the yearbook, too. It just came in. I'll overnight it—"

"E-mail me the names first and hold on to the yearbook for now. I might want you to scan some pictures for me."

"I'm already ahead of you. I sent the e-mail before I called."

"Thanks. And Griff?"

"Huh?"

"I'm sorry about Ron Delaine. I hate that—"

"Yeah, me, too. Delaine was only twenty-nine. He was engaged to a real cute girl from his hometown. He was thinking about moving back home to Shreveport and opening his own P.I. business." Griffin cleared his throat. "Go check that e-mail. Then give me a call and let me know about the yearbook."

Jim hung up the phone and turned to Bernie. "Griff's e-mailed me the list of students from Heather's junior year at Leighton Prep."

"You're looking for the boy Mrs. Ogletree told you about, aren't you? Melvin somebody-or-other. You think he's the Secret Admirer killer."

"I'm ninety-nine percent positive. And if his name is listed as a student, then let's hope he didn't miss picture day."

Jim went straight to Outlook Express and downloaded the e-mail. Bernie stood up, moved in behind Jim and looked over his shoulder. Griffin's list consisted of fifty-six names, all juniors at Leighton Prep twelve years ago.

Together, they scanned the names.

"There," Jim said. "Melvin J. Smith. It's got to be him. He's the only Melvin on the list."

"Do you think if we see a picture of this boy when he was sixteen, we'll recognize who he is? You think he's someone here in Adams Landing, don't you?"

"I hope so. God, I hope so." Just as Jim reached for the phone to call Griffin, it rang. Jim yanked his hand back, a knee-jerk reaction. "Damn."

He picked up the receiver and identified himself.

"Jim, it's Charlie Patterson. I've got some interesting in-formation I thought you needed to know ASAP."

"And that would be?" Jim asked.

"Who is it?" Bernie asked.

He mouthed the word *Charlie.*

"We dug out four bullets from the wall and floor at Robyn Granger's fitness center," Charlie said.

"Yeah?"

"All four bullets were identical. And all four were fired from Ron Delaine's weapon."

"That's not possible. What about the bullet that went through Scotty Joe's arm?"

"It seems there was blood on one of the bullets from Delaine's gun."

Jim's stomach knotted. "Shit! Look, let's keep a lid on this info, okay?"

"Okay, for now. Is there something else going on, something I don't know?" Charlie asked.

"Maybe," Jim replied. "I'm not sure, but you'll be the third to know."

"The third?"

"Yeah, I'll be first, Bernie will be second and you'll be third."

"Whatever's going on, don't do anything without me," Charlie told him.

"I haven't forgotten the Sheriff's Department and the ABI are in this thing together." Jim glanced at Bernie, whose eyes were filled with questions. "Look, I've got to make a phone call. I'll get back in touch with you soon."

Still holding the telephone, Jim hit the OFF button. Bernie grabbed his arm.

"Tell me?"

"The crime scene investigators found four bullets at Robyn's gym. All four came from Ron Delaine's gun." Jim quickly dialed Griffin's private number. "One bullet had blood on it."

Bernie stared at him in disbelief. "If that's the case, then . . . No. No, it's not possible."

Griff answered on the second ring.

"Check the yearbook for a photo of a kid named Melvin J. Smith."

"Hold on."

Bernie shook Jim's arm. "You can't possibly think that—"

"Jim?" Griffin said.

"Yeah?"

"I found him. He's a nerdy looking kid. He was on the debate team and belonged to the Van Gogh Club. I imagine that was some kind of a club for artists."

"Scan his picture and send it to me ASAP."

"You got it."

Jim sat at the computer. Waiting. Bernie stood behind him again, then leaned over, wrapped her arms around his neck, and pressed her cheek against his.

In no time at all, the second e-mail from Griffin came through, this one with an attachment. Jim sensed that Bernie was holding her breath. Hell, even he was.

He opened the attachment and the scanned school photograph of Melvin J. Smith. He studied the boy's features, mentally removed the glasses, and added twelve years and seventy pounds of hard muscle.

"What do you think?" he asked Bernie.

"I'm not sure. I see a resemblance, but . . ."

"I think it's him."

She nodded. "Yes, I think it is, too. So what do we do now?"

"Not we, honey. Me. You're on temporary leave, remember?"

Jim picked up the phone and dialed Griff's number again.

"I'm already on it," Griff said. "We're doing a search to find out if Melvin J. Smith legally changed his name."

"How soon should you know?"

"If we're lucky, a couple of hours."

"Then pray that we're lucky."

Chapter 32

Once Jim learned that Melvin J. Smith had legally changed his name before he went into the army ten years ago, he knew he possessed the identity of their Secret Admirer killer. But knowing her abductor's identity didn't mean they could save Robyn. They could arrest him, put him behind bars, and throw away the key, but if their suspect didn't admit that he'd taken Robyn and tell them where he'd hidden her, Bernie's sister would probably die before they could find her. As difficult as it had been for them to bide their time, to wait even a few hours for their suspect to make his next move, they'd known that, for Robyn's sake, they had no other choice.

But as luck would have it, they hadn't had to wait long. Only until nightfall that same day. Their killer had made an unexpected move, forcing them to act quickly. As far as Bernie knew, Jim was with John Downs right now, search warrant in hand, going through the suspect's home. She had no idea that while John searched the apartment, Jim and Charlie had set in motion a plan to rescue Robyn.

He and Charlie had agreed that the only way to make this

work was if one man followed the suspect at a discreet distance. And the two of them had also agreed that Bernie and R.B. would be kept out of the loop for the time being. They couldn't risk R.B. going off half-cocked, acting like an outraged father and screwing things up. And Jim didn't want Bernie worrying herself sick about him for any longer than necessary or feeling as if she should be in on her sister's rescue.

Jim had gone in alone. The ABI had provided him with a car, a late-model inexpensive sedan. Nondescript. Not likely to be noticed. The perfect vehicle to use for tailing someone.

As Jim made a slow, easy turn, he kept his gaze focused on the taillights of the SUV a good ten-car distance ahead of him. He had to be careful, even risk losing the guy, in order to keep the son of a bitch from spotting him. If Robyn's abductor even suspected he was being tailed, it could cost Robyn her life. It had been three days since she'd disappeared, three days without food, possibly without water. Three days all alone and scared out of her mind.

Jim hadn't done much praying in his life, but he prayed now. Prayed that God was looking after Bernie's little sister.

When the SUV made another turn, Jim cursed under his breath. He knew where the guy was headed. Goddamn it! Why hadn't he figured it out sooner? It had been right there in front of him, right under his nose.

He called Charlie. "He's got her stashed away somewhere at the community college."

"What? How do you know?"

"He just turned off on Baker Lane."

"That doesn't necessarily mean—"

"Yes, it does. My gut instincts are screaming at me."

"Be careful, Jim. We're about three miles behind you."

We meant the Sheriff's Department's Special Operations

Group, consisting of one sergeant and six deputies, all trained in SWAT tactics, each officer a crack shot.

"For God's sake, don't move in until I tell you to," Jim said. "We can't spook this guy."

"Then keep in touch on a regular basis. Every five minutes."

"Every ten."

"Damn."

"He's pulling into the parking lot at the college right now," Jim said. "I'm going to take the back way in and park behind the school, then try to catch up with him on foot."

"Hey, before you sign off . . ."

"I'll check in again in ten minutes." Jim ended the conversation.

He parked the car, got out, and raced around the building, doing his best to avoid the security lights, trying to stay in the shadows. Breathing hard, adrenaline pumping, Jim took cover behind a huge Dumpster at the side of the secluded lot where their guy had parked his vehicle. After scanning the scene, Jim realized the SUV was empty. And there was no sign of the driver. He'd been in a hurry to go to his latest victim, eager to abuse her.

God, don't do this! Don't let it happen. I've got to find Robyn and I sure could use some help right about now.

Knowing their guy could have gone anywhere, into any of the buildings, Jim accepted temporary defeat. If he went searching for him right now, the odds were not in his favor. Jim hurried back to his car, got in and contacted Charlie Patterson again.

"What's wrong?" Charlie asked.

"I lost him," Jim said. "He's here at the college somewhere, in one of these buildings, but it could take days to search the place, and I don't think Robyn has days. Because of his injury, this guy hasn't been able to get to her since he abducted her. There's no telling what he'll do to her as soon as he gets his hands on her again."

"We need to be able to narrow it down, to figure out exactly where he stashed her. There can't be that many places at the college where he could keep her that she'd go completely undetected for days, even for a couple of weeks."

Jim knew Charlie was thinking about the other women who had been held for thirteen to sixteen days. Where on this campus could a woman be held captive without anyone even suspecting she was there?

"We need to talk to somebody who knows every nook and cranny of this college," Jim said. "Somebody who knows if there are any secret places."

"R.B. might know," Charlie said. "And if he doesn't, he'll know who to contact to find out."

"Call Bernie. Tell her what's going on, then have her explain the situation to her father. Tell her to have R.B. call me directly."

"Yeah, will do."

Jim leaned over the steering wheel, lifted his hand and rubbed his forehead. All he could do for now was sit and wait.

And do a little more praying.

When they approached the front door, Deputy John Downs hesitated. Bernie paused, turned and looked at him. "What's wrong?"

"Nothing. It's just I'm beginning to think your coming along on this search might not be a good idea. What if we find what we're looking for?"

"I hope we do."

"When Jim finds out that—"

"Jim will understand that I needed to do this, that I had to do something to help with this investigation, to help nail the guy who kidnapped my sister."

"Yeah, I know."

Bernie motioned to the three backup deputies accompanying them to take their positions. Then using the key the landlord had provided, she unlocked the front door. With her weapon drawn, as a precaution only since she knew Jim and Charlie were pursuing the suspect at this very moment, she entered the apartment. Thank God that John had felt compelled to update her on the situation, even if Jim had decided it best to keep her out of the loop.

She wanted to be with Jim, wanted to take every step he took, be at his side to protect him. She wanted to be the one to rescue Robyn and bring in her potential killer. Or bring him down.

Logic dictated that because she was the victim's sister, she couldn't be objective in her thinking or her actions. So, she was doing what she could do—trying to find the evidence they needed to prove their suspect was the Secret Admirer killer.

When they were certain the apartment was clear, no sign of the resident or anyone else for that matter, they began their search. It didn't take long for Bernie to discover the condemning items inside a desk in his living room. After returning her weapon to the holster, she donned a pair of gloves and sorted through the items, lifting them from the drawers and spreading them out on top of the desk.

"What have you found?" When John saw the items on the desk, he let out a long, low whistle. "Good God!"

Bernie stared at the array of snapshots, all of young, pretty brunettes. Jacque Reeves. Stephanie Preston. Thomasina Hardy. Abby Miller. Bernie's hand trembled as she lifted a single snapshot of Robyn.

John looked over her shoulder. "This is our guy all right. He's got pictures and sketches of all the victims. And"—

John pointed first to one small container and then to another—"there's a box filled with pink nail polish and lipstick, and that one has little perfume bottles in it and . . . Son of a bitch! He bought these things in bulk."

"I don't want anything touched," Bernie said. "Leave everything for the ABI's CSU people. Seal off this apartment and post a guard at the door."

John nodded. "I need to contact Jim and Charlie, let them know they're definitely pursuing the right guy."

"No, you handle things here. I'll get in touch with Jim and Charlie."

"Bernie?" John frowned. "Are you sure? Jim really wanted you to stay—"

"I can't stay out of it. Not now. Jim will understand."

Jim's phone vibrated. He'd turned off the ringer and set it to vibrate instead.

"Yeah?"

"Jim, it's R.B. Look, I've talked to the college president and he's given us permission to search the entire college. But I don't think it'll come to that. I told President Corbitt that I remember the campus includes an old building that years ago was an auditorium/lunchroom. That building is used now only by the drama department for plays and the choral department for their annual musical. And for the D.A.R.E. program lectures."

"Damn!"

"Here's the thing—in the early fifties, a part of the basement was converted into a bomb shelter consisting of several rooms, all of them virtually soundproof, and one room not accessible except through a hatchlike door. That part of the basement hasn't been used in twenty years, not even for storage."

"Then that's where he's holding Robyn."

"I agree."

"I'll find her, R.B. And I'll get him."

"Listen, boy, there's not going to be any way to sneak up on him."

"I know."

"President Corbitt gave me instructions on how to get to the bomb shelter," R.B. said. "It's fairly simple, if you know where you're going."

Jim got out of the car and headed toward the old building, following R.B.'s directions, step by step.

Lying on the bed, staring up at the ceiling, Robyn thought she heard something, but chalked it up to her imagination. Her wild imagination. Her insane fears.

I'm going crazy. I'm losing my mind.

She had no idea how long she'd been trapped in this single concrete room. She thought it had been only a few days, but it could have been longer. She hadn't eaten, and for a while she'd been hungry, but not any longer. Thankfully, she had water, had been able to use the sink for drinking water and to keep herself washed off a little. No towel and washcloth. And the only soap was out of reach, in the makeshift shower stall on the other side of the sink and commode.

Where is he? Why hasn't he come for me?

She heard the noise again. Overhead. She rose slowly into a sitting position. Someone was opening the door.

Her heart raced maddeningly. Had he come back? Or was it possible someone else had found her? Should she cry out or remain silent?

"Hello," she called. "Who's there?"

"It's me, darling. Have you missed me terribly?"

Oh, God, no . . . No!

* * *

Jim's phone vibrated just as he reached the basement in the old building. Following the directions R.B. had given him, he had broken into the auditorium through a back door. He had breathed a heavy sigh of relief after he punched in the security code President Corbitt had given R.B. and the green light had come on at the control panel.

Pausing in a dark corner, Jim flipped open his phone. "Yeah?" he whispered.

"Jim."

"Bernie?"

"Look, I'm going to make this quick, okay? I went with John to search our guy's apartment. We found everything— photos of all his northeast Alabama victims, a box filled with pink nail polish and lipstick, all the other gifts and—"

"Honey, I've got to go. Thanks for confirming what I already knew in my gut."

"Wait. What's happening?"

"Call R.B. He'll fill you in."

Jim closed his cell phone, clipped it to his belt, then turned on his flashlight and slowly, carefully made his way down the pitch-black hallway.

Weak, fatigued and scared out of her mind, Robyn did not fight her captor when he unchained her and led her across the room and into the shower. He had stripped off his clothes before he freed her, and now they stood together, both of them naked, beneath the cool, pelting water.

She noticed the ugly, bruised wound on his arm. What had happened to him? *Think, Robyn, think back to when he killed Agent Delaine.* The private bodyguard had used his gun. She distinctly remembered hearing the shots. Had one of his shots hit this madman?

He lathered his hands with soap. Starting at her neck, he

washed her body. Every muscle tight, every nerve rioting, she stood there and allowed him to touch her intimately, to scrub her breasts, rake his nails over her nipples, to put his hand between her thighs and—*No, please, don't.* He stuck two fingers up inside her. She tensed. He eased his other hand down over her buttocks, slipped his fingers in the crease of her cheeks and inserted a finger into her anus.

"Relax, my darling. You know you love it when I touch you. Here—" He jabbed his fingers in and out of her repeatedly.

She whimpered.

"Oh, poor baby, you want my dick inside you, don't you? You're tired of me playing with you." He paused his thrusts, lowered his head and bit her neck. She shivered. "Ask me nicely."

No, I won't do it.

"Robyn, I told you to ask me."

Silence.

"Bad girl. I'll have to punish you. You have to learn that when you defy me, there are consequences."

Before she realized what was happening, he yanked her around, shoved her up against the concrete shower stall wall, then lifted her up just enough to ram his penis into her anus. She screamed with pain.

Standing over the open hatch, feeling grateful that their guy hadn't closed and locked the only access into the room below, Jim heard a woman's screams. Goddamn it, he was hurting Robyn, torturing her.

Take a couple of deep breaths. You need to be thinking straight and your nerves need to be steady when you go down there. Robyn's life depends on you. If you fuck this up, Bernie will never forgive you. And you'll never forgive yourself.

Jim turned off his flashlight, drew his Glock, and headed down the rickety wooden stairs, completely aware of the fact that his only protection was the Kevlar vest beneath his shirt.

Robyn's tormented screams echoed inside Jim's head as he stepped down onto the solid concrete floor. Scanning the area hurriedly, he froze to the spot when he saw, there across the room, an open bathroom area. The guy had his back to Jim. He was pumping into the woman he had pressed against the wall.

Jim lifted his pistol and aimed it at the back of the guy's head. But before he could get off a clean shot, Scotty Joe Walters whirled around, putting Robyn directly in front of himself, his hands at either side of her neck.

"Hello, Captain Norton."

Jim swallowed hard, but his hands remained steady. He kept the gun aimed at Scotty Joe. "Let her go."

"You're a lot smarter than I gave you credit for," Scotty Joe said. "How'd you figure out it was me?"

"I said, let her go."

"I can't do that."

Robyn's eyes widened in terror.

"It's over, Melvin," Jim said. "We know everything. All about how the Sable Girls humiliated you, about your nervous breakdown. We know about your metamorphosis while you were in the Army, changing from skinny, nerdy Melvin Smith into macho guy Scotty Joe Walters. And we know you killed Heather and the other Sable Girls. Then when that didn't satisfy your thirst for revenge, you began killing their look-alikes."

"You've been a busy boy, haven't you, Captain?"

"Let Robyn go. If you don't, I'll have to shoot you."

Scotty Joe laughed, the sound maniacal. And unnerving.

"I can break her neck before you can shoot me." He tightened his fingers around Robyn's throat.

"Are you willing to bet your life on it?" Jim asked.

"Are you willing to bet Robyn's life?"

Without another word, without another thought, Jim pulled the trigger. Robyn screamed. The bullet entered Scotty Joe's head, dead center between his eyebrows. When he fell, Robyn fell with him.

Jim ran across the room, his weapon in his hand. He knelt and inspected Scotty Joe's body. The guy was dead. He returned his gun to the holster, then reached down and rolled the young deputy over and off Robyn. He scooped her shivering body up into his arms. As he carried her past the metal bed, he reached out, yanked off the top sheet and wrapped it around her.

She lay cuddled in his arms, weeping softly, clinging to him for dear life. He paused at the bottom of the steps. "I'm going to toss you over my shoulder until we get out of this hole."

When they emerged from the bomb shelter dungeon, Jim paused long enough to call Charlie Patterson. "I've got her. We're coming out."

"What about Scotty Joe?" Charlie asked.

"The son of a bitch is dead. You'll find his body in the bomb shelter."

The moment Bernie saw Jim walk out of the old building, with Robyn in his arms, she raced toward them. Her father and Raymond were only a few steps behind her. In the background, a cheer rose from the deputies.

Bernie caressed her sister's pale face; then she leaned over and kissed her forehead. Tears streamed down Bernie's cheeks, over her mouth and dripped off her chin.

"I—I'm alive," Robyn said. "I'm alive."

"You sure are, baby girl." R.B. grabbed Robyn's limp hand, brought it to his lips and kissed it.

Bernie looked at Jim and mouthed the words *Thank you.*

Jim glanced at Raymond, who stood there crying and trembling. Jim handed Robyn over to Raymond, who immediately opened his arms and took her from Jim. Holding her close and pressing his face against hers, he said, "You're going to be all right, sweetheart. There's an ambulance waiting."

"Don't leave me." She clung to Raymond.

"Never."

When Raymond turned and headed for the ambulance, R.B. started to go after them. Jim reached out and grasped R.B.'s arm. "She'll always be your little girl, but it's time you turn her over to another man. The man who loves her and wants to take care of her."

With tears trickling down his weathered face, R.B. nodded, then glanced from Jim to Bernie and then back at Jim. "I suppose you want me to turn this one over to you."

"Damn straight," Jim said.

R.B. reached out and shook Jim's hand. "Thank you, son." R.B. swallowed. "I need to call Brenda and tell her to meet us at the hospital." Making direct eye contact with Jim, R.B. asked, "How bad did he hurt her?"

Jim hesitated. "She's alive. That's all that matters."

R.B. clenched his teeth tightly, then walked toward Charlie Patterson, leaving Jim and Bernie alone. R.B. pulled out his cell phone, hit his home number and spoke to his wife.

Jim turned to Bernie and held out his hand. When she put her hand in his, they headed across the parking lot toward her Jeep. Pausing by the SUV's hood, Bernie faced him.

"How will I ever be able to thank you for solving the case and saving my sister?"

Jim slid his arm around her waist and yanked her up against him. "I think spending the next forty or fifty years with me should be thanks enough."

"The next forty or—Jim Norton, was that a proposal?"

"Yeah, I guess it was."

"It wasn't a very romantic proposal."

"Honey, I told you that I'm not a romantic kind of guy."

Bernie lifted her arms up and around his neck, then kissed him. All the while thanking God for sparing her sister's life. And for giving Jim and her a second chance at love.

Epilogue

Brenda and R.B. Granger celebrated their fiftieth wedding anniversary surrounded by their two daughters, their two sons-in-law, and their four grandchildren. The gala event was held at—where else?—the country club. Bernie and Robyn had spent months preparing for the lavish party, every detail discussed with and approved by their mother, of course.

After Robyn's terrifying experience with Scotty Joe Walters, she had spent months in therapy. With the love and support of her family and her fiancé, she had recovered by slow degrees. Although she had returned to work almost immediately, it had taken her over a year to begin living her life without fear, to be able to plan and prepare for her wedding. Robyn and Raymond shared their big day with over three hundred people, on a warm, sunny day in June. Bernie had been the matron of honor, since she and Jim had married on New Year's Day the year before, having chosen the date because it represented new beginnings. Bernie and Jim's wedding had been simple, held in her parents' home, with only immediate family and close friends in attendance. It had been what they'd both wanted.

Brenda and R.B. were in their element as grandparents, first with Kevin, then with the other three. Both had been ecstatic when, only six months after her elaborate June wedding, Robyn announced she was pregnant. Rea Long was as beautiful as her mother and grandmother before her, but Robyn liked to point out that Rea had Raymond's gorgeous eyes. The precocious little imp had every man in the family eating out of the palm of her delicate seven-year-old hand.

Rea sashayed up to her grandmother and announced in a loud yet ladylike voice, "Grandmother, Bobby ran into Brenda Anne and she spilled punch on my new patent leather shoes. Those two little cousins of mine are absolute hooligans." Rea sighed dramatically.

Brenda managed to mask her smile. "Since you're seven and they're only five, it's your responsibility to set a good example for them."

Bernie grinned at Robyn and shrugged. "Sorry, Sis. If Rea's shoes are ruined—"

"Don't worry," Robyn replied. "I'm sure the punch will wash right off." Then she whispered, her words for Bernie's ears only, "That crack Rea made about your twins being hooligans—you know that didn't come from Raymond or me. She just repeated what she's heard Helen say. That mother-in-law of mine!" Robyn rolled her eyes upward and sighed as dramatically as her daughter had only moments ago.

Five-year-old James Robert "Bobby" Norton chased his twin sister, Brenda Anne, around the gift table, and just as his foot caught on the edge of the tablecloth, his big brother, UT senior Kevin, scooped him up into his arms. Jim eased in behind his daughter and grabbed her up and off the floor. Both twins giggled and squirmed.

Bernie smiled at her husband, a feeling of complete happiness enveloping her. It wasn't that their life together was perfect, but it was good. Damn good! Just when she'd given up hope of having Jim's baby, they'd found out she was carrying twins. Bed rest for six months and a lot of prayers had helped bring two healthy babies into this world. Not a day went by that she didn't thank the Lord for her many blessings, not the least of which was Kevin. Although she hadn't given birth to him, she thought of him as her son. He was the child of her heart, a young man so very much like his father.

Six months after Mary Lee's surgery, she and Jim had worked out a joint custody agreement so that they shared their son equally. Then less than a year later, shortly before Kevin's fourteenth birthday, Allen Clark had been offered the job of a lifetime—in Singapore. After he and Mary Lee moved out of the country, Kevin had come to live with Jim and Bernie full time, but he spent a month each summer with his mother and stepfather overseas.

With Brenda Anne on his hip, Jim walked over to Bernie. Kevin followed, his little brother, Bobby, in tow.

"Sheriff, I think these two heathens need to be put in the hoosegow," Kevin said jokingly.

"What's a hoosegow?" Bobby asked, looking up at his big brother.

"It's a bad place," Brenda Anne said, then smiled at Jim. "Isn't it, Daddy?"

"You don't have to worry, sugar pie," Jim said. "Nobody is ever going to put you in a bad place."

She wrapped her pudgy little arms around Jim's neck. "That's 'cause you and Mommy won't let them. 'Cause you and Mommy are the sheriff."

When everyone laughed, Brenda Anne narrowed her gaze and glared at her relatives.

"Mommy's the sheriff," Bobby said. "Daddy's the chief."

"Then I guess when we grow up, I'll be the sheriff and you'll be the chief," Brenda Anne said.

Everyone laughed again. Brenda Anne frowned.

Jim slipped his free arm around Bernie's waist. "Sounds like our younger two plan to keep the Granger tradition going for another generation."

"The Granger-Norton tradition," she told her husband.

Jim grinned. "Yeah, the Granger-Norton tradition."

Dear Reader,

I truly hated to say good-bye to Bernie and Jim and the residents of Adams County, Alabama. I hope that while reading their story, *Close Enough to Kill*, you became as deeply involved with them as I did while writing about them. When I finished *Killing Her Softly*, I knew I had to write a book for secondary character Jim Norton, and I also knew at that time I would have to make another secondary character—wealthy, debonaire lawyer Judd Walker—the hero of his own book. So, in my next romantic suspense novel for Zebra Books, I'm leaving Jim and Bernie to live happily ever after and am traveling slightly northeast of Adams County, Alabama, to Chattanooga, Tennessee, a city I consider my second home.

Judd Walker, the hero of my next Zebra book, was born with the proverbial silver spoon in his mouth. Rich, handsome, intelligent, married to former Miss Tennessee Jennifer Mobley, Judd lived the good life until an unforeseen tragedy struck, destroying what mattered most to him. Filled with anger and rage, obsessed with only one goal, Judd becomes a man that his best friend wouldn't recognize—a single-minded, ruthless vigilante seeking revenge.

In Judd's book, you will be reintroduced to Jim Norton's old UT buddy, Griffin Powell, the mystery man, the multi-millionaire who heads up the prestigious Powell Private Investigation Agency, home-based in Knoxville, Tennessee. And you'll meet Lindsay McAllister, a former Chattanooga police detective who now works for the Powell agency, a lady as determined as Judd is to find a diabolical killer to whom murder is simply a game.

But before my next novel comes out in April 2007, I have a very special project set for release in February 2007. Lisa Jackson, Wendy Corsi Staub and I have collaborated on a romantic suspense novel, MOST LIKELY TO DIE. Bad boy Jake Marcott was brutally killed at a high school dance on Valentine's Day and his murderer never caught. Now, twenty year later, when Jake's old classmates return to Portland, Oregon, for a high school reunion, the killer strikes again and the victims are all women with a connection to Jake.

I enjoy hearing from readers. You may contact me through my Web site at www.beverlybarton.com, or by writing to me in care of Kensington Publishing Corp.

Warmest regards,
Beverly Barton

Please turn the page for an exciting sneak peek of
Beverly Barton's
newest romantic suspense thriller
coming in 2007!

The intensely bright lights blinded her. She couldn't see anything except the white illumination that obscured everything in her line of vision. She wished he would turn off the car's headlights.

Judd didn't like for her to show houses to clients in the evenings and generally she did what Judd wanted her to do. But her career as a realtor was just getting off the ground, and if she could sell this half-million-dollar house to Mr. and Mrs. Farris, her percentage would be enough to furnish the nursery. Not that she was pregnant. Not yet. And not that her husband couldn't well afford to furnish a nursery with the best of everything. It was just that Jennifer wanted the baby to be her gift to her wonderful husband and the nursery to be a gift from her to their child.

Holding her hand up to shield her eyes from the headlights, she walked down the sidewalk to meet John and Katherine Farris, an up-and-coming entrepreneurial couple planning to start a new business in Chattanooga. She had spoken only to John Farris. From their telephone conversations, she had surmised that John, like her own husband, was the type who liked to think he wore the pants in the family. Odd how considering the fact that she believed herself to be a thoroughly modern women, Jennifer loved Judd's old-fashioned sense of protectiveness and possessiveness.

When John Farris parked his black Mercedes and opened the driver's door, Jennifer met him, her hand outstretched in greeting. He accepted her hand immediately and smiled warmly.

"Good evening, Mr. Farris." Jennifer glanced around, searching for Mrs. Farris.

"I'm sorry, something came up at the last minute that delayed Katherine. She'll be joining us soon."

When John Farris raked his silvery blue eyes over her, Jennifer shuddered inwardly, an odd sense of uneasiness settling in the pit of her stomach. *You're being silly,* she told herself. Men found her attractive. It wasn't her fault. She didn't do anything to lead them on, nothing except simply being beautiful, which she owed to the fact she'd inherited great genes from her attractive parents.

Jennifer sighed. Sometimes being a former beauty queen was a curse.

"If you'd like to wait for your wife before you look at the house, I can go ahead and answer any questions you might have. I've got all the information in my briefcase in my car."

He shook his head. "No need to wait. I'd like to take a look around now. If I don't like the place, Katherine won't be interested."

"Oh, I see."

He chuckled. "It's not that she gives in to me on everything. We each try to please the other. Isn't that the way to have a successful marriage?"

"Yes, I think so. It's certainly what Judd and I have been trying to do. We're a couple of newlyweds just trying to make our way through that first year of marriage." Jennifer nodded toward the front entrance to the sprawling glass and log house. "If you'll follow me."

"I'd be delighted to follow you."

Despite his reply sending a quiver of apprehension along her nerve endings, she kept walking toward the front steps, telling herself that if she had to defend her honor against unwanted advances, it wouldn't be the first time. She knew how to handle herself in sticky situations. She carried pepper spray in her purse and her cell phone rested securely in her jacket pocket.

After unlocking the front door, she flipped on the light switch, which illuminated the large foyer. "The house was built in nineteen-seventy-five by an architect for his own personal home."

John Farris paused in the doorway. "How many rooms?"

"Ten," she replied, then motioned to him. "Please, come on in."

He entered the foyer and glanced around, up into the huge living room and to the right into the open dining room. "It seems perfect for entertaining."

"Oh, it is. There's a state-of-the-art kitchen. It was completely gutted and redone only four years ago by the present owner."

"I'd like to take a look," he told her. "I'm the chef in the family. Katherine can't boil water."

Feeling a bit more at ease, Jennifer led him from the foyer, through the dining room and into the galley-style kitchen. "I love this kitchen. I'm not much of a cook myself, but I've been taking gourmet cooking lessons as a surprise for my husband."

"Isn't he a lucky man?"

Jennifer felt Mr. Farris as he came up behind her. Shuddering nervously, she started to turn and face him, but suddenly and without warning, he grabbed her from behind and covered her face with a foul-smelling rag.

No. No . . . no, this can't be happening.

* * *

Beverly Barton

Had she been unconscious for a few minutes or a few hours? She didn't know. When she came to, she realized she was sitting propped up against the wall in the kitchen, her feet tied together with rope and her hands pulled over her head, each wrist bound with individual pieces of rope that had been tied to the door handles of two open kitchen cabinets.

Groggy, slightly disoriented, Jennifer blinked several times, then took a deep breath and glanced around the room, searching for her attacker. John Farris loomed over her, an odd smile on his handsome face.

"Well, hello, beautiful," he said. "I was wondering how long you'd sleep. I've been waiting patiently for you to wake up. You've been out nearly fifteen minutes."

"Why?" she asked, her voice a ragged whisper.

"Why what?"

"Why are you doing this?"

"What do you think I intend to do?"

"Rape me." Her voice trembled.

Please, God, don't let him kill me.

He laughed. "What sort of man do you think I am? I'd never force myself on an unwilling woman."

"Please, let me go. Whatever—" She gasped, her mouth sucking in air as she noticed that he held something shiny in his right hand.

A meat cleaver!

Sheer terror claimed her at that moment, body and soul. Her stomach churned. Sweat dampened her face. The loud rat-a-tat-tat of her accelerated heartbeat thundered in her ears.

He reached down with his left hand and fingered her long, dark hair. "If only you were a blonde or a redhead."

Jennifer swallowed hard. *He's going to kill me. He's going to kill me with that meat cleaver. He'll chop me up in little pieces . . .*

She whimpered. *Oh, Judd, why didn't I listen to you? Why did I come here alone tonight?*

"Are you afraid?" John Farris asked.

"Yes."

"You should be," he told her.

"You're going to kill me, aren't you?"

He laughed again. Softly.

"Please . . . please . . ." She cried. Tears filled her eyes and trickled down her cheeks.

He came closer. And closer. He raised the meat cleaver high over her head, then swung it across her right wrist.

Blood splattered on the cabinet, over her head, and across her upper body as her severed right hand tumbled downward and hit the floor.

Pain! Excruciating pain.

And then he lifted the cleaver and swung down and across again, cutting off her left hand with one swift, accurate blow.

Jennifer passed out.